Romeo

A Dark Knights MC/Blood Fury MC® Crossover

Jeanne St. James

Jeanne
ST. JAMES

———

Credits:
Photographer/Cover Artist: Golden Czermak at FuriousFotog
Cover Model: Ché Myers
Editor: Proofreading by the Page
Beta Readers: Alex Swab, Author BJ Alpha and Sharon Abrams
Logo: Jennifer Edwards

———

www.jeannestjames.com

Sign up for my newsletter for insider information, author news, and new releases:
www.jeannestjames.com/newslettersignup

Warning: This book contains explicit scenes, some possible triggers and adult language which may be considered offensive to some readers. This book is for sale to adults ONLY, as defined by the laws of the country in which you made your purchase. Please store your files wisely, where they cannot be accessed by under-aged readers.

This is a work of fiction. Any similarity to actual persons, living or dead, or actual events, is purely coincidental.

————

AI Restriction: The author expressly prohibits any entity from using this publication for purposes of training artificial intelligence (AI) technologies to generate text, including without limitation technologies that are capable of generating works in the same style or genre as this publication. The author reserves all rights to license uses of this work for generative AI training and development of machine learning language models.

————

Dirty Angels MC, Blue Avengers MC & Blood Fury MC are registered trademarks of Jeanne St James, Double-J Romance, Inc.

————

Keep an eye on her website at http://www. jeannestjames.com/or sign up for her newsletter to learn about her upcoming releases: http://www.jeannestjames.com/newslettersignup

Author Note

Romeo, the president of the Dark Knights MC, was first introduced in Crash: A Dirty Angels MC/Blood Fury MC Crossover.

He showed up once more in the epilogue of Blood & Bones: Easy (Blood Fury MC, book 12). The prologue of Romeo's book starts there.

He again shows up in Beyond the Badge: Nox (Blue Avengers MC, book 6). Now, he gets his own story. I hope you enjoy the ride... And the downfall of this heartbreaker.

Glossary of Terms

Sled - biker slang for a motorcycle

Cage - bike slang for a vehicle with four wheels instead of two.

Strange/Randoms - sexual partners who are strangers/random people

Bid - Prison term

DAMC - Dirty Angels MC

BFMC - Blood Fury MC

BAMC - Blue Avengers MC

DKMC - Dark Knights MC

NFL - National Football League

NHL - National Hockey League

MLB - Major League Baseball

Character List

The Dark Knights MC

Romeo - President
Bishop - Vice President
Magnum - Sergeant at Arms
Sigh - Secretary
Cue - Treasurer
Cisco - Road Captain
Sully - Chaplain
Wick - Member
Slick - Member
BamBam - Member
Booger - Prospect

The Blood Fury MC:

Trip - President
Sig - Vice President
Judge - Sergeant at Arms

Ozzy - Secretary
Deacon - Treasurer
Cage - Road Captain
Shade - Member; Maddie's Stepfather
Castle - Member
Easy - Member

Others:

Aaliyah - aka Liyah/Ali-Cat - Magnum's oldest daughter; married to a Blue Avenger
Cait - Magnum's wife; Dawg's oldest daughter (Dirty Angels MC)
Chelle - Maddie's mother; Shade's ol' lady/wife
Josie - Maddie's younger sister
Gabi - Rescued by the Blood Fury MC from a cult at 14 yro, lives with Crash (DAMC) and his ol' lady, Liz
Jude - Maddie's adopted brother
Coop - Dirty Angel MC member; manager at The Iron Horse Roadhouse
Zeke Jamison - "Little Z" or "LZ" - Dirty Angel MC member; son of the DAMC president, Zak Jamison and his wife, Sophie
Roger Smith - Owner of Smith's Sports Therapy & Rehab Center; Maddie's boss
Russos - The Pittsburgh Mafia aka La Cosa Nostra
Autumn/Red - Sig's ol' lady/wife
Stella - Trip's ol' lady/wife

Prologue

ROMEO TRACKED her as she walked across the Blood Fury MC's courtyard.

The young strawberry blonde with the big brown eyes.

The same as her mother.

The same as her younger sister.

She wore no one's colors, despite being old enough to be an ol' lady. From what he could tell, she had to be only a few years younger than him.

His best fucking guess? She was at least twenty-one now since she was drinking. Not that her doing so was a perfect indicator. Romeo doubted the Fury gave a shit about underage drinking.

He could be wrong—that happened sometimes—since he heard Trip, the Fury president, was pretty damn strict. Totally fucking opposite of him, the president of the Dark Knights.

But then, he was younger than either president of the Fury or the Dirty Angels. Add in the fact he also liked to party fucking hard and often, he wasn't enough of a dick to police anyone in his club—or even anyone connected to his club—unless he had no damn choice.

And anyway, he had his no-fucking-nonsense sergeant at arms to do that shit for him. No matter that Magnum no longer had youth on his side, he still fucking had it in him to pound someone into the ground or make someone shit their pants with one cocked eyebrow.

Romeo licked his lips as he thought about Magnum's hot-as-fuck, much younger wife.

That had him turning his wandering thoughts back to the woman heading toward the covered pavilion. Right now the popular gathering spot was too crowded for him to approach. He didn't want anyone listening in on his "game." He'd find a better time when she wasn't surrounded by others who might fuck up his plans.

When he could speak to her in private. Turn on his charm.

Test the waters.

Because he planned on having her before this wedding weekend was over.

The fuck if he was leaving Manning Grove without finding a willing woman to warm his bed. It didn't have to be the same woman each night. He wasn't picky. His only requirement was soft thighs, big tits and an ass that wouldn't quit.

A mouth that wouldn't quit, either. And he didn't mean when using it in conversation.

He was currently drawing a blank on her name because—between the three clubs, all their sweet butts, hang-arounds and others who had descended on the Blood Fury's farm for the wedding between the Fury member named Easy and their president's sister—there were way too many goddamn people to remember.

If he had to be honest, he really didn't give a fuck what her name was. The second he kicked her out of his bed, he'd forget it anyway. What he wouldn't forget was if her pussy was tight, how wet she got, or how skilled she was with those soft, plump lips.

A grin crossed his face as he closed his eyes and imagined her spread naked in the bed in his rented RV. The one parked in a field on the same farm where he stood.

Since the motels in town were booked solid due to the weekend-long wedding, he had no choice but to rent one. Unless he wanted to pitch a fucking tent.

And not one in his jeans.

Romeo did not sleep on the fucking ground. Ever.

Unless he was passed-out drunk.

Or someone happened to be lucky enough to knock his ass out.

If he was out cold—by either booze or a sucker punch—one of his brothers better move him somewhere more comfortable. One of the many perks of being voted in as prez.

Not even an hour later, when his eyes scanned the crowd and the courtyard, he spotted her again. Mostly because she was so damn hard to miss.

The problem was, he wasn't the only one watching her.

He heard rumors about her stepfather—or whatever the fuck Shade was—watching over his ol' lady's hot daughters like a fucking hawk.

Magnum could be in-your-face deadly.

Shade went about it quietly.

He was the kind who'd slice your throat and disappear before you even knew what the fuck happened. Breathing one second, bleeding out the next.

With one last glance at the strawberry blonde and the

group she was with, he wandered away to find himself a cold beer.

And while he was sipping that beer, he'd work on his plan of attack.

————

HER BACK WAS PRESSED to one of the pavilion's wood posts. Above her head, so was his forearm. Romeo leaned into it and dipped his head until their eyes locked. Her big brown ones held a gleam, and her mouth curved up at the corners as she stared back up at him with those inviting lips slightly parted.

He remembered her name now after hearing another man mention it. So, at least he didn't have to ask and risk her putting him off because of it.

Women liked to be remembered. They never wanted to be forgettable.

But again, names weren't at the top of the list when it came to what was important to him.

"How old are you, Maddie?"

"Why?"

"Just wanna make sure you're legal."

"For what?"

For you and me to share a little skin-to-skin contact. "To make sure you're supposed to be having that beer."

She lifted the red plastic cup. "You mean this one?"

"That one."

She put it to her lips and swallowed a mouthful. When she was done, she smiled. "Why does what I do concern you? I get enough of that around here from Shade and the rest of the Fury. I don't need it from you, too."

"He keep you on a short leash?"

Her eyebrows knitted together. "Who? Shade?"

He nodded and took a tiny step closer, closing the small gap between them. The visible pulse pounding in her neck drew his attention for a hot minute.

"No, but that doesn't mean he doesn't pay attention. You, out of anyone, should know how a club works. Anyone with a vagina is property for them to protect."

"You don't wanna be protected?"

"I don't want to be dictated to. I'm an adult, a college graduate and about to head to graduate school."

Damn. Proof she was too damn far out of his league. But, *fuck*, he didn't want to discuss Shakespeare with her. He only wanted to share some basic human urges.

Like procreating.

Without the "creating" part.

As far as he knew, he didn't have any of his DNA waddling around on two short, chubby legs. He was good about making sure he collected it in a wrap and tossed that shit in the garbage.

Where it belonged.

Where it didn't force him to make child support payments. A sentence of eighteen to twenty-one years.

Too many of his brothers paid out the ass every month for the mistake of not wrapping it tight.

He wanted to wrap it tight with Madison. He only needed to convince her that it was a good idea.

That might be the difficult part.

"A smart, independent woman," he murmured, sliding his fingers down her arm. "Ain't nothin' wrong with that. It's a turn-on for me."

Goosebumps appeared on her previously smooth skin and her breathing quickened.

Oh yeah. She wasn't immune to his charm.

"Let's be real... I'm sure it doesn't take much to turn you

on, Romeo."

He shrugged one shoulder. "Love a variety of women. All colors, shapes, and sizes." He pressed the tip of his index finger against her chest. "Ain't the outside that turns me on, it's the inside."

She rolled her lips inward for a second. "*Uh huh.* Do you stick around long enough to discover what's beneath the surface?"

"Doin' that now, ain't I?"

"I don't know, are you? I figured this was your attempt at greasing my waistband to help my pants slide off a lot faster and easier."

His attempt at what?

Damn. He needed to up his game if he wanted to win it.

Good thing he liked a challenge. And Maddie decided she was going to make herself one.

Challenge accepted.

"Nothin' wrong with a brother wantin' to be with someone so damn beautiful."

"*Mmm hmm,*" she murmured.

"Ain't lyin'."

Using her finger, she drew a pattern on his chest. "Romeo..."

He snagged her hand and pressed it to his lips. "Yeah, baby?"

"I'm going to share something with you that I don't share with many people."

Hot fuckin' damn. "Gonna make me feel special by sharin' a secret with me."

"It might make you look at me differently."

"You only like chicks?" If so, that would fucking suck, and he was wasting his damn time.

She tucked her bottom lip between her teeth and shook her head.

Why the hell was she teasing him like this?

"Then what? You can tell ol' Romeo your deepest, darkest secrets." He patted his own chest. "I'll keep them locked in here and promise not to spill them."

"I'm a virgin."

His head jerked back, and he barked out a laugh. "Funny." Now she was fucking with him.

Only, she didn't laugh with him. One side of her mouth pulled up and she shrugged.

He blinked. *Holy fuck.* "Wait. You fuckin' serious?"

"I figured that little tidbit would scare you off."

"Then, it's a lie." Because if it was true, it was hardly a fucking little tidbit. This was huge.

And he wasn't sure if he was happy about it.

When she didn't answer and her eyes sliced from his face to over his shoulder, his stomach dropped.

He might have to find a new plan because he didn't fuck with virgins. "It's a lie, right? How old are you?" He never did get that answer. Because there was no fucking way...

"How old are *you*?" she countered.

"Twenty-nine."

"You look older."

Was that supposed to be a compliment or a fucking insult? "What about you?"

She lifted her glass. "Old enough to drink, apparently."

"So, twenty-one."

"Add another year onto that."

She was twenty-two and still a goddamn virgin? No fucking way. That had to be bullshit. What female graduated college still a virgin?

Hell, would he even know? When the fuck did a college girl ever look at him twice?

Fucking never.

He barely got his high school diploma. He wasn't good enough for any of them.

Not even for a night.

Or an hour.

Unless they used him as a revenge fuck.

"Your man piss you off? Wanna get back at him? I'm available. If you're hot, no charge. If you're not? We can negotiate the terms."

He didn't have a problem with that. For the right woman, he'd even volunteer.

But a fucking virgin?

She was definitely fucking with him. He decided to go along with it and see where it led him. "Can help you with that."

"With what?"

This girl had to be playing him. "That pesky hymen."

"I haven't found it to be bothersome. Maybe I want to save my virginity until I find the love of my life."

"Yeah? You can pretend."

"Pretend what?"

"That I'm the love of your life."

"You mean if I close my eyes while you're splitting me in two and pretend you're someone else while you're doing so?"

He turned his choking into a chuckle. "Fuck, baby, I like you."

"Why's that?"

"What's not to like? You're hot as fuck. You got an ass I wanna smash. And since you're good at school, I bet your easily teachable. Even if you *are* a virgin."

14

Her eyebrows, the same color as her hair, stitched together. "Do lines like that get you laid?"

"Usually don't gotta work so fuckin' hard to get laid."

"I bet not with sweet butts at your beck and call. They can't say no, right?"

"They can say no."

"Not if they want to remain a sweet butt."

She was right. But this was not the path he wanted to head down tonight. He wanted them to take the path to his waiting RV, instead.

Her eyes flicked from his face back to over his shoulder. Her spine snapped straight at the same time she whispered, "Shit."

Of course that made his spine tighten, too, but before he could turn around to figure out the issue, the issue was standing next to them.

"Let's go," Shade ordered Maddie in a low tone that screamed he didn't want an argument.

"I'm fine here," she told him.

"No you ain't. Let's go, Maddie. He ain't for you."

Romeo turned to face Shade but remained standing between the Fury member and Maddie. "Why? 'Cause I'm Black?"

Shade's dark eyes narrowed on him. "'Cause you're a fuckin' dog sniffin' around someone you shouldn't be."

"She's an adult and I thought you ain't her pop, so not sure why you get to tell her what to fuckin' do," Romeo told him.

Everything went completely still on Shade, except his lips. "My job to protect her."

"From me?"

"From anyone lookin' to take advantage of her. You need to fuckin' respect that."

This exchange was the most words he ever heard the Fury member say, not that Romeo had been around him much. But the man was known to speak few words and when he did, he spoke softly and slowly like he chose his words carefully.

Unlike Romeo. He tended to let shit fly. "We're only havin' a bit of fuckin' conversation, that's it."

Shade's tight jaw shifted. A second later he focused on his stepdaughter, if that was what she was to him. He still didn't know that answer. If truth be known, he also didn't fucking care.

"Let's go, Maddie."

Romeo took offense when Shade curled his hand around her forearm and tugged. "Maybe she don't wanna fuckin' go."

Romeo felt the other presence before he saw it. "It" being a him.

Judge. The Fury's sergeant at arms.

"Brother," was all the tall, bearded man rumbled.

Romeo wasn't sure if the warning was directed at him, at Shade, or the both of them.

"Let's not ruin this fuckin' day. Or our alliance. When you're in our territory, gotta respect our rules."

Romeo frowned and asked Judge, "What rule ain't I respectin'?"

"When the man don't want you fuckin' with his daughter, you gotta respect that."

"Is she his daughter?"

"Close enough. Family don't gotta be blood around here, just like I'm sure it is in your club. If the man got a problem with you hittin' on his girl, then you move the fuck on. Plenty of other women here for the weekend who might be willin'. Would be in your best interest to find one of them instead."

Clearly, Judge was running interference. Because while

the tall man talked, Shade had convinced Maddie to go with him. But Romeo did note, that while she trailed behind the long-haired Fury member, she did not look happy about it.

He waited until Judge turned to follow them before he let himself smile.

He didn't give a fuck about these so-called rules or what anyone thought about him. He planned on getting some of that.

And the fuck if he was leaving this damn farm until he did.

Game fuckin' on.

Chapter One

Five years later...

Romeo sucked on a fat blunt. With a half-full bottle of whiskey on the floor by his boot and his knees spread wide, he slouched in the recliner tucked in the corner of his room while keeping his eyes glued to the bed.

When the smoke rolled out of his mouth, he inhaled it again through his nostrils and back down deep into his lungs as he contemplated the situation before him.

What bugged his ass the most was, he should be rock hard about now. He should have his dick in his hand and be stroking it until he rode that sweet, sharp edge. Until he was ready to take part in what was happening on his mattress.

But he wasn't.

For some fucking reason, this shit tonight wasn't doing it for him.

Maybe he was sick. Though, he didn't feel ill. Just...

Bored as fuck.

That realization just made this whole goddamn thing worse.

Sweet butts weren't a fucking challenge. All he had to do was order them to show up and they did.

No backtalk.

No attitude. No spirit.

Nothing but fucking boring.

He could tell them to do anything he damn well pleased and if they wanted to remain a sweet butt in his club, they had to do it. For the most part.

Again, boring.

He was in the mood for a woman—or even more than one —with fight and fire.

Someone to get his pulse pounding, his blood rushing, and his dick hard enough to ache.

He was far from that right now. In fact, he had to smother a fucking yawn.

Not just one, either.

Were Tink and CeeCee great at eating pussy? Seemed to be by the sounds coming from them both as they enthusiastically munched down on each other in a sixty-nine position.

Could he order one or both of them to come over to him, get on their knees and suck him off until he blew his load down their throat? Hell yeah.

Did he want to? Fuck no.

Christ. Something was definitely wrong with him. Since when did two horny women going at it hot and heavy not get him off?

If he wasn't sick, he had to be fucking broken.

Because for him, this shit wasn't normal.

Maybe he needed a goddamn shrink.

Or less whiskey.

Regrettably, maybe less pot.

He frowned.

Fuck that. Overindulging never once made him not want to have sex in the past. Normally, he was always ready to go no matter how badly he was wasted.

That was another sad fact tonight...

He wasn't even buzzing yet.

"Kiss each other," he barked before tucking the lit joint between his lips.

Tink lifted her face from between CeeCee's thighs as the other sweet butt turned her head. Both stared at him with their lips shiny and their eyes glassy.

He might not be buzzing but the two of them certainly fucking were.

Damn.

When they untangled their limbs and sat up, their tits hung heavily, and their nipples were tightly pebbled.

He picked these two tonight out of the ever-changing stable of sweet butts because they both had thighs thick enough to rub together. Just how he liked them.

Don't give him a damn thigh gap. He didn't want to see a sliver of fucking light between their thighs. When he went down on a woman, he wanted to be temporarily blind and deaf because his face was buried deep within some womanly flesh.

White boys liked skin and bones. Gaps between a woman's thighs large enough to drive a Harley through.

Romeo was certainly not fucking white. Nor did he want to be.

He was the goddamn president of the Dark Knights. And to be in his MC, you had to be dark. Or at least be some shade of black.

As for the club's sweet butts and ol' ladies? Not the same

requirement. They could be any color in the damn rainbow as long as they had tits and a pussy.

And put out. Willingly.

In fact, Tink was Asian and CeeCee was... He didn't fucking know or care. Basically, she was pale. All he cared about was that her pussy was pink, and it didn't smell like a wet fucking dog.

For fuck's sake. The two of them tangling tongues and twisting each other's nipples also didn't do shit for him tonight.

Something had to change. It had to be either him or them.

He decided it was them.

The second they paused from eating each other's face, he ordered, "Get out."

"Romeo..." CeeCee whined with her two over-plucked eyebrows pinched together so tightly, they became one thin line that looked like someone had drawn it on with a damn Sharpie.

"Get the fuck out. Done with you two."

"But we—"

This was not the kind of attitude he was looking for. It wasn't a challenge, it only pissed him the fuck off. "Said get the fuck out! Find somewhere else to fuckin' be. Anywhere but here," he bellowed, crushing the lit end of his blunt between his fingers.

When he surged to his feet, his boot kicked over the bottle of whiskey and it skidded across the floor. At least the fucking thing didn't break, because that would be a waste of good booze.

It was bad enough he just wasted his damn time.

"Givin' you five minutes to get the fuck out and get gone." With that, he spun on his boot heel and climbed down the loft steps, keeping one ear on the sweet butts to make sure they were doing what he ordered.

He shook his head when he heard them scrambling and asking each other what they did wrong, then he headed outside and took long, determined strides toward Dirty Dick's.

Of course, that trip only took a few seconds since his place was directly behind the Knights-owned bar. It used to be Magnum's crib until the man got hitched to his ol' lady and decided to knock her up.

Twice.

Caleb and Asia were younger than some of the enforcer's goddamn grandkids. Instead of coasting into old age, here he was raising more crib lizards.

Fuckin' fool.

Worse, Magnum now put his family over the damn club. He was still supposed to run the bar, but who ended up doing it most of the time?

Romeo.

Because Magnum was nowhere to be seen. Thank fuck for Wick, since the bartender and his DKMC brother kept shit under control.

Romeo flung open the back door and kept moving. He quickly scanned Dirty Dick's kitchen on his way to see if the establishment was hopping tonight.

Of course it would be, it was a Saturday night.

For fuck's sake, a Saturday night and here he was not even getting his dick wet. Maybe he could find someone in the bar to change that.

Someone with sharp teeth and claws.

"Everythin' fuckin' good?" he shouted without breaking stride.

He heard a couple of mumbled, "Yeahs," before he

slammed both palms against one of the swinging double doors.

The strong smell of tobacco and weed along with the faint stink of vomit hit his nostrils as he made his way over to the long, packed bar that ran along the rear of the room.

He gave a chin lift to a few of his brothers gathered around a table playing cards and probably betting their last fucking dollar.

One difference between the Knights and some other clubs was, they didn't have an official clubhouse. Dick's was their church.

It wasn't supposed to be that way but once they bought the place, that was how it ended up. Prior to that, the club had a shitty little building that was a joke. And embarrassing. But that was all before his time.

The state seized that building and tore it down when the Knights didn't maintain it and stopped paying the taxes on the property. No fucking loss from the pictures he'd seen.

Should they have an official church other than a bar open to the public? Probably.

Did he give a shit? Fuck no.

Did any of his brothers give a shit? He heard no complaints.

Unlike the Iron Horse Roadhouse, owned by the Dirty Angels, Dick's had a basement. They used that when they needed privacy. Like for officer or club meetings.

Or a beat down.

The space worked for them because it was pretty damn flexible, even if it wasn't fancy.

Like the kitchen, the bar itself was busy tonight. And not only with his brothers. With actual paying patrons.

Customers who didn't give a shit about rubbing elbows with Black bikers.

Customers who didn't clutch their fucking pearls when it came to patronizing a MC-owned bar.

Customers who knew to keep any bullshit comments to themselves about the Dark Knights or bikers in general.

To Romeo, seeing how packed Dick's was meant a hell of a lot of scratch would be hitting the club's coffers. Some of that would also find its way into his own pocket.

That thought actually improved his mood.

"Wick!"

"Yeah?" the older Dark Knight muttered as he made his way down the bar.

He slammed a hand on the scratched and nicked bar top. "Gimme a whiskey!"

Wick's expression pinched. "Took a whole fuckin' bottle with you."

"Yeah? And now I wanna shot or two from another bottle. Why the fuck you questionin' me?"

"'Cause I can," was the bartender's answer.

Romeo shook his head. The attitude he wanted from a woman was the attitude he was getting from Wick, instead.

However, he had no desire to fuck Wick. Romeo's club brother would need much bigger tits and to shave the goatee off his face. Not to mention, he'd need a plump pussy that could take a good pounding.

When a full shot glass was slammed on the bar in front of him, some of the whiskey spilled over the edge. "Jack. Double. Neat," Wick announced before sauntering to the other end of the bar.

After downing it in one swallow, Romeo swiped the back of his hand across his mouth before drawing his fingers over his beard to make sure there weren't any droplets clinging to his pride and joy.

He might no longer be able to grow a full head of hair,

but his thick facial hair made up for it. It made a good partner with his tongue when he was tickling a woman between her plump thighs.

It was a tight fit when Coral sidled up to him by squeezing her big hips between him and the patron on the next stool.

His hand automatically went to the sweet butt's ass where he had no problem getting a good grip. "What's up, *chica?*"

Maybe he should've invited Coral into his bed tonight. She was the spiciest Puerto Rican he'd ever known. And that was saying something since most *Boricuas* were spicy as fuck.

Only she wasn't down with threesomes. She'd do it if told but would make her displeasure known often and loud. For him, it wasn't worth the fucking heartburn.

However, she was a pro with her mouth and if he couldn't find anyone else to get him off tonight, he could always get her to give him head. And maybe even a quickie against a wall.

The night was young, though, so he had time to decide on his next course of action.

She dug her sharply pointed nails into the back of his neck causing his dick to take notice. "Where's Tink and CeeCee?"

And now his dick went back into hibernation mode. "You ask them?"

"No."

"Then why you askin' me? I look like I fuckin' work in an information booth?"

"Because they left with you, Rome."

He beat back his irritation. "So?"

Coral sighed.

He grabbed her chin and twisted her head towards him. "You just fuckin' sigh at me?"

Without even a hesitation... "Sure did."

He released her chin. "Go get me another whiskey. Double. Neat."

"I know how you like your whiskey."

"Then why the fuck ain't there one in front of me?"

"What's up your ass tonight?"

"My goddamn balls are blue."

She shook her head, her level of annoyance now matching his. "Want me to take care of that for you?"

He considered her. The woman didn't have a damn gag reflex, so, again, he was tempted. The only problem was, if he was still feeling this restless once he blew his load, he would be even crankier afterward.

What the fuck was wrong with him?

He used to be perfectly fucking fine with either some sweet butts or strange in his bed.

Since when did he get so goddamn picky?

Maybe it was time to straddle his sled, go for a long damn ride and let the wind clear his fucking head.

Chapter Two

It was late but the night was absolutely beautiful, as well as peaceful. And peace was badly needed after the week she had.

Maddie sat at a picnic table under one of the parking lot lights and contemplated the fat burger she just unwrapped. Her mouth watered as she got a good grip on it and lifted it to her lips. A second later she shoved it into her mouth and took the biggest bite she could.

She closed her eyes and savored the juicy beef, the salty bacon, and the tangy slice of melted cheese, as well as the crunch of the crisp lettuce and the sweetness of the ripe tomato slice.

Perfection.

She deserved this meal tonight. This past week had been hell at work. She almost quit fifty times in the last five days alone. Okay, that might be a slight exaggeration. It was more like forty-seven and a half. But really, who was counting?

Her boss at Smith's Sports Therapy & Rehab Center was

a dick and a cheap ass, so they were always understaffed. That meant her and her co-workers were run ragged.

It only got worse when high school sports were in full swing.

She had a variety of patients. Kids competing in school sports or on travel teams for their sport of choice. Teens hoping to get a college recruiter to notice them. College students hoping to get drafted by a professional sports team.

Marathon runners... Olympic swimmers... Tennis players...

The variety of athletes she worked with was endless.

She loved what she did, she just hated where she did it. She had to tell herself on the daily to stick it out and do her time so she could land the job she really wanted.

Her ultimate goal? Being a sports physical therapist for the Pittsburgh Steelers. And if she couldn't land a position with the popular NFL team, she'd take a spot with the Pirates baseball team. Or the Penguins NHL team. Any of those professional teams located in her favorite city.

That was the whole reason she had moved down to this area. Plus, there wasn't an overabundance of need for what she did up in Manning Grove.

The deep, throaty sound of straight exhaust pipes had her head automatically twisting in that direction. It was a familiar sound since, unofficially, she was a part of the Blood Fury MC.

Claimed, more like it. And only because her mother fell head over heels in love with a Fury member.

"Holy shit," slipped from her lips as she recognized the biker getting off the Harley.

She spun on the picnic bench until her back was to him. She wasn't sure if he'd recognize her, but she wasn't taking that risk.

She had no desire to talk to him.

Enough had been said five years ago. And she wasn't in the mood to rehash that tonight.

Or ever.

All she wanted to do was enjoy her damn burger and fries. The problem was, if he spotted her, she might not be able to do that.

She peeked over her shoulder to see where he went.

To order at the take-out window, of course, you dolt. Why else would he come to the burger joint?

However, she ate here often and never once had she spotted Romeo doing the same.

Had she seen members of the Dirty Angels here? All the time.

The Blue Avengers? Absolutely.

But the Dark Knights? For some reason, never. So, she believed it was safe.

She guessed there was a first time for everything. Except, if she had to run into a Knight, she only wished it wasn't this one in particular.

She figured she was bound to run into him one day since she worked and lived on the border of the Knights' territory. Yet, she somehow managed to avoid it in the last year and a half.

Apparently, tonight her luck had run out.

If she didn't breathe, didn't say a word, didn't look in his direction or make eye contact, he might not even notice her. Once he left, she could go back to enjoying her burger along with her much-needed peace and quiet.

She'd rather deal with a cold burger than a hot biker. The problem being, the one ordering take-out was a womanizer. One who acted like women were only good for one thing. Or a couple things, depending on her skill set.

Five years ago, her skills were limited.

She had wanted to expand them. She simply picked the wrong man to do it with. She should've waited for someone she cared about. And one who cared about her.

Her mistake.

But making mistakes were a way to learn and grow. And that was how she used that experience.

The biggest lesson she learned was, selfish, misogynistic bikers—cocky enough to think the sun both rose and set in themselves—were not for her.

Over the years, she also grew into her sexuality.

Had Romeo broken the seal for her? Sure.

Did he take advantage of her?

She sighed. Maybe, maybe not. He saw an opportunity, the same as she did, and he jumped on it, as did she.

Truthfully, she really had no one to blame but herself. But that didn't mean Romeo was a mistake she ever wanted to repeat.

Live and learn.

To avoid him noticing her, she sat perfectly still with her ears open, and her eyes averted.

I'm invisible.

Hopefully, he'll concentrate on his meal and shoving it down his gullet before it gets cold.

She mourned the fact that her meal was doing just that as she waited for him to leave.

Her spine stiffened and her teeth clenched as she heard the distinct crunch of stone under heavy biker boots heading her way.

The picnic table actually shook slightly when the person she was hiding from in plain sight sat down. Her ears picked up the crinkle of the paper as he unwrapped his burger.

Holy shit. Who would've thought that imagining herself invisible didn't work?

She pulled in a breath, braced, and turned to face him, only to find him staring at her as he chewed.

After swallowing the bite, he made the straw squeak obnoxiously against the flimsy plastic lid by sliding it up and down several times, Unfortunately, the steady rhythm of the annoying sound reminded her of sex.

"Fuck, that shit's good," came out on the heels of a satisfied sigh after chasing his bite of hamburger with a long sip of the freshly squeezed lemonade.

She forgot the deep and rich tone of his voice.

She forgot how he smelled. A mix of warm leather, exhaust, and a hint of some sort of cologne. Not overbearing, unlike his personality.

She certainly forgot how intense the man sitting across from her could get.

"And you are?" she asked smartly.

He snorted, shook his head, and took another massive bite out of his burger. Maddie watched his tongue jut out to capture the juices running down his fingers.

She quickly grabbed a napkin from her small pile and tossed it in his direction, even though it was too late. Instead of the temperature dropping as the night got later, watching what he did with his tongue suddenly made it heat up.

It became uncomfortably warm.

It had to be her hormones, even though she was way too young to be having a hot flash. "What are you doing here, Romeo?"

His burger was temporarily forgotten in his fingers when he said, "Funny, was gonna ask you the same thing."

"I'm here having dinner."

He lifted his burger. "Same."

"I was looking for peace and quiet."

He shrugged and repeated, "Same."

"I never saw you here before."

A grin flirted with his full lips. "Same."

"I'm surprised you remember me." She glared at him while warning, "Don't you dare say 'same.'"

"Hard to forget someone who gave up—"

She raised her hand to stop him. "Don't."

He put his burger down, took another long sip of his sweet drink, popped four fries into his mouth and chewed as he asked, "What're you doin' here, Maddie?"

She swept a hand over her own half-eaten burger and barely touched fries. "Eating my dinner. I thought that was obvious."

"Know what I meant. What are you doin' *here*?"

"I live here. Well, not *here*," she pointed at the ground, "but near here."

His head twitched. "Since when?"

"Since I packed up my car and drove down here."

His nostrils flared and his lips pressed together. "Ain't an answer."

"It was but you just didn't like it."

"No one told me you were livin' down here."

"I didn't know you had signed up for the email notifications. Did you check your spam folder?"

When he continued, she couldn't tell whether her comment went over his head or if he chose to ignore it. "Last I fuckin' checked, you're part of a club the Knights got an alliance with. A heads up woulda been nice so we could keep an eye on you."

"Well, see, that might be the issue... I don't need anyone to keep an eye on me."

He didn't appear convinced. "The DAMC don't know you're livin' down here?"

"They do, but not because they were given a heads up. It's only because I run into them on a regular basis." If they had been given a heads up, no one mentioned it to her.

His brow furrowed so deeply, it reminded her of the Grand Canyon. "You hangin' with them?"

She easily read into that question. He wasn't asking if she spent time with the Angels, he was asking if she was hooking up with any of them.

Truthfully, whether she was or wasn't, wasn't any of his business. However, she had learned over the years how damn stubborn these bikers could be. If she didn't give him a decent answer, he wouldn't quit prodding until he got one that he considered satisfactory.

Maybe if she gave him that, he'd move along sooner than later. "I occasionally grab a drink at the Iron Horse. But I don't *hang* with them. I have no desire to be an ol' lady or... whatever."

That "whatever" covered everything a woman could be within an MC. Everything *but* a member. Because, *shudder*, equal rights were scary to big, badass bikers.

Well, except for the Blue Avengers. As far as she knew, they now had at least two female members, but the BAMC was more of a riding club than a whole damn lifestyle.

She studied the man across the picnic table from her. Being a biker defined him. It was who and what he was and always would be.

Like the Mafia, getting in or getting out of an MC wasn't so easy. But unlike the Mafia, you didn't need to die to get free.

Usually.

Despite not wanting that life for herself, she loved

everyone in the Blood Fury MC. They were truly family and had fully embraced Maddie, her mother, and her younger sister. The members, their ol' ladies and possibly even some of the sweet butts, would do anything for her. She also wouldn't hesitate to do the same for them.

Truthfully, they were the most loyal people she knew.

When Shade and her mother found each other...

She closed her eyes.

One day she hoped to find a love like they had. A partner totally dedicated to her. As she would be to him.

Yes, that was what she wished for, not someone who stuck his dick into any welcoming hole.

Romeo lived life as if he had to hit a certain number of notches on his bedpost before time ran out. Like it was a race to the grave.

He'd been handy to get the job done. But once that task was over, she walked away.

Or more like it, she did the walk of shame.

Luckily, no one saw her stumble out of Romeo's RV with her clothes wrinkled and her hair a tangled mess. And if they did, they kept it quiet.

If any of the Fury members had known she was in Romeo's RV that weekend losing her virginity, most likely a war would've broken out between at least two of the clubs, if not all three.

She had no doubt that Romeo would've been dragged right out of his rented Winnebago and made an example. Whether by the Fury president Trip or by Shade. Then she would've been the cause of that chaos, along with possibly destroying the club alliance.

All because she had been selfish and wanted to take care of a problem that she now knew was never a problem in the first place. At the time, she'd been foolish enough to think she'd been "missing" out. That she should be embarrassed being a college graduate who never went "all the way."

Even so, causing chaos was the last thing she wanted during the celebration of Easy and Tess's wedding, so, afterward, she walked away from that RV and avoided Romeo for the rest of the weekend.

Despite him trying to catch her attention on numerous occasions.

She didn't want anyone getting suspicious and asking questions.

Digging deeper on why she hadn't slept in her own bed all night.

Wanting to know why she snuck into the house before sunrise not quite looking the same as she left it the day before despite wearing the same outfit.

Or asking the biggest question of all…

Why Romeo?

Chapter Three

"How come you moved down here?" Romeo's question drew Maddie back to the present.

"It was *strongly suggested* that I live and work in one of the MC alliance's areas." Since the "alliance" consisted of three MCs, the Blood Fury—the club to which her stepfather belonged—the Dirty Angels and the Dark Knights—Romeo's club—it gave her practically all of western Pennsylvania to live.

She picked up her burger and took another bite. While it was no longer hot, it still remained tasty, and it would be a tragedy to waste a Bangin' Burger.

"If that's true, you coulda reached the fuck out and told me you were down here."

"That wasn't a requirement," she answered after swallowing the mouthful. And, truly, if she had complained enough, they would've let her move anywhere.

Let her.

She mentally sighed. Like she needed anyone to "let her"

do anything. At twenty-seven, she was an adult, made her own money and was quite capable of making good decisions.

Luckily, she loved Pittsburgh, and the sports teams tied to the city, so the location happened to align with what she wanted. She only let them think she was going along with Shade's and her mother's demands since it made them happy and not stress over her moving away from Manning Grove.

And away from Shade's eagle eyes.

She understood why they worried. After years of dealing with the crazy people up on the mountain, aka Hillbilly Hill, the Fury was overly cautious. However, the thorn in the Fury's side, the cult known as the Shirleys, was now gone and the club no longer had any enemies.

For now, anyway.

"You blame your pop for makin' you stay in the alliance's area?"

Did he forget? Or did he just not care enough to pay attention? "Shade's not my father. My father died while serving in the Army."

"Might not've been his seed that was planted, but your mama's ol' man stepped in to help raise you."

Well, there it was. Proof he hadn't paid attention. "You might've missed the part where I was already twenty when he came into our lives."

"Age don't mean shit. Family's family, no matter the age. You don't like him?"

"I love Shade, but he's not my pop, as you called him." Even though he acted like both Maddie and Josie, her younger sister, came from his loins.

He was actually more protective than most biological fathers, but he had a reason to be that way that had nothing to do with being a member of the Fury. He'd been abducted as a young child and sold into sexual slavery. Because of that, Shade and her mother also "adopted" Jude, who Maddie now considered her younger brother, after Shade found him down in a basement locked in a cage, waiting to be auctioned off.

Her heart raced simply thinking about that dangerous situation and how much more damaged Jude would be right now if Shade hadn't rescued him when he did. It was bad enough that her brother still suffered through a lot of dark moments and thoughts caused from that experience, amplified by the loss of his mother.

All because of sick sexual perverts.

"Goddamn semantics, girl."

What? Damn, she needed to stay focused.

She especially had to stay on her toes with the man sitting across from her. Romeo was slick and before she knew it, he could be talking her out of her clothes and right back into his bed.

"Speaking of semantics... I'm not a girl. I wasn't a girl when you met me the first time and I'm not a girl now, Rome."

"Woman, then," he corrected.

"The fact is, there aren't enough jobs up in Manning Grove for what I do. My options were better closer to Pittsburgh."

When his head tipped to the side, his gaze raked from the top of her head down her chest, only stopping when the table blocked his view of the rest of her. "What d'ya do?"

Did the man really care? Or was he only trying to work her? "I'm a sports physical therapist."

"A what?"

"I'm a physical therapist for athletes," Maddie explained. "You know what an athlete is, right?"

He grunted in response to her question but didn't take the bait. "Where at?"

"A rehab center, but I'm hoping to get hired by a major sports team."

His brow dipped low. "What kinda team?"

"A professional one. Preferably with the NFL or MLB."

"Like the Steelers or Pirates?"

"Since those are professional teams, yes." She knew she was being a smart ass, but she didn't feel the need to explain herself, or her career, to Romeo of all people. Since when had he shown real interest in anyone without a dick between their legs? She was damn sure he pretended to care only enough to get them to bend to his will.

His reputation was well known since he used women simply for his own satisfaction.

Maybe in the past five years, he turned over a new leaf.

Wait. She glanced up to the dark sky. Did a pig do a fly-by?

His "Why?" pulled her back to the conversation.

"Why not?" she countered.

"Like workin' with men?"

Why did he assume all athletes were men? "I like working with... people. All kinds." She loved helping people either heal from a sports-related injury or to be the best athlete they could be.

No one was more surprised than her mother when she went into this line of work since Maddie had never been an athlete herself. In high school, she never ran track or played on any teams, like volleyball, softball, or field hockey. But she had always appreciated the hard work and dedication it took to become a top-notch athlete.

To her, it seemed like too much pressure to perform.

However, she didn't hold that goal against anyone and in fact, was happy to help people achieve it.

"Make a lot of scratch?"

"I do all right." But she could do a lot better once she had more experience under her belt. That was why she had to suck it up and stick it out at Smith's unless something better popped up. She had to keep reminding herself that her current employer was only a stepping stone to bigger and better opportunities.

"Yeah?"

"Yeah," she echoed softly.

"You touch men?"

She mentally sighed. She should've expected that he wouldn't let that particular point go. "I touch a lot of people."

"Like men."

"Yes, I touch men, but not in a creepy way, Romeo. I'll leave that to you." She ate a few more fries. Like the burger, they were cold, but she certainly wasn't going to waste them.

"Don't fuckin' touch men."

She lifted her gaze from her food to the man across the table. "I meant women."

"Don't touch anyone who don't want me touchin' them."

"They probably only regret it after it happens."

"Damn, woman."

She shrugged. "Am I wrong?"

"You regret me touchin' you?"

"I don't want to hurt your feelings," she warned, even though she wasn't sure if Romeo even had any.

He blinked at her.

She grinned at him.

He scowled.

Her grin grew.

His scowl deepened and his burger sat forgotten. "It was great, right?"

"Great is being... generous."

His spine snapped straight, and his heavily bearded chin jerked up. "What the fuck d'you mean?"

She shrugged and pointed a fry in his direction. "I had nothing to compare it to back then. Now I do." She popped it into her mouth and waited while she chewed.

"Now you do?" exploded from him. "What the fuck does that mean?"

"Do I have to explain it to you?"

His deep brown eyes narrowed on her and she swore his voice dropped a whole octave when he asked, "How many?"

Maddie held those eyes with her own. "What does that matter?" That was nobody's business but her own.

"It don't."

"Seems like it does. Otherwise, you wouldn't have asked."

Did he just grind his teeth?

The horn dog was bothered by someone else having sex? Or more likely, a woman having sex with someone other than him?

That was plain stupid. They had sex five years ago. Once.

It had been a mistake.

Not because he was awful in bed. She learned later that he'd been better than most, but the mistake was having sex with him for the wrong reason.

And that reason made her as selfish as him.

"Wanna come back to my crib?"

What? Was he serious? The man clearly didn't know how to read the room. Or picnic table. "You have an actual place? Or is it a room in the Knights' church?"

"We got a bar. Ain't a barn with livin' quarters behind it, like the Fury."

44

"You live in a bar?"

"Live behind a bar."

"In an actual house?" Was Romeo somewhat domesticated and not a complete feral tom cat?

"Got four fuckin' walls and a roof, so guess you could call it that. That make a difference for you to say yes?"

"No."

"Well?"

"That was my answer."

"Figured you needed a reminder on how great it was. Willin' to give you that reminder."

She somehow managed to keep her eyes from rolling out of her head. "Don't take it personally, Rome. It's normal that someone's first time isn't great." Especially with someone they didn't share an emotional connection.

They had flirted and joked around. She thought he was hot. And from what he said, he thought the same about her.

But that was where the connection ended.

She figured out of anyone, Romeo—a known womanizer —wouldn't care that she wasn't experienced. She also figured since he was so self-centered and only worried about his own needs, he'd power through no matter how awkward or uncomfortable it was for her. Or, *hell*, the both of them.

She also didn't want to "break the seal" with anyone she'd see on a regular basis. She was sure a few Fury members without an ol' lady would've been more than willing to volunteer to help with her dilemma.

She was also aware of the fact that doing so could be dangerous for them if Shade found out.

Plus, after seeing each other naked, it would be even more awkward to look whoever it was in the eye later.

More importantly, she certainly wasn't looking to hook up long-term with any biker. Not a Blood Fury member. Not a Dirty Angel. Or—she met Romeo's eyes across the table—a Dark Knight.

When she found the love of her life, he wouldn't be wearing a leather cut and riding a Harley. But then, to find the love of her life, she'd have to be looking.

She wasn't.

Right now, her focus was on her career and getting hired by a professional sports team. She wanted to prove to herself that she could do anything she put her mind to. Like professional athletes, she also had a goal and was sprinting towards it. She didn't want anyone tripping her up along the way.

Or a man thinking that he could tell her what to do and how to do it.

"Well?" he prodded again.

"Thank you for the invitation. Although it's hard to resist such a generous offer, I'll have to pass."

"Your place is okay, too."

"Okay for what?"

"For a repeat."

"You might have missed this in health class, but I can't lose my virginity a second time."

She didn't realize his full lips could get so thin.

He reached across the table with his hand open and his palm up.

She frowned as she considered it. "What? Do you want the rest of my burger?"

"Phone."

"For what?"

"Gonna give you my number. You need anythin', you fuckin' call me."

"You mean if I need to get stoned or get drunk enough to get into a fight, or I'm just looking to get laid without any strings attached?"

"Maddie..." he growled. "Call me if you're in a fuckin' jam."

"Oh, got it. So, the word Knight in your MC's name isn't just random, then."

He got up from the bench, snagged her cell phone from where it sat near her drink, and before she could duck, he held the screen up to her face to unlock it, then scrolled.

"Can I have my phone back?" she asked as calmly as she could, even though the panic was rising.

"When I'm fuckin' done with it."

This was exactly what she *wasn't* looking for in a man. One who made demands and thought he can dictate how she lived her life. "That's theft."

"Ain't stealin' it. Just borrowin' it."

Romeo continued to do whatever he was doing. Most likely inputting his number into her contacts. When he was done, she heard his cell phone ring.

Shit. Now he had her number, too. She should've launched herself across the table to steal her phone back before that happened.

Without warning, he tossed her phone back to her, but luckily, her reflexes were quick enough to catch it. She didn't bother to delete her newest contact entry since he now had her number, anyway. And, truthfully, she didn't dislike the guy. It was the opposite.

But he wasn't for her.

Even if the sex wasn't bad.

The problem was, if she succumbed to temptation a second time, he'd figure out just how much she had enjoyed it the first time.

Was it awkward and uncomfortable? At first, yes. But surprisingly, he made sure it wasn't for long. Because of his reputation, she hadn't expected him to think about someone other than himself.

He also didn't have to do that.

But he did it for her.

And that had bothered her the most about the whole interaction.

Chapter Four

HAD it really been five fucking years since he'd seen her?

The couple of times the clubs got together he had asked about her, but not in an obvious way that would draw suspicion.

He had been told she was away at school.

When they hooked up during Easy's wedding weekend celebration, she was already a college graduate. That meant she had gone back to further her education.

She might have mentioned it back then, but her schooling hadn't been the focus of his interest.

Even so, that hammered home the fact that she'd been out of his league before... But now? She probably had some impressive degree. Unlike his wrinkled and stained high school diploma he received by the skin of his teeth. Did he need that damn piece of paper? Hell no. He made something out of his life without it.

He might not be considered "successful" in a lot of circles, but he didn't give a fucking shit what others thought about him.

Romeo might not have book smarts, but he had street smarts. To run his MC. To make scratch. Even to stay alive.

And to him, that was more important.

He only needed to be respected as the president of an ever-expanding MC that had grown to thirty-two members. Their brotherhood was now larger than either the Dirty Angels or the Blood Fury, even though the Fury was now running a close second.

While the three MCs in the west formed a formidable army, he was more interested in growing one of his own. That way, in a pinch, the Knights didn't have to rely on anyone else. It would also guarantee they'd be a force to be reckoned with if another president was voted in for the Fury or the Angels and decided to turn on the Knights in an attempt to take their territory.

Having numbers on their side would make sure that wouldn't happen easily, if at all.

Romeo wasn't a fucking fool. He knew the next in line to hold the Angels' gavel was Z's son, Zeke. While Zak had a laid-back personality and a good head for biker business, his son was young and cocky. Then there was the fact that Little Z was already doing stupid shit. The kid needed to get some of that out of his system before taking the reins of a long-established, well-respected MC.

The wrong president could destroy a club. The right one could make it invincible. He considered himself the second type. He figured his brothers did, too, since he kept getting voted back in as prez year after year after the former prez stepped down.

He was slowly replacing his executive committee with younger blood but there were still some old timers hanging on.

Like Magnum. However, his sergeant at arms had created

a stronger bond with the DAMC by making Cait, the daughter of one of the Angels, his ol' lady, wife, and the mother of his two youngest offspring.

It wouldn't hurt to create that same bond with the BFMC.

Only he wasn't looking to "settle down" with an ol' lady. He certainly wasn't looking for a fucking wife or to have crotch droppings. At only thirty-four, he was still living life to the fullest and had a long way to go before tying himself to one woman screwed that up.

Could he have an ol' lady and still fuck around with other females? No fucking doubt, but that would cause a lot of damn headaches he didn't want to deal with.

Unfortunately, most women didn't like to share.

Life was hell of a lot simpler when he stuck to sweet butts, hang-arounds and strange he could easily scrape off.

As he steered his sled into the parking lot of Dirty Dick's and continued along the side of the building to the rear, the memory of Maddie spread naked on the bed in his rented RV flashed before him.

He couldn't fucking believe he ran into her tonight.

He pulled up next to the side of his crib and shut down his sled.

No, he couldn't fucking believe she'd been living in the area for a year and a half—according to her before they parted ways—and no one ever mentioned it.

If Dark Knights property moved up north, he'd be on the fucking phone letting Trip know so they could watch out for her.

That was what allies did for each other. They had each other's back.

That covered family and property, too.

Once he no longer straddled his ride and his feet were

planted on the ground, he pulled his cell phone from the inner pocket of his cut and glanced at the time.

It was after eight. The old man could already be in bed.

He texted Magnum anyway. *U no the Fury's Maddie is livn down here?*

He headed inside and set his phone on the counter while he grabbed a cold beer from the fridge.

By the time he twisted off the cap, successfully lobbed it into the trash like an NBA All-Star and guzzled about a third of the beer down into his gut, he finally got a response.

As expected, it was short and to the point. *No.*

Romeo quickly texted back. *I wake u, old man?*

No.

He snorted. Magnum hated texting, so that alone probably chapped his Black ass. *Think Z knows?*

Y dont u fuckn ask him steada me?

Romeo shook his head and grinned. *Someone's prostate swollen or what? Should have that looked at.*

Gonna drop my fuckn pants n u can check it 4 me next time I c u.

Romeo warned, *Don't threatn me with a good fuckn time.*

Next, he found Z's number in his contacts and shot the Angels' prez a text. *U no Maddie from the Fury's livn in the area?*

By the time Z answered, Romeo was already on his second beer and was stripped down to only his boxer briefs while lounging on the couch. He flipped through endless fucking television channels looking for something to get his mind off the woman he ran into tonight.

Porn would be the answer. It might be the only thing that would distract him. Especially since the curvy, formerly strawberry blonde was wedged firmly in his noggin.

It was hard to tell with the outdoor lighting at Bangin'

Burgers, but he could swear her hair was now darker than it had been previously.

Truthfully, he didn't give a shit about the color of her hair. It could be bright pink, and she'd still be as sexy as shit. He considered her even hotter now that she had filled out more than the last time he saw her.

She had been a touch too thin for him last time.

Now?

He blew out a breath.

Goddamn perfection.

Zak's text drew him from his perverted thoughts. *Yeah. Knew it. What about it? There a problem?*

Romeo asked, *Trip give you the heads up?*

Shade did, came Z's answer.

Y didn't he tell us?

Y u askn me? Ask him.

He was tempted to shoot back the same reply he sent to Magnum, but Romeo needed to keep things cool between the clubs. It was one thing to bust on one of his own. It was another to bust on the prez of another club, despite him and Z being solid.

There a problem I need to know about?

The problem was that the Fury didn't feel the need to let him know one of their own had flown the coop and landed in the area.

But, apparently, the only one thinking it was a problem was Romeo.

No problem. Ran into her. That's all.

When the next text was only a thumbs up emoji, he tossed his cell phone on the couch next to him and tucked his hand into the elastic waistband of his boxer briefs.

Pursing his lips, he considered the TV show on the screen.

Whatever it was wouldn't get his mind off Maddie and that spot of blood he found on the sheet after she booked from his RV in the early morning hours like her ass was on fire.

Of course, she had told him she was a virgin, so seeing the proof hadn't surprised him. But still, it was a stark reminder of what he had taken from her.

Something she'd never get back.

He shouldn't feel guilty about accepting what was freely offered. But for some fucking reason, in this case, he had.

To this day, it still bothered him.

He gave her what she wanted.

He hadn't taken any more than what she'd been willing to give him.

He even took his fucking time and kept the fact she was inexperienced at the forefront in his mind so he wouldn't forget and get too rough or demanding.

Normally, he didn't give much thought to the women he had under or on top of him, but with her...

It had been different.

And look where it got him.

Nowhere.

She most likely went on to fuck a bunch of other men and probably never gave Romeo a second thought.

He clenched his teeth.

What the fuck? Was he getting soft?

When the fuck did he grow a pussy?

Why was he letting any of what happened bug the shit out of him?

After powering off the TV, he threw the remote across the room—not giving a shit where it landed—before picking up his phone to find what he really needed.

Something that wouldn't cost him a damn thing.

Unlike the formerly strawberry blonde with the big brown eyes and tight as fuck pussy.

With the plump lips he wanted wrapped around his cock as he pumped in and out of her mouth.

With the one spot he guaranteed no one else had ever touched after he popped her cherry.

He scrolled through the site until he found the clip he was searching for. One with a brown-eyed woman and head of strawberry blonde hair.

Then he settled in for the next hour.

Only, it turned out he needed less than five minutes.

But no one had to know that.

Chapter Five

Trip's deep voice filled Romeo's ear. "There's a reason we didn't give you a heads up, Rome."

"And that reason is?"

"You really gotta fuckin' ask?"

Did they actually know or only suspect? Or was the Blood Fury president just shooting blanks?

He couldn't imagine that Maddie had told anyone about what happened.

"Stay away from her."

Too late.

"She ain't for you, brother."

Should he be offended? He felt like he should be fucking offended. Time to do a clap-back. "Wouldn't blame you if you're savin' that sweet, young thing for yourself."

He knew that wasn't true. He'd witnessed the connection the Fury president had with his ol' lady. That man didn't have eyes for anyone other than Stella, his wife and mother of his two sons.

Some bikers he knew might not be loyal, but Trip wasn't one of them.

Sucker.

"Gonna end this conversation now. If we don't, it could fuck up our clubs' alliance."

"How would it get fucked up?"

"When you do."

Damn. "Why the fuck would I get fucked up?" This conversation was not going as planned.

"By tryin' to get with our girl."

"Your girl," Romeo murmured into the phone.

"Wears our colors. Under our protection."

"When I ran into her last night, she wasn't wearin' anyone's colors." Fact.

"Then, you're fuckin' blind."

"Could see her just fine." And how fine she looked.

"Pretend you can't."

For fuck's sake. He was hoping Trip would tell him to look after Maddie, not stay away from her. That kind of put a kink in his plan.

"Look, was reachin' out 'cause our clubs are supposed to have each other's backs. Had no fuckin' clue she was livin' down here. If you didn't wanna tell me, you shoulda shared that info with Magnum, at least."

"Magnum knew."

Hold up...

"Told him not to tell you."

Now Romeo's blood pressure was spiking. "Why?"

"'Cause you got a reputation, *Romeo*. No, ain't a fuckin' reputation, it's reality. You stick your dick into anything. But let me clue you in... Ain't gonna be stickin' it in her."

Romeo muttered, "Such goddamn disrespect."

"Am I wrong? Think it didn't go unnoticed when you

were sniffin' 'round her every damn time we had a gatherin' you were at? Think we didn't hear those inquiries about her whereabouts when she wasn't there?"

Shit. Had it been that obvious? He thought he'd been slick about it.

"Think we don't know how you earned your goddamn road name?"

Romeo was batting a thousand here.

"Not hearin' your answers," Trip prodded.

Because Romeo didn't have any.

He couldn't deny it. It was all true. "Called to help a brother out and all I get is this bullshit."

"Tell me, why do you give a shit that Maddie's down there?"

"Like I said, was tryin' to do our part since we're allies. That's it. Don't gotta read anythin' more into it."

Silence filled Romeo's ear. He didn't take that as Trip realizing Romeo was right, but as the Fury prez trying to avoid pissing off another club's prez even more.

Between the clubs, Trip's hair-trigger temper was as well-known as Romeo's quest to put so many notches in his bedpost, nothing would be left except a pile of sawdust.

He wiped his grin away with his hand as if Trip could see it. "All right... Figured I'd help a brother out but can see my efforts ain't appreciated."

"If I believed you had good intentions, Romeo, I *would* appreciate it. But like I said, Magnum got a heads up."

He was going to have a little discussion with his enforcer. Especially after he lied and told Romeo he didn't know. The fucker wasn't supposed to keep secrets about shit like that. At the minimum, that info should've been shared in an exec committee meeting.

"Guessin' that means if anyone from the Knights moves

north, you expect me to contact Judge 'steada you?" Judge was the Fury's sergeant at arms.

Once again silence hit his ears.

Yeah, just like he fucking thought. Trip only bypassed him to keep Romeo in the dark about Maddie.

Finally, Trip said, "On the rare chance that happens, got no problem with you reachin' out to Judge."

Bullshit. "Got it." He was so fucking done with this conversation. "Have a good one."

"You, too, Rome. And don't worry about Maddie. We got it covered."

Romeo ended the call and stared at his phone.

Good thing the alliance was formed long before Romeo became president, otherwise, there wouldn't be one.

Not after that fucking phone call.

But he still had one more fucking bone to pick. This time it was with one of his own.

———

"You said you didn't fuckin' know."

Magnum grunted and pushed past Romeo.

"You kept shit from your goddamn president."

Magnum didn't even grunt this time, he ignored Romeo and kept moving. Romeo followed right on the big man's heels.

"Had a little convo with Trip and he said he told you she was livin' down here."

Magnum suddenly stopped and spun to face Romeo. "Why the fuck do you care if she's livin' down here?" His chin pulled into his neck. "Only one reason... And it's exactly why Trip didn't want you to fuckin' know."

"I expect respect from not only my own fuckin' brothers, but from the other clubs, too."

"You had a daughter, you'd understand."

"She ain't Trip's daughter," Romeo exclaimed.

"Don't matter. What fuckin' matters is, she's still under his protection. He did what he thought was best for her. Like any goddamn president worth bein' a goddamn president would do."

"You sayin' I shouldn't be president?"

"You hear that shit come outta my mouth?"

"Better not hear that shit come outta your mouth," Romeo warned him. "I was unanimously voted in and keep get voted in. That's gotta say somethin'."

"Says nobody else wanted that fuckin' spot. That's what it says."

Damn. What crawled up his ass tonight? "Cait got you in the doghouse or somethin'?"

Magnum scowled. "What the fuck you talkin' 'bout?"

"If not, you gotta have problem with me to be talkin' shit like that."

"Again, you're puttin' goddamn words in my mouth. Got no problem with you bein' president, but gonna have a fuckin' problem if you cause trouble with the other clubs. All over a piece of ass. The Knights are so much damn stronger havin' the Angels and the Fury at our back. You get that, right?"

He did.

Magnum wasn't finished. "Had that alliance in place long before you became a prospect and take my word for it, we don't wanna lose the support of those fuckin' clubs. Shit's so much better now. Since the alliance ain't a secret, other clubs don't wanna fuck with us. What d'you think stopped the Deadly Demons from movin' more north than they did?"

"The fact the Angels would've crushed them like a fuckin' roach?"

"The Angels couldn't've done it on their own."

"They got the Shadows at their back," Romeo reminded him. And that group of former military special operators wasn't a crew to fuck with, despite them now leaning more toward the geriatric side.

He also considered Magnum's age as the big man said, "They also got us. And the Fury. You don't think that stops stupid fucks from testin' their boundaries?"

Romeo couldn't disagree with that fact, so he didn't.

"Not sure why this whole thing with Maddie's such a big fuckin' deal to you..." Magnum shook his bald head. "No, I fuckin' know. Don't fuck with her, Rome. You do, you'll be playin' with fire. You fuckin' with her can fuck up our alliance."

"Or make it stronger."

"You ain't makin' shit stronger. You'll fuck her, then fuck her over. That'll make her cry to her mommy and mommy's gonna cry to her ol' man. Shade's either gonna get pissed and kill your dumb motherfuckin' ass in your sleep or he's gonna say somethin' to Trip. And you know how fuckin' short that man's temper is. Ain't gonna be good either way. Did my job as the goddamn enforcer of this club and made a decision to protect, not only my president and our fuckin' club, but our alliance. You don't like that fuckin' decision, too fuckin' bad."

Damn. "I might not've been part of this club when you met your ol' lady, but from what I heard, you were warned off her 'cause she belonged to the Angels. Am I right?" When Magnum didn't answer, Romeo continued, "Not only did you take her for yourself, but it also made the bond between the Angels and our club even stronger. You can't fuckin' say it didn't."

"Didn't fuck her over, Rome. Fuckin' married her and gave her babies. That's the goddamn difference."

"Who says I'm gonna fuck over Maddie?"

With another grunt, Magnum shook his head again and continued through the busy Dirty Dick's kitchen and to the back corner of the building where the steps to the basement were located. They were heading downstairs for an executive meeting.

"Got all the free fuckin' pussy who'll do whatever the fuck you want and here you got a hard-on over one you shouldn't even be lookin' at."

Nothing wrong with wanting a taste of forbidden fruit. Even though he already had a taste. After running into her, he realized he was hungry for more. "You didn't have a problem when I was eyein' up Aaliyah."

Magnum's oldest daughter was hot as fuck, despite being a few years older than Romeo. Even better, she had plenty of scratch. The woman busted her ass and was rolling in the dough.

After yanking open the door to the basement, Magnum glanced over his broad shoulder at him with his eyes narrowed. "Truth is, knew my girl wasn't gonna ever give you the time of fuckin' day. She's too good for your fuckin' ass."

"But not too good for a pig."

He just brought up a sore subject since his daughter was once again married to a damn badge, just like her first husband. She also gave the newest one a kid, too.

"Think I like that shit? Only tolerate it 'cause he makes my girl happy and takes care of her. He's also a damn good father to my latest grandbaby and my grandsons."

"He's a wannabe." Aaliyah's pig husband was a member of what Romeo considered a "pretend" MC, the Blue Avengers.

"Pretend" because it was full of law enforcement members, and they didn't live the life. And that was what being a true biker was... a lifestyle. The Knights' lives revolved around their MC; the Blue Avengers' lives revolved around their badge.

"I woulda been loyal to her." At least he would've tried. Whether he was successful or not was another story.

Magnum snorted, shook his head, and began to lumber down the steps.

Romeo followed. "Ain't gonna bring this up tonight with the other officers, 'cause I wanted you to give it some thought first, but... think you need to step down as the club's sergeant at arms."

He almost slammed into Magnum when he stopped abruptly at the foot of the steps and bellowed, "For what fuckin' reason?"

Romeo moved around him and out of reach. Just in case. He normally could hold his own but, age aside, Magnum wasn't anyone to fuck with when he was pissed. "Gettin' long in the tooth, brother. Time to pass that job on to someone younger."

"Like who?"

Romeo shrugged. "Whoever wants their name thrown in the hat and can handle the job."

"Think I can no longer handle it?" As Magnum's temper got shorter, his voice tended to get louder.

Despite that, Romeo wasn't backing down from this conversation. He'd been putting off having it, but Magnum keeping Maddie a secret was a good reason to finally bring it up. "Didn't say that."

"Sure fuckin' sounded like it. Been doin' this since you were just a tadpole in your daddy's nut sack."

"And that's what I'm fuckin' sayin'. You're slowin' down,

old man. Wouldn't you rather be home loungin' in a recliner and bouncin' your grandbabies on your knee?" Maybe even an arthritic knee at that.

"Right now the only grandbaby I got small enough to be bounced on my goddamn knee is Destiny."

Destiny was Aaliyah's latest kid with her current badge-carrying ball-and-chain.

"How 'bout you ask the rest of the officers if I should be fuckin' replaced? See what they say. Like you bein' prez, I'm pretty fuckin' sure our brothers think I'm still good enough to be this club's enforcer. Any-fuckin'-way, it's the membership's fuckin' decision, not yours."

Magnum wasn't wrong. He'd have to be removed from the position for a valid reason. Unless he quit. Otherwise, Romeo would have to wait until the next election and try to convince someone to run against him.

"Do we got enemies?"

Romeo answered, "No."

"You want enemies?"

"No."

"Then the right person's in the fuckin' position."

"Just figured you'd wanna slow down and enjoy life instead. You're also supposed to be managin' the bar. You're hardly ever here. I gotta step in all the fuckin' time."

"Wick's got shit under control. You only step in 'cause you're much closer now that you're livin' in my old place."

"But you're still takin' a cut of the profits as fuckin' manager."

"Why you such a fuckin' whiny bitch tonight? You on your period or somethin'?"

Romeo's head snapped back. "Brother, you're talkin' to your goddamn prez."

Magnum leaned closer and looked him directly in the

eye. "Know who I'm talkin' to. Believe it or not, I always got your back, brother, that's the whole reason I didn't fuckin' tell you about Maddie."

Romeo got it but that didn't mean he had to like it. "You want me to fuckin' thank you for that?"

"Yeah. That woulda been better than all the bullshit you just shoveled. 'Specially since I was tryin' to keep you breathin'. But go fuck with her and see how that works out for you."

"As long as I don't end up married and givin' her babies like you, I'll be fuckin' golden."

Magnum snorted, shook his head, then headed over to this spot at the table. That conversation was over as soon as the rest of the committee wandered downstairs.

Romeo decided not to bring it up during the meeting.

But that didn't mean he wouldn't bring it up again.

Chapter Six

Maddie sat in her car in the parking lot at Smith's Sports Therapy & Rehab Center and stared through the windshield at the building in front of her.

Her place of work should really be in her rearview mirror right now since normally she'd be heading home for the night. Instead, she sat contemplating on whether to put her Toyota in Drive, smash her foot on the accelerator and plow through the front of the building.

Would it be stupid? Yes.

Would it make her feel better? Also, yes.

At least, until the reality of her actions set in.

Her fingers choked the steering wheel, and every damn muscle was tense. One of the massages she gave to her patients to relieve knotted muscles would be great about now.

She really needed to keep pushing at getting a job with a professional team, but if she applied for them now, she'd get turned down without even an interview since she needed more time and experience under her belt.

Hence, the reason she still worked at Smith's.

She also needed a good reference. Another reason she wasn't ramming her SUV into the building.

A regular paycheck would be nice, as well, so she could eat, put gas in her vehicle and pay rent. She might even need bail money if she ended up taking her frustration out on her asshole boss.

All this was why she was leaving her car in Park and only shooting daggers at the building instead of creating a new entrance with her Toyota.

The pros when it came to working at Smith's: her patients and getting the experience she needed to advance her career to the next level.

The cons: too many to fucking list.

However, at the top of the list of cons was one Roger Smith. She didn't think anyone could be more arrogant or cocky than a biker. Time and time again, "Roger Dodger" proved her wrong.

Every time her mother called to check in on her, Maddie donned her game face and lied about how she loved her job. The last thing she wanted was to tell her the truth.

Because one, they might insist she move back home. And that was happening... Never.

Two, Shade might pay Roger a visit. That was something else she needed to prevent.

Shade was overly protective of his blended family. Not only of her mother Chelle, but of Maddie, her younger sister Josie, and her adopted brother Jude.

When it came down to it, also Gabi, currently living with Crash and Liz in Shadow Valley. For a short time, she had lived with Maddie's family after she was rescued from the Shirleys on Hillbilly Hill.

But since Gabi and Jude had formed some sort of deep connection in that short amount of time and were considered too young to act on it, Crash and Liz from the Dirty Angels welcomed her into their household.

Doing so prevented a lot of problems and temptations. It also gave both Gabi and Jude stable homes and families.

Maddie spent a lot of time with Gabi since she was now almost twenty-one. So, even if Trip hadn't notified Zak when she moved down here, Gabi would've known and shared that info.

When it all boiled down to it, Romeo was bent out of shape for nothing.

With the three clubs being so interconnected, Maddie couldn't escape the MC life. Or their meddling. No matter how much she might want to.

For a hot minute, she did consider moving to Thailand.

Or Antarctica.

She loved her family, both immediate and the Fury, she really did. She received plenty of love, support, and protection. Even if, at times, it felt a little smothering. However, if she needed anything, it was only a text or phone call away.

If she was short on money one month, a deposit would appear in her bank account.

If her SUV needed serviced, she could either get it done for nothing in Manning Grove at Dutch's Garage or here at Shadow Valley Bodyworks, a garage owned by the DAMC and run by Crash.

Anything she needed could be covered by one of the three clubs. So, she really shouldn't complain about the MC life. It took good care of her.

Unlike the asshole owner of Smith's Sports Therapy & Rehab Center.

If her Toyota broke down causing her to be a few minutes late to work, he'd dock her pay by an hour.

If she tripped over a piece of equipment, he'd loudly call

her a klutz, or worse, in front of all the patients and employees.

If a client complained over the smallest reason, he'd write her up and mention it in her employee evaluation, using it as an excuse not to give her a decent raise.

He also insisted on calling her Mad instead of Madison or Maddie.

And quite frankly, that made her... mad.

He thought the nickname was funny. She didn't agree. Maybe if anyone else but him used it, she'd think otherwise.

His biggest—and lamest—joke was, "Are you Mad?" Then he'd guffaw so much and so obnoxiously, she wanted to knee him in the nuts. That would stop the stupidity.

It would also get her fired.

Not to mention, ruin her future as a sports physical therapist for the Pittsburgh Steelers. Then she *would* have to move to Antarctica and work with penguins. The actual birds, not the NHL hockey team.

She blew out a long breath, started her car and forced herself to turn the steering wheel. She needed to head out of the parking lot before she made a mistake she wouldn't be able to undo.

Today had been extra difficult.

So, if she couldn't ram her car into the building, or kick Roger in the nuts without fucking up her future, she needed a damn drink. It was too bad Gabi's twenty-first birthday hadn't come and gone yet.

Soon. Then she'd have someone to go out with to the bar or club. A "wing-woman." Unfortunately, since Gabi was still underage, Maddie had to go out on her own.

She really needed to make more of an effort to find friends around here. Even if they were some of the women from the Dirty Angels. But until then, she could head to her regular drinking spot... The Iron Horse Roadhouse.

Or...

She *could* go to Dirty Dick's.

She'd be safe at either location. She wouldn't have to worry about protecting her drink when she wasn't looking. She wouldn't have to worry about being accosted in a dark parking lot. She'd also be taken care of if, for some reason, she drank too much.

However, at Dick's she'd be worried about running into Romeo. She already fended off one aggravating man today, she didn't want to deal with another.

She was tired and her patience was non-existent.

That decided it.

The Iron Horse it was.

———

ROMEO CRAB-WALKED his sled backwards into the spot next to another Harley, shut it down, pulled off the bandana that kept bugs from getting stuck between his teeth and shed the clear protective glasses he wore when it was too dark to wear his shades.

He decided to leave his skull cap and of course, his cut in place. The DAMC had no problem with other clubs wearing their colors in their establishment as long as it didn't cause issues. If it did, that cut, along with the troublemaker wearing it, was quickly ejected out the front door by the prospects playing bouncers that night.

But now that the Shadow Warriors MC was long gone and what was left of the Deadly Demons on life support, trouble usually didn't find its way into the Iron Horse Roadhouse.

Unless they considered Romeo trouble. Some of the Angels might.

Hawk had previously run a tight ship and now shared manager duties with Coop. The DAMC vice president was about as present in their bar as much as Magnum was at Dick's. Basically, he kept himself scarce. While Coop, along with the other long-time DAMC members, kept the bar running smoothly.

As soon as Romeo yanked open the thick, bullet-proof door, the deep bass of loud rock music smacked him right in the chest.

He recognized the song immediately as one belonging to Dirty Deeds, Nash's band. The band still did well but could've been a national—or even international—success if the Dirty Angel hadn't settled down with Cross, his badge-wearing pig husband, to raise adopted twins.

The band still toured, but not like it used to. The Knights occasionally hired them when they threw a big bash or event.

The Iron Horse played their music a lot, both recorded and live. When it was live, they were a huge draw, and the bar was usually packed shoulder to shoulder. Tonight, Dirty Deed's music was recorded, and the bar was about as busy as any drinking hole would get on a Thursday night.

Not very.

That made it much easier to spot the person he'd hoped would be here.

He had a fucking hunch she might show up at the Iron Horse only because she had mentioned the other night that this was where she drank.

Her mistake was his advantage.

He grinned.

Since she was playing pool, her back was to him when he strode straight to the bar to grab a beer.

He slid his ass backwards onto a stool and only twisted his head enough to give Coop a chin lift in greeting.

Instead of returning it, Coop came over. "Brother."

"Whassup? Need a cold one."

"Tap or bottle?"

Romeo answered, "Whatever's on the house."

"Nothin's on the fuckin' house 'cept conversation. And maybe a bowl of stale peanuts."

"Whataya got on tap?" Romeo asked him.

"Probably the same shit you have on tap at Dick's. Why you here?"

"Damn! Can't a man come in here and have a fuckin' beer?"

"Sure. But if you wanna drink for free, Dick's got you covered. Maybe you're lost."

"Ain't lost. Can't hang out here? Jesus fuckin' Christ. Hawk know how you're treatin' your customers?"

"Since when are you a customer?"

"When I gotta fuckin' pay!" he just about shouted. With a grumble, he dug out his wallet and thumbed through his cash. He turned and slapped a fiver on the bar.

"You're short."

"I'm goddamn six-one. How the fuck am I short?"

Coop snorted and tipped his head toward the five-dollar bill. "It's six now for a draft. And that don't include the generous tip you're gonna leave me."

"Here's a fuckin' tip for you..." Romeo flipped Coop the bird, then jabbed it at him. "See the tip of my finger?"

"You're goddamn hilarious, Rome. You should do fuckin' standup."

"Prolly should."

"Okay, cheap ass, draft or bottle?"

"Whatever that five spot covers."

"That'll get you a glass of tap water. Without ice."

Romeo shook his head and gave the man his back again so he could concentrate on the woman playing pool.

Now that she was standing under a light, he noticed he was right about her hair being slightly darker. Nothing drastic but it didn't seem as blonde as when he last saw her. It was now more of a reddish brown.

Either way, it was still long enough to fist a handful of it as he pumped in and out of her sweet lips.

Anyway, he didn't give a fuck if her hair was neon purple, the woman was still fuckable. If her hair distracted him, he could turn off the lights. Or cover her head with a pillow. Or something.

The plunk of a bottle on the wood bar top behind him made him glance over his shoulder. "That water's a weird fuckin' color. Better have your plumbin' checked."

"Lucky we fuckin' like you, brother. Otherwise, for five bucks I would've poured you a half a draft. You could take tiny fuckin' sips all night to make it last."

"Maybe *you* should be the fuckin' comedian." He turned back to watch Maddie work the pool table.

She was damn good. Much better than he would expect. He wondered who taught her how to play that well.

He eyed up her partner next.

Zeke Jamison.

Romeo wondered if the next in line to hold the DAMC gavel had managed to get down her pants yet. Knowing Little Z—a nickname the kid now hated—he most likely had worked her hard. Whether she fell for his game or not was another story.

Romeo knew LZ wasn't even twenty-one yet. Was she into younger guys? Rome might be seven years older than her, but LZ was seven years younger.

Was she doing him?

He was damn sure Maddie would prefer a man over a boy.

He could definitely be that man for her. He only needed to get her away from Zeke and convince her Romeo was what she needed in her life.

For a night.

Maybe two.

Chapter Seven

"SHE WHY YOU'RE HERE, ROME?" Coop asked.

Fuck. "I say that?"

"Makin' it pretty obvious since you're talkin' to me while starin' at her."

"You ain't as hot as her, Coop. If your ass and tits looked that fuckin' good, I might stare at you, too."

"With the lights off and your eyes closed, it wouldn't be any different," Coop joked. "And rumor has it that you ain't picky, anyway. Any hole will do."

"Got me fuckin' confused with Nash since he swings both ways, so any hole *will* do."

"*Nah.* Nash ain't doin' anyone but Cross. He ain't fuckin' up that marriage."

Romeo sucked on his teeth. "Not sure why anyone would wanna tie themselves down to one person for the rest of their fuckin' life. Everyone knows variety is the spice of life."

"You and I might agree with that, brother, but not everyone else does. You do know who she is, right?"

"Of fuckin' course I know who she is."

"She know you? Or you just bein' a creepy moth-erfucker?"

Since she saw him naked one night in an RV, he'd say she knew him. "Knows who I am."

"That means you know who her stepdaddy is, right?"

"Coop," Romeo growled, "mind your own fuckin' biz. Also, don't need a goddamn quiz."

"Just tryin' to make sure you don't fuck up and end up dead."

"Ain't gonna end up dead. Now, can you fuckin' stop jawin' in my ear? Will let you know when I need another fuckin' beer."

What the fuck was with him rhyming? Coop must've caught it too because he chuckled before rapping his knuckles on the bar and sauntering away.

About fucking time. Now he could focus, without distractions, on the reason he was at The Iron Horse. He certainly wasn't there for the beer since he could drink himself under the table for free in his own bar.

His jaw tightened when he saw how LZ and Maddie interacted with each other. Like they knew each other pretty damn well. Laughing, grinning, smiling. They stood close a few times and talked quietly. Zeke would lean in even closer to give her pointers on her next shot... By putting a hand on her back, hip or arm, or whispering shit in her ear...

Romeo pulled a breath in through his flared nostrils.

Zeke was definitely working her by flirting, joking, touching...

Was she falling for his play?

Either way, Maddie must not have a problem with smoking since LZ had a lit cigarette dangling from between his lips. Seeing that surprised Romeo since he assumed Zeke's generation all vaped instead of smoked.

Guess not.

But then, he wasn't up with the newest shit. If he was going to smoke—weed or otherwise—he would do it like a real man, not some punk sucking on some bullshit battery-operated pen. Or whatever the fuck it was. He didn't give a shit because he was never using one. He'd be laughed right out of the president's spot.

If he saw one of their prospects or younger members using one, he would rip it right out of their fucking mouth and smash it under his boot heel. They should put it in the bylaws outlawing that bullshit.

He sighed. He just distracted his own damn self over something stupid.

Back to the subject at hand...

And that hand was LZ's touching Maddie when it should be Romeo's, instead.

Time to make himself known. Otherwise, if LZ was successful in luring Maddie upstairs to his room in the Angels' church—conveniently attached to the back of The Iron Horse—Romeo might lose his shit.

If he even saw the two of them heading that way, he'd step in. Of course, that could cause an issue between the two clubs. So, to keep the peace, he needed to be on the offensive, not defensive.

"Coop!" he called down the bar, still keeping his eyes glued to Maddie's ass as she bent over and lined up her next shot. He wasn't the only one staring at it. Only LZ could get a much better look from where he leaned nearby on his cue stick.

For fuck's sake.

Do not fuckin' introduce your fist to the DAMC president's kid's face.

"Don't gotta fuckin' shout. Only two fuckin' feet away. Guess you're distracted."

Romeo ignored the amusement in the Angel's tone. "Get me whatever she's drinkin'. Get me a fresh one, too."

Coop's lips twitched. "You payin'?"

Romeo sighed, jerked his chain wallet back out and pulled out a twenty. When he tossed it at the other biker, it fluttered to the bar.

Coop snatched it up, "That should cover both beers and my tip," and headed down the bar.

Romeo turned back around to make sure Maddie hadn't left with LZ when he hadn't been paying attention.

Not even two minutes later, Coop dropped off two fresh beers.

"Change?"

Coop laughed and walked away.

"Asshole."

"I'm in good company," Coop threw over his shoulder.

After grabbing the two bottles, Romeo hauled his ass off the stool and across the bar toward the pool tables.

He couldn't believe Maddie hadn't noticed him yet. The bar wasn't that damn busy. He had no fucking clue how she didn't notice a six-foot-one, handsome-as-fuck Black man wearing a Knights cut in a sea of white folk.

Maybe LZ's flirting was working, and she didn't have eyes for anyone else.

Romeo was about to change that.

"I'm up next," he announced as he reached the table, then greeted his competition, ignoring Maddie for the moment. He'd get to her in a minute. "LZ."

"Rome."

They clasped hands and bumped shoulders.

"What are you doin' here?" LZ asked. "Dad know you're here?"

Romeo pulled his chin into his neck. "I need to clear it with him first?"

LZ took a long drag on his cigarette. "No, just figured you two mighta had a meetin' or somethin'." He tipped his head back and blew the smoke up toward the ceiling.

"Nope. Here for pure pleasure." Romeo made sure to look at Maddie when he said that.

LZ's eyes narrowed on him, as did Maddie's. "What kinda pleasure you findin' at The Iron Horse that you can't find at Dick's?"

"Ain't I allowed to enjoy a beer?"

"Sure. Dick's got beer, too."

What the fuck. Between Zeke and Coop, he wasn't feeling very welcomed.

"You're double-fistin' beers, brother. Must be really fuckin' thirsty." LZ once again tucked his cigarette between his lips, moved down the table and took his next shot, cleanly sinking the pool ball into a side pocket.

"Both ain't for me." Romeo placed the second bottle on the table's rail in front of Maddie and tipped his head toward it. "That's for you."

"You didn't have to do that—"

"Wanted to."

"Since I don't pay for my drinks here," she finished.

What the fuck?

LZ chuckled around his cigarette and moved to take his next shot.

Romeo shook his head when he glanced over to the bar to catch Coop wearing a cocky grin.

Asshole.

Maddie rolled her lips inward and the corners of her eyes crinkled. "But thank you for bringing it over to me. That's very kind of you, Rome."

"He ain't bein' kind, Maddie. Don't fall for his bullshit." LZ completed his next shot successfully and when he straightened, he gave Romeo a cheesy grin. "You know he sniffs after anyone with tits."

The fucker was trying to be a cock-block. He would make sure LZ failed.

Romeo tipped his beer to his lips and downed about a third of it before setting it on a nearby high-top table. "How 'bout you finish your fuckin' game so I can rack next?"

"You wanna play the winner, put your quarter up on the rail," Zeke instructed him like Romeo never played a game of fucking pool in his life.

He managed to bite back his typical clap-back and instead said, "Ain't playin' the winner. Playin' her."

"Hear that, Maddie? Told you. He wants to play you." LZ wiggled his dark eyebrows.

Romeo's fingers automatically curled into fists. *Dig deep and find that fuckin' patience, brother, before you do somethin' stupid.* "You no longer a prospect, LZ?"

Zeke took another long drag on his cigarette. "My man, you see 'prospect' anywhere on my fuckin' cut?" He blew a stream of smoke out of the side of his mouth.

"Wasn't lookin' that closely at you."

He hooked a thumb over his shoulder, pointing it at the back of his cut. "Got my full set of patches a year ago." He dropped another ball into the corner pocket with ease.

The kid probably played pool ever since he was big enough to hold a cue stick. He was probably an expert at darts, too.

But, *guaran-fucking-teed*, Romeo had him beat in the bedroom.

What would impress Maddie more? An expert at playing pool and darts, or at eating pussy?

His guess would be the second one. And that was only where Romeo's skills began.

He was goddamn well-rounded.

He also appreciated well-rounded women. Tits. Ass. Hips. Lips.

They watched and waited as LZ cleaned up the rest of the table. He didn't even give Maddie another chance to make a shot. "Ain't much of a gentleman if he can't even let you win," he told her out of LZ's hearing.

"What do you know about being a gentleman? Would you let me win?"

Romeo wasn't as good as LZ because he hardly played pool. But, *hell*, he'd love to go head-to-head with Z's oldest son in a game of dice. He'd clean out that kid's wallet and maybe bruise that ego a bit.

"If that's what it takes."

"Takes for what?"

He glanced down at Maddie to see her staring at the table and not him.

"I've never seen you here before," she murmured. "Not until I mentioned the other night that I come here."

She turned in place until she was staring up at him. He knew exactly why. She wanted to watch his face.

He schooled his expression carefully. "Been busy, that's all."

"You mean with your *own* bar? You know, the bar where you can drink for free?"

Maddie was fucking smart. She knew what was what.

A rough clearing of a throat had them both turning toward the person who did it.

LZ smirked. "Good game, girl."

"I wasn't even close to winning," she admitted with a shrug.

"Gettin' much better with my help." When LZ said that he met Romeo's eyes.

"No one in the Fury taught you pool?" Romeo asked her, surprised.

"I only knew the basics of Eight Ball. I wasn't any good at it."

"Gonna teach her to be a pool shark, so when she goes home, she can clean up and rake in all their scratch. She'll be laughin' all the way to the fuckin' bank."

"Whatya mean, 'go home?'" Was she moving home soon? It didn't sound like that the other night when they were at Bangin' Burgers.

"For a visit," Maddie clarified.

Romeo waited for LZ to head to the bar to grab another beer before telling her, "He's not the only one who can teach you pool."

"I really wasn't looking for lessons. Zeke volunteered."

"But you didn't say no."

"Because I'm enjoying the game. However, I don't care about being any shark. It's fun. So, how about racking those balls?"

"How 'bout you rack my balls?" almost spewed from his mouth without thinking. Thank fuck he caught it in time.

Maddie wasn't a sweet butt. She wasn't a hang-around trying to sink her claws into a Knight in hopes to become an ol' lady. She also wouldn't put up with any bullshit with the goal to become one. Or at least become a regular piece.

He had no doubt that was the last thing she wanted.

Bottom line was, she was Fury property. So, if he wanted her to land in his bed again, he needed to be careful. He needed to do it right.

Only, he had no fucking idea just how to pull that off without pissing off a fuck-load of people.

Including his sergeant at arms.

Chapter Eight

IT SEEMED as if Romeo wanted a repeat of what happened all those years ago in his rented RV. However, she wasn't sure why. He had no reason to chase her since he had plenty of available and willing women at his fingertips.

Why did men always go after what they couldn't or shouldn't have? Was it the challenge? Or their ego?

With Romeo, it could be both.

Maddie watched him set the balls perfectly and slide the full rack into place before lifting the wooden triangle.

Her heart skipped a beat when he stepped back from the table and gave her a cocky grin. The man knew he was hot and handsome. The problem was, he was also a handful.

He might want a challenge, but she didn't. And dealing with Romeo would be one.

Even for only one night.

She knew if she simply made the suggestion to go back to her place—or his—he would jump on it.

She wasn't stupid. The DKMC president didn't hang out at The Iron Horse Roadhouse. His club owned Dirty Dick's.

Obviously, he was only here for one reason, even if he didn't want to admit it.

Her.

Why?

He tipped his head toward the table. "You take the first shot."

Of course, since he racked, she got to break. Zeke had been helping improve her game, but that wasn't why she occasionally hung out at The Iron Horse or with the DAMC president's son.

Despite Zeke being a few years younger than her, she liked him. Not romantically or even sexually, but as a friend. He also tended to be protective of her if any man in the bar stepped over the line.

But then, so would Coop, Hawk or any of the Angels, including the prospects, working at, or hanging around in the bar. They all knew who she was. They all respected the Fury and in turn, for the most part, respected her.

If she really wanted to, she was welcome to drink at their private bar in their clubhouse, conveniently attached at the rear of The Iron Horse. However, doing so would make her feel like she was intruding. Plus, some of the club's sweet butts didn't like her in their territory. They looked at her as competition.

They shouldn't. She had no desire to date, or even mess with, anyone in the DAMC. Just like she had no desire to date or mess with anyone in the Fury or the Knights, either.

If she was going to date anyone, she'd find a nice, boring, regular guy. Not one with a deeply possessive "touch her and you die" vibes, where almost everything was seen as a damn threat.

A grumbly, "Maddie," had her shaking her wandering

thoughts free and getting a better grip on her cue stick. "Know how to break?"

She nodded and approached the table. "Yes, but don't expect it to be anything spectacular."

One side of his mouth pulled up. "I can help."

Funny how he didn't even ask her if she wanted to play this next game with him. He simply assumed.

Since he came to The Iron Horse specifically for her, she'd be kind enough to play one game with him. Maybe during that time, she could make him realize that she had no desire to be anything with him other than acquaintances. At best, maybe friends.

And that didn't mean friends with benefits.

She specifically picked him five years ago because it was well known he was a player. She assumed—maybe wrongly—that meant he had the experience to know what to do, to do it right and after that night, move on to his next conquest.

That was what was *supposed* to happen.

Clearly, tonight was proving that it didn't.

Did he only see her as an easy mark? An opportunity for a quickie?

Even if he did, it still made no sense. He had plenty of women at his disposal he didn't have to work hard at getting into his bed.

Had there been a spark between them all those years ago? Of course. Add on the fact that Romeo was slick. He knew how to flirt like a pro. He was skilled at making a woman feel special, even if in his eyes, he didn't believe it was true.

Women were the target, and he was the damn arrow.

Since he hit Maddie's bullseye last time, maybe tonight he was ready to take another shot.

And not only in the game of pool.

She moved to the end of the table and eyed the neatly set

pool balls and for some reason became nervous. She had to remind herself that this was a game, not a life-or-death situation. Should she really care if she messed up the break shot? This was supposed to be a fun, casual game and not a serious competition, right?

Nothing was riding on this game. Yet... But she expected him to change that.

"Before you take that shot, wanna make a bet?"

Just as she thought. "I think I have about five bucks on me," she answered.

"Ain't about money."

Of course, it wasn't. She played along. "What's it about? You certainly aren't here to witness my lack of billiard skills."

"I win, you come to my place afterward. You win, I go to yours."

She straightened and frowned. That bet was even worse than she expected. But of course, no surprise. "How is that even a bet? I'm the reward in both situations."

"Ever think I'm the fuckin' reward?"

She turned her face enough to make sure he could clearly see her eyes roll. Hard. "You benefit whether you win or lose."

"So do you." He pursed his lips as he considered her. "Willin' to help you win."

Mmm hmm. "Can you please explain how I'd be winning?"

"Get to spend time with me and everythin' that goes along with that."

She shook her head. "Man, Rome, you're really full of yourself."

"Can fill you up, too."

She groaned. "Seriously?" Did women normally fall for that type of talk? She guessed she had in the past but then, at the time, she was only twenty-two. She was a lot more experienced now.

He laughed. "Yeah."

"If a bet is required, I don't want to play. Find another sucker."

As she began to step away from the table, he grabbed her arm and pulled her to a stop. "Just fuckin' with you."

Sure he was.

"We don't gotta bet. Take the shot."

They stared at each other for a little too long. Neither wanting to be the first to break eye contact.

Finally, Romeo murmured, "Take your shot, Maddie."

A shiver shimmied down her spine.

Why the hell did he affect her so much and, worse, with a simple statement?

"Just for fun," she confirmed.

"Always for fun."

After she got into position and was concentrating on where to hit the cue ball to make sure her shot wasn't a complete dud, his heat wrapped around her seconds before his big body did.

She wasn't very petite, but Romeo was much thicker and taller than her. When he placed his hands over hers, the contrast of their size difference and skin tone was startling. Her much smaller hands, her unmarked skin versus his tattooed arms, the rich darkness of his skin over her own pale coloring...

It did make her aware that she needed to get out in the sun a bit so she wasn't the same shade as a damn corpse. But to do that, she needed to not work so many hours.

Once again, that brought her back to her cheapskate boss and how understaffed they were at work. And the whole reason why she had come to The Iron Horse tonight.

To forget her problems. Or one problem in particular.

"Why so tense?" He seemed a bit offended.

She explained it away with, "Long day."

Luckily, he accepted that and didn't push. "Anytime you need pointers on pool, come to Dick's. I can teach you how to handle balls better than that kid. He's still wet behind the ears," he murmured in her ear.

Another shiver slipped down her spine and caused goose-bumps to break out all over her.

With his chest pressed to her back and his crotch to her ass, he caged her in by placing his hands on top of hers, all in the guise of helping to guide her shot.

"He's just a friend." *Damn*, why did she sound so out of breath?

Why the hell did he affect her like this? Was it because it brought back the memories of their one and only night together?

Was it she who wanted the repeat?

No. That would be stupid and another mistake since these bikers tended to get possessive if you weren't a sweet butt or some random. They might not want a relationship, but they didn't want you wanting anyone else, either. You were only supposed to have eyes for them while their eyes landed on anyone with tits and ass.

Was that fair? Hell no. But this was one reason most MCs considered women as property and not as equals.

As for Romeo, he had a reputation. He didn't deny it. He owned it.

"He don't wanna be a friend, Maddie. He ain't helpin' you with pool outta the goodness of his fuckin' heart. He wants somethin' from you."

Well, wasn't that ironic? "You mean, like you do?"

"Just lookin' out for you."

"I'm perfectly capable of knowing who's a true friend and who... isn't." They needed to get this game started because she was beginning to like his embrace a little more than she should. "How about this bet? You win, I come over to your place. I win, I don't."

Suddenly, he released her hands and stepped back, giving her some breathing room. He grabbed her chin and turned her head, attempting to read her expression. "Know you're gonna lose, right?"

She shrugged. "If I do, I do."

"Then, gonna take that fuckin' bet."

She figured he would grab the carrot she dangled in front of him.

He locked his dark eyes with hers. "Just wanna be clear... Comin' over to my crib don't mean you comin' over for a cuppa coffee and some conversation."

"I'm aware of what it means." She certainly was.

With a cocky grin, he released her chin and tipped his head toward the table. "Then, break."

He thought it was going to be an easy win. She'd have to do her best and prove otherwise. "Now you won't help me in hopes I lose?"

"You're gonna lose and I can't fuckin' wait. Don't wanna hear any fuckin' complaints when you do."

Jesus. The arrogance.

That only bolstered her determination to win.

After lining up her shot, she pulled back the stick, then struck the cue ball with as much force as she had.

The crack of the balls striking each other was even louder than the music. She held her breath while they headed off in different directions. Just like she hoped, one solid colored ball dropped into a side pocket, and another fell into the far corner pocket.

With her eyes wide, she whispered, "Wow."

"Beginner's luck," he muttered.

"I'll take any luck I can get." She analyzed the table and where all remaining solid balls stopped.

To win, she had to pocket five more solids before sinking the eight-ball. All without missing a shot. Without scratching. Without launching a ball over the rail. Without accidentally knocking in one of his striped balls.

She glanced over at Romeo. "Are we calling pockets?"

His lips twitched. "No need."

Oh yes, he was so damn arrogant.

She shrugged and studied the table again with her bottom lip gripped tightly between her teeth.

"Just take your time," he encouraged.

But she heard it in his voice. He didn't believe she'd make the next shot.

It was highly possible that she might not.

She purposely picked a super easy shot any beginner would be a fool not to take and...

Dropped the ball into the other corner pocket.

"Too fuckin' easy. Try somethin' harder. Let's see how gooduva teacher LZ is."

She ignored him as she circled the table searching and concentrating. Zeke had taught her how to do bank shots, but the stakes were too high with this game to risk taking one. Instead, she found another sure shot and quickly took it. The number six ball fell right into the side pocket.

She heard a noise from where he stood, but didn't spare him a glance. She continued to search for the next shot and took it, sinking that ball, too.

She wanted to gloat but tried desperately to hide her satisfaction in how far her skills had come.

She only had one solid ball left before she had to sink the eight ball. The ball needed to win both the game and the bet.

Her heart was now pounding. In her chest, in her ears and also in her throat.

Focus.

She steadied her hands and ignored everything around her, including the big burly biker standing nearby, waiting for her to screw up.

Maddie needed to stay out of her own head, concentrate and look at the next shot logically. Size, age, gender had nothing to do with how well a player did. It all relied on physics by using momentum, impulse, and kinetic energy.

She broke down the next shot in her head first, then put her plan in motion, successfully sinking the three ball.

She managed to swallow her excited squeal. This wasn't the time to celebrate. The next ball was the most important of all.

Everything rode on the solid black eight ball.

All she had to do was get it into a pocket without scratching or knocking in one of his striped balls instead.

Not an easy feat with all seven of Romeo's balls still on the table.

She used the tip of her cue stick to tap the side pocket. Now she only needed to make the shot.

She picked a spot on the cue ball, lined up her stick, pushed all the breath from her lungs to try to slow her racing heart...

Then went for it.

Chapter Nine

"WHAT THE ACTUAL FUCK?" burst from Romeo the second the eight ball tipped over the edge and landed in the pocket. "What the actual fuck, Maddie? That ain't no fuckin' beginner's luck. You fuckin' played me."

Not so cocky now, was he? "I did. In pool."

A muscle jumped in his cheek. "Not what I fuckin' meant."

"Sounds like you thought you could take advantage of me but failed." Maddie shrugged and, with a grin, placed her cue stick in the rack on the wall. She then headed over to him where he still stood in shock and anger. Using his shoulder for balance, she rose onto her tiptoes and leaned in close. "You think I didn't notice you come in the door? You're hard to miss, Rome. Especially in here."

Not waiting for that to sink in, she quickly moved away from him and, while meeting his eyes, put the beer he bought her to her lips and took a long sip.

When she was done, she sighed loudly and shot him a smile.

As soon as she had spotted him coming into The Iron Horse, she and Zeke jokingly devised a half-assed plan while Romeo sat at the bar. She had no idea that plan would actually come into play, and he would walk right into it.

Shame on him for underestimating her.

Maddie already knew the basics of pool before moving to Shadow Valley. Zeke only helped hone her skills.

On a rare occasion, they worked together to make some spare cash by pretending she was still a beginner. She'd bet an unsuspecting Iron Horse customer and when she won, would act like it was beginner's luck. Just like she did with Romeo. But with the others, the bet had nothing to do with sex.

Romeo's vision of a "sure thing" was now destroyed.

His cockiness possibly taken down a peg.

He also now knew she wasn't a pushover.

Chuckling, Zeke came back to the billiard area and slapped Romeo hard enough on the back to make him lurch forward. "Better luck next time, brother."

Oh shit. Romeo was already annoyed, but to have Zeke rub his loss and the fact Maddie pulled one over on him in his face...

Not smart.

She opened her mouth to tell Zeke to let it go. Before the first word slipped past her lips, it turned into a squeak when Romeo grabbed her wrist and began to take long strides toward the exit with her in tow.

"Romeo..." She kept her voice calm and low to avoid Zeke freaking out and coming to her rescue.

The big man didn't stop until they were outside and away from the door. Once they were, he backed her against the exterior wall, dropped his head and locked eyes with her. "That was fuckin' bullshit."

She lifted her chin. "You only think that because you lost. Bet you wouldn't think it was bullshit if you had won."

The second he released her wrist; she spun in the direction of her car. He quickly stopped her by slamming a hand against the side of the building, blocking her path. When she spun the other way, he barred her escape with his other arm, caging her in.

"Let me leave, Romeo."

"Ain't leavin' 'til I'm fuckin' done with you."

Oh yes, the man was not happy.

"I'll leave when I want to leave. You have no right to stop me." Could he detect the tremor in her voice?

Was she stupid to push him like that?

She knew him but she didn't know him *that* well. Even so, she never heard of him abusing or hurting women. He only used women sexually. But it was always consensual, like with her five years ago.

However, he had no reason to get this pissed. The only thing he lost was a game of pool. He wasn't scammed out of anything of value. Her plan had been to only put him in his place.

Zeke had no idea that Maddie and Romeo hooked up during that weekend up in Manning Grove. As far as she knew, nobody did. She hoped like hell it stayed that way.

Zeke only went along with the plan because he thought it would be funny that big, bad Romeo would be beaten by a "girl."

"Maddie, you okay?" came from behind Romeo.

Speak of the devil.

"She's good," Romeo growled, still keeping their eyes locked.

"Wanna hear it from her," Zeke insisted, his voice dropping an octave, too.

Romeo's nostrils flared and she swore he was grinding his teeth.

She would not be the cause of a brawl between Zeke and Romeo. That would cause issues. Not only for Romeo and Zeke, but between the Dirty Angels and the Dark Knights.

She would not be the reason their long-standing, solid alliance cracked or even became shaky.

"I'm fine, Zeke," she reassured him.

Romeo continued to intensely stare at her, but they were both fully aware of Zeke still standing behind the Knights' president, ready to step in to rescue her.

"Don't be a goddamn sore loser, Rome. She beat you fair and square."

Zeke assumed this all had to do with the game. That maybe Romeo was embarrassed by his loss to Maddie.

He had no idea what they had bet. And, judging by his reaction, it was best if he didn't know. Despite them only being friends, Zeke still had that typical "touch her and you die" attitude. Unfortunately, that mindset could be dangerous.

"Don't look fine. You wanna be there?"

Not really, but Romeo wasn't hurting her. "We're simply having a discussion," she assured him.

"Pretty fuckin' close discussion," Zeke pointed out.

"It's fine, Zeke. As soon as I'm done talking to Romeo, I'm heading home."

Zeke still stayed where he was.

"I appreciate you looking out for me but it—"

"Ain't needed," Romeo finished for her.

"I'm not likin' this, Maddie."

"Ain't for you to like," Romeo informed him.

She had to admit, Romeo was very confident in himself since not once did he look at Zeke. He kept his back to the younger biker, making it clear Romeo was dismissing him without worry.

She had no doubt that Zeke took that as a slight since it meant Romeo didn't fear or have any concern about what the younger biker might do. And that would knock the DAMC's president's cocky son down a peg or two. No different than Maddie getting one over on the man caging her in.

Both men had their ego checked tonight. All Maddie wanted to do was enjoy a couple of beers, play some pool, hang out with her friend, and forget about work for a few hours.

She said under her breath, "If I promise not to hightail it out of here, will you back off, so Zeke does the same?"

With his lips pressed into a tight, thin line, he pulled in a deep breath, then straightened. After a slight hesitation, he took a small step back and dropped his arms to his side.

She did not miss that his fingers were loosely curled into fists or that he still stood close enough, so his thick body blocked her view of the man standing behind him.

Romeo made a damn good wall and a terrible window.

But that also meant that Zeke couldn't see her. She raised her voice to make sure he could hear her. "Everything's fine, Zeke. Nothing to worry about. Romeo and I have a lot to catch up on."

"Didn't know you were that close to have shit to catch up on." Of course, Zeke sounded skeptical since he was far from stupid. He got his looks from his father, his intelligence from both of his parents, but somehow his father's laid-back gene had skipped him.

"Of course. We became friends years ago." They had never been friends. They had flirted plenty and had sex once, but that was where the relationship ended.

"All right," Zeke muttered. "Text me if you need anythin'."

As soon as she answered, "I will," Zeke grumbled something under his breath, turned and headed back inside, finally leaving her and Romeo alone.

When Romeo stepped closer, she expected him to cage her against the side of the building again, but he didn't. Even though he wasn't touching her, he stood in her personal space, demanding, "Was he in on it?"

"In on what?"

"You playin' me like that."

"You don't like being played, Rome?" she asked so sweetly, she gained five pounds.

WHAT THE ACTUAL FUCK? "Wasn't my goddamn question."

"Are you mad?"

"I look fuckin' happy?"

"You thought your win was a sure thing. That *I* was a sure thing. You're mad because I'm not."

He couldn't argue that point because it was true, but her gloating was pissing him off even more. "You're gettin' back at me 'cause you think I used you that night." That had to be it.

"Well, didn't you?"

"Didn't you?" he countered.

"Can we both admit we used each other? I can admit it. But isn't using women your M.O.? Don't pretend like it's not."

His head jerked back. "Love sex. Need women to have sex." He might not've done great in high school biology, but he knew that fucking much.

"Not really." She smirked and pumped her fist in a jerk-off motion.

If he wasn't so damn pissed right now, he'd think that was funny. But he was, and it wasn't. "Ain't the same."

"Because when you're done, your hand's still attached? Unlike all the women you like to pull a dip and dash."

Dip and dash?

Why the fuck was he bothering with her? He didn't need this shit.

He had plenty of women at his fingertips. None that took work to get naked and into his bed.

And even though she wouldn't admit it, he had no fucking doubt she plotted with LZ to fuck with him.

If Romeo was still the Knights' president when LZ took over at the head of the Angels' table, the alliance might be at risk. He wasn't sure he could be an ally to a cocky kid.

Especially, not after this shit with Maddie.

She wasn't DAMC property. She wasn't LZ's, either. The kid needed to mind his own fucking business and stay out of Romeo's.

"You mean the same way you dashed from my RV that night?"

"It was morning," she corrected.

Jesus. "Middle of the fuckin' night."

"*Aww*, Rome. Did you want to cuddle afterward?"

He didn't give a fuck about cuddling. Maybe pussy-boy LZ liked that kind of shit. What he had really wanted at the time was to fuck her again. When she wasn't dealing with the discomfort of losing her virginity to a man with a big fucking dick.

He'd been careful the first time. He hadn't planned on being so careful the second. But he wasn't the one who "dipped and dashed" that night.

It was her.

And that never fucking happened to him. If anything, he

had a hard time kicking some clingers out of his bed. Especially the ones with the hopes of becoming his ol' lady.

Maddie had snuck away the second he closed his eyes and drifted off. It was almost as if she had taken a page out of his playbook. "Yeah, you owe me a cuddle."

"I gave you my virginity. That wasn't enough?"

Fuck no, it hadn't been enough. And he didn't give a fuck about her virginity. He usually avoided inexperienced women.

He'd been into Maddie, not her sexual status.

She was why he came to The Iron Horse tonight. It had taken him a while to push her out of his mind, for the memory to fade, after that weekend five years ago. But running into her at Bangin' Burgers returned that memory front and center into his brain.

He didn't like that.

In fact, it bothered the fuck out of him.

He never chased a goddamn woman before and here he was...

He needed to walk away. Leave her be and forget about her. Go back to Dick's, find a sweet butt, and do the nastiest shit possible with her to push Maddie out of his thoughts.

Did his stupid ass do that? Fuck no.

What did he do instead? Something he normally wouldn't unless he was out of his fucking mind. Right there out in the parking lot of The Iron Horse, right in DAMC territory, he used his chest to bump her backwards and pin her against the wall.

"Ro—"

He swallowed his own name as he captured her mouth.

She didn't claw out his eyes but instead, dug her fingers into his arms. Not to push him away, but to pull him closer. To encourage him to continue. To keep them connected.

He wedged a knee between her thighs, drove a hand into her hair and pinned her against the wall using his chest to continue to do what she wanted... plunder her mouth.

Her body, her reaction, confirmed what he already suspected.

The woman was putting on a goddamn front. Pretending she didn't want him when that was the opposite of the truth. But she wasn't the only one unable to hide her reaction. In an instant, his dick turned into a steel pipe and ached to be inside her.

Despite it being her first time that night, she had been surprisingly responsive. She hadn't laid there like a corpse but had met him thrust for thrust.

He wanted a repeat of her naked and squirming under him, digging those nails into his back instead of his arms.

Was she still as tight as she was five years ago when he had gone where no man had gone before? He wanted to find out.

Tonight, his tongue explored every inch of her mouth, twisted, and tangled with hers. Her lips were warm and soft as they moved against his. When she slightly tilted her head, he took the kiss deeper.

A groan slipped up her throat and her nails dug even deeper into his flesh as she clung to him.

It was stupid to start this here where they couldn't finish what they both wanted.

Because if those fucking groans and whimpers were any indication, her denying that she wanted him would be a lie.

It was when Maddie began to grind against the thigh he had planted between her legs, he knew this had to stop. Because if she didn't... Shit might get real really quickly.

He was not fucking her in her goddamn cage in the parking lot of The Iron Horse.

For fuck's sake, at this point he didn't want to fuck her at all. He was only trying to teach her a lesson about playing him. Get her all worked up and then pull the rug out from underneath her. Like she did with him.

She should know that paybacks were a bitch.

However, it might turn into a failed lesson if he didn't stop now.

It took everything he had to rip his mouth from hers and step back, freeing her. Freeing himself from temptation.

His hard-on kicked in his jeans when he saw her lips were parted, her chest pumping with each ragged breath and her eyes squeezed shut.

Yeah, he did that.

She couldn't deny he was the cause of that reaction.

When her eyelids finally lifted, he drew a hand down over his thick beard to smooth it back into place and said, "Guess you're gonna be missin' out on where that woulda led."

With that, he set his jaw and did something so damn difficult. He turned and strode to his sled, leaving her standing against the wall still in a daze.

She thought she outplayed the player.

And maybe she did.

This time.

But next time he'd be prepared.

Because he was nobody's bitch.

Not even Maddie's.

Chapter Ten

MADDIE GLANCED at the large clock on the wall. The one she watched between patients. She always counted the minutes until she could walk out the door.

Roger had been gone all day doing who knows what—not that she cared—and that made her workday more pleasant than usual. Not only for her but for everyone working at Smith's. All the employees—from physical therapists to the back-office workers—seemed more relaxed today. They chatted, they joked, they even smiled when the unbearable asshole wasn't breathing down their necks and looking for any reason to criticize, to write someone up, to dock their pay...

The list was too long.

Roger Smith was a fucking tyrant. He crowned himself the king of his own castle and ruled his kingdom with an iron fist. He was the reason the business had a constant turnover of employees.

It was no surprise that when someone quit, Roger called

them "soft," "lazy," "stupid" and worse. Sometimes he even used slurs.

She had just finished working with her last patient of the day and was anxious to get the hell out of there when the front door opened and the man himself walked in.

Her groan was followed with a whispered, "Fuck," as she ducked behind a large, square column to hide. Usually with Roger, it was out of sight, out of mind. Everyone knew not to make quick moves to draw his attention.

All the employees remaining on the floor most likely had their fingers crossed behind their backs, hoping he'd go directly to his office at the rear of the building. But to get there, he had to walk through the large, open room where they all worked with their patients.

Everyone quickly made themselves scarce or pretended they were busy. Nobody made eye contact if they could help it.

Pressing her back against the column, she closed her eyes and held her breath, listening carefully.

Suddenly, it wasn't Roger she was thinking about. Because the last time she had her back against a wall...

She could once again feel the press of Romeo's solid body and his hard, thick cock. The way he gripped her hair. The way he took control of her mouth in a kiss that made her knees buckle and her heart race. The way one of his massive thighs smashed against her throbbing pussy. The way his beard scratched against her skin.

His heat. His scent. His taste.

The intensity of his deep brown eyes once he broke off the kiss.

All of it came flooding back. Playing out on the back of her eyelids like a 3D movie, causing her pussy to clench with wanting a man she shouldn't mess with.

She didn't want to want him.

Her body and her brain warred over that fact.

Common sense told her getting involved with the president of the Dark Knights would be just plain stupid.

She jumped out of her skin when she opened her eyes and found Roger standing only a couple of feet away from her with his blond eyebrows pinned together and his cruel mouth twisted.

"What are you doing?"

Hiding from you. "I was... feeling dizzy." Not a complete lie. Her memory of the kiss with Romeo had made her a bit weak in the knees all over again.

"No surprise. Because you *are* dizzy."

Why the hell did she continue to work here and put up with his bullying?

Oh, that's right, she wanted a job with a professional sports team and, unfortunately, Roger had connections.

That meant, if she flipped him the bird, told him to go to hell, and stomped out, she'd be lucky if she got a job working with a local Little League team. He'd make sure she was blackballed in all of the Pittsburgh area.

Why did assholes have all the power? Most likely because they stepped on the "little people" as they worked their way to the top.

She fought the urge to peek around the column at the clock. If he caught an employee clock watching, he called them out on it. Loudly. Not caring if he embarrassed the person he was berating. Not caring if patients were in the room, including children.

Actually, Roger didn't care about anyone but himself. The narcissist's only other love was money. During the last year and a half, she had never once heard the man mention family or friends. Or even a pet.

She might complain and get annoyed sometimes with her MC family but at least she had people who loved her, looked out for her, and would come stand by her side if she called them.

It was pretty much a guarantee if one of Roger's employees was behind the wheel of their vehicle and he tripped out in the parking lot and fell to the ground, he'd end up as a speed bump. Several times over.

"Since you have fifteen minutes before the end of your shift and you're only holding up that post, why don't you go clean the restroom." It wasn't a request but an order.

What an asshole.

She was a certified physical therapist, not a custodian. Cleaning toilets was not in her job description or in her future career plans. Did he fire the night custodians because he was such a cheap fucker?

Or did he insult the cleaning company's workers enough, so they quit? She wouldn't put it past him if he called them some sort of racist slurs.

The only good thing about working at Smith's, despite the owner being a douchebag, was that it had a great reputation for helping athletes. But that had more to do with the caring physical therapists he employed, not Roger. It also meant they were always busy and that usually helped the day go faster.

Should she tell him no? If she did, would he be a total dick? Or would he fire her for insubordination? If he did, he could fight her getting unemployment compensation while she searched for a new job.

Then she wouldn't have her rent or any money at all. If that happened, she'd have to move home. Eventually, she'd also get sick of hearing how she shouldn't have moved away in the first place. And how life was better in Manning Grove than anywhere else.

Sure it was. If you loved small town living. If you loved everyone being all up in your business. As well as having an opinion on everything you did with your life and not being afraid to share that opinion. Out loud.

And dating? It was slim pickings up there unless she wanted to be with a biker.

She did not.

At least long term.

Because after that kiss, that toe-curling reminder two days ago, one night with a biker able to keep his mouth shut might not be so bad.

Wearing a scowl, Roger barked, "Why are you still standing there?"

He always expected everyone to jump the second he ordered them to jump. He managed the business using fear and intimidation, then put on a fake front when dealing with his clients and vendors.

Someone needed to put Roger in his place. But until she had something better lined up, it wouldn't be her.

"If you hustle, you can get the toilets scrubbed in the next twelve minutes, so get to it."

"I didn't spend years getting my graduate degree to clean toilets." At least toilets anywhere other than in her apartment.

Roger leaned in closer and sneered, "I don't pay you to not follow my orders. Do you think you're too good to clean them?" He glanced at his watch. "Time is ticking, Mad. I don't care how late you have to stay to get it done. When I tell you to do something, I expect you to do it."

The metallic taste of blood filled her mouth from biting her tongue so hard.

She had a decision to make. Do what he demanded and keep her damn job or refuse and watch her career fall apart when he damaged her good reputation as a sports physical therapist.

Roger would no doubt lie to destroy her. Again, typical narcissist behavior.

Unfortunately, the decision she *really* wanted to make—kneeing ol' Roger in the balls—would get her arrested for assault. Instead, she would fantasize about doing that while she scrubbed the damn toilets.

She should've moved to another area with other professional sports teams and skipped Pittsburgh completely.

Too late.

Even so, she had a goal, and no one was going to derail it.

Not even Roger Smith.

She was determined to get what she wanted, despite him and his asshole ways.

———

It didn't take her twelve minutes. It took her over an hour to get all the disgusting toilets cleaned inside and out. "Gross" didn't even cover it. She now had the utmost respect for people who cleaned for a living. They certainly weren't getting paid enough to scrub piss covered floors or toilet seats. Or to pick up questionable items off the floor.

Once again, she sat in her car in the now empty parking lot while staring at her closed place of employment and contemplating her life choices.

After she finished with her assigned task and walked out of one of the bathrooms, she almost smacked right into Roger. Apparently, he'd been inspecting her work.

He was the asshole-ist asshole in a world filled with assholes.

It had been on the tip of her bleeding tongue to tell him that.

She didn't. She swallowed it back down, squeezed past him, grabbed her things, and walked out the front door with her head held high since it was never smart to reveal your weakness to a narcissist.

She waited for him to call her back or complain about something she'd done. To make her do it all over again. He was lucky he didn't.

Actually, *she* was lucky she could keep her thoughts contained. As difficult as that was.

She sat in her Toyota Highlander while he closed up and locked the front door. She sat in her car as he walked to the spot reserved for him near that front door. She sat in her Toyota as he slid into his Porsche.

And she remained sitting in her vehicle as he drove out of the lot without even a glance in her direction.

If looks could kill, his Porsche would've exploded with how hard she glared at it.

The clock on the dashboard said it was only a few minutes away from five-thirty. Her day was supposed to be done at four. Would she be paid for that extra hour and a half? Of course not. Be a few minutes late and get docked pay. Stay late and her time was a donation.

She wasn't sure how much longer she would last at Smith's. But it also wouldn't look good on her resume if she job hopped.

Or couldn't get a good reference.

Or was lied about.

And she was pretty damn sure if she told Roger to take

this job and shove it, then he'd make up all kinds of stories about her.

She grabbed her phone out of the center cup holder and pulled up her contact list. She scrolled until she found Zeke's number.

Maybe some time with her friend would help get her out of her miserable mood.

After three rings, she expected it to go to voicemail.

It didn't.

A female answered on the other end. "Yeah?"

Yeah? "I'm looking for Zeke."

"Who's this?"

Maddie pulled in an irritated breath. "A friend."

"He's busy with another *friend* right now. You'll have to wait your turn."

She wasn't stupid enough to ask what he was doing with that "friend." She could guess. Especially since he was too busy to answer his own phone.

"Who's this?" she asked the woman.

The phone went dead.

Maddie pulled it away from her ear to confirm the woman hung up on her. She quickly texted Zeke's number. *Call me when you're not busy. Hopefully you're okay.*

Just as she was about to toss her phone on the passenger seat, her phone dinged with an incoming text.

The second she pulled it up, she regretted it. It was a photo of Zeke with one naked woman sitting on his face while another sucked his cock. The message with it read: *He looks okay to me.*

The only reason she recognized him was due to his tattoos. Otherwise, since his face was covered, it could be any photo of a man having group sex. But she really doubted

Zeke would keep those kinds of photos on his phone. Naked women? Probably. A naked man? Not likely.

She quickly deleted the photo and wondered what she should do next.

The best thing would be to go home, have a couple glasses of wine, and watch a rom-com or something. Anything to get her out of this foul mood.

She searched through her contacts. She could call home and talk to her mom or sister. She could also call Jude.

She could even call Shade. With him, she just wouldn't be able to vent about work. Otherwise, she might end up jobless and not because of being fired, but because her boss would no longer be breathing.

That was also her fear when it came to talking to the rest of her family. If Shade caught wind of her troubles at Smith's, he just might hop on his sled and take a trip south.

She had to protect her stepfather from himself.

Instead, she continued to scroll. She could text Gabi and see what she was up to. See if she wanted to grab dinner or something or even come over to watch the movie with her.

But before she found Gabi's number, another entry caught her eye.

BBC.

Was that a joke? It had to be a joke.

She didn't put that in her contacts—

No damn way...

Holy shit. She forgot that Romeo put his number in her phone at Bangin' Burgers.

Should she call him? Or just try to ignore that he existed?

Or she could call him.

Just to give him shit about the whole BBC thing.

But maybe that was why he did it. To get a reaction from her.

She should ignore it.

She should.

But did she?

Of course not. She clicked on the number and pressed Send.

Her excuse? She really needed to take her mind off work that didn't involve a lot of alcohol. He might be able to do that without her getting buzzed to do so.

The man with a "BBC," as he self-proclaimed, might be her solution.

His phone only rang once before he answered. "'Bout time."

She rolled her eyes at that greeting. "BBC? Really?"

A deep chuckle filled her ear. "Know what it means?"

"Why don't you tell me, since you're the one who put it in my phone?"

"Would rather show you."

"I've seen it."

"Worth takin' another look."

"Then, you can send me a pic." A dick pic, that was.

"2D pics don't do it justice. It's more impressive in 3D."

"Honestly, Rome, at the time, I didn't know better. Now I know you're only average."

"Damn," came his whisper.

"I don't know who's cockier. You or Zeke."

"Guess you could say I'm cockier since mine's bigger."

Maddie groaned and rolled her eyes even harder this time. "I haven't seen his to compare."

She couldn't even see it in the picture she deleted. A woman's head with long bleach blonde hair had censored it. However, she did note that someone needed her roots touched up.

But that was neither here nor there.

"He's a bit young for you, dontcha think?"

"Well, I'm pretty sure the age difference between me and him is the same as me and you. Am I too young for you?"

That shut him up. At least for a second or two.

"Whataya doin'?"

Funny how he wanted to change the subject instead of answering. "Sitting in my car talking to you."

"Why you in your cage?"

Good thing she knew that "cage" was biker slang for her vehicle. "I'm trying to decompress."

"From what?"

"Work."

Silence filled her ear for a few seconds. "Whataya doin'?"

What? "I just told you—"

"No. Whataya doin' callin' me?"

"I figured that's why you put your number in my phone. So I'd call it." *Duh.*

"Whataya lookin' to get outta this call?"

"A conversation?" She didn't realize Romeo was so damn dense.

"That ain't it."

"It isn't?"

"What d'you want from me, Maddie?"

"I just said a conver—"

He cut her off again. "Ain't it."

"Okay, then tell me why I'm calling you."

"Want me to take your mind off whatever's makin' you need to decompress."

Well, that was true. Maybe she was wrong, and he wasn't so dense after all.

"Know plenty of ways to do that," he went on.

That might be true, too. "How?"

"First, I'm gonna spread you wide, bury my face between

117

your sweet fuckin' thighs, then use my tongue 'til you scream for me to stop. 'Til you buck off the bed. 'Til you come so many times, you can't even fuckin' move."

His crudeness should be a turn off. It was the opposite.

Why did his deep voice combined with dirty words light her on fire?

"Then, I'm gonna—"

"Romeo," came out on a ragged breath in an attempt to stop him.

She didn't need to hear him explain it, she could already picture it in her mind.

Her pussy clenched violently and began to throb. Her fingers and toes curled. Her pulse pounded in her ears.

He needed to stop before she climaxed right there in her driver's seat in the parking lot of Smith's.

She never had phone sex before, but she imagined this came damn close.

"Gonna fuck me over again or you gonna lemme fuck you?"

"I didn't—"

"Be at Dick's. Twenty minutes. You don't show up, delete my fuckin' number."

"Are we going to play pool?" Despite trying to be a smart ass, her breathless voice gave her away.

"We're gonna play somethin' and it ain't gonna be pool."

Chapter Eleven

ROMEO SNAGGED the Jim Beam off the top shelf behind the bar and cracked it open. He kept his eyes glued to the entrance of Dirty Dick's as he poured the bourbon into a short glass.

He downed it in one shot, then dragged the back of his hand over his lips.

Maddie had five minutes left to show. If she didn't, he was heading back to his place, locking the damn door, and forgetting the woman existed.

He refused to get played again.

Unfortunately, forgetting her might be impossible.

He thought he had until the night he spotted her at Bangin' Burgers. Since then, he hadn't been able to stop thinking about her. Especially now that her hips were a little rounder, her ass extra pound-worthy and those tits a bit heavier.

She'd matured a fuck of a lot more since he last saw her naked.

No lie, the past five years had been good to her. And that wasn't always the case when it came to women getting older.

Not that Maddie was old. *Hell*, she hadn't even hit thirty yet. Unlike him. He passed that point a few years ago.

"What's goin' on, prez?"

Romeo took his eyes off the door for the second needed to see BamBam approaching. "Nothin'. Whataya doin'?"

"Just checkin' to see who's on the menu tonight."

"Tink, Coral and Keisha's 'round here somewhere if nobody's snagged 'em yet." He hadn't paid much attention since his mind was on another female.

One not a sweet butt shared with his brothers.

"Was hopin' for Nia. You see her?"

"I mention her name?"

BamBam chuckled as he poured himself a draft. "Could be keepin' her for yourself tonight. Woman's got a fuckin' mouth on her, but it's easy enough to keep her quiet when she's on her fuckin' knees."

"Just don't piss her the fuck off. She's got some sharp teeth."

BamBam snorted and slapped Romeo on the back. "Sounds like you know from experience."

Romeo shook his head. He did, but he wasn't going to admit it. They both learned a lesson that day. Romeo discovered he shouldn't piss off Nia when she was in the middle of giving him head and Nia learned to never bite his dick again.

For the most part, the Knights were generous, as well as lenient, with their club girls. They were treated well and had the run of Dick's, meaning they could eat and drink as much as they wanted whenever they wanted. If they needed a roof over their head or a cage to get around, one was found for them. They were also under the club's protection. However, Romeo drew the line when it came to almost being neutered.

When he turned to place the bottle back on the shelf, he heard BamBam release a low whistle. "Damn, look what just wandered in lookin' like she's lost. Guess it's up to me to go help her find her way."

As BamBam turned to head over to the newcomer, Romeo stopped him by grabbing his arm. "You ain't doin' shit. She ain't lost. She also ain't here for you."

His fellow Knights' eyebrows rose. "Know her?"

"Yeah."

"She here for you?"

Romeo sucked loudly on his teeth before answering, "Yeah."

BamBam elbowed him. "Willin' to share her?"

"Fuck off, brother. Go find Nia."

Romeo agreed with his brother's observation, though. Maddie did look slightly lost since she had never stepped into Dick's before. *Hell*, he wasn't even sure if she ever stepped into Knights' territory before.

With her being Blood Fury property, she would normally need permission to be in another club's territory. But that rule wasn't enforced due to the BFMC and the DKMC being allies. All three clubs had the freedom to come and go through each other's area without making a request first.

While she scanned the bar looking for him, all his brothers were scanning her in return. So were some of the customers.

"Nia can wait. Now I gotta stick around to fuckin' watch this."

"Nothin' to watch." He needed to go claim Maddie before anyone else approached her trying to do the same.

When Romeo rounded the bar, she spotted him and headed in his direction. He stopped long enough to watch the roll of her hips and the bounce of her tits.

Yeah, she'd definitely filled out in the last five years.

He fucking liked it.

More than he probably should.

Tonight, she was dressed like the girl-next-door. Worn denim hugged those rounded hips and her jeans were short enough to show her ankles. Some sort of slip-on sneakers or shoes covered her feet, a T-shirt advertising Mansfield University snuggly fit across the tits he wanted to bury his face between and a black baseball cap with a big red M embroidered on it covered her head. Her hair—whatever the fucking color was now—was pulled into a ponytail and stuck out of the back of the hat.

If she wore any makeup, it wasn't much.

She wasn't dressed to impress but for comfort. Despite that, she was still hot as fuck to him.

Short shorts and miniskirts where a woman's ass cheeks were hanging out had its place... On a sweet butt. Not Maddie. He would've lost his fucking mind if she walked into Dick's dressed like a club whore.

He pinched his nose, closed his eyes, and shook his head at his reaction to that thought. Why did it make his fucking blood pressure rise? Why should he care how she dressed? She didn't belong to him. She wasn't his ol' lady or even one of his regulars. She was only a woman wanting some dick tonight.

Dick he was more than willing to provide.

When he opened his eyes, Maddie had disappeared. Someone had blocked both her path and his view.

That someone wore a Knights' cut.

Fuckin' Slick.

Just like Romeo, Slick got his name for good reason.

Sucking on his teeth again, he went to run interference. And make it clear Maddie was here for him.

Nobody else.

Not BamBam. Not Slick. Not any of his brothers.

When he got to them, he "accidentally" bumped into Slick hard enough to dislodge the hand holding her chin and tipping up her face.

From Maddie's expression, it seemed as if she wasn't buying any of the bullshit spewing from his lips.

Good. Because Slick was skilled at sweet-talking women into his bed.

He was almost as good as Romeo.

Almost.

But Romeo was about to cock-block him.

When he immediately grabbed her hand and tugged her to his side to claim her, Maddie looked relieved to see him.

"She's with me," he growled at Slick. Without waiting for a response from his brother, he next ordered Maddie to, "Let's go."

"Damn, brother..." he heard behind him.

Luckily, she followed without resisting or complaining in front of Slick. Once they were far enough away, she asked, "Where are we going?"

"Somewhere private." After releasing her hand, he curled his around the back of her neck to steer her toward Dick's kitchen. He escorted her through the swinging door, ignoring the stares from the two kitchen employees, and kept her moving.

Once they were outside, she repeated her question. "Where are we going, Rome?"

"My place."

Halfway between the bar and his crib, she slammed to a stop. "You live *there*?"

"Where the fuck d'you think I live? In a fuckin' tent?"

"*Umm.* I figured a cardboard box on the sidewalk. I'm not sure that's much better."

"Funny," he muttered.

"*I* thought so."

"You don't hear me fuckin' laughin'." He squeezed her neck slightly. "Let's go."

He admitted his place wasn't much to look at from the outside, but it was kept that way on purpose. At first glance to an outsider, the building looked similar to an oversized storage shed.

Despite how the exterior appeared, it was far from a shed on the inside. It might be simple but simple was all he needed. Once Magnum married his ol' lady and began making more hump dumplings, the club's enforcer needed to find a bigger place, so Romeo jumped on the chance to take it for himself. He was president, after all, and outranked anyone else interested.

Better yet, club funds paid for it all since it sat on the same property as Dick's. For only the cost of his monthly dues, he got a cool place to live, all the utilities paid, and access to a full bar and commercial kitchen only a few yards away.

Plus, sweet butts were always close at hand.

It was a sweet fucking deal.

He only needed to remain president to keep it. He had no doubt that if he ever gave up the gavel—willingly or unwillingly—someone else on the Knights' executive committee would be fucking in his bed, lounging on his couch, and watching his massive TV while drinking free whiskey.

When they reached the windowless, metal side door, Maddie asked, "Is this really your place?"

"Yeah."

"Is it a barn or a shed?"

"It's where I'm gonna fuck you."

A ragged exhale was heard behind him as he unlocked the door.

"Maybe I only wanted to spend some time with a friend."

Romeo snorted and pulled open the door. "You wanted a friend you woulda called LZ."

"He was busy."

"Then Gabi. She's former Fury, bet you're friends with her."

"I am, but..."

"But you wanted dick, and she don't got one," he finished for her.

"I'm only looking to take my mind off work."

"Dick will do it." Especially his.

"You have a lot of confidence that your dick will solve my problems."

"Didn't say solve them but will make you forget them for a while."

"Since when is thirty seconds considered 'a while?'"

"Once again, your attempt at bein' funny ain't it." He stepped back, placed his hand on her lower back and shoved her inside.

He had to chest bump her to get her to move farther into his place so he could step inside behind her, close the door, and lock it.

All three locks. The one on the handle, the slide latch, and the deadbolt. He also set the security bar in place.

He did not want what they were about to do to be interrupted.

He turned to see her brown eyes wide.

"Do you really need all of that?"

"Yeah," he answered simply.

"Is this a bad area?"

"Nothin' to do with the area since we rule it. Has to do with me bein' prez of the Knights."

"Are you paranoid?" she asked.

"Realistic."

"Have you had threats against you?"

"Not lately, no. That don't mean there won't be in the future. The Knights and the Angels had an issue with those fuckin' Shadow Warriors before they were dealt with. Then we had to deal with those motherfuckin' Deadly Demons more recently."

"Who are the Deadly Demons?"

"One-percenters that got too damn big for their fuckin' britches. They got decimated."

Her eyebrows rose. "By your club?"

He pulled in a breath. They had a hand in it but only because the outlaw club took Aaliyah, Magnum's oldest daughter, against her will. They swiftly dealt with the two MC members that snagged her after La Cosa Nostra dealt with the remainder.

The rest of the cleanup was done by a fucking federal task force. One that Ali-Cat's hubby had been a part of.

Romeo's upper lip pulled up into a sneer as it always did when he thought about Magnum's pig son-in-law and baby daddy of his latest granddaughter Destiny.

"By your club?" she prodded.

He answered, "No," because they did not talk about what happened the day they found the two Demons, T-Bone and Saint, at a motel with Magnum's oldest daughter. The Knights only assisted karma when those two motherfuckers disappeared that day and were never seen again.

"So, if that club was decimated, why worry?"

"Ain't worried. Bein' smart. Never know what evil lurks

outside that locked door." He pushed past her, headed to his right and into his open kitchen. He opened the refrigerator. "Beer?"

She nodded.

He grabbed her a cold bottle, twisting off the cap and handing it to her before grabbing one for himself.

When he turned with his beer in hand, she said, "Not much food in there."

"Don't need much. Got a whole damn kitchen with a walk-in fridge only yards away."

Surprise colored her tone when she asked, "You cook?"

He huffed out a breath.

"You have your kitchen staff make it for you?"

"Them or the sweet butts." Another perk of being president of a strong, growing MC.

With her expression closed, she stared at him for a whole damn minute before asking, "I should've asked this before, but you're single, right?" then taking a swig of her beer.

Chapter Twelve

"You don't have an ol' lady or a girlfriend?" Or a wife? Why didn't she ask this prior, instead of only assuming he was free? It was Romeo. Maddie doubted he showed any woman loyalty. Wife, ol' lady or otherwise. "I don't want to step on another woman's toes by being here." He might not care about that, but she did.

"No toes to step on."

After a quick glance over at him to make sure he didn't appear to be lying, Maddie wandered from the small kitchen that was to the right of the side door to the open living space that took up the majority of the building. Or house. Whatever it was considered.

The structure had a ceiling two stories high with what looked like a loft. She could barely get a glimpse of a big bed up there. Under the loft on the main floor were shelves, closets, and a door to what was most likely a bathroom.

His place pretty much reminded her of a studio apartment and was about the size of one, too.

To her left and along the side wall was a very narrow,

very steep stairway that led to where he slept. It wasn't much more than a ladder on steroids, and she couldn't imagine trying to climb up or down the steps while either drunk or exhausted.

That was a disaster waiting to happen.

"This place is... interesting." Despite being small and basic, it was surprisingly nice inside. Super clean? No. But it wasn't a pigsty, either.

She had no doubt since the sweet butts cooked for him, they also cleaned his place.

As well as did other things.

She knew how the whole club girl thing worked in an MC. She'd also witnessed them being used by members of the Fury more times than she'd like to admit.

After some of those incidents, the need to bleach her eyeballs was strong.

Those same eyeballs noticed that not much decorated the walls. And what did was more a generic decor and not at all personal. If she had walked in without him, she never would've guessed it was his place.

That was a bit strange to her since as soon as she moved into her current apartment, she couldn't wait to make that space her own. To turn it into her home. To put up pictures of her family and some of Jude's drawings. To decorate it as she pleased.

"It's a place to lay my fuckin' head and get some privacy. That's about it. Don't need to be fancy."

She turned. "No, it doesn't." She tipped the bottle to her lips and the cool liquid slid down her throat. She needed the beer to take off the edge because right now she was a ball of nerves.

If he broke out a joint, she might even take a hit, even though she normally didn't smoke, pot or otherwise.

Of course, the second she thought it, he pulled what looked like a fatty as well as a lighter out of his leather cut's inner pocket. He tossed both onto the low table in front of the couch, shrugged out of his colors and hung the worn vest on a hook next to the door. He probably never walked out of his place not representing the Knights.

That was typical MC behavior. She rarely saw anyone in the Fury not wearing theirs unless they had a good reason. Shade for sure, because he usually removed his cut as soon as he entered the house.

With a tip of his head toward the couch, he scooped up the joint and lighter as he rounded the table. Then he dropped his big body onto the couch.

She was really surprised Romeo wasn't immediately dragging her upstairs to his bed. He acted as if he was in no rush to have sex. Like the two of them normally hung out together. As if they were best buds.

Was it that obvious that she was a bit wired, and he thought the weed would help?

He patted the seat next to him. "C'mere." He lifted the joint. "This'll take the edge off quicker than beer. And I want you fuckin' sober."

She pretended to misunderstand. "Sober for what?"

"For what you came here for."

As she headed over to the couch—and him—she asked, "What did I come here for?"

"We playin' dumb now? Or you just fuckin' with me?"

She sat next to him but, unlike him, she perched on the edge. "I wouldn't have come at all if I was fucking with you, Rome."

He tucked the blunt between his lips and lit the rolled tip. He took a few quick puffs until the end burned steadily, then took a long pull. While he held the smoke deep down in his lungs, he offered it to her.

She stared at it a few seconds, debating whether she should or shouldn't.

Fuck it.

She came here to get her mind off work. And Roger.

If a combination of sex and pot was what it took, then... When in Rome...

She took the rolled joint from him and tentatively took a hit. When it reached her lungs, she began to hack.

A deep chuckle came from the man sitting next to her. He plucked the joint from her fingers, taking another long drag on it.

She wrinkled her nose and rubbed her chest since her lungs were still on fire.

"You smoke weed before?"

"A few times, but not regularly. I'm assuming that's not the case with you."

He held the joint out to her again and shook his head. "Nope. Helps keep my temper in check."

"You have a temper?" That was surprising. She was used to Trip's hair trigger temper but wasn't aware of Romeo's.

"Got no patience for bullshit."

She took the hand-rolled joint from him. "That makes two of us." After taking another hit—definitely not as long as Romeo's—she did her best to keep the smoke in her lungs for a few seconds without coughing before blowing it up and away from them.

The burn wasn't so bad the second time.

Even better, it was starting to work its magic. The ball of stress in her chest was beginning to unravel.

Maybe she didn't need to have sex with Romeo. Maybe all she needed was to get stoned. Or at least buzzed.

After grabbing her beer off the floor where she'd left it, she scooted back and sank into the very comfortable couch with a sigh.

His body heat practically seared her where their thighs and arms pressed together, but she didn't move away.

"When did you get your road name?"

He snorted. "When I was about sixteen."

She bugged her eyes out at him. "Really? You were a dog as a teenager, too?" *Figures.*

His cocky grin made her pulse speed up and warmth swirl through her until it landed between her legs.

Her head knew he was trouble. Apparently, the rest of her didn't care.

"Always loved the ladies."

"But they don't always love you," she countered.

"Ain't lookin' for love."

"No, just wet pussy, right?"

Holy shit, did that just come out of her mouth? She glanced at the blunt still in his thick fingers. It must be some good shit. But then, he probably had the right connections.

She took another swig of her beer in an attempt to douse the fire in her belly. She needed to keep her head about her.

Maybe smoking pot and drinking beer wasn't the best idea to do that.

"Never promised shit to any of 'em."

"No, you only did a bunch of sweet talking, right?"

"More like talkin' dirty."

"Well, you do have a way with words, Romeo."

"My way must not be so fuckin' bad seein' you're here."

Yes, she was. But she was fully aware of the kind of man he was. And tonight, she was okay with that. She only wanted the same as what she wanted from him that night five years ago in his RV.

Nothing more.

Nothing less.

The only thing different tonight would be her level of experience. As well as being in a structure that had a foundation instead of wheels.

She held out her hand.

He shook his head, took his sweet ol' time licking his fingers, then pinched the end of the joint to extinguish it before tossing what was left back onto the table in front of them.

She stared at it with longing since she was now relaxed. Even so, him cutting her off was most likely for the best. She already felt like she was floating and also had the strong urge to take a nap.

Only, she didn't come over here for a slumber party.

"Do you mind if I grab another beer?" Maybe that would wake her up a little more. She pushed herself to her feet, but before she could take a step toward the kitchen, he grabbed her arm and tugged her sharply, making her land on his lap.

"No."

His thighs were thick, warm, and hard.

"No? Then what can I have?" she whispered.

His thighs weren't the only thing hard. "You're lookin' at it."

She turned herself until she straddled his lap, and their faces were only inches apart. "I am now."

She met his brown eyes. So dark that she couldn't see where the dark iris ended, and the black outer ring began. But that wasn't all she noticed.

His eyes held heat and a promise, making her pussy quiver and her nipples peak.

She combed her fingers through his thick beard. "When's the last time you've seen your cheeks?" *Good lord*, her breathless question gave away how much she wanted him right now.

She didn't understand the attraction. For her, anyway. He chased anyone with tits and a few available holes.

"Long time. What's with all the fuckin' questions?"

She yanked one shoulder up in a half-shrug. "Maybe I want to get to know you better."

He cocked an eyebrow. "Why?"

So she didn't feel guilty about doing exactly what Romeo normally did? Using someone simply for sex? Only wanting to bang and bounce?

Not being worried about strings? Not having to deal with a possessive man trying to rule her life afterward?

Truthfully, all of that sounded perfect. It was exactly what she needed. Nothing more. She was fine with one night of bumping and grinding.

"You're right. There's no valid reason to get to know you at all, Rome. Beyond what I already know, anyway."

His eyes narrowed on her. "Just here to use me."

She cocked an eyebrow back at him. "That's right. Do you have a problem with that?"

"Long as you don't gotta problem with me doin' the same to you."

"I wouldn't be here if I did."

Instead of him looking relieved at her words, his expression turned sour.

Chapter Thirteen

HOLY SHIT. Was Romeo bothered by the fact a woman would actually *want* to have sex with no strings attached? Women beside sweet butts, that was.

That couldn't be rare in his world, could it?

It was only logical to assume some women wanted to hook up with him with the end game of wearing his cut. Being the ol' lady of a club president held some status and power in the MC world.

While technically MC "royalty" didn't exist, Stella, Trip's ol' lady, was certainly considered the queen of the Blood Fury's kingdom. But then, she was the perfect partner for the BFMC's ruling "king."

"You don't have to worry about me wanting anything more than the sole reason I came here for. You can breathe easy, Rome."

He cupped her ass and gave it a firm squeeze. "Ain't havin' a problem breathin', woman. Just wonderin' why the quiz before we fuck, that's all."

"I won't ask any more questions, then. I'll simply stay blissfully ignorant about you, if that's what you want."

When he pinned his lips together, she grinned and grabbed his bearded face, got a good grip on the black, wiry hair, and pulled him forward as she leaned in.

"We don't need to talk at all," she whispered once their mouths were only a hairsbreadth away.

"Just how I fuckin' like it," he murmured back.

When she drew her tongue over her lips, his gaze followed. As soon as she was done, his eyes lifted and met hers.

Everything inside her clenched with what she saw in his. In that moment, she had no doubt that tonight he would deliver what she ordered.

He didn't wait for her to close the slight gap. He took her mouth like it belonged to him, causing an electrical current to crackle and pop down her spine.

His full lips were soft, but firm, as they moved over hers. His tongue traced the seam of her mouth, encouraging her to open and let him in. She welcomed him.

Their tongues touched and took turns exploring.

She tasted beyond the beer and pot. She could taste him.

They hadn't really kissed the last time they had sex. Instead, his lips had been busy everywhere else in his attempt to keep her mind off what came next. His intent was to get her so worked up; she'd forget she was a virgin.

Tonight, she was far from innocent, and she appreciated how well he kissed. Honestly, that surprised her. She figured, just like the first time with her, that he normally didn't waste time on anything so intimate. That he only wanted a physical connection. One that was shallow, not deep.

But maybe kissing wasn't a big deal for him. That it went along with the rest of it. He probably did whatever was needed to remove a woman's clothes. And if kissing was the key to unlocking that next step...

Either way, she was overthinking it. She shouldn't be concerned with what he did with other women, she should only be concentrating on this moment.

Bottom line, he was a damn good kisser, and she wouldn't complain about taking time to lock lips with him, instead of immediately moving on to the main event.

Her moan ended up caught between them when he dug his fingers deeper into her ass and began kneading her cheeks with some enthusiasm.

At the same time, Romeo stole her breath before giving it back to her. Their tongues sparred for a few seconds before he used his to explore every inch of her mouth.

A groan worked its way from deep inside her when she dropped all of her weight onto his lap and ground against his hard cock. Circling her hips, she rode his denim-covered erection while his fingertips dug so deeply into her ass, it caused discomfort.

Despite that, she didn't want him to stop.

When she continued to grind against him, he thrust upward over and over, giving her a preview of what was to come once they got naked. However, if they didn't stop, she might come simply by dry humping the fully dressed man beneath her.

Was that a problem?

Not in her eyes.

She doubted it would be in his, either.

Most likely he'd be amused over the fact she could get off so quickly and without much effort.

Was it like that with everyone? Absolutely not. But there was something about Romeo...

Ooooh. Helloooo.

As expected, an orgasm ripped through her, making her gasp and rock herself over his steely length.

What she hadn't expected was it to be that intense.

"For fuck's sake," he groaned the second he ripped his mouth free from hers. Holding her hips, he jammed his face between her cotton-covered breasts. Was it to hide his rapid panting? "So fuckin' hard right now."

He certainly was. It had to be uncomfortable.

Wrapping her arms around his head, she pinned him to her chest as tiny aftershocks continued from her powerful climax.

"Need this off you," came muffled from her T-shirt. "Need everythin' off you. Like fuckin' yesterday."

She wanted to see every inch of him, too.

Her memory of what he looked like had faded over the last half a decade. It was time to refresh that memory. The one she had compared every man to for the first couple of years afterward and was disappointed when they didn't measure up.

"Are we going to have sex on the couch?" She hoped not.

He only hesitated for a heartbeat. "Fuck that. Want you spread naked on my bed."

Using a bed got her vote, too.

His thighs were almost as rock hard as his cock. "You feel tense."

"Tryin' not to blow a goddamn load in my fuckin' jeans. You comin' like that..." He huffed out a breath. "For fuck's sake..."

He pulled his face away from her. Oh yes, he appeared a bit tortured. She was surprised he wasn't sprinting for the loft.

"Would carry you up but don't wanna fall down those fuckin' stairs and die."

"Not dying sounds like a solid plan," she agreed.

One side of his mouth pulled up. "Figured it would."

He surged to his feet at the same time cradling her in his arms as if she weighed nothing, despite knowing for a fact she weighed something. A whole bunch of somethings.

She hooked an arm around this thick, corded neck and grabbed one of his bulging biceps as he carried her the short distance across the room. While she wanted to avoid tumbling down the steps to her death, she also didn't want to hit the tile floor, either.

The second he reached the base of the steps; he dropped her to her feet. "Get upstairs before I fuck you right here on the floor."

She wrinkled her nose. "The floor's dirty."

"Right. Get the fuck upstairs, then."

When she reached the third step, he slapped her ass hard, making her lurch forward and her heart do a somersault in her chest. She clung to the wooden banister by her nails. "Rome, don't! I don't want to fall."

"You do, gonna catch you."

"What if I knock you backwards and we both end up in a crumpled heap?"

"I'll break your fall."

"And I might break your bones."

"Then hurry the fuck up."

"Who designed these?" The steps were crazy steep. It would only take one misstep…

"Want me to research that, or do you wanna get fucked?"

"It was actually a rhetorical question."

"Yeah? So was mine. Keep goin'."

She pursed her lips and turned her attention back to the top. She was not fond of heights. At least the loft had a cable railing that would keep her from falling off the edge and to her early and tragic death.

As she worked her way up, the heat at her back told her that he was following closely behind her, but she wasn't turning around to confirm.

She breathed easier when she reached the top and both of her feet were finally planted on a floor. Then, more panic ensued when she realized the loft didn't have a bathroom. She'd have to climb back down if she needed to go.

"Do you sleep up here when you're drunk?"

"Never drunk."

A peel of laughter escaped her. "What? Now, I know that's a damn lie."

He grinned. "Couch is pretty fuckin' comfortable."

"If I lived here, I'd buy one with a pull-out bed."

She glanced around. She thought the loft only held a bed. She was wrong. Personal photos decorated the opposite wall.

She immediately went over to a framed photo of a woman holding the hand of a child. She leaned closer and squinted as if that would help her recognize the people in the picture.

But the kid...

"Is that kid yours?" Was Romeo a father?

She heard a snort behind her. "The kid's me."

She glanced over her shoulder. "That's you? But you look so sweet and innocent."

"At ten, probably was."

"But at eleven you turned into a badass gangster?"

When he huffed, "A gangster?" she giggled.

"The woman's your mother?"

"Aunt."

She found it interesting that he pronounced aunt differently than she did. He said it like "awnt," while her whole life she always said it like "ant." *Huh.*

She quickly scanned the rest of the framed photos. One posed shot included him and a bunch of other Knights. Next to it was a candid shot of Romeo. The smile he wore in the picture was blinding.

Jesus, he looked so damn young. And the cut he wore... "Prospect?"

"Yeah, was just handed my cut."

"Beginning of the end, right?" she teased.

"As soon as I put that motherfucker on, my end goal was prez."

She turned. "You go after what you want."

"Don't you?"

"And you get it."

"Don't you?" he repeated with a cocked eyebrow. "Wanted me and here the fuck you are."

Of course he'd say that. She smothered a grin and turned to face him. "So... your aunt, huh?"

"Woman raised me."

That was it? That was all he had to say? "What happened to your mother?"

His grin disappeared. "Story for another day."

A day she doubted would ever come. They wouldn't be best friends after this.

He grabbed her arm and pulled her away from the wall of photos. "Got better things to do than jawin' 'bout nothin'."

She doubted it was nothing. She had seen the way his expression changed when she asked about his mother. After that, she certainly wasn't asking about his father.

"We doin' this or what?"

"I didn't climb those neck-breaking stairs for nothing," she informed him. She needed a reward for taking that risk.

She took in his king-sized bed. It was a mess. Like he woke up and simply rolled out. "When was the last time your sheets were washed?"

He glanced over at this bed. "Gotta ask Tink."

"Tink?"

When he opened his mouth, she gave him "the palm" to stop him from answering. "Never mind. I can figure it out."

He tugged on his beard. "Got a problem with sweet butts?"

"Not as long as they don't have a problem with me."

"Used to them, right?"

"I guess so. But I've never..." She was about to say that she never shared a man with them before. But then, Romeo was the only true biker she ever had sex with. And she could guarantee he slept with plenty of them. She didn't even have to ask.

Some of the single Fury members showed interest in her but they thought twice about it when it came to dealing with Shade afterward. Not that Maddie would've turned that interest, or even their innocent flirting, into anything more. She didn't want to deal with the crap that went along with alpha-holes.

She stepped closer and tipped her face up to his. "Promise me you won't tell anyone about this."

"I run my fuckin' mouth the last time?"

"Not that I'm aware of." Another reason why she picked him back then. Despite having plenty of conquests, she never heard him brag about any of them. Most likely because he forgot them the second he pulled his jeans back up.

A lot of bikers didn't see women as equals. Romeo was no different. To him, women had one function. To serve him. In bed. In the kitchen. Or by doing his bidding, whether it was doing his laundry or cleaning his place.

That was confirmed when she asked about his bedding. He didn't know the last time they'd been washed because he had a sweet butt—apparently, one with the name of Tink—do it for him.

Her train of thought brought her back to something she should've asked five years ago. "You always use condoms, right?"

"Think I'm fuckin' stupid?"

"A lot of men are."

"If you think bein' stupid's limited to men, you'd be fuckin' wrong."

He was getting irritated. They needed to stop talking before he decided she wasn't worth the effort and told her to go pound sand.

Though, she did already climax once tonight...

And it hadn't been disappointing.

Even so...

She stepped back, raked her gaze down him from his smooth, bald head to his biker boots. "Let's get naked."

The corners of his lips curled up in a wicked grin. "'Bout fuckin' time."

Chapter Fourteen

"Too much fuckin' chatter and not enough action goin' on."

After she rubbed one off on his hard as fuck dick, Romeo had been left hanging by a thread, so this shit needed to move faster.

Maddie had caught his interest long before he ever took her virginity. But now with a few more years and pounds on her...

Jesus. She was a fucking wet dream.

His, anyway. He didn't give a fuck what any other men thought of her. In fact, he hoped they didn't think about her at all.

She might not be his, but that didn't mean he wanted her to be anyone else's. *Fuck that.*

Was that selfish? Hell yeah it was, but he didn't give a fuck.

Perching on the edge of the bed, he removed his boots and socks. As soon as his feet were bare, he sat up and noticed she hadn't moved a damn inch. Even more disappointing, *nothing* on her was bare. Not even her head.

Un-fuckin'-acceptable.

"You change your mind?" If so, he'd do his fucking best to change it again. No way was he missing out on what she had to offer.

"Again, I didn't climb those stairs for nothing. I expect you to make it worth my while."

Thank fuck.

He surged to his feet, tempted to help her get naked by ripping off her clothes. But if he did that, she'd have nothing to wear after he kicked her out of his bed.

"Then, get naked, Maddie. Don't want me helpin' you 'cause I don't got the fuckin' patience right now to not tear your clothes if I gotta do it." With that, he grabbed the bottom of his T-shirt and yanked it over his head.

Hearing a sharp intake of breath, he glanced up to make sure she was getting her ass in gear.

She wasn't.

She was staring at him.

"Maddie," he growled.

She seemed to struggle to raise her gaze from his bare chest. "What?"

Did it turn her on or off?

More importantly, did he care? Fuck no. "Get fuckin' naked. Now."

"Did Crow do all of your tattoos?"

"Some. But we're done with fuckin' words, woman. Actions speak louder..."

When she smiled, something he didn't recognize went through him. Besides the urge to fuck her.

Normally a smile could light up her face, but this smile...

It told him that she definitely liked what she saw and that made his dick twitch in his jeans.

She really needed to hurry the fuck up. "You ain't undressed by the time my Black ass is, I'm rippin' off your clothes. And when I say rippin', I mean rippin'. If you wanna keep those clothes in one piece, I suggest bein' quick about it."

She better heed his second warning because that was the final one.

His threat flooded her cheeks with color and had her jerking into motion.

Wearing only his jeans, he stood with his hands on his hips, watching her pull the hat from her head.

He wasn't sure what hair color he liked better. Her natural strawberry blonde or the more reddish brown. Either looked good on her. She could probably rock purple hair, too.

But he really didn't give a shit what color it was since he wanted to fuck her, not braid her damn hair.

She toed off her shoes next, then unfastened the button on her jeans and unzipped them. Wiggling the denim over her curvy hips and down her thighs, what remained behind was a pair of peach-colored panties.

He licked his lips. "Keep goin'."

"Are you only going to stand there and watch?"

"Yep."

A gleam filled her brown eyes. "Are you sure you don't want to help?"

"Not unless you wanna go home lookin' like you escaped a lion's cage."

She pressed a hand over her tits. "I kind of like this shirt." Her head disappeared for a moment when she pulled her T-shirt up and over it.

His fingers twitched with the urge to touch her.

149

He had plenty of time for that. For now, he would watch the rest of the show since it might be the only time he got to do so.

But instead of removing her bra and panties, she walked toward him and when only a few inches away, she turned.

His eyes skimmed the line of her spine, the flare of her hips and roundness of her ass.

Goddamn perfection.

"Unclip me."

When he skimmed the back of his fingers down her smooth skin, from her neck to her bra strap, she shivered, and goosebumps broke out all over. His big fingers made short work of unhooking her bra, but since she kept an arm barred across her tits, the bra remained in place.

She took two steps away, then turned to face him again. "Your turn."

His turn? *Oh yeah.*

He quickly shucked his jeans. Since he wasn't wearing anything under them, he was now completely naked. His dick practically stood straight out from his body and the head glistened from the smeared precum.

She closely watched him when he fisted the head and squeezed out another drop. "Like what you see?"

"It's not bad," she teased. "On a scale of one to ten, I'd say you're..."

He cocked an eyebrow.

"An eight," she finished.

"You talkin' about me or my dick?"

"You. Since your cock is attached."

"Should be a ten."

Her eyes flashed. "Nobody's perfect."

He snorted. "Gonna rate you next. Lemme see those fuckin' tits."

When she removed her arm, her bra fell to the floor.

Fuuuuuck. He could suffocate in her rack. Now that he thought about it, it actually wouldn't be a bad way to die.

"Panties."

He held his breath as she pulled them down and stepped out of them once they dropped to her feet.

At least she didn't shave her pussy bare. He hated that shit. He wasn't into out-of-control bushes, but he also didn't like scorched earth.

"Hair down."

"So demanding." He detected a shake in her voice.

When she reached behind her head, her tits pulled higher, and his eyes were drawn to the tightly puckered nipples. He couldn't wait to get his mouth around them.

Once her long hair was free, it framed her face and fell like a curtain around her shoulders.

Holy fuck. The girl next door was gone, and a vixen replaced her.

"Think you lied about nobody bein' perfect. You're a goddamn ten, Maddie."

"Hardly."

"It's my ratin'. Ain't for you to say otherwise. Come to me."

"Being the Knights' president, you're probably used to giving orders, aren't you?"

"Somebody's gotta keep those fuckers in line."

"Well, I'm not one of those *fuckers* and I thought it was Magnum's job that kept everyone in line."

That reminded Romeo that Magnum had kept the fact Maddie was living in the area from him. That still pissed him the fuck off.

He could've had what stood before him so much fucking sooner.

Magnum was a goddamn cock-block.

Fucker.

Romeo tamped down his rising annoyance and concentrated on the woman in front of him. He held out his hand. "Told you to come here."

With one side of her mouth pulled up, she took her time closing the gap between them. And he enjoyed watching every step she took.

Tonight, he would be one lucky fucker. Even better, he didn't have to share Maddie with any of his brothers. She would be his and his alone.

If anyone else tried to touch her, he'd break their fucking fingers.

After she grabbed his outstretched hand, he lifted their clasped fingers over her head and spun her slowly in a circle, appreciating every inch.

Once she faced him again, he tugged her hard, slamming her into him and effectively sandwiching her soft tits and his hard, aching cock between them.

When she tipped her face up to his, he lost his damn breath. The last time that happened to him was the first time he slid inside her and knew he was taking something from her she could never get back.

He normally didn't give a shit about virgins, mostly because they were a pain in his ass. The ones he had in the past didn't know how to please a man, but Maddie...

To know he was the first one to have her...

To know she chose him over anyone else, even though she probably had a long list of dicks chasing her. *Hell*, in just the Blood Fury alone...

"Why you here, Maddie?" Maybe she had an ulterior motive for choosing him again.

"I already told you why."

He couldn't stop paranoia from creeping in. Being president of a powerful MC, he always had to watch his back. Even with females. "Why me?"

"Because you don't like commitment."

"So, anyone not lookin' for a ball and chain would've done?"

She only hesitated for a second. "I wanted someone I could trust."

"Some might say you're a fuckin' fool for trustin' me."

"I value my own opinion over others."

"Don't know me well enough."

"You didn't screw me over five years ago. You just screwed me," she reminded him.

"Just what you wanted."

She nodded.

"The same as you want tonight."

She nodded again.

"Sex without strings," he confirmed.

"Weren't you the one complaining about not enough action?"

He grinned. She was right. They were wasting time.

But really, was it truly a waste of time when he had a hot as fuck woman standing naked before him?

Any sane man would answer that with a *hell no.*

He drew his knuckles along her jawline, then trailed the pad of his thumb over her bottom lip. "How 'bout you show me what your mouth can do besides talkin'?"

"Sing?"

He shook his head.

"Whistle?"

He shook his head again.

"Are you going to reciprocate?"

"Gonna bury my face in your pussy and make you come. Want your juices coverin' my whole face."

She quivered. *Oh yeah*, she wanted that, too.

"Sit," she said.

His eyebrows rose when she suddenly took charge, pulling away from him and pointing to the end of the bed.

His aunt didn't raise no fucking fool, so he sat where she indicated. And as soon as he did, she used her knee to push his wider, giving her plenty of space to kneel between his legs.

She dug her fingers into his thighs as she lowered herself to her knees.

Too damn slowly.

The anticipation was more like torture.

"Your thighs are like tree trunks."

"So's my dick."

"You mean like a sapling?"

"More like a hundred-year-old oak."

Her dark eyes tipped up to his. "Hard to lie when I'm staring at it directly in the eye."

"Stop usin' your fuckin' eyes and start usin' your mouth. It ain't gonna suck itself."

As soon as he said that, her expression closed up.

For fuck's sake, he needed to remember she wasn't a sweet butt. He needed to treat her differently. Carefully.

She didn't have to come to him. She did.

He couldn't fuck this up. He almost did.

Maybe he just needed to keep his fucking mouth shut so she didn't bail before they even got started.

Chapter Fifteen

Why the hell did she contact him?

Why did she think he was what she needed to get her mind off work? She had to be crazy to think it would go any other way than it was.

He was used to women doing whatever he demanded. She should've known better than to think he'd treat her any differently.

Fool that she was, she was now totally naked on her knees on the floor.

She had lost her mind for a minute, but reality was now setting in.

The bad part of this whole thing... He was Romeo, a known user of women. The good part... He wouldn't tell a damn soul they had sex. Did the pros outweigh the cons?

His cock was nice. So, there was that.

From what she remembered, he also knew how to use it. As well as his mouth.

Her decision at this point was to either deal with his bossy biker bullshit or leave.

He *did* have a nice cock. And he was easy on the eyes.

He had more tattoos than she remembered. She swore he was also bulkier in size. Not fatter, simply... beefier.

Nothing about him turned her off except his attitude.

Should she grin and bear it?

She mentally sighed. Of course she would.

Wrapping one hand around the root of his erection, she took the tip into her mouth. His cock might not be as thick as a tree trunk, but it wasn't small, either. A salty tang hit her tongue as she swirled it around the head.

His groan hit her ears at the same time his fingers drove into her hair and pulled tight. When he whispered, "That's it, baby," her pussy clenched so hard, she thought she might actually come again.

Solely from the way he said it. *Damn.*

She took in as much of his length as she could without gagging. Though, he probably wouldn't care if she did. She'd seen some of the Fury guys face fuck women so rough and deep that tears ended up running down their face, strings of saliva clung to their lips and snot ran out of their nose.

Maddie thought that was gross. The guys? Not so much. Hopefully, Romeo wouldn't try to "skull fuck" her like that. If he did, she had no qualms about tapping out.

She traced her tongue along the thick ridge running along the underside of his cock before swallowing as much as she could again.

His fingers flexed rhythmically in her hair, loosening and tightening. And his hips jumped a couple of times off the bed. But at least he didn't force her head down while thrusting his cock deeper.

"Fuck," he groaned as she continued to suck and lick.

She didn't have to tap, but, surprisingly, *he* did when she took his balls in her mouth while using her fist to pump his steely length.

Using her hair, he yanked her head away.

"Fuck," he groaned. "Look at you. Cheeks flushed. Lips swollen and shiny. That's hot as fuck."

"Are you done?"

He shook his head slowly. "Not done."

As she went to take him into her mouth again, he stopped her. "Meant you're done. With that. We ain't done with the rest." When he got to his feet, his veiny cock bobbed violently. "Switch spots."

Once again, he was giving orders, but this was one she didn't mind. If memory served her right, he was very good at what he was about to do next.

Her reaction when he had eaten her out that first time had amused him. It could've been because she released a high-pitched squeal and practically jumped out of her skin when she had an unexpected orgasm.

This time she'd be looking forward to it and what he could do with that tongue. The man might be a womanizer, but he did have some amazing skills.

Her opinion was, he could get away with being like that because the man knew he wasn't hard to look at. He also knew he was good in bed. Herein lied the problem. If he wasn't either of those things, he'd be a lot more resistible and unable to get whatever woman he set his sights on.

Like her.

She fell into that trap.

"On my hands and knees? On my back? How do you want me?"

"How don't I want you is the fuckin' answer. But for now, on your back with those legs spread wide as fuck. Show me that pretty pink pussy."

Pretty pink pussy?

Did that really come out of Romeo's mouth?

Was all the blood in his cock making him delirious? Or maybe she was so wound up herself that she was mishearing things.

Before she could climb onto the bed, his large hands gripped her ribcage and she found herself tossed on the bed as if, once again, she was as light as a feather.

The man was nothing if not strong.

Once she landed with a bounce, she quickly scooted backward until her head rested on one of his pillows.

"Show me." His deep, delicious growl made everything inside of her burn hotter.

Without hesitation, she pulled up her knees and spread them.

"Spread your lips," came his next demand.

She almost asked him which ones to tease him, but right now, she wasn't in any sort of mood to joke around. This was serious business.

The hunger in his dark eyes made her breath catch, her nipples ache and her thighs shake. She stroked her pussy lightly first before making a V with her fingers and spreading herself wide for his viewing pleasure.

A rush of air slipped from between his lips. "What a fuckin' sight."

She'd have to assume that was a compliment and not an insult since she kept up on her personal grooming. Not for any particular man, but for herself.

Watching sweet butts the last few years made her not want to cater to anyone with a dick. No matter who he was. Any man she might be with long term, she wanted to be treated as an equal, not like an object.

Tonight would be the exception. She would deal with his biker attitude solely to get what she wanted.

She wanted Romeo for a night, not a lifetime.

Just the same as he wanted her.

A simple mutual arrangement.

The bed dipped under his weight as he climbed on, his eyes not straying once from the apex of her legs.

She stopped breathing for a second when his fingers dug into her thighs and spread her even wider.

"I'm a big fuckin' boy. Need some room to work."

"Less talk, more action," she reminded him with a playful tug on his beard.

His eyes lifted to her face for a few seconds, then he tipped his head and dropped to his belly, pushing her fingers out of the way, and putting his mouth in their place.

Her back arched as he sucked on her clit and his beard scraped roughly against the delicate flesh of her folds. The man did not hold back. He was all in and definitely trying to give himself a facial with her arousal.

She'd be happy to help.

He sucked, licked, nibbled, and nipped.

Oh yes. She was right to contact him. This was just what the doctor ordered after a shitty end to her day. *Hell,* she'd be fine with it if she ended every day like this. She'd have no complaints.

Even better, Romeo ate her like he hadn't eaten in a month. Everything he did kept her hips hopping off the bed and her fingers digging into his smooth skull. She flung her head back and closed her eyes, appreciating his cunnilingus skills.

She *really* appreciated those skills.

But when he sucked on her clit and began to finger fuck her, all of her spinning thoughts were flung from her head.

She was hyper-focused on what he was doing with his mouth and fingers.

And what she *was* doing was losing her damn mind.

Every bone turned to liquid as he continued the delicious onslaught on her pussy. He'd drive her to the brink, then rudely yank her back from the edge before shoving her back toward the precipice until she teetered there again, only hanging on by her fingernails.

While more than ready to have another orgasm, she also wanted him to continue.

She was torn. Let herself come or hold out as long as she could?

If she was nice, she'd consider Romeo's patience. She was damn sure he was ready to get to the main event.

She considered him. Being a biker, like the majority, Romeo would never do what he didn't want to do. That included a marathon session of eating pussy. So, maybe she shouldn't worry about him and only worry about herself.

If he didn't like it, he'd have no problem making that known. Loudly, too.

That was one good thing about bikers. They did not beat around the bush. They could be painfully direct and didn't care what anyone's opinion was about that.

She drew in a breath before releasing it just as slowly and decided to let him continue until she couldn't take anymore. She brushed her thumbs back and forth over the warm skin of his smooth noggin.

His skin was soft. His beard rough.

And, even though she could no longer see it, she was damn sure his cock was still a steel rod. Most likely leaving a mess on his sheets.

Her head slammed back into the pillow and her whole body twitched uncontrollably when he added another finger to the mix. But unlike the first two, the third one went south to touch her somewhere she'd never been touched before. At least by a man.

Oh... Hold on...

She wasn't sure she was comfortable with his new playground. It didn't feel bad but... different.

She'd give it a chance before telling him not to go there.

Since he took her virginity, did he now want to claim that spot for himself, too? She wouldn't doubt it.

He was the type to push for claiming a woman in all ways but not to keep her permanently. He'd work to get what he wanted, then move on. Maddie had been fine with that five years ago and she was also fine with that tonight.

She didn't want to wear his cut.

Or deal with his regular biker bullshit.

She only wanted to orgasm a couple more times. And if he was good enough to give her more than that, she wouldn't be disappointed. She would climb back down those neck-breaking steps satisfied.

More than satisfied. Actually, with a grin and a spring in her step.

Maybe even with a new outlook on life.

He pressed lightly on her anus, but didn't break the plain. Was he testing her reaction?

As soon as she realized she had tensed up in anticipation, she forced herself to relax again. He knew what he was doing and wasn't some bumbling teenager. She could trust him during sex. If she couldn't, she wouldn't be in his bed right now. In fact, she wouldn't be anywhere near him while naked.

In the end, he didn't push any farther than that, instead he kept stimulating her there, sucking hard on her clit while alternating stroking her slick folds with the flat of his tongue, and curling his fingers deep inside her to find that other very important spot.

A man with the knowledge of a woman's G-spot location was, in her opinion, priceless. But she wasn't telling Romeo that, it would only make his head—the one between his shoulders—swell even more.

Instead, she let him do his thing.

And, *boy*, could he do it.

Teasing her clit, her G-spot, and her anus all at once made the fire in her belly flare even brighter as if someone threw fuel on it.

Her back arched and she cupped her own breasts, squeezing and pulling, twisting her own puckered nipples.

Everything on and in her began to pulse, meaning she was close. It wouldn't take much more to push her over that sharp edge.

And when she finally tumbled, her orgasm rushed up to catch her and sweep her away.

Chapter Sixteen

Now *that* was a fucking orgasm.

Romeo grinned against her very warm, very slick pussy.

Mission fucking accomplished. Now that it was, it was time to move on and get his own relief.

When he lifted his head, Madison appeared passed out, with her lax expression and limp body. She must have lost all control of herself.

Fuck yeah. He still had it. Not that it was ever in doubt. But for some reason, he needed to make sure Maddie was well-satisfied.

Did he want to ask himself why? Fuck no.

Did he ever give a fuck about leaving a woman satisfied? Not usually. But, again, for some reason, in his head, Maddie was different from his normal conquests.

She shouldn't be. She should be like any other hole he wanted to plug.

It bugged the shit out of him that he put her in another category all together.

So what if he took her virginity? He didn't owe her shit for that.

Sitting up on his knees, he raked his gaze over her. Even lying there lifeless, she was hot as fuck. And more than tempting. "Like that?"

Of fucking course she did. It was obvious.

Her eyes fluttered open and a soft smile curled the corners of her mouth. "It was okay."

He huffed out, "Yeah, right. Had better then?"

Her brown eyes locked with his. "Do you want me to rate you?"

"By the looks of you, that was a solid ten."

Her smile grew and she sat up, scraping her fingers through her hair to tame it back into place. "*Mmm.*"

"You sayin' it wasn't?"

"Do you need validation? That makes you sound a bit insecure."

He shook his head. "Don't need shit."

"That means you don't need an answer."

For fuck's sake. Maddie must have turned into a smart ass in the last few years. He normally preferred women more compliant over one that had strong opinions. But then, this wasn't long-term so he could deal with her mouth for the short period of time she'd be in his bed.

And if he got his ass moving, she'd be out of his bed sooner than later.

That was what he wanted, right?

He frowned.

"What's the matter? Do you have a cramp or something?" she asked.

"If I did, guessin' you can relieve it." Especially with her being a physical therapist. She probably put her hands on all sorts of fucking people.

Including men.

He sucked on his teeth.

"I do have knowledge in that area. Show me where you're tense."

He sat up on his knees and pointed to his hard as fuck dick. "Only one fuckin' way to fix that."

"I can think of a few."

"Only one that matters right now."

"What are you waiting for, then?"

"You in a rush?"

"I'd like to get out of here at a decent hour," she answered.

What the hell? "You got jokes."

"I wasn't joking. I have to work tomorrow."

"Bang off."

Her forehead wrinkled. "Bang off?"

"You know, call in sick."

Her expression closed up. *Fuck.* It was time to take this to the next step and stop flapping their fucking gums before shit went south. Because if she left before he got to fuck her, he'd be pissed.

He crawled up her body until he was face to face with her. "You came here to forget about work. I almost fucked that up."

She cupped his cheek and murmured, "Then do something to fix it."

"Don't gotta tell me twice that you want my dick."

Her expression smoothed out and her lips twitched with amusement. Dipping his head, he took possession of those very lips and slid the back of his fingers down her soft cheek and along her jawline before curling them around the front of her throat.

His thumb traced back and forth along her wildly

pounding pulse. Whether that was from what they were doing now, or from her orgasm, he didn't know.

He adjusted his hips until he was settled between her spread legs, then it hit him he didn't put on a wrap.

Of course that was a goddamn requirement. He did not fuck any female without one. He didn't give a shit if they claimed they were "taking care of it." *Fuck that.* He had gone thirty-four years without having any crotch goblins and wasn't planning on having any soon, either.

In fact, wrapping his dick up tight was one of the first things he usually thought about, no matter if it was a sweet butt or some strange. Maddie was neither, but that didn't mean he didn't want to protect them both.

He was damn sure she wouldn't want his kid and the fuck if he'd be bent about that fact. He wanted to fuck her, not produce spawn with her.

With a groan, he broke off the kiss.

Her brow furrowed. "Something wrong?"

"Need a wrap."

"Yes, you do."

"Fuck," he grumbled, rolling over her and toward the edge of his king-sized bed. He hoped to fuck he had at least one left. He had used three the last time he had a couple of sweet butts fucking him in his bed and he forgot to check his supply afterward.

That was goddamn stupid. He should have wraps on auto-delivery. Doing that would be fucking cheaper than diapers and child support.

Ice slid down his spine at the thought of being financially responsible for a kid for a minimum of eighteen years.

He ripped open the top drawer of the old chest of drawers he used as a nightstand and blindly reached in, feeling around for the box.

He better have some left or this whole thing would be stalled. She'd leave and he'd be forced to take care of his release on his own. That would suck, when he currently had a willing, curvy woman waiting in his bed.

For fuck's sake.

When his fingertips brushed against the box, his relief was short-lived. Worst scenario, it could be empty. Snagging it, he yanked it from the drawer, did a little prayer to the condom gods and peeked inside.

Thank fuck he had two more. He rolled one of those fuckers on as fast as possible since it was past time to ease his suffering...

Romeo rolled back over a patiently waiting Maddie and once again settled his hips between her thighs.

"Do you have your act together now?" Her brown eyes held a gleam.

"Again, you got jokes," he grumbled.

"It wouldn't have been funny if you didn't have condoms."

No truer fucking words. He might've actually shed a damn tear or two if this opportunity slipped through his fingers because of it.

But since that wasn't the case, it was go time.

Fuuuuuck yeah.

Then it dawned on him that he'd been waiting for a second shot at Maddie ever since he executed the first one.

He finally had it within his fingertips, so he couldn't fuck it up.

Goddamn it. Why the hell did he give a shit? The last time he cared about what a woman thought of him was when he was fifteen. Back then, instead of taking shots, he got shot down.

Then he matured. Bulked up. Grew a beard. Added a tattoo, or two, or twenty.

He also became a self-proclaimed badass.

Jesus, he was an asshole. He had a gorgeous woman naked beneath him and his damn thoughts were wandering.

Was he fucking broken? Would no women ever scratch all of his itches?

He mentally shook himself, grabbed his dick, lined it up and pulled in a breath. "Ready?"

"I've been, Rome. Not sure where you just went, but it seemed farther than that box of condoms."

His answer was thrusting inside her.

When he hit the end of her, he paused, closed his eyes, and appreciated the warm, slick fist of her pussy.

Her legs wrapping around his hips had his eyelids lifting to see hers tightly shut.

Fuck that shit. She needed to know who was inside her and not be having some fantasy about some other man.

"Look at me," he ordered.

When her eyelids lifted, her pupils were wide, her mouth slack and a flush ran up her chest and throat.

Her legs were long but not long enough to completely encompass his hips. She squeezed him tighter and pulled him deeper.

"Gonna fuckin' start movin' and when I do, probably ain't gonna stop 'til I'm done," he warned her.

"What about me?"

"Gonna make sure you're done, too."

"I'm okay with that, then."

"Wasn't askin' your approval."

She rolled her eyes and dug her heels into his thighs. "Well, you got it, anyway. Deal with it. Now fuck me like you mean it."

Damn.

He drove his fingers into her hair, dropped his head to pull her nipple into his mouth and he did what they both wanted... He moved.

With his knees drilled into the mattress, he began to power up and into her. He drove his dick home over and over.

He didn't go slow. He wasn't gentle. He didn't treat her like she was delicate or breakable.

If she wanted fucked, she was getting *fucked.* He would treat her like anyone else landing in his damn bed. She was no fucking different.

She was *no* fucking different.

Her long, low moan had him lifting his eyes to meet hers since they were still open and focused on watching him suck on her tits.

Her flush had crept into her cheeks. Her eyes were unfocused. Through parted lips, she panted softly.

Fuck yeah, she liked it.

He pounded her a little harder to see if she could take it and continued to piston in and out of her like the machine he was. He slammed his dick so hard inside her, her whole body jerked from the impact.

She didn't tell him to stop or slow down. Instead, she dug her fingernails deeper into his ass in encouragement.

This was totally different from the first time, when she was more tentative and inexperienced.

He was liking it, too.

But he also wasn't.

How many times had she been fucked this hard? And by who?

He pushed that out of his head, reminding himself that this was only a one-time thing. She didn't owe him shit and he owed her the same.

No strings. No chains. No goddamn cock cage.

Right?

Fuckin'-A right.

Chapter Seventeen

MADDIE HAD NOT FORGOTTEN his well-oiled hips. She was glad he hadn't changed. This was *heaven* and she had zero regrets.

So far, anyway.

The harder he pumped in and out of her, the deeper she dug her nails into his ass. The muscles flexed powerfully beneath her fingertips.

Wrapping her legs tighter around him, she tilted her pelvis to make sure he hit all the right spots. Every thrust was accompanied by a deep grunt that fueled the fire in her belly.

Sucking her nipple farther into his mouth, his teeth scraped against the beaded tip, making her back arch and a whimper escape. Using both fists full of her hair, he tipped her head back and drew a damp path with his tongue from her breast to the hollow of her throat and beyond. His thick beard tickled both the underside of her jaw as well as the skin of her neck as he clamped those soft lips on her throat.

Letting her eyes slide shut, she lost herself in his smooth moves and in the sounds he made. She released one ass cheek and slid her hand up his spine, feeling his back muscles tighten and loosen as he fucked her.

The man was pure power.

And, no surprise, it was a damn turn-on.

For a second, she wondered if she could make this a regular thing with him without it getting sticky. She would love to be able to call or text him whenever she needed a stress reliever but still keep her independence.

She refused to give up her freedom in exchange for sex. Not today, not tomorrow, not ever. She had too many things on her to-do list and one of them was not being tied down to a man.

Did she want to one day get married and start a family? Yes, but not until after she landed her dream job. That was her main focus right now.

Well, right now her focus should be the man on top of her.

"Woman," came out on a tortured groan.

She *hmm*'d since she didn't think she'd be able to answer in actual words. She doubted she could stitch enough together to make a coherent sentence.

And, honestly, that was a good thing.

"Waitin' on you." He put an exclamation on that statement with another hard thrust.

She appreciated the fact he wanted her to have another orgasm before he had his. Truthfully, she figured Romeo wouldn't give a shit whether she did or didn't. Maybe he could actually be considerate in some cases?

Meh. She wouldn't give him credit for that just yet.

He fisted her hair hard enough to make her scalp sting and slammed into her again.

Oops. He was still "waitin' on her."

She was grateful for his endurance. And patience. Though, it surprised her that he had the second one.

Girl, he's going to leave you in the dust if you don't orgasm soon.

She cleared her mind and attempted to get back into the moment. As soon as she did, an orgasm built quickly with his thick cock stroking her insides. With his firm lips on her skin. His long fingers in her hair. His warm breath beating against her neck. His heart knocking against her chest. And the power of his thighs, making this the best sex she'd had in a long time.

However, she'd keep that her little secret. The man tended to be cocky and telling him he "gave good dick" could make that worse.

Continuing to take full strokes, he removed one hand from her hair and drove it between them, quickly—and expertly—finding her clit.

Someone was now getting desperate and trying to hurry this along.

Did she blame him? No. Since she would also benefit from this latest move, she had no complaints.

And, *damn*, what a move it was. He kept proving that he knew how to use his fingers, mouth, and cock expertly.

Oh yes, he had been the right choice.

When her hips surged up to meet his, the intense waves of orgasm started at her core and spiraled out, managing to suck all the oxygen from her lungs as well as curl her fingers and toes. When her mouth opened, nothing came out.

"That's it, baby," was groaned against her ear as she rode out the just as intense aftershocks. "*Fuuuuck.* That's it."

His cock seemed to swell even more as his hips rolled smoothly before pounding into her. A sure sign he was getting close.

Right before his own climax, he sealed his lips over hers, stealing the little air she had left and giving her back a groan when he powered deep one more time.

When he tensed and stilled, her pussy clenched even tighter around his cock at the knowledge he was coming.

After a few seconds, he twisted his head to break the lip lock, but didn't immediately roll off her. Instead, he buried his face in her neck again and panted.

Romeo was solid and heavy, but she didn't mind his weight on her. At least not for the short amount of time it would be there. Instead of pushing him off and sprinting for the exit, she lazily dragged her fingers up and down his spine, feeling his back rise and fall with each labored breath.

Without any words of warning, he rolled to his side and onto his back, tucking one bent arm under his bald head and ripping off the full condom with his other hand.

She debated whether to head out or wait until he said something. Because he continued only lying next to her, gripping the used condom, and looking more relaxed than ever. If his eyes shut and he started snoring, she was getting the hell out of there.

She should leave, anyway. She hadn't lied when she said she needed to work tomorrow and she certainly wasn't spending the night. Even if she wanted to—she didn't—she doubted he'd want that, either, because she couldn't imagine he woke up next to any of his conquests.

She could safely bet that Romeo wasn't into cuddling or sharing breakfast and coffee the next morning.

Again, it was time to go since she got what she came for and had no other reason to stay.

She inched her way to the edge of the bed. "I need to clean up. I guess the only bathroom for me to use is downstairs." She'd simply grab her clothes and not climb back up those treacherous steps.

But before she could get to her feet, he grabbed her arm and yanked her back to the spot next to him. "Got you."

He got me?

Her eyes tracked all his naked glory when he climbed out of bed, still carrying his own DNA, and quickly disappeared down the steps.

Sitting up, she listened carefully to make sure his naked ass didn't tumble down them. Because if he did, she'd do enough to make sure he was still breathing, cover his important bits with a towel and dial 911.

They could deal with his crumpled ass. She was a physical therapist, not an ER nurse.

A soft snort escaped her.

If the man only knew her thoughts...

But really, why was she waiting?

Before she could once again try to escape his bed, his head appeared at the steps followed by that heavily tattooed, drool-worthy body.

Damn it.

In one of his big paws, he no longer held the used condom but what looked like a wet rag.

This couldn't be his normal routine, could it?

Her guess was many women had his footprint on their backs from him kicking them out of his bed.

Approaching the bed, he held out what she now could see was a washcloth and not some random rag.

She still wrinkled her nose as he held it out to her. While that was a really nice gesture... "Was it clean?"

"Nah, wiped my ass with it first. Of course it was fuckin' clean. Whataya take me for?"

She pressed her lips tightly together to prevent answering

that and snagged it from his fingers. "I assumed most bikers stood outside and hosed themselves off."

His lips twisted and he shook his head. "That what the Fury does?"

"I really don't ask them their hygiene routine."

"What about your stepdaddy?"

She shrugged. "I don't follow him into the bathroom, either."

"Ever see him outside buck naked with a hose?"

While normally she'd find that question amusing, she couldn't when it came to Shade. With his tragic situation growing up—and she'd been spared most of the grizzly details—she wouldn't doubt he'd had a hose turned on him. Unfortunately, the reason for it would be no laughing matter.

"I should go," she murmured as she quickly swiped the damp cloth between her legs and over her inner thighs.

"Where you gotta go?"

"Home."

"What's there?"

She frowned at this unexpected line of questioning, scooted off the bed and to her feet. "My bed." She grabbed her clothes and began pulling them on.

"Maddie..."

She raised her eyes to him. "Yeah?"

He was staring a little too hard at her. "Lookin' goddamn fine, woman."

"There's been some changes since the last time you saw me naked." She didn't like all of them, but there was only so much she could do.

"Nothin' wrong with that. No man in his right mind wants to gnaw on a fuckin' bone without any meat."

"Dogs do."

"Ain't a dog."

She went back to pulling on her pants. "I'm not sure you can say that."

"And that's a problem."

It wasn't a question, but she answered it anyway as she slipped her feet into her shoes. "Not for me, it isn't." When she was done, she pulled her hair back into a ponytail, grabbed her baseball cap and slapped it back onto her head. "Well, it's been fun."

"That it?"

She glanced at where he stood naked with his hands on those awesome hips of his. His spent cock was still impressive. As well as tempting.

Time to go.

She could see him becoming a dangerous bear trap that she needed to avoid stepping into and getting caught. If that happened, she might have to gnaw off her own leg.

"Am I forgetting something?"

He sucked on his teeth and slowly shook his head. "No."

With a nod, she headed toward the steps, took her time carefully climbing down them and walked out the door.

She did not backtrack through Dirty Dick's since she didn't want to draw any attention. Instead, she skirted the exterior of the bar and headed back to her Highlander.

During the drive home, she realized, as she hoped, Romeo had helped her forget all about her asshole boss.

At least for a little while. Unfortunately, morning was right around the corner. And with it, another day at Smith's Sports Therapy & Rehab Center.

Chapter Eighteen

ROMEO SAT BACK and slowly stroked his beard as he contemplated his fellow Knights joining him around the long table where the president's gavel sat only a couple of inches from his left hand.

His nostrils flared as he pulled in an irritated breath. He wouldn't be surprised if he started grinding his teeth, too.

But here they were.

His gaze bounced over his executive committee. From Bishop, his VP, sitting to his right, to Sigh the club secretary, to their treasurer Cue, Cisco the road captain, and he finished with Magnum, sitting at his left.

The only Knight with an official title not in attendance was Sully because their chaplain didn't get a vote. Or get to make decisions. They only had a club chaplain because Sully asked for the title a long time ago after becoming an ordained minister. The previous president granted his request, and it was no skin off Romeo's nose for the long-time member to keep it.

He side-eyed his sergeant at arms again. The man who

kept Maddie's living arrangements secret. And that still chapped Romeo's ass.

Magnum's eyes narrowed on him. "What the fuck you do?"

"Didn't do shit," he responded. "Let's get this meetin' started."

The big man to his left wouldn't be happy if he found out Romeo dipped his dick in Blood Fury property. Especially without first asking permission from the Fury member she belonged to.

But then, Romeo didn't ask Shade if he could fuck his stepdaughter five years ago, either.

He wasn't stupid.

Okay, maybe he was. Sometimes.

He had taken his life in his own hands by taking Maddie's virginity. Despite her being a willing participant. But now she was on her own and not in the Fury fold. And he was damn sure that Maddie didn't run anyone she fucked past Shade beforehand.

He realized going to Shade first would've shown some respect. But he had no doubt that the Fury member would've told him to fuck off and leave his girl alone.

That wasn't going to happen.

Especially after the other night. He hadn't fantasized about any other female since. All he could think about was how wet, warm, and tight Maddie's pussy was. How her tits rocked and rolled every time he slammed his dick into her.

Her face when she came.

Her face when he came.

Unfortunately, now was really not the optimal time to relive that night.

Especially when Magnum leaned closer and tried to catch Romeo's eyes. "You did somethin', asshole, didn't you?"

"Yeah, called a fuckin' meetin', so let's get to it."

A muscle ticked in Magnum's smooth cheek.

Did Romeo look guilty? He shouldn't.

Maybe Magnum heard chatter about Maddie coming to Dirty Dick's. His brothers all like to run their mouths like a bunch of high school mean girls. He should've been smarter and met her somewhere else.

Too fucking late.

"Maybe it's got to do with that hot young thing that showed up the other night," Cisco mentioned with a grin.

For fuck's sake.

Romeo kept his mouth shut since he knew better than to respond. If he scrambled for excuses, he'd look guilty as fuck.

Magnum asked Cisco, "She got reddish blonde hair?"

"She got somethin'," Cisco answered.

"Why the fuck are we wastin' time here? A female walkin' into Dick's ain't nothin' new. No goddamn reason to discuss that kinda shit at this table." Romeo jabbed his finger against the worn, scarred wood. "Got real business to discuss."

"If you touched another club's property, that's club business," Magnum told him. "The fuck if we need to cause issues with an ally."

"Ain't gonna be any issues."

One of Magnum's thick black eyebrows rose up his huge forehead. "'Cause you didn't touch Fury property, that right?"

His first instinct was to lie but if he got caught in that lie later... That could create a clusterfuck. Still, he wasn't going to admit shit during an officer meeting. They weren't there to discuss their latest conquests. Or their sex lives. Or even their fucking family life.

They were there to take care of Knights business.

"Know you too well, brother. You can't keep your dick in your fuckin' pants."

"Nothin' new," he admitted.

Cisco dropped his head and snorted. Sigh grinned and Cue nodded, also smiling like a fucking fool.

Bishop bitched, "Christ, if we're gonna talk about Rome's latest fuck every goddamn time we got a meetin', then that's all we'll be talkin' about. Move the fuck on. He steps on Fury toes, then he can deal with it."

Magnum's jaw tightened. "Don't fuckin' work that way. He steps on Fury toes, we're all gonna be dealin' with it."

"If he steps on Shade's toes, Rome won't be sittin' at the head of the table anymore. Problem solved." Cue shrugged.

Sigh added, "Yeah, he's gonna find his Black ass buried in some deep grave somewhere."

"Missin' skin and flesh. Maybe even without that tongue he likes to use so damn much." Cisco stuck out his tongue and made a sawing motion like he was cutting it off.

Romeo fought a grimace and a shudder. "Then, good thing Shade's got no reason to do that."

Magnum huffed and shook his head. "Better be true."

"Need to stop questionin' your president."

"Once you stop doin' stupid shit," Magnum countered.

"Expectin' miracles, brother," Bishop told their sergeant at arms on a laugh.

Magnum leaned toward Romeo and growled, "Don't fuck up our alliance. Got no goddamn enemies right now 'cause of it. We lose that, we could have other clubs testin' us."

Romeo jerked his chin toward the gavel. "See where that's sittin'? Ain't in front of you, brother."

"After the next election, might not be sittin' in front of you, *brother*."

This meeting was going sideways. He needed to rein it in.

He picked up that gavel and slammed it on the table. "Done chit-chattin' like a bunch of bitches. Let's get serious."

———

ROMEO COULDN'T GET out of the basement fast enough. Magnum burned a hole in the side of his face during the whole fucking meeting. If his enforcer was trying to make him crack, he failed.

Dick's was quiet tonight as was typical on Tuesdays. It was one reason they held their executive meetings that particular night of the week. That way they could hear themselves think.

He headed straight behind the bar because after dealing with that bullshit, he needed a fucking drink.

And a full bong. With some really prime Kush.

While plenty of perks existed for being the Knights' prez, it involved plenty of headaches, too. Whiskey and weed would serve as his aspirin.

Just as he finished downing his first shot of Jack Daniels, the entrance door opened and someone he didn't expect walked in.

What the actual fuck? Of all nights she had to show up on a fucking Tuesday?

Without giving him a heads up?

Holy shit, this could end up being a fucking disaster. Especially after that whole shit with Magnum.

Worse, the man hadn't left yet. Magnum was most likely still down talking to Cisco. That meant he could come upstairs at any second.

Romeo quickly skirted around the bar and headed in Maddie's direction. As soon as he got to her, he angled his body to block anyone coming up from the basement from seeing her. But that was only a temporary fix. Maddie did not blend in well at Dirty Dick's. Her presence drew attention, as was obvious with the majority of men's eyes turned her way. "What the fuck you doin' here?"

Her eyebrows pinned together. "I texted you and you didn't answer."

That was because he hadn't checked his damn phone during the meeting. Even if he saw it, he never responded immediately to any female. If he did, they might think he was waiting to hear from them. He wasn't. Usually. "So, you just show the fuck up without knowin' if I'd be here?" Or busy with some other female?

The crease in her forehead deepened. "I didn't know it would be a problem."

The problem's name was Magnum. Romeo's eyes sliced to the far back corner of Dick's and the door that led to the basement.

Fucking fuck.

"If it's not a good time—"

He firmly grabbed her elbow and used it to hustle her toward the kitchen. He did not want to deal with more of Magnum's paranoid bullshit.

Hell, right now he didn't want to deal with the man at all. What Romeo did with Maddie wasn't the sergeant at arms' goddamn business.

It was no one's beside the two people involved.

"Why you here?" he growled after shoving her through the swinging door into the kitchen.

"I can leave," she snapped back. "Jesus, I didn't think you'd be such a bitch about me showing up at a *public* bar."

Hold up. She was fucking copping an attitude with *him?* "Ain't any public bar and you know that shit."

"I still don't see the problem."

Of course she didn't. Should he warn her about Magnum sticking his nose where it didn't belong and potentially contacting her psycho stepfather? If he did, he might lose out on the most likely reason for her showing up tonight. He considered his options. "You ever talk to Magnum?"

Her forehead scrunched up again. "Why would I talk to him?"

That was all he needed to hear. "Just wasn't sure if he checked in with you."

"No reason for him to do so."

Romeo agreed. He hoped like fuck that Magnum wouldn't recognize Maddie's cage.

"Are we going to your place?"

"We sure ain't in the kitchen to make fuckin' tacos."

"Well, it *is* Taco Tuesday."

His feet stuttered to a stop. Then he shook his head and kept moving. He'd feel safer once they were behind closed doors. In his crib. With all the locks securely set.

Not even two minutes later, he was turning all of those same locks and finally breathing in relief.

He turned to check out the woman who had hunted him down. Not that she had to search hard. "You come back for a second helpin'?"

"A second helping?"

She knew exactly what he meant. But if not, he'd help her out. "Yeah, of this..." He grabbed his dick and shook it.

She rolled her brown eyes. "Classy."

"You want classy, you're in the wrong fuckin' place, woman."

"Oh, thanks for clarifying. Now, do you want to unlock the door so I can find someone with some class?"

When she approached, pretending she wanted to leave,

he grabbed her hand and pulled her into him. "Nope. Came lookin' for me for a reason. Tell me what that is."

She turned her eyes up to him. "What do you think?"

Those eyes held a bit of naughtiness. She was clearly playing with him. "Was right, then, yeah? You want what only Romeo can give you."

Her soft smile got him in the fucking gut. "I wouldn't say you're the only one. My vibrator can give me a hell of an orgasm."

"If it could do as good a job as me, your ass would be usin' it right now. You're not. You're here. Can't fuckin' fool me."

"Maybe I like a bit of variety."

He pursed his lips as he stared down into her face. She was pulling his chain. "Definitely not your normal variety."

She cocked one eyebrow. "Are you not?"

What was she indicating? "How many brothers you been with?"

"Brothers, as in bikers?"

"Not what I fuckin' meant and you know it."

She lifted and dropped one shoulder "Like you, I don't talk about my past conquests."

He sucked on his teeth. "Thought I was special."

"Oh, you're special. But our meaning of that word might be different."

"Again, you got jokes."

"I was being serious." A huge grin spread across her face.

He shook his head, dug his fingers into her hips and pulled her even closer. Until her tits were smashed flat against him. Tonight, she wore a shirt with a deep V that showed off those tits perfectly.

He couldn't wait to get his mouth on those nipples poking through her shirt. "Why you here, Maddie? For real."

186

His eyes were drawn to her throat when she swallowed. Her teasing turned serious, and her eyes turned troubled.

Fuck.

Was it her fucking job again? "What's the issue at work?"

She sighed out a, "Nothing."

When she avoided his eyes, it was clear she was lying. Something with her job was really getting to her. Most likely her shitty boss. He wondered if the man was on a power trip.

He placed a thumb under her chin and tipped up her face, forcing her to look at him. "Bullshit."

She twisted her head free and again avoided his eyes. "It's mentally and physically exhausting, that's all. Since we're always shorthanded, we're super busy but despite that, the days still feel like they drag on forever."

That wasn't it. She was still lying. Or at least downplaying whatever it was. "Quit and go somewhere else."

She scowled. "I can't just quit. My boss has a lot of connections. Connections I can't sever if I ever want a job with a professional sports team. I'm just doing my time until that happens."

"A job shouldn't be like doin' time in the fuckin' joint."

"You're right, it shouldn't. But like being stuck in prison, we don't always have a choice."

"Always got a choice."

"You chose to do time?"

No one *chose* to do time. "Chose to break the law. Ain't stupid. Knew the consequences of gettin' busted and did it anyway. Just like you chose to get a job there and you choose to stay."

"I wish it was that simple," she murmured, pulling free of him.

Again, she was hiding something. She was trying to keep

whatever was going on at work from her expression, but he spotted it before she could hide it completely.

She didn't want to share with him whatever it was. Of course, there had to be a reason for that. What that reason was, he didn't fucking know.

If he really wanted to figure it out, he had his ways. For now, he'd let it go. If whatever it was continued to be a problem, he'd find a solution for her.

That was what allies did for each other.

If one club had a problem and another one in their alliance had a solution, they worked together.

He was pretty damn sure that the Fury would appreciate Romeo stepping in if their girl was dealing with some shit.

At least that was what he told himself.

Magnum might not agree. But then, he was the damn president, and he didn't give a fuck what his enforcer thought. The prez outranked the sergeant at arms every damn time.

Whether the big man liked it or not.

Chapter Nineteen

MADDIE DIDN'T WANT to go into details on why she had another shitty day. It would just get her blood pressure spiking again. She tracked down Romeo so *he* could get her blood rushing, not that asshole Roger.

Her boss was such a dick, and she was tired of telling herself to hang on because doing so would pay off in the end.

If she only knew when that "end" would be, dealing with him might be a little easier. Only, it seemed too far off in the distance. Worse, there was no guarantee staying would ever pay off. The fingernails she was using to cling to the faith that it would were starting to rip off.

"Do you mind if I get some water?" She glanced over her shoulder to see him push away from the door and stalk toward where she stood by the kitchen.

She could really use a beer instead, but her stomach was still twisted in knots from dealing with Roger and his undeserved cruel insults.

"Only got shit from the tap," he said. "Nothin' fancy."

"That's fine." She hoped sipping some water would help settle her stomach.

With a single nod, he grabbed a glass out of the cabinet and filled it with ice and water from the refrigerator door dispenser. She hoped the glass was clean. She assumed he didn't do his own dishes since he had sweet butts to do his bidding.

While she waited, she fingered a piece of mail sitting on the kitchen counter addressed to a Marvin.

Did Romeo get someone else's mail by accident? "Who's Marvin?"

When he didn't respond, she glanced up. His expression said it all. "Hold on. Is that you? Is your real name Marvin?" She giggled, then leaned closer to read the rest of the name. "Marvin Lee Carter... The third?"

"Nothin' wrong with that name. It's a family name."

"Of course there's nothing wrong with it." Only, it was hard to look at Romeo and see a Marvin. In fact, Romeo was as far from a Marvin as one could get. "Why don't you use it?" She rolled her lips inward, trying not to grin like a lunatic.

"You know why," he grumbled, placing the glass of ice water on the counter in front of her.

She danced away from him, still laughing. "I'm calling you Marvin from now on."

"The fuck you will."

"What will you do if I do?"

"Spank your ass."

She slid to a stop and spun to face him keeping the kitchen island between them to stay out of his reach. "No, you won't."

"Wanna bet?"

Her eyebrow rose. It had to be an empty threat. He wouldn't dare. "I'll bet."

"It's a bet you're gonna lose."

"We'll see about that, Marvin."

"Madison," he growled.

"Oh, now I know you're serious since you used my full first name." She shivered with fake fear before sticking out her tongue at him. "So scared."

"Should be."

This was what she needed tonight. Some teasing and laughter. Someone who could take a joke without getting bent out of shape.

Romeo might act like he was annoyed with her learning his birth name but in truth, his eyes said otherwise.

"Do your brothers know your real name?"

He shrugged.

"So, they don't? Holy shit, do I actually have something to use as blackmail against you?"

"Got something you want from me that I ain't willin' to give?"

She pursed her lips and considered him. "You'd give me anything I asked?" Of course not, she was only playing with him. She didn't expect anything but sex from him. He owed her nothing and she owed him the same.

"Within reason. Can't give you a fuckin' million dollars or a Ferrari. But can give you a ride somewhere." He tipped his head toward the full glass. "Or a drink. Maybe some free advice. Can't guarantee that advice won't suck ass. And if you want an orgasm or two, can give you that."

That he could. "The last one is why I'm here."

"No shit." He jerked his chin toward the untouched water. "Can you manage to carry that upstairs?"

If the stairs were normal, yes, but his were far from that. "I wouldn't risk it."

"Then drink your water 'cause I'm about to make you thirsty all over again."

"Promises, promises," she murmured, snagging the glass off the counter. When she finished downing a third of it, she noticed him staring at her. "What?"

"Nothin'."

She was lying when she gave him that exact answer earlier. Now he was doing the same.

When she licked her lips—on purpose—his eyes followed the path of her tongue. Despite the water, her throat quickly went dry. "I think we need to go upstairs now."

"Good fuckin' idea. Otherwise, gonna fuck you on that counter and you won't gotta worry about climbin' those fuckin' stairs."

Not only did a wildfire sweep through her and land between her legs, her cheeks even became heated. She couldn't be blushing, could she? She pressed a hand to one.

She certainly was.

Why did this man turn her on so much? It didn't make sense. He was everything she didn't want. Mainly, a biker in an MC. *Hell*, not just a biker but an MC president and one with no filter at that.

A man with no fucks to give at all.

But for the next hour or two, she also would have zero fucks to give. Tomorrow was another day to worry about what waited for her at work.

———

AFTER WAKING UP ALONE, Romeo headed downstairs with disappointment weighing on him. Maddie must've slipped out after he drifted off. Somehow, she managed to leave without waking him. Not an easy feat.

Her stealthy escape proved she only wanted one thing from him.

She had said it, but most women said shit and either didn't mean what they said, or the meaning went far deeper than their words. Of fucking course, men were just supposed to figure that shit out on their own. Like a mind reader.

And if they didn't, they got nothing but hell for it.

It was one reason why he had no intentions to have any woman wear his cut. They were too damn confusing.

Sometimes even annoying.

Someone needed to write an instruction manual. Though, if he had to be honest, he doubted men would read it.

While he should be happy about not having to kick her out of his bed for lingering too long, it also bugged him for a reason he didn't want to dig into.

The sex with Maddie was fucking great. But he'd had plenty of great sex before and never cared if the woman left immediately after. Actually, if a woman didn't leave on her own, he would encourage her departure. Even assist with it.

Bottom line, when he was done, they were done.

Once they were out of sight, they were out of mind. At least until they landed in his bed again.

But not all of them got that privilege, especially if the sex sucked.

Or they never shut the fuck up.

Or they were catching feelings.

Or made demands.

But none of that applied to the woman who snuck out last night. Maybe that was why it bugged him so damn much.

It also bugged the shit out of him that she was keeping the

issues she was having at work so damn close to her chest. He even asked her again after her third orgasm what the problem was.

And again, she refused to say.

Maybe he needed to find out for himself.

That was what good allies did for each other, right? Sure it was.

Since Magnum was so damn dead-set about not fucking up their strong alliance with the Fury, he couldn't possibly have a problem with Romeo helping them out.

He should find out where she worked and go scope out the situation. Because whenever he asked Maddie for details, she blew it off.

While he figured Magnum knew where she worked, Romeo couldn't ask him. Not without starting a shitstorm. But he did have someone he could call. Someone with the expert skills to locate anyone anywhere.

Someone on a team capable of hacking into databases— even the government's—and not get caught.

Hunter would have no problem finding out Maddie's place of employment and her home address. He would also keep his mouth shut about Romeo's request.

He would only owe one of Diesel's Shadows a favor in exchange. Whatever that ended up being might be worth it.

———

"Maddie, your new patient is here," she heard called out.

Her *new* patient? She should've looked at her schedule closer.

She weaved through the equipment on her way to the front of the building where the receptionist greeted anyone walking through the door. Maribeth also checked them in for their appointment and made sure they filled out their forms completely and correctly.

The second Maddie saw her new "patient," she almost tripped over her own feet.

What the hell? Since when was Romeo an athlete needing physical therapy? His sport of choice was sex. And maybe drunken fist fights. He certainly didn't suffer from tennis elbow or a torn Achilles tendon from running track.

The only running the Knights president probably did was from the law. And he wasn't using his legs for that, she was damn sure he would have his powerful sled between his thighs.

So, why the hell was Romeo here at Smith's?

She glanced over her shoulder to make sure Roger wasn't lurking around. While she didn't see him, that didn't mean he wasn't watching. He was a sneaky bastard. She had no doubt he watched the security cameras, waiting for someone to do something he didn't like. He looked for any excuse to write someone up or degrade them verbally.

Because of that, she had to treat Romeo as she would any other patient. She gritted her teeth and kept going.

When she got to the front where he waited, she ignored the grinning man and asked Maribeth, "Did he get all the appropriate forms filled out?"

The receptionist held up a clipboard. She took it and glanced at the top sheet. "Old school, huh?" She lifted her gaze to meet Romeo's.

The fucker was now smirking.

"You do know you could've filled these out online, right?" And saved a tree or two.

"Mr. Carter made a last-minute appointment," Maribeth explained like Romeo couldn't speak for himself.

Maddie turned enough to make sure Maribeth couldn't see her eyes rolling. "Come with me, Mr. Carter." Not waiting to see if he followed, she strode toward her "office."

Truthfully, calling it an office was a joke since it was about the size of a linen closet. It barely fit a desk—half the size of a regular one—and two chairs. Luckily, they all used tablets to keep their patients' files and notes. Fitting a file cabinet in her space would be impossible.

Not that she was in her office often. She tried to stay out on the floor as much as possible so Roger couldn't catch her in there and be an asshole behind closed doors. If he was going to be a dick, Maddie wanted everyone to be a witness.

With Romeo's bulk, as soon as they stepped into her office, it felt even tighter than it was in reality.

The biker was not a small man. Anywhere. He might not be quite as bulky as Magnum, or even Diesel, the DAMC's enforcer, but he was damn close.

"Close the door," she told him. After leaning back against her desk, she pointed to the chair in front of her. "Sit."

No surprise that mischief filled his eyes as he took a seat. His fingers "accidentally" brushed against her thigh and caused a shiver to shoot through her.

She shook her head. "Really?" What was he up to?

He shrugged. "Kept askin' what problems you're havin' here. Wouldn't tell me, so came to see for myself."

She sighed. "It's not your problem, Rome. To be clear, I didn't ask for your help." At least help in any form other than a little sex.

Or, preferably, a lot of sex.

His nostrils flared and his expression turned serious. "Maddie, you belong to the Fury. The Fury's our ally. That means if you got a problem, we all got a problem."

She was tired of the ally excuse. "Bullshit."

Chapter Twenty

"Did you not come to me for help?" Romeo asked.

"Not this kind of help. I went to you for stress relief. And only a certain kind. That's it."

"Just here to figure out the source of that stress. If I can solve it, gonna do that. Should be thankin' me, not givin' me shit."

"Yes, I'm *sooooo* thankful you made up an excuse to become my patient so you could stick your nose in my business. You do realize that if you solve my stressful situation, I will no longer need sex from you?"

Maddie purposely said "need" instead of "want." Because after the two nights she'd went over to his place recently, she'd still be tempted to swap some bodily fluids with him. Forget the stress, it would simply be for pleasure.

His expression told her that he must not have thought that far ahead.

She lifted the clipboard and drew a finger down his intake paperwork. "Let's see what excuse you used."

"Strained my hamstring fuckin' you."

"Bullshit," she repeated, then lifted her eyes and met his. Her pounding heartbeat jumped into her throat. "You didn't tell that to Maribeth, did you?" Again, this man had no filter. She wouldn't put it past him to tell the receptionist they'd had sex. Of course, at the same time flirting with the woman.

"Said I tweaked it."

She raised an eyebrow. "On your morning jog?"

"Somethin' like that."

She pulled in a breath and shook her head. "You know, now I have to treat you like a real patient. Let's not forget, bill you like one, too."

"You can give me a discount."

"I can't. That's not up to me. I'm not sure if you looked at our rates, but our services here aren't cheap."

"How you gonna service me?"

She tapped her fingertip against her lips as she pretended to seriously consider his fake injury. "Well, we could start out with some exercises—"

"Naked?"

"Like hamstring curls. Then move on to some hip extensions and wall stretches."

"Any of that hands on?"

"You mean like a massage?"

"Yeah, I'll take one of those."

"No, not for a strained hamstring. Should've come up with a better fake injury if you wanted a massage."

He jerked his chin toward the clipboard she was holding. "Can I get that paperwork back?"

"Nope. But I can easily rip it up and on your way out the door, you can inform Maribeth that you've decided you can't afford PT and will let it heal on its own." Problem solved.

His brow creased. "Who the fuck said I can't afford it? Think I can't pay?"

"I was giving you an out," she answered.

"You're givin' yourself a fuckin' out."

That, too.

"Just here to help you, woman," he grumbled.

"Help I didn't ask for," she hissed. A knock on her office door had her whispering, "Shit."

"Who's that?" Romeo asked.

She bugged her eyes out at him. "I won't know until I answer the door." She had a good idea, though.

She looked from the door back to Romeo. At least he'd been smart enough not to wear his cut while trying to pull off this ruse.

Without waiting for her to answer it, the knob turned, and the door opened, getting jammed against the back of the chair Romeo sprawled in with his boots and thighs spread wide.

"I see I'm interrupting." Roger peeked his head around the partially open door. His eyes sliced from Maddie to Romeo. "A new patient?"

"That'd be me," Romeo answered, staring at her boss over his shoulder. He didn't move a damn inch or even shift the chair enough to allow the door to open fully.

Good. Her office wasn't big enough for both men's egos.

Roger wedged himself into the gap, jutting out his hand. "Let me introduce myself. I'm Roger Smith, owner of this center. I see you picked a good therapist to work with."

What? Did an actual compliment pass Roger's lips? Maddie didn't think it was possible.

She waited for Roger to self-combust from his attempt at being nice. It had to be a struggle.

Without bothering to get up, Romeo twisted around to squeeze Roger's offered hand. Hard.

Roger's slight wince almost made her smile, but Maddie knew better than to let him see her enjoying his discomfort.

But... Was Romeo so damn astute that he already figured out what her problem was at work? Or more like *who* was her problem?

That couldn't be possible. Maybe he was only testing the waters.

When Romeo finally released Roger's hand, her boss pulled it into his chest with a frown. "So, what injury brings you here? What sports do you play?"

———

Romeo stared at the intruder.

Some people rubbed you the wrong way the second you met them. Roger Smith was a damn good example of that.

Did the owner greet all new patients? Or was he particularly interested in Maddie's?

Was he her problem? Was he harassing her for sex?

Was he fucking touching her without permission? Did the fucker not know how to take "no" for an answer?

His jaw tightened and shifted. He forced himself to remain seated and not launch himself at the guy simply because of a gut feeling. If he ended up behind bars for knocking out a guy possibly innocent, he couldn't help Maddie with her problem.

"All kinds, Roger. Like to keep in shape, so I work out a lot. Love to wrestle." Naked. "Play a little ball." Especially with the ones hanging between his legs.

"A little B-ball?"

"Didn't say that, Roge. Shouldn't assume I play basketball 'cause I'm Black."

Ol' Roger paled at Romeo calling him out for a stereotype. Hopefully, his asshole was puckered, too.

"Prefer golf. A bit of tennis. Some pickleball." How the fuck did he even say that shit with a straight face? He deserved one of those gold statues they gave movie stars.

"You sound like a well-rounded athlete, then," Smith murmured.

"Ain't an Olympian, but I'll admit I like to have a bit of fun." With women. And currently with one in particular.

Smith clapped his hands together once. "All right, well... It was nice meeting you..."

When Maddie's boss left that hanging, Romeo supplied, "Mr. Carter."

"Mr. Carter," Smith echoed. "I'm sure Mad here will take good care of you. She's one of our best."

When he heard a noise come from Maddie, Romeo glanced at her, missing the moment Smith ducked out and closed the door.

"He fuckin' calls you *Mad*?" he just about bellowed. Somehow, he managed to keep it at a non-deafening level.

She sighed. "I've asked him not to, but..."

"He touchin' you?" Unfortunately, that came out a little louder. He wondered about the thickness of the office walls. Smith could be a nosy fucker and have his ear plastered to the door.

"What? No. Why would you think that?"

Her look of disgust told him she wasn't lying. So, being sexually harassed by her boss might not be the problem.

"Assholes like him tend to think they can do whatever the fuck they want."

Her eyebrows rose and she gave him a pointed look. "Oh, really? I wonder why you'd think that?"

"Might be a lotta damn things, but never had to force myself on a woman." And never would.

"Not when you have sweet butts at your beck and call."

His spine tightened with what she was insinuating. "Nothin' to do with sweet butts. Ain't ugly. Ain't stupid. Got a pretty fuckin' impressive dick. Got more positives than negatives."

When she dropped her head to hide her face with her hair, her body shook. Was she laughing at that?

"You sure didn't have a problem gettin' naked with me."

"It was only a test drive. I wasn't looking to buy."

"Again, you got fuckin' jokes." She needed to reevaluate her comedic material.

"Oh, you giving me a short list of your attributes wasn't supposed to be amusing?"

"Heard no complaints when my dick was splittin' your pussy in two last night."

It only took a fraction of a second for her cheeks to bloom red. Now the tables were turned, and he was the one amused.

She glanced at the door in panic.

He peered over his shoulder to make sure her boss hadn't poked his head in again.

Maddie sighed. "All right. Can we end this farce now?"

"Gonna tell me what's stressin' you the fuck out?"

She hesitated, but only for a second. "I don't need you getting involved, Romeo. It'll only create more issues."

"Might be able to solve them for you."

"Not without making a bigger mess."

"Maddie..."

"No, Romeo. I don't belong to you. I don't belong to the Knights. It isn't your job to step in." She pushed off her desk and grabbed the clipboard. "I'll walk you out. You can tell Maribeth that... Actually, I don't care what excuse you give, just come up with one on why you won't be a patient here."

He remained seated. "Ain't gonna do that."

"Do it for me."

It was her obvious rising panic that decided his next actions. "That's who I'm fuckin' doin' it for. So, you don't wanna be my physical therapist? You got it."

When he finally rose from the chair the room was so damn tight, they stood toe-to-toe.

He dipped his head and locked eyes with her. "But gonna give you what you want and go talk to Maribeth. Gonna tell her to set me up with someone else. You don't like it? Too fuckin' bad."

"Rome..."

"Fuck that shit. Nothin' you say's gonna change my fuckin' mind."

"You're stepping where you don't belong."

"You keep thinkin' that."

She swallowed hard enough it was noticeable. *Yeah,* another sign he shouldn't let it go no matter what she said.

"Why are you so damn stubborn?" she hissed.

"No more than you," he answered.

"I can't burn any bridges, Romeo. This job could determine my future."

He considered her whispered plea. What kind of man would he be if he let her continue to suffer? He wouldn't be able to live with himself if he just let it go.

Was he benefitting from whatever was going on? Of fuckin' course he was. It also drove him goddamn crazy that he didn't know what was causing that suffering. And even if he found a solution for her, it didn't mean the sex had to stop.

"You gonna help me out with my injury or you gonna make me find someone else?"

"I came to you because I didn't want anyone barging into my life. I didn't think you'd give a shit."

Normally, he wouldn't. However, he was finding this situation far from normal for him. "Guess you were fuckin' wrong. I give a shit."

"Can you not?"

"No."

"If I tell you what it is, will you leave?"

"Depends."

"I need a guarantee."

"Then, no."

She blew out a breath, closed her eyes and shook her head. "You're an asshole, Rome."

"Yep. And if you think callin' me an asshole's gonna bother me, that's one guarantee I can give you... It won't."

Chapter Twenty-One

No matter how tempted she was to call or text Romeo to hook up again, she refrained. She figured it would create less drama if she used her vibrator instead. A couple of nights she met up with Zeke at The Iron Horse for a drink and a few games of pool.

She spent last weekend with Gabi having a "girls' weekend," too.

Unfortunately, despite trying to find an alternative, the only way to get Roger completely free from her mind after a bad day was getting naked with Romeo. But after what he pulled at Smith's, it made her hesitate.

If possible, she needed to find a substitute. Someone *not* a biker. With plenty of hookup apps out there, the right man couldn't be impossible to find, could it?

Since the apps could be risky, she wasn't really keen on them, especially since she preferred her skin not be turned into a leather coat. Or her teeth into a necklace. Or to be buried without her limbs in some random spot out in a field.

But if she could find someone to have sex with—someone

who was good—without dying or becoming a sex slave, it could be an option.

When Romeo came in for his initial appointment, Maddie had escorted him back to the receptionist desk and Maribeth assigned him to another physical therapist. She refused to let him be so damn intrusive and if he insisted, he could crack open his wallet and continue the injury ruse with someone else.

She also made sure Maribeth assigned him to a man instead of a woman he could flirt with. For her, that made him sticking his nose where it didn't belong all a little more palatable. She had a feeling Romeo would soon get sick of having appointments with Chuck, as well as watching his wallet get thinner and thinner.

When she wasn't busy with a patient of her own, she watched Romeo and Chuck work together, knowing full well the biker was faking his injury.

She had to give the man credit for sticking with it for the last two weeks and, despite it being annoying, for being so damn dedicated to discovering her "problem."

Luckily, since he only came in twice a week, she managed to avoid Roger every time Romeo was in the building. So far. But that wouldn't last for long. She was damn sure he'd witness her boss's bad behavior if the Knights' president didn't throw in the white towel soon.

She was grabbing a snack in the break room between patients when Chuck cornered her.

"Your friend's on my schedule in fifteen minutes." Her co-worker glanced at his watch and his mouth twisted. "Though, he tends to run late."

No surprise. She didn't know any biker who watched a clock. They tended to live their life on their own time and terms.

"He says he knows you very well."

Damn it. Should she pretend Romeo was nothing more than a distant acquaintance?

If he was fishing for details on her and Romeo's "relationship"... *Good luck, Chuck.* "We do know each other, but not as well as he tends to insinuate."

Chuck's dark eyebrows rose. "But you didn't want him as a patient?"

"I figured you'd be better suited to work with him." That wasn't quite a lie.

Her coworker frowned. "Don't you think it's kind of odd that he self-referred himself into our care instead of going to a doctor first?" Chuck turned and leaned back against the counter with a coffee mug in hand.

"Ro—" Her brain glitched. If she called Romeo by his road name, it would only spur more questions. "Marvin tends to march to the beat of his own drum."

"I've experienced that," Chuck said dryly. "He tried to tell me how to do my job."

Oh shit. But that wasn't surprising, either.

Maddie rolled her lips instead of her eyes. "He's not being cooperative?"

"Oh, he is, but he has some very strong opinions."

That he did.

"That he shares. Often."

"On therapy?"

"On everything. And he asks a lot of questions about Roger. For some reason, he seems to be obsessed with our asshole boss."

Of course. "Be careful. You don't want to get caught complaining about *you know who.* That will only make it worse."

"I've managed to dodge most of Marvin's questions."

Good.

"Are you sure you don't want to take him for your patient roster?"

The pleading in Chuck's eyes had her feeling guilty for pawning Romeo off on him. However, not enough to agree to take him back. "I don't think it would be appropriate," was the last thing she said before slipping out of the break room with a peach swiped from her own lunch bag.

As she was about to head back out onto the floor, she noticed the man they were just discussing coming through the door.

She turned her head and called out, "Chuck, your appointment is here."

"Already?" came his response.

Apparently, Romeo wasn't late every time. Or Chuck learned to tell him an earlier time to make sure he arrived *before* his appointment started, instead of after.

That trick was used often by women tied to bikers. If their ol' ladies wanted them somewhere at eleven, they told them ten-thirty. It worked until the men caught on.

"Can you tell him I'll be out in a few minutes?" Then she heard mumbled, "I should make him wait as long as he makes me wait."

Maddie pulled in a breath before reluctantly answering, "Sure." She wouldn't do it for Romeo, but as a favor for Chuck since he took the stubborn Knight off her hands.

As she headed toward the front, she glanced longingly at the peach clutched within her fingers. She had hoped to eat it before her next appointment showed up.

She ignored the fact her heart did a tumble, and her pulse quickened the second Romeo spotted her heading his way and blinded her with a 100-watt smile.

Then took his time inspecting her from head to toe.

She almost smoothed her hair into place, then got annoyed with herself for even having that urge.

She stopped at Maribeth's desk. "I'll take him back for Chuck. He's running a little behind."

She missed the receptionist's response because Romeo was staring at her so hard, Maddie swore he had X-ray vision and could see right through her clothes. Especially when he said, "Nice peach," in a way that made her pussy clench.

"Come with me, Mr. Carter," came out more breathless than she'd like. Annoyed at her own reaction, she set her jaw, turned, and strode past a few other patients working with their therapists. "You should probably wear sneakers for your appointments. Does Chuck let you wear your biker boots while he's working with you?"

"Think I fuckin' got sneakers?"

Who didn't own a pair of damn sneakers? "Weren't you wearing them while running that marathon? If you ran over twenty-six miles in heavy biker boots, no wonder you pulled your hammy."

She heard a snort behind her. "Woman's got plenty of jokes."

Making light of the situation was the best way to deal with it.

She stopped at a matted area along the wall and pointed to a large inflatable exercise ball. "You can sit on that and wait. I'm sure Chuck will be with you shortly."

Of course, he didn't follow her directions. Instead, he turned to face her. "Don't give a fuck about Chuck. Ain't why I'm here."

"So, how are you recovering from that devastating injury?" Maddie asked. "Are you enjoying Chuck's massages? He's got some very strong hands and a special touch, doesn't he?"

"The best," Romeo muttered.

She finally lifted her eyes and met his. "When are you going to end this farce?"

"Soon's I find out the info I came for."

"I can't believe you continue to go to this extreme. It has to be costing you a fortune."

"Think about what you just said. Coulda told me the problem when I asked. Now it's costin' me. Doin' this for you, Maddie, not me."

"If it's costing you, that's on you, not me, because I asked you not to get involved. You should've respected my request to stay out of it."

"Stubborn."

Hold up. He was calling *her* stubborn? "Huh." Trying to avoid more verbal sparring, she took a bite of her peach. Riper than she expected, the juice ended up dribbling down her chin. She should've grabbed a napkin or two. Or ten. Her mistake.

Since she didn't want to use her sleeve, she turned to head back to the kitchen to grab one. Romeo jerked her to a stop by grabbing her arm, making her very aware of her messy face. When she went to clean it off herself, he batted her hand away and wiped the sticky juice away with his thumb. He kept his heated gaze locked with hers when he plugged that thumb into his mouth.

Holy shit. It wasn't just the action but the way he did it that made her weak in the knees and regret avoiding his bed lately.

Why did this particular man make her so damn weak? Why couldn't it be anyone else?

When he pulled his clean thumb from between his lips, his voice was low and grumbly. "Haven't been over lately."

"Did—" She cleared her tight throat and tried again. "Did you miss me?"

He grabbed his crotch but didn't hold onto it long enough for anyone to notice. Other than her, at least. "Hard not to think 'bout you and that pussy."

Her peach ended up forgotten in her hand as they stared at each other.

Chuck came rushing over. "Thank you, Maddie. I got it from here. Come with me, Mr. Carter, and we'll get you started."

Romeo just got her "started."

Resist, Maddie.

She hoped like hell that Chuck did not hear the last thing Romeo said.

"Are you okay? You look really flushed. Are you having a hot flash?" Chuck asked.

"I'm not old enough for a hot flash." She pressed a hand to her hot cheek. "I'm just a little warm."

"Maybe you should cancel the rest of your appointments and go home and rest. You might be catching something."

She caught something all right.

When she heard "Mad!" yelled through the building, she actually thought Chuck's suggestion might be a good one. Because that voice only belonged to one person.

A quick glance at Romeo showed her that he was searching the room for the one bellowing her name.

"Mad!"

Fuck. Fuck. Fuck.

She heard a muffled growl—that did not come from Chuck—over the sound of her gritting teeth.

She needed to find Roger before he found her. And before he continued to spew shit loudly. Maybe she could head him off and quiet him down.

It turns out she didn't move fast enough.

Roger beelined over to where they stood, appearing out for blood. Only she worried it wouldn't be her blood spilled.

"Your patient is waiting for you. What are you doing?" His eyes dropped to the peach. "Not only making your patients wait but eating out on the floor? You know that's not allowed. Besides, it's piggish. Are you a pig, Mad?"

She waited for him to start oinking. He had done it before when someone spilled their snack.

"You know the rules. I'm going to have to write you up for that. That's your third write-up this month. You know the three-strike rule, now I'm going to have to dock your pay."

This was nothing new. Roger purposely looked for excuses to write up his employees. Even for the most trivial reasons so he could dock their pay. That put more money back in his pocket.

Greedy asshole.

"Remember me, Roge?"

Oh shit.

When a searing heat hit her back, the fine hairs on the back of her neck stood up. Roger had awakened the beast. The whole reason she wanted Romeo to stay out of it. If he handled this badly, she could lose her job and, knowing Roger's pettiness, he could blackball her everywhere.

This could turn into a complete nightmare.

"Mr. Carter... How could I forget? Hopefully, your therapy is proceeding nicely."

"Would be if I wasn't so fu— disturbed with how you speak to your employee. Makes me wonder if I made the right decision comin' here."

"We have rules, Mr. Carter. Just as I'm sure your employer does, too. Without rules, it's mayhem."

Oh good lord.

"It's a fuckin' peach, Roge."

"While it might only be a peach this time, if I let it go, what about next time? I maintain strict rules for a reason. If Mad can't follow them, then she doesn't belong here."

Maddie jolted forward slightly when Romeo's chest bumped her back. "Her goddamn name is Maddie. Or Madison. Or even Ms. Goddamn Goodson. It ain't *Mad*."

Roger blinked at Romeo's unexpected fury. "If she doesn't like me calling her that, she would've told me."

She did. Most likely a dozen times before she gave up.

"Tellin' you... Don't fuckin' call her that again."

Roger's brow dropped low. "No reason to use profanity."

"Got every damn reason to use it. You're disrespectin' your employee."

"By telling her to follow the rules? Rules she agreed to when she was hired?"

She didn't remember any rules about eating out on the floor, but that was neither here nor there right now.

Maddie pulled in a breath and turned, placing a hand on Romeo's chest. She caught his gaze and widened her eyes at him in a silent plea. "It's fine. I don't mind."

"You fuckin' mind. You told me that."

"Rome..." *Fuck.* "Marvin, I appreciate you standing up for me, but it's unneeded."

Chapter Twenty-Two

UNNEEDED? The fuck if it was unneeded.

Romeo's growing suspicion that ol' Roger was the source of Maddie's stress was now confirmed. All she had to tell him was that her boss was a dick. Actually, more than a dick. He was bordering on abusive.

Romeo found that un-fucking-acceptable.

And the fuck if he would let it continue, no matter how much Maddie wanted him to stay out of it.

Fuck that shit.

"I'm sorry, Mr. Carter, but it looks like you might not be a good fit for my establishment after all. I'm going to have to ask you to leave since you can't control yourself. I'll refund your visit today if you've already paid."

Romeo spun on the man, making him lurch back a step. Even pale slightly like the little bitch he was. "You think I ain't in control? I'm fuckin' in control. You wouldn't want to see me when I lose my shit."

Smith was the kind of pussy-ass bitch who'd press charges if Romeo even poked him with a finger.

But he certainly wouldn't be poking the guy. He'd be hauling off and planting a fist right in her boss's mouth. And once he was down, maybe even crushing that motherfucker's face with one of his boots.

But Romeo was in control.

Barely.

It was time to leave before that changed and shit went sideways. He normally didn't wear any jewelry, so cold metal cuffs were not his style.

When he turned towards Maddie, he noticed she was frozen in place. Not only that, he didn't think she was aware she held the peach in a death grip and its juice was dripping off her fingers and onto the floor mats.

Smith must have spotted that at the same time, too.

"You made a mess, Mad. Now go get something to clean it up. This is a perfect example on why food isn't allowed out on the floor."

Romeo pulled in a deep breath, jerked his head to the left, then to the right to crack his neck, then forced his fingers to uncurl.

The asshole didn't know when to shut the fuck up.

Smith was also pushing his luck by calling Maddie "Mad" after Romeo made it quite fucking clear not to do that again.

When Maddie lifted her hand, her face changed the second she saw what she did. Her eyes flicked to the floor.

"Now!" Smith barked. "Someone could slip and fall on that mess, and you know who will be getting sued? Not you."

"Sorry." The second she jerked into action, so did Romeo. But not to haul off and teach Smith a lesson.

Not here, not now.

When the man least expected it. When there wouldn't be

witnesses. Some would call it a "random" act of violence. Romeo would call it karma.

Smith's time was coming.

Tick motherfucking tock.

He strode after Maddie as she headed toward the back of the building.

"Mr. Carter, you need to leave. You're heading the wrong way."

Romeo ignored Smith and instead called out, "Maddie!"

When she stopped and turned, she lifted her hand with the mangled peach. "I need to throw this out."

"In a second." Closing the gap between them, he tucked his thumb under her chin to lift her face to his and lowered his voice. "Gonna go before I end up locked in a concrete box, but want you to go, too."

"I can't," she whispered. "I need this job."

Romeo sucked on his teeth and a muscle jumped in his cheek. "If you couldn't tell, that wasn't me askin' you, woman. That was me tellin' you. So, gonna make it fuckin' clear... you ain't stayin' here. Plenty of other jobs out there. Don't gotta deal with his bullshit."

"I told you why I stay," she whispered more fiercely. "He's got important connections in the industry. I only have to hold on a little longer."

"How much longer?"

He was making a point because even Romeo knew it was a crapshoot whether this job would end up leading her to bigger and better things. Her boss was a narcissistic dickhead. That was never going to change. He was the kind of motherfucker who only did anything that would benefit himself, not others.

In the short time he'd been coming to her job, it was pretty damn clear her boss ruled his employees with fear, not respect. At first, Romeo hadn't seen it with Maddie, but now that he had...

When she closed her eyes, his anger spiked through the roof. He understood that she was torn. She had a career goal. She thought this was the only path toward it.

The truth was, that was total bullshit. There had to be another way to get what she wanted.

And if he needed to find that alternative for her, he would. Because the fuck if she was going to continue to be verbally abused by that asshat.

Not on his watch.

———

Romeo stood outside of unit number twenty-two and pounded on the door.

Noises came from the other side before he heard a muffled, "Who is it?"

He sighed. "Got a peephole. Know who the fuck it is."

"Do you have a good reason to be here?"

He shook his head. She was testing his patience. "Seriously, woman? Open the fuckin' door. Otherwise, I'm gonna embarrass the shit outta you 'til you do."

"By doing what?"

He leaned closer to the door and warned, "Really want to find out?"

"With you, it could be anything."

She wasn't wrong.

He listened carefully for the slide of a chain and the click of a deadbolt to make sure she kept her door locked.

The second she opened it, he barreled right past her and inside her place.

"Come on in," she said dryly.

"Why don't your place have an elevator?"

"Why doesn't yours? And if you haven't noticed, my apartment complex is small. I'm capable of walking up a flight of steps. Apparently, you are, too, since here you are!" She tipped her head to the side and raised both eyebrows.

With his head on a swivel, he checked out her crib. At least the parts he could see from where he stood.

From what he could tell, her apartment was tiny. "You live here alone?"

"No. With my lover."

His head spun toward where she still stood by the now closed door. She had a damn good poker face. "He got the initials LZ?"

"You know Zeke has a room at the Angels' church."

"Lotta MC members keep a room at church. Don't mean they don't sleep elsewhere." Or bounce from bed to bed, depending on what female they were fucking that night.

"You must've forgotten. We already had a discussion about Zeke."

With his hands on his hips, he turned to face her. "Women lie."

She frowned. "You're calling me a liar? That's rich."

"Ain't you lyin' about havin' a lover?"

"I was only joking."

"Yeah. Your jokes don't make me laugh."

"That's why I'm a sports physical therapist and not doing standup."

"Gonna give me the nickel tour?"

"It's going to cost you more than a nickel. Have to account for inflation, you know."

He dug into his front pocket and pulled out a quarter. He flipped it in her direction. After catching it, she turned it within her fingers. "Not sure this will cover the cost of you being here."

"Me bein' here ain't costin' you nothin'."

"Unlike you coming to my job."

He had no idea what happened after he left Smith's earlier because she refused to leave with him. Since he wasn't in the mood to spend a night or ten in the slammer, he reluctantly left without her.

She headed into the small kitchen to the left of the entry. Only a half wall separated it from where he stood, and the living room situated to his right.

He followed her.

She went over to the stove. "You never said why you're here."

"Wouldn't come to me, so came to you, instead." He figured he'd hear from her once she left work. All he got was radio silence.

"Anyway... How do you know where I live?"

"Got my ways."

"By following me?"

"No need." He also had no need to explain where he got his info. He flared his nostrils and breathed deeply. Whatever was on the stove smelled really fucking good. "Whatcha makin'?"

Stepping closely behind her, he glanced over her shoulder at what looked like a pot of chili.

"Dinner. You know, the meal most people eat before bedtime."

"Usually eat pussy before bedtime."

"Like I said... *Most* people."

When he whispered, "Expected you to come over to my place," close to her neck, he grinned because he caused goosebumps to break out.

Fuck yeah. She wanted him. Even if she tried to deny it, her reaction gave her away.

"Expectations aren't always met."

"*Mmm.*" He blew lightly on the back of her neck.

She shivered and waved a hand over her shoulder in his direction. "Stop."

"Gonna share that with me?"

"I only made enough for one."

"There's enough fuckin' food there to feed ten."

"Maybe I'm really hungry."

"Or maybe you just like bein' difficult."

She shrugged and turned. "Not sure why you'd think that?"

"What woman ain't difficult?"

"I could say the same for men."

"We ain't difficult. We're just dicks."

"With dicks."

He *mmm'd* again and stepped back, giving her space to work.

She gave the chili a last stir, turned off the heat and moved the pot over one burner. His eyes were glued to her ass as she opened a cabinet and pulled down a bowl, placing it on the counter next to another empty one.

Then she dug out a second spoon.

Someone was going to be eating good tonight. He hoped to be that someone.

A little homemade chili followed by some pussy for dessert.

That might end up being his new favorite meal.

She spooned half of a bowl for herself and a full bowl for him. She held them both out to him. "Put these on the table." She quickly moved out of his reach to pull some napkins from a holder, then placed them next to the bowls where he had set them across from each other.

Just like he owned the place, he headed to the fridge and opened it without even asking.

"Help yourself," she muttered.

"Planned on it," he answered with his back to her as he dug around, searching for beer. He didn't have any luck.

He held up a bottle with a familiar name. Of course he knew Smirnoff made vodka, but this shit wasn't clear, it was pink. "What's this shit?"

"You never had hard lemonade before?"

Hard what? "Don't need lemonade to make me hard."

She groaned. "Don't the Knights own a bar?"

Of course she knew his MC owned a damn bar. She'd been in it. "This shit ain't ever bein' served at Dick's."

"Shame. It might attract some new women into your establishment."

"Then, guess I'll get some ordered." He twisted off the top and took a sip. He grimaced. "Women like this shit?"

She plucked the cold bottle from his fingers. "Yes, we do."

"Got no beer?"

She shook her head.

"Whiskey?"

She shook her head again.

"Nothin' but that piss?"

"I like that piss." She took another long sip and placed the bottle on the table next to her bowl.

"Seein' as you fucked me twice, figured you got good taste. Guess I was wrong."

She tipped her head and said with a straight face, "You were wrong."

Damn.

"Came back for seconds, though."

"Ever hear the saying, 'desperate times call for desperate measures?'" She took her seat and pointed at where his bowl was on the table. "Sit and eat before it gets cold."

He watched her spoon chili into her mouth, close her eyes and swallow it.

"Man, that's good. I'm a damn good cook if I say so myself."

He went back into the fridge and grabbed another bottle of the spiked pink piss.

When he turned, she was staring at him. "I thought you didn't like it?"

"Desperate fuckin' times call for desperate fuckin' measures," he repeated, yanking out the seat across from her and sinking his ass into it. His mouth watered just seeing and smelling the homemade chili.

Grabbing the spoon, he dug in. Once it hit his tastebuds, his head jerked back.

Holy shit. It was the best damn chili he ever had.

He stared at the woman across from him. She was not only hot as fuck, but she could cook?

The corners of her lips curled up slightly. "Good?"

She fucking knew it was. And was gloating about it.

He'd give her that because... *Damn.* He could eat that whole pot himself. Just maybe not in one sitting.

His brothers would fall over themselves to slob down some of this.

Was he sharing? Fuck no.

The sweet butts occasionally cooked for him, but he mostly ate whatever he could grab from the kitchen at Dick's.

It had been a while since he sat down at a table and shared a meal with a woman. In fact, the last time was most likely last Christmas. Cait, Magnum's ol' lady, always invited him over to spend the holiday with their family.

He used to go over every year just to try to get down Ali-Cat's pants. But now Magnum's oldest daughter was married to that pig and had a piglet with him.

And his sergeant at arm's younger daughter Asia was too damn young. Like jailbait young. And the fuck if he was into that.

He liked his women ripe. Just like that peach Maddie had earlier today.

Sweet and juicy.

Chapter Twenty-Three

"Why are you staring at me like that?"

"Like what?" Romeo pretended he wasn't looking at her in the same way he was looking at the chili. As if she was edible and he was a starved man.

Maddie circled her spoon in the air at the same level at his face. "I can't tell if you're in shock that I can cook or if you're going to launch yourself across the table to eat me instead."

"Maybe it's both." He shoved another generous spoonful into his mouth. "If you want a new job, got a spot for you in Dick's kitchen."

She huffed, "I have a career already and it's not as a line cook."

"Could be temporary 'til you find somethin' better."

"So, about that…"

"Shoulda walked out when I did."

"Well, I know this is a difficult concept for you to understand, but let me explain it, anyway… I don't belong to you, so I don't have to follow your orders."

She didn't have to wear his cut for him to want to protect her. "No reason to stay in that fuckin' job, woman, and keep lettin' him abuse you."

"Did you only come over to rehash this? If so, I'm going to tell you, you made things tense for me at work today. I told you to stay out of it and you didn't. I could've gotten fired. I'm sure Roger seriously considered it. Oh wait. You know how I know that he did? He told me at least a half dozen times that I'm 'lucky' he didn't fire me."

That asshole needed to be taught a lesson... More like Smith needed a beat down. "Worried about you."

"Don't be. I've survived working there for over a year now. How he acts isn't new. He's been like this from the start. Anyway, it's not only me, he treats everyone like shit. It's the whole reason there's a high turnover rate."

"Surprised nobody snapped and cut the bitch."

She raised both eyebrows at him. "Could it be because doing so is illegal? In case you're unaware, stabbing someone is a crime, being an asshole isn't..." Her lips twitched. "Or you'd be doing life behind bars."

Once again, she had jokes. "You sayin' I'm an asshole?"

"Am I wrong? Didn't you say that men are dicks?"

She wasn't wrong.

"Luckily," she continued, "I'm used to dealing with men with egos bigger than a hot air balloon."

"You been in one?" He'd need to be knocked the fuck out first before stepping into what looked like a wicker picnic basket attached to a huge balloon that couldn't be steered or stopped.

Fuck that shit.

"No, but bikers tend to be full of hot air."

"Ain't blowin' any hot air. You give me the okay to rough

that motherfucker up in a dark alley one night, gonna do that."

"I'd prefer you avoid committing crimes on my behalf."

"Just sayin'."

"While I appreciate your dedication to being my personal Batman, I'm good, Rome. If you go to prison, don't expect me to visit."

"Wouldn't even put any scratch on my books?"

"Nope."

He raised one eyebrow. "No conjugal visits?"

She shook her head. "Definitely not."

"Not even a phone call?"

Using the universal hand sign for a phone, she placed it to her ear. "New phone, who dis?"

He almost spat out his mouthful of chili. Wasting any of it would be the true crime.

The woman had a sense of humor, was smart, could cook, was more than easy on the eyes, responsive as fuck in bed and knew the MC life...

She'd be perfect if he was looking for someone to wear his cut.

He wasn't. But that didn't mean he couldn't enjoy some of those assets on the list.

Even though Smith didn't fire her... "What happened after I left?"

"I was written up. Again."

What the fuck? "For what?"

"Making a mess out on the floor. With both the peach," she bugged out her eyes at him, "and you."

"Wrote you up. That it?"

"He also docked my pay."

He fucking did what? "Can he do that?"

"He can do whatever he wants since he owns the place.

I've been told many times that if I don't like the way he runs things, I can leave."

Romeo agreed that she should leave. "You should."

"Thanks for confirming where you stand," she raised a finger and added, "on something that doesn't concern you."

With his jaw tight, he closed his eyes and pulled in a breath. He wasn't backing off on this. But he realized in the future, he'd need to keep both his thoughts and actions about it secret.

"Heartburn?"

"Not from the chili," he muttered.

"Is it because I won't kowtow to you?"

"Kowtow? That some kinda new sexual fetish I don't know about? 'Cause I'm game for new shit."

Her spoon scraped the bottom of her bowl as she finished the last of her chili. "For most bikers, it's not a new fetish."

This was news to him. "It involve bondage or somethin'?"

"Sort of. But not in the way you're thinking."

"Fuckin' explain, then."

She shrugged and set her spoon in her now empty bowl. "Bikers tend to like their women submissive. They want them to do whatever they say."

He stared at her. "Are you fuckin' kiddin' me? You might not know any of the Knights' ol' ladies, but you damn well know the Fury's and probably most of the Angels'. How many of their ol' ladies are fuckin' submissive? How many of them talk back to their ol' man?"

He was spitting out facts she couldn't deny. The only ol' lady he knew was truly submissive to her man was Syn. But that was more of a sexual dynamic between the two. "Even Dodge don't stop Syn from havin' an opinion and sharin' it. So, not sure where you get that submissive bullshit."

"What about the sweet butts? They have to do what any of you demand."

"But they ain't..." It was probably better if they dropped this conversation. He wanted to get laid tonight. If this discussion went sideways, that might not happen.

"Aren't what?" she prodded. "Women with valid thoughts and feelings?"

"No one's forcin' anyone to be a goddamn sweet butt. Their choice. They don't like it, they can leave."

The second she tipped her head to the side and raised her eyebrows at him, he realized he fell into her trap.

"Boy, that ultimatum sounds familiar. But they don't leave, do they? Why?"

"'Cause they wanna be there. It ain't a fuckin' career. If they were abused, they'd—"

She cut him off with, "Skull fucking them to the point of tears running down their faces, snot coming out of their nose while gagging isn't abuse?"

"They..." *Fuck.* He scraped his fingers through his beard and sighed. "Chili's damn good."

She slid her chair back and stood. "Nice deflection."

He focused on the sway of her hips and the luscious curves of her ass as she walked her dirty dishes over to the sink. When she turned, she noticed him eye-fucking her.

Not that he gave a shit.

He came over to her apartment for two reasons. To find out what happened after he left and to plant his beard between her thighs. If she wasn't aware of the second reason, she would be soon.

Long gone was the polo shirt with the embroidered "Smith's" logo above her left tit. Or the nerdy tan pants she wore earlier. Or the plain white sneakers. She had changed into plain cotton shorts that showed off her smooth legs, one of those snug camisoles that framed her tits so perfectly that he wanted to smother himself between them and her pink-tipped toes were bare.

By the time she finished the short walk to his side of the small table, her nipples were poking through the stretchy cotton.

He suddenly lost his taste for the chili and had a hankering for something else.

"Finished?"

The huskiness in her voice made him believe she'd be fully onboard with his after-dinner plans.

When she reached for his partially empty bowl, he scooted back his chair, grabbed her hips, and yanked her into his lap.

Instead of pushing him away, she settled in, hooking an arm over his shoulders and combing her fingers through his thick beard. "I guess you're finished."

"Yep. Soon time for dessert." Especially since his idea of dessert had nothing to do with food.

She shifted. "What's poking me?"

"My dick?"

"Feels like you have two guns locked and loaded. One in your jeans and one in your cut. Do you always carry?"

"Yeah."

"Why?"

Because he wasn't stupid. "Evil lurks everywhere. Bein' part of the Fury, you should know that."

"The evil's lair in Manning Grove was blasted to oblivion."

That it was. "More than one fuckin' evil, Maddie. Hell, you work for someone in that category."

"I thought we were off that subject."

He squeezed her hip. "We are. Now you're on my fuckin'

lap and we can talk about the future. Like what's about to happen in the next few minutes."

"I need to clean up." When she shifted again, he had to bite back a groan. Did she grind against his hard-on on purpose?

"Not for me, you don't."

"I meant the kitchen."

"Kitchen can wait. The dick you're sittin' on can't."

"Aren't you attached to it?"

"Yeah, and I'd like to keep it that way."

"Has someone ever threatened to cut it off?"

He snorted. He had a long damn list of crazy fucking women who had rolled in and out of his bed. He was damn sure plenty of them wouldn't hesitate to slice off his dick if given half a chance.

After he moved into Magnum's old place, he became more cautious about the women he actually allowed in the same bed he slept in. Maddie was one of less than a handful —beside sweet butts—permitted to know where he lived.

If he wasn't sure about some random, he tended to go to her place or a motel. Or use a back seat. Or the bathroom at Dick's. Really, all he had to do was open his jeans enough to pull out his dick to get the job done. It was safer not to let them know where he laid his head at night. It also made it easier for him to scrape them off after the hookup.

However, he was in no rush to scrape off the warm, soft woman currently in his lap. If anything, she'd be the one kicking his ass out the door after he made her come.

Shoving his chair back even further, he got a good grip on her ass and surged to his feet. He grinned when she hooked her arms more securely around his neck and wrapped her legs around his waist instead of insisting he put her down.

He carried her down the hallway and quickly discovered her place was even smaller than he thought.

"One bedroom?"

"That's all I need. Why pay for space I'm not going to use? Less to clean, too. And, anyway, your place doesn't even have one bedroom."

"Got a loft."

"Not the same."

"Less to clean," he echoed, heading into her bedroom.

She did a snort-laugh. "Right. Like you clean."

He shrugged. "Less for the sweet butts to clean. Means they can get the job done quickly." And then get the fuck out of his domain.

She shook her head at his answer.

With his hands still planted on her ass cheeks, he let her slide slowly down his body until she stood on her own two feet, but he didn't release her. Instead, he dipped his head and held her gaze. "Gonna fuck you."

A flush hit her cheeks, and a gleam filled her eyes. "I figured."

"Got fuckin' jokes about that? You do, get 'em out now."

She grinned. "Or forever hold my peace?"

"Good with that."

"I'm sure you are, since you don't find my sarcasm funny."

He slipped one thin strap of her cami off and nibbled across her shoulder. "Tastes better than that damn chili," he murmured against her skin. "And that shit was the best."

"Not as spicy?" Her whisper held a shake.

"You still got a fuckin' bite, though."

"Are you saying that even though my chili didn't give you heartburn, I will?"

"Don't gotta say it, you just did."

"No one's forcing you to be here."

"You are."

When she pulled her head back, her eyebrows were pinched together. "How am I forcing you to be here? I didn't even invite you over."

He pushed the other strap off her shoulder and dragged his tongue along her collarbone. "'Cause you're a goddamn irresistible temptation."

"Should I apologize?"

"Are we done fuckin' talkin' yet?"

"Are you?"

Chapter Twenty-Four

APPARENTLY, Romeo *was* done talking since he shuffled them over to the bed, yanked her off balance and caused them both to crash land onto the mattress. When he rolled, pinning her underneath him, Maddie stared up into his intense, dark eyes and her heart did a somersault.

None of it made sense. Why did she find Romeo so damn hot? So sexy? She never wanted a biker before, even for a fling, so why did she want a womanizer like him?

Not permanently, of course.

But naked.

The man was drool-worthy when only wearing his tattoos. He was also orgasm-inducing because he knew how to use that beard to his advantage.

Beards had never been her thing. Mostly because most men didn't know how to care for them properly and the longer they got, the scragglier they became. In the past, she'd seen beards that resembled a tumbleweed glued to a man's chin and cheeks.

Unlike some other bikers, Romeo seemed to take real pride in his facial hair. Maybe because he had no hair on top of his head. Not only was his thick, jet-black beard well-groomed, it fit his face. In truth, it fit him.

"Problem?" came his grumble.

"Only that we're still both dressed."

One side of his very kissable mouth pulled up. "Anxious for my dick?"

Oh, someone was getting even cockier than normal. "Is that what I said?"

"Ain't blind. Can see it in your eyes, woman. Can also see how fuckin' hard your nipples are. Bet if I touched your pussy, it would be soaked."

That same pussy clenched in anticipation of his touch. "Why me, Rome?"

He narrowed his eyes on her. "Whataya mean?"

"Why me? You have plenty of women at your disposal, why are you chasing me?"

That cocky expression quickly dissipated. "Ain't chasin'. Don't chase after any damn female."

Huh. Why did he look insulted? "You came to my job. You came to my apartment," she reminded him. That sounded like chasing to her.

"Yeah, and you hunted me down at Dick's. So fuckin' what?"

"We could've simply had sex that night and after I left, you never had to see me again. I was okay with that, I figured you would be, too. Isn't that how you normally prefer it?"

"Says fuckin' who?"

"Says your past actions. Tell me, how often do you do a repeat? Other than with sweet butts, of course."

A deep crease appeared on his forehead, and he growled, "Whataya doin', Maddie?"

236

She thought it was obvious. "Trying to figure out how I'm different from the other women you smash and dash."

He rolled off her and sat up, giving her his broad back and a clear view of his cut with its rockers and patches. It was a good reminder that the Knights were a huge part of his life and always would be. He lived and breathed that club. Most loyal MC members did. Being a biker was their life, not a hobby.

"What the fuck you doin', Maddie?"

Did he not like being called out? That surprised her. She figured he wouldn't care since Romeo had a reputation he normally embraced. "Trying to protect myself."

"From?"

"You."

He scrubbed his hand back and forth over his smooth scalp. The jerky motions were evidence of his annoyance. "Didn't think you wanted anythin' more than dick."

She thought she'd been pretty clear about it. "And that's true. I only wanted to forget my work situation for an hour or two. You seemed like an easy solution since I assumed you didn't like strings."

When his head jerked sharply, she also sat up.

"But then you stuck your nose in my business by coming to my place of employment and now here you are in my bedroom." To her, that felt like strings. Maybe they weren't quite as heavy as chains, but more like thin dental floss.

"To fuck."

No, it was more than that. "You came to my job and pretended to have an injury so you could fuck me again? Of course you didn't. One didn't have anything to do with the other. You said you wanted to protect me. That's not typical behavior for someone who prefers one-night stands."

He sucked on his teeth loud enough for her to hear it.

Did he not like being in the hot seat? *Huh.* Pity.

She added, "And don't give me that bullshit excuse about the Fury being an ally, Rome."

"Ain't an excuse when it's fuckin' true."

"Okay," came out on a sigh.

"Okay what?"

She shrugged. "Just okay."

His expression turned hard, leading her to believe that he didn't like that response. Most likely because he realized it was her attempt to end that line of conversation.

It was obvious he was only using the Knights alliance with the Fury as an excuse. Because if he was really worried about her situation, as the Knights' president, he could have easily reached out to Trip, the Blood Fury's president, and shared his concerns.

Would she have been pissed about him doing so? Of course. Because like him showing up as a fake patient at Smith's, Romeo was still sticking his nose where it didn't belong.

Despite his opinion on it.

Despite her telling him multiple times to mind his own business.

When he stood and took a couple of steps away from the bed, she figured he was leaving. At least until he stopped.

Once again, she focused on the back of his cut, a harsh reminder of who and what he was.

That ended up being a fleeting thought when her gaze drifted down to his ass and she had a flashback of her fingers digging deep into his well-developed glutes, experiencing the power behind each forceful pump.

Her pussy pulsed at that particular memory, plus everything else that happened while they were naked.

The truth was, she didn't want him to leave.

Not yet, anyway.

Was that selfish? Possibly. But she couldn't imagine that Romeo would say no if she asked him to stay. "Are you leaving?"

He turned, wearing a scowl. "Want me to leave?"

"Isn't that why you got up?"

"Got up to take off all this shit."

Well then...

In this case, she didn't mind being wrong.

However... she wondered how often Romeo got fully naked with his conquests or if she was a special case. She was afraid if she asked, it might bring them back to their previous conversation. Not only was that conversation beating a dead horse, she preferred to get to where they weren't having any conversation at all.

The whole reason they were in her bedroom.

It was also safer that way since, apparently, they didn't see eye to eye on certain topics. One being her personal life.

"Do you need help?" she offered. "I'm available and eager to assist."

"All that chili made me pretty fuckin' tired, so could use the help."

She liked the direction of this conversation a whole lot better. He probably did, too. "Do you at least have enough strength to take off your boots?"

"Probably can manage that."

She definitely preferred this playful teasing over the more serious stuff. Plus, the fact he could lighten up made him even more attractive in her eyes.

After unlacing his boots and yanking them off, his socks quickly followed. She was pleasantly surprised that they didn't have any holes with his little piggies jutting out.

Of course, that thought led her to wondering if he

shopped for his own clothes or if he sent one of the club girls to pick him up packs of socks and boxer briefs. If they did his laundry, Maddie wouldn't doubt they went that extra mile for the Knights' prez.

She would never understand a sweet butt's need to please these bikers, despite being treated like indentured servants. The reality was, they chose to live that lifestyle and none that she knew were being held against their will.

Once he was barefooted, he held his arms up and out to the side in an unspoken message for her to take over.

She would be happy to do so.

She got to her feet and walked slowly toward him, deciding where to start.

His cut, of course. A biker's pride and joy. Also as important as his sled since it was proof of his brotherhood and his way of life. His cut defined him.

"Turn around."

When he did, she slid her hands up his arms and under the shoulders of the leather vest before carefully slipping it off. The heaviness of the gun was unmistakable, and most likely hidden somewhere in the liner.

"Careful with that."

"With that comment, I'll assume it really is locked and loaded."

"Ain't worth shit otherwise."

She went over and hung his cut on the hook attached to the back of her bedroom door. When she turned, he was watching her intently with his expression blank and his dark eyes unreadable.

His body language also gave nothing away.

Was he trying to hide something? Or was she over-thinking it?

She stopped toe-to-toe with him and grabbed his shirt, peeling it up and off him, to expose his very impressive, tattooed chest. She smoothed both hands over his heated skin and followed the contours of his muscles.

He continued to hide his thoughts and, surprisingly, had zero reaction to her touching him. So, she bent her knees enough so she could draw her tongue from his belly button up his abs and between his defined pecs.

He fisted her hair tightly like a ponytail and growled, "Woman."

Well, *that* got a reaction.

She paused to flick one of his dark, pebbled nipples with the tip of her tongue before doing the same to the other. When she straightened, the look on his face made her pussy pulse with every thump of her heart.

It was also getting slicker by the second.

They needed to get this moving before she ended up in a huge puddle at his feet.

Leaning into him, she drew her nose along his throat while inhaling the scent typical of a biker—exhaust, leather, weed and something else she couldn't identify—at the same time working his belt buckle open and unfastening his jeans.

Heat radiated from him like a furnace and seared her everywhere she touched. But it also drew her like a moth to a flame.

She shouldn't like him.

She shouldn't want him.

She shouldn't have let him into her apartment.

But she did.

She didn't know what his "secret sauce" was that made him so damn irresistible but now she semi-understood why he had plenty of women at his fingertips for his use and disposal.

Maybe after tonight, she'd be the next one kicked to the curb.

He might even block her number and tomorrow night be on the prowl for his next conquest.

Would she care? She wanted to say no, but that might no longer be true.

Doing this was not a good idea.

In fact, all of this was a very bad idea.

Despite her gut instinct, she shoved his jeans and boxer briefs down anyway.

Or until they got hung up on his erection. The second she freed him, he grabbed his cock to slowly stroke his length as he stepped out of the jeans and underwear nested at his feet.

It was no lie that Romeo was quite a specimen. It always surprised her when bikers worked out. Before her family became a part of the Fury, she didn't know much about bikers or motorcycle clubs and would've thought they all had beer bellies and violent tempers.

It was obvious that Romeo took care of himself. Maybe to get more women? Maybe for his own pride? She didn't know, but she appreciated the effort he put into his physique.

While he was naked, she could forget for a while that he was a biker. Being naked, she saw him as she would anyone else.

"Now you."

His voice was so deep and gravelly, it caused tingles to explode through her, made her nipples ache, her pussy clench and her breathing to become a bit ragged.

"You're not going to help?" The huskiness in her own voice caught her off guard.

"Fuck no. Gonna watch you get naked." Her split-second hesitation had him growling, "Woman, do it now," next.

Another good reminder of who he was.

A bossy biker. Whether wearing his club's colors on a cut or inked onto the skin of his bare back.

Everything she thought she did *not* want in a man.

Chapter Twenty-Five

As ROMEO WATCHED Maddie take her time peeling off the little she wore, he slowly stroked his rock-hard dick.

When she was finally naked, they stared at each other from only a few feet apart. The distance might as well be the width of the Allegheny River. She was too fucking far away, and he was dying for her to be pressed against him. Despite that, he first wanted to appreciate the woman before him by using only his eyes.

He'd get to touch and taste her soon enough.

Her breathing shallowed and a flush worked its way up her chest into her cheeks when her heated gaze followed his fist sliding up and down his hard length.

Her hair draped loosely around her slender shoulders and was long enough for a few stray strands to fall across her full tits. Both her puckered nipples and the anticipation of tasting her cunt again made his mouth water.

The chili had been damn good, but if asked, Maddie would be his preferred meal.

She was so fucking tempting.

And too damn addicting.

Normally, if he was interested in a woman, he simply turned on the charm and it usually didn't take much effort to get her exactly where he wanted her. If she ended up being a pain in the ass, he quickly moved on and turned his attention to the next woman who caught it.

Plenty of warm, slick pussies existed out there. No reason to work too hard to get one.

If he struck out, he could easily text a sweet butt to come see to his needs. But right now, he didn't want a club girl. *Fuck that.* Everything he wanted tonight was within his reach.

He was damn sure he'd get tired of Maddie sooner than later. That was always the way for him. Normally, one night with any woman was more than enough.

On the rare occasion, a woman might last more than one fuck as long as she didn't have a damn pie hole that flapped needlessly, and constantly spewed a bunch of bullshit, giving him a headache.

For him to even consider being with a hookup more than once, she had to be top fucking notch. Give him a mouth so skilled it could suck the cum directly from his nuts and a pussy tight enough to cut off the circulation to his dick.

Since Maddie had neither, he didn't "get" his abnormal obsession with her. Especially since this was the third fucking time they were naked together.

What made his gut twist was the fact he had zero urge to scrape her off. He wasn't experiencing the choking of an invisible collar around his neck or a cock ring on his dick. The second he felt either tightening the slightest, he was bolting out the door.

But *fuck him*, right now the urge wasn't to run, it was to stay.

However, that wasn't what disturbed him the most about this whole fucking thing. It was the fact he had the urge to possess her. To protect her.

To claim her as his.

For fuck's sake, he couldn't even say that was weed talking. He was stone-cold sober. He had to be broken.

Or something.

He'd worry about that shit later. After he fucked her. After he chowed down on that sweet pussy. After he heard his name cross her lips when she came. After he blew his load deep inside her.

Sex was the only reason he should be at her place. Not to give a fuck about what happened at Smith's after he left.

Her "Something wrong?" detoured him from the path of doom. *Thank fuck.* Because if he kept traveling down that road, he'd be jerking on his clothes and truly sprinting for the door.

Even before he got to fuck her.

The problem was, if that happened, he'd end up in his own bed obsessing about her all night. He'd also have a chafed dick and blisters on his hand.

Reality wasn't always better than imagination. But in Maddie's case, it was. He knew that for sure because he tested that option.

A few times.

"Only fuckin' thing wrong is that my face ain't covered in your pussy juices yet."

A ragged breath slipped from between her parted lips. "Well, we can right that wrong."

"Sure as fuck can. By you sittin' on my face."

"That's going to be hard to achieve with you standing there. I'm not a gymnast."

"Easy fuckin' fix." It was time to get this party started.

Stepping closer, he wrapped his fingers around the back of her head and pulled her into him for a thorough kiss. One that made her melt against him, because, *fuck yeah*, he had some damn skills.

When he was done, he rounded the bed and climbed on. Two seconds later, he was sprawled out on his back. "Hop on."

He smoothed down his beard as he waited for her to follow him onto the bed. It had to be a great mattress since it hardly moved when she climbed on and straddled his head.

His senses went into overload with seeing her perfect little pussy just inches from his face. He caught a whiff of how aroused she was, too. He closed his eyes and inhaled even deeper.

Best fuckin' perfume ever. It wasn't fancy or expensive, but definitely his favorite.

Now he needed a little taste.

When he opened his eyes, he met hers for a second before grabbing her hips and pulling her down.

"Am I crushing you?"

His answer was to bury his nose and tongue in her cunt to get the full experience.

Goddamn perfection.

When he alternated fucking her with his tongue and sucking on her plump folds, it didn't take long before her thighs began to tremble as well as squeeze his head.

When he sucked on her clit, she rocked her hips.

When he blindly reached up, found those hard as fuck nipples, and twisted them, she ground her cunt harder against his mouth.

She could smash that bomb-ass pussy against his face until he passed out from a lack of air, and he wouldn't give a shit. He'd think he'd died and went to heaven. But as soon as he came to and found himself still on Earth, he'd be ready to chow down again.

Romeo wouldn't deny it, both oxygen and pussy were a requirement for him to live. After, everything else needed in life was a distant second.

If he was stranded on a deserted island, he might miss his sled and brothers, but the fuck if he could go without a woman for more than a few days. He might as well dive off a goddamn cliff headfirst into the rocks below.

Life would no longer be worth living.

A bit fucking dramatic? Not if it was true.

Her fingers wrapped around his head, and she began to ride his face as if she was a drunk country bar patron and he was a mechanical bull.

"Rome," she groaned.

Hell yeah.

His name, her moans, her whimpers were music to his sandwiched ears.

It didn't take long before her fingers dug even deeper into his skull and she shot upward, dislodging his mouth when she came. He quickly jerked her back down so he could taste the results of his efforts. He couldn't lap it up fast enough.

Fuck yeah. She was definitely ready for his dick.

His face and beard were a mess, and he didn't give a fuck. Wearing her arousal was a badge of honor.

Not every woman liked getting her pussy eaten.

Not every woman could come like that just from getting eaten out.

Thank fuck Maddie was not every woman.

While that should be a good thing—and not troublesome — it only made him want her more. And to do it again.

That was not normal for him.

None of this was fucking normal.

He released her hips and tipped his head back so he could breathe easier. When he saw her eyes were still closed, her head drooping forward and her lips parted, his erection twitched to remind him that it was impatiently waiting.

Soon, he told it silently. *Gotta wrap you tight first.*

For fuck's sake, he should've thought of that before they both got naked.

He stared up at the woman still straddling his head. "You got wraps within reach?"

He wasn't sure if he wanted to hear that fucking answer. If she did, that meant he wasn't the first man in her bed. In this apartment, at least.

If she said no... Then he'd have to get his ass up and grab one from his wallet.

For some reason, he preferred the second option.

Inconvenient? Fuck yeah.

Worth the fucking hassle? No doubt.

He clamped his teeth together to avoid saying shit that would piss her off and end the night too damn soon when she stretched as far as she could to reach the nightstand and yank open the drawer.

He guessed that was his answer.

After a quick glance at the box when she removed it to see if it was sealed or open, he closed his eyes.

He didn't want to fucking know. It would only piss him the fuck off.

Just the thought of someone—other than him—sliding into that warm, wet pussy would make him want to shank someone. Slip that blade right between the ribs. Maybe even twist it a little. And once they were down, he'd keep them there with a boot to the throat.

What the actual fuck?

Now he was pissed at himself for letting that shit bother him.

Yeah, none of this was fucking normal.

He should go. Free himself from whatever the fuck was happening before it was too late and he couldn't free himself at all.

Who was he shitting? His ass wasn't going anywhere.

Especially once Maddie pulled a condom from the box, ripped it open and settled herself once again by straddling his gut. Her wet pussy smeared along his skin as she worked her way further down and across this throbbing dick. She didn't stop until his erection was in front of her, giving her easy access to roll the wrap down his length.

He was damn pleased that she took the initiative. Women who didn't lift a damn finger during sex were always one and done for him. With those, imagination *was* always better than reality.

Once his dick was gloved, she held it straight up.

Fuck yeah, he definitely liked a woman who took the initiative. Not only did she ride his face, she was about to do the same with his cock.

And the fuck if he was going to stop her. *Hell no.* He would lie back and enjoy every damn second of it. She could set the pace, and he could watch.

Hearing her "Ready?" had him lifting his gaze from where she held his dick to her face.

His dick was rock solid in her fist. "Any doubt I am?"

She smirked. "I figured consent was important before I just... climbed on?"

"Don't gotta ask, just—" He groaned out a, "*Fuuuuck,*" when she lined him up and sank down on his dick.

She stilled when she had him buried as deep as he could get. "You feel so much bigger in this position."

Say what? "That good?"

When she wiggled like she was testing him out, he bit back a groan.

"You're a bit much like this," she admitted.

He grinned. "Sounds like a good thing."

"Bigger isn't always better," she shared.

"Ain't gonna convince me of that."

With her bottom lip caught between her teeth, she planted her hands on his chest and leaned forward. Most likely to relieve any discomfort. "Okay," she breathed. "That's more like it."

Hell yeah, it was.

"Going to move now," she warned.

"My dick ain't an airport. Don't gotta announce it, just—"

His thoughts became scrambled, and he forgot what he was about to say when she did what she said she would do. She *moved*.

And he was there for it.

Up. Down. Back. Forth. Round and round.

She rode him slow. She rode him fast.

She paused at the top. She paused at the bottom.

Somewhere along the way, he lost the little bit of sanity he normally clung to. Because she was driving him crazy.

Not that he gave a shit because it was worth it.

The only problem he had was, he wasn't sure where to focus. On her expression? Her tits bouncing wildly? His dick disappearing and reappearing over and over as she turned back into that drunk wannabe rodeo queen?

She became so damn soaked, her arousal began to drip down his dick and gather at the base.

Watching her made him lose his damn breath. Watching her made his chest ache. Watching her made him question his life's fucking choices.

All of them.

Hold the fuck on... What?

Yeah, he was losing his shit, and it was all her fault.

Did she have some magical pussy or something?

That had to be it. She put some bullshit spell on him.

He was pulled from his whacked thoughts when she dug her nails so deeply into his chest, he swore she drew blood.

He didn't give a fuck about that, either.

Since her pussy was pulsing around his dick, she had to be close to coming.

Then she threw her head back and slammed down on him, grinding him even deeper as the ripples of an orgasm squeezed and released him to the point he almost shot his load right then and there.

He clenched his teeth to keep his shit together since it was too soon to finish. He wanted more of what she was willing to give.

With a long moan, she collapsed on his chest, her heavy breathing rapid and her thumb trailing back and forth over his nipple.

It was time to take over.

Chapter Twenty-Six

AFTER WRAPPING an arm behind her back and while still buried deep inside her, he flipped her over and stared down into her hooded brown eyes. "Now... *You* ready?"

A smile spread across her relaxed face.

He was about to change that.

Driving his knees deeper into the mattress, he drove his dick home.

His brain glitched. *Fuck me,* her pussy *did* feel like home.

He ignored the invisible, ice-cold fingers strolling down his spine.

Of course, good sex normally left him feeling satisfied, but this was different. A strange itch he refused to scratch below the surface.

For fuck's sake, he couldn't get caught up in her. He had a name to live up to. A lifestyle to maintain. Maddie was a threat to all of that.

He'd seen some of his brothers—even fellow brothers with the Dirty Angels or the Blood Fury—fall victim to love, then go from an endless selection of pussy to being stuck with only one. While they seemed happy, even content, Romeo figured it had to be all smoke and mirrors. Being with only one woman for the rest of his life sounded like fucking torture.

He also didn't want to deal with any ol' lady drama of him having side bitches to get his variety fix. Most women didn't like it when they were loyal, and their man was not.

"Rome!"

He shook himself mentally and realized he'd stopped moving. He had gotten so fucking lost in his head, he forgot where he was and what he was doing for a second.

What he was supposed to be doing was Maddie, but instead he was panicking. For no damn reason.

He wasn't putting "a ring on it." He sure as fuck wasn't handing her his cut to wear. He wasn't even taking her for a ride on the back of his sled.

He was doing what Romeo did best. Fucking her. Nothing more, nothing less.

Nothing more, *you asshole*, nothing less.

"You didn't come already, did you?" Her question might as well have been a bucket of ice tossed on his naked ass because the fact that she thought he came that quickly woke him the fuck up.

It also rubbed him the wrong way since he was no damn two pump chump.

"Didn't come, woman. Gimme a sex... sec... *fuuuck*." The last came out on a groan.

He was losing his shit. He needed to focus on what he was doing and afterward, focus on the exit.

"Okay, well... We don't have all night."

If that was supposed to be another of her damn "jokes," he wasn't laughing. "You in a fuckin' rush?"

"I have to—" Her words were lost in a gasp followed by a long groan as he slammed into her.

This time he wasn't stopping. Not until she exploded all over him again. Not until he busted a nut.

He sucked her nipple into his mouth, not being gentle. If it was too rough, she had a voice. She could tell him to lighten up or stop. So, unless he heard otherwise, he would keep doing this the way he wanted, which was pulling out all the stops.

This time had to count since it would be the last time. It had to be, since it was one more fuck opportunity than he gave anyone else. It would be stupid for him to do this again.

Dangerous, too.

Not only because of the threat of getting caught up in her, but because of a biker named Shade. Romeo would prefer to keep his vocal cords intact and also safely in his damn neck.

After leaving one nipple shiny and peaked, he moved to the other. The harder he sucked, the more her back arched and the deeper her nails dug into his back and ass.

A quick glance showed that her eyes were squeezed shut and her lips parted. He took that as visual encouragement for him to take it even further.

He circled one areola with the tip of his tongue, before picking a nice tender spot on her tit to sink in his teeth.

Again, she didn't tell him it was too much or that she didn't like it. Her body language told him the opposite. So he did it again, this time hard enough to leave a slight mark on her ivory skin before brushing his lips lightly over it.

When he bit her, she had thrown her head back, exposing the delicate column of her throat. Since it called out to him, he collared it with his hand and drove his other arm under her hips, lifting them slightly. Now she was at the perfect angle.

Digging his knees deeper for leverage, he slammed into her over and over, causing her tits to jerk back and forth and the breath to rush from her with each forceful thrust.

She didn't stop him. She didn't tell him to slow down or demand he fuck her more gently.

She ate up everything he gave her.

He wondered how far he could push it. How rough she liked it.

He had pushed boundaries before but only with sweet butts. They were usually up for anything. But when he was fucking strange, he tended to not push it. He didn't want to end up in a concrete cell for some goddamn misunderstanding.

However, this was Maddie. She'd have no problem telling him to switch gears.

While she never asked him to slow down, he had to, anyway. He was dangerously close to coming. His balls were pulled high, his dick was pulsing, and the pressure was building.

He ground his teeth and slowed his roll before he lost his load too quickly.

Since this was the last time, he had to make it count for Maddie, too. Even though she wasn't aware that this couldn't happen again.

Not one to normally say no to free pussy, in this case, Romeo would have no choice. That fucking sucked but it was better than falling down some damn rabbit hole and not being able to escape. This was the first time in his thirty-four years on this fucking planet that he worried about that happening.

Again, his thoughts being pulled in a direction he wanted to avoid forced him back to the matter at hand...

The woman under him.

The woman he was plunging in and out of.

The woman whose little noises and hot, slick pussy were driving him to the point of no return. He was barely skirting that edge, so she needed to come soon before she didn't get to fucking come at all.

Thank fuck it turned out that he wasn't the only one about to bust. Her nails raked down his back so hard and deep that, for a second, he worried about his ink getting fucked up. Her legs squeezed him even tighter, and she began meeting him thrust for thrust.

When she grabbed his ass and tried to pull him even deeper, he felt it... The small pulses growing more intense and coming faster. Her pussy squeezing him and getting even slicker.

Jesus, that wasn't helping him keep his shit together, but the fuck if he was stopping.

No fucking way.

Once again, he told himself that since this was the last damn time, he needed to make it worth it. For her. For himself.

This *was* the last damn time, he swore it. He needed to stick to his fucking guns. If anyone had the goddamn willpower to do that, it was him.

"Fuck, woman," he groaned, hanging on only by a quickly unraveling thread. "Come, goddamnit."

"I don't want to," she moaned back.

"Why fuckin' not?" She was going to kill him.

"It's... It feels... so damn good."

One side of his mouth pulled up, but only for a second before he pinned his lips together and carried on. Instead of pumping into her, he changed tactics. He began to roll his hips and grind deep, while jamming his hand between them to thumb her clit. He also tightened his grip on her neck so he could feel her throat working beneath his fingers.

"Rome..."

He did his best to ignore his name and focus on the end game... making her come.

"Rome..."

He closed his eyes because he couldn't watch her face twist in pleasure. Pleasure *he* was giving her.

"Rome..."

Wait. Maybe it wasn't pleasure. Was something wrong?

He lifted one eyelid to check. *Oh, fuck no.* Nothing was wrong, everything was right.

Like him, she was only losing her mind. In the best way possible.

He continued to circle both his hips and her clit until...

Thank fuckin' fuck.

The second the ripples turned to a full-blown orgasm, he chased her down that path and they both arrived at their final destination only seconds apart.

That was far too close for his liking. He had a reputation to protect. Not only being a lover of the ladies but being good in bed. Coming before Maddie would have fucked that up.

Happy that he was still king, he released her throat and replaced his hand with his face instead. It remained buried in her neck until his breathing slowed a bit and his dick began to soften. When it did, he quickly secured the wrap at the base and reluctantly slipped from her.

With a groan, he rolled off and onto his back, staring up at the ceiling, and wiped a bead of sweat from his forehead with the back of his hand. With the one not holding the full wrap, of course, because having a latex tube full of cum slap him in the face was not on the agenda.

With a satisfied moan, Maddie stretched her arms over her head and pointed her toes before twisting her head to stare at him. He didn't have to look at her to know she was doing it, the heat of her stare burned into the side of his bald head.

"Bathroom's in the hallway. Throw that in the trash and don't flush it. I don't need a bill from the landlord for a clogged toilet."

What the fuck? That was what she had to say? Nothing about his skills or how intense her orgasm was or how he was the best fuck she ever had?

Just... don't clog her damn toilet?

Maybe she needed to hear some appreciation on his end first. "Perfect night. Good food. Good woman."

She tipped her ear forward. "What was that?"

"Heard me."

She smiled but didn't return the same recognition. Or, *hell*, any.

For fuck's sake.

"All right..." She slipped from the bed and headed to her pile of clothes.

"Watcha doin'?"

She began to get dressed. Unfortunately, covering up the body he preferred naked. "I need to clean up the kitchen."

"Now?" he barked.

She glanced at him as she finished pulling up her shorts. "No, a week from now. When the chili has mold growing on it and the dishes need to be sandblasted."

His eyebrows pinned together. "When'd you get such a smart mouth?"

"When was it dumb?"

He shook his head and grumbled, "The jokes." Was she trying to ruin a good night?

"I figured you'd have a sense of humor."

"Got a sense of humor."

"You could've fooled me."

"Maybe you just ain't funny."

She shrugged. "Now, this was great, but I have stuff to do."

"You're kickin' me out?"

"I thought we were done. What am I missing?"

I thought we were done. He pulled in a breath and stared at the now clothed woman he just fucked. "Didn't know you were in a fuckin' rush to get it over with."

Her eyebrows hiked up her forehead. "*Huh.* You don't like it when the shoe's on the other foot?"

"What you talkin' about?"

"Aren't you the king of hit and run?"

His brow furrowed. "Hit and run?"

"Smash and dash? Hump and dump? Pounce and bounce? Dip and duck? Fuck it and chuck it?"

"Jesus fuck," he muttered. "Know what the fuck hit and run means. Just surprised to hear you use it."

"Do you think I've never been a victim of a hit and run?"

His head jerked. "You fuckin' ran quicker than shit after that night in the RV."

"I didn't know you wanted me to linger."

At the time, he didn't because he preferred to stay breathing. Something her stepdaddy could easily change if Shade caught the two of them together. *And* found out Romeo took Maddie's virginity.

The truth was, he'd most likely remain breathing while the Fury member skinned him alive first. He'd stop eventually but only after fucking suffering for longer than he'd like.

So, fuck no, he didn't want Maddie to linger in his bed that night since he didn't have a fucking death wish. He had been only doing her a solid, anyway, by doing what she asked for. Nothing more.

He didn't take advantage of her; he'd only been accommodating. But he doubted Shade would believe that.

"Whatever," he muttered and hoofed it out to the only bathroom in her small apartment, tossed the used wrap into the garbage after tying it shut, took a piss, cleaned off any remaining pussy juices, checked his teeth for any pubes stuck between them and rinsed out his mouth with the mouthwash on the counter.

Once he jerked the door open again, he heard her putting around the kitchen. He shook his head with annoyance, headed back into her bedroom to get dressed and pull on his cut, then he headed toward the exit.

Since she was done with him, he might as well take that as a sign. He had been good for only one thing.

He waited for her to call out to him to at least say goodbye or thanks or something, but he heard nothing but dishes clanking. When he peered into the kitchen on his way to the door, her back was to him at the sink.

He paused, opened his mouth, then shook his head, and decided it was best to keep moving and not say shit.

Good thing he wasn't some sensitive pussy, because he might be feeling some kind of way with her blowing him off like that.

In less than a minute, he was down at this sled, straddling it. He stared up at her apartment while running everything that happened through his mind.

He considered his options, even though he only told himself earlier that this was the last time.

He sucked on his teeth at his own lies.

Then it hit him...

Madison didn't seem the type to be clingy, so what would it hurt to make her a regular?

That didn't mean he couldn't fuck anyone else. Or order a sweet butt to drop to her knees so he could face fuck her and shoot his load down her throat.

No, he could add Maddie to his regular rotation. The best part about that would be, unlike a sweet butt, he wouldn't have to share her with any of his brothers. He'd squash any interest they had in her with a quickness.

But that didn't address the problem of the woman being considered BFMC property. More concerning, belonging to the most dangerous Fury member.

Shade would not like the fact that Romeo was only using Maddie to get his rocks off.

In truth, he couldn't imagine Trip would be okay with that, either. The man was overprotective of everyone tied to his club. Just as a good president should be. Though, he was more intense than most.

Romeo sure as fuck didn't rule his MC with an iron fist. That was too much damn work. If one of his brothers needed an attitude adjustment, that was why he had a sergeant at arms to do the dirty work.

With one last glance up at her apartment window, he grinned. He needed to come up with a plan where she should only fuck him, while he could do any woman he wanted.

Damn, he liked that plan even though she probably wouldn't. It would just take some careful convincing.

Wearing a grin, the roar of his sled filled the night as he sped away.

Chapter Twenty-Seven

I NEED THIS JOB. *I need this job. I need this job.*

She swore that was now her daily mantra.

Take it one day at a time, girl. It'll be worth it in the end.

Hopefully.

At least that was what she kept telling herself. She could kick herself later if it turned out to be untrue and all she did was waste the last year and a half at Smith's while taking the abuse.

Her tongue was particularly bloody today from biting it one too many times. She only stopped once Roger walked out the door and left her alone to close up.

She loved seeing his back as he walked away. It was his best side. Both for her and the rest of his employees.

Tonight, she was the last one to leave because Roger cornered her after she finished up with her last patient. As soon as she saw him striding in her direction, dread overcame her. She knew instantly she would be stuck doing some bull-shit job. One she couldn't refuse.

Roger had her trapped in his tiny iron fist and he knew it.

The day that changed, she would tell him what a piece of shit he was. Most likely through an anonymous email since she couldn't say it directly to his face without him putting a black mark on her career.

Tonight's bullshit reason for her to stay late was to wipe down the strength equipment out on the floor. Forget the fact that the therapists sanitized each piece of equipment after a patient used it. Apparently, Roger's excuse was that he didn't "trust anyone to do it properly." Funny how he trusted her to do it right?

Whatever.

He'd been slightly more of a dick than normal—Was that even possible?—after Romeo confronted him. Proof Roger didn't like anyone challenging his ass. So now she was being punished more than normal on a regular basis.

She would've blown off cleaning the equipment and headed home if cameras weren't all over the place. Watching. Recording. Like big brother.

Maddie didn't doubt that Roger also kept an eye on the live feeds on his cell phone. The last thing she needed was to be written up again or docked any pay for "insubordination."

Her only choice was to suck it up and get it done before leaving for the evening. Only, in the end, it took her an hour and a half past her quitting time. Time she'd never get back or be compensated for.

Because her boss was a user and a loser.

The other night she had a dream that he tripped in front of her and, instead of helping him up, she ended up kicking him while he was down. She wasn't sure if she should admit that she woke up with a smile. Maybe she'd keep that to herself. But remembering that brought another smile to her face.

Until she stepped outside.

Before she could turn and lock the door, she saw that her vehicle wasn't the only one parked in what should be an empty lot. Right next to her Toyota sat a Harley. And on that Harley sat a man. And on that man was a leather cut proclaiming he was the president of the Dark Knights MC.

She sighed.

Maddie hadn't heard from him in about two weeks. Not that she reached out to him, either. The reason she hadn't texted or called him was...

She liked having sex with him way too much.

Way too much.

She had picked up her cell phone several times in the last couple of weeks to arrange a "meet," but seconds later she set that same phone down. She didn't want to start relying on him. Not for protection. Not even for sex.

She also didn't want him to think she needed him. For anything. That could be dangerous when it came to overly protective, possessive bikers.

With a shake of her head, she turned and took her time locking the front door to Smith's. After releasing another loud, long sigh, she headed over to the man waiting for her.

A black silky do-rag covered his dark, bald noggin and dark sunglasses hid his just as dark eyes, even though the sun had begun to set.

Those glasses followed every step she took across the parking lot. Of course he had parked right next to her driver's door. Was he afraid she'd try to avoid him?

If she had to admit it—though she'd never say it out loud —the man looked damn good straddling his badass sled. Especially with his skilled hands planted on those thick thighs.

She stopped next to him. "At least you waited until Roger left." The man might actually have some common sense.

"Been waiting here for a while."

Her head jerked back. "How long?"

"Long enough to see your asshole boss leave along with all your fuckin' co-workers. Why'd you stay?"

If she told him the truth, he would only give her a rash of shit for it and tell her that she should leave this job for the thousandth time.

She didn't want to hear it. She was tired. She was hungry. Her feet ached. "I had a few things to finish up."

"Like?"

"Like work."

His brow furrowed. "What kinda work? That dick insist you stay late?"

"No."

The big man could move fast when he wanted to. Because suddenly he was off his bike and toe-to-toe with her. With a tight grip on her chin, he raised her face so she couldn't avoid him.

She lifted a hand to stop whatever he was about to spew. "I don't want to hear it, Rome. I'm done explaining. If you can't accept that, then leave."

His nostrils flared, a muscle jumped in his cheek and his grip tightened to the point it bordered on painful.

She needed to stop him before he started in on her. If he did, she might go off on him, tell him to fuck off and the next thing she knew, he'd be telling Shade that she was having issues with her boss.

That could be a fatal mistake.

For Roger.

"I see you setting to go off... but please... just don't," she finished on a whisper.

That had him pinning his lips so tightly, they ended up in a slash.

"Why are you here?" Maybe she could get him off track.

"You were here a goddamn hour and a half longer than everyone else, Maddie."

Oh, *he* was pissed? He wasn't the one wiping down already clean equipment. "Tell me something I don't know. Why are you stalking me?"

His bearded chin jerked back into his neck. "Ain't stalkin' you."

"You still haven't said why you're here."

"Figured you might wanna get fed and fucked."

While that sounded tempting, taking him up on that offer would have her skidding down a slippery slope. The one she was trying to avoid. "Is that some sort of spa package?"

"Yeah. You qualify for the president's special. Limited time only."

"Maybe I don't want it."

His sudden smile wasn't a "happy" smile, but one more predatory. When he added a deep, grumbly, "Want me to prove you're a damn liar?" it made her toes curl and heat pool between her legs.

Damn it.

She cleared her throat so her voice wouldn't crack when she responded, "No need."

"Thought that'd be the case."

"So damn cocky," she mumbled under her breath.

His head tipped to the side. "You want my cock? That what you just said?"

"I said you're damn cocky." This time she said it loud and clear so there was no "misunderstanding."

His smile grew and he shoved his sunglasses to the top of his head. Why did this man look so damn fine?

It was frustrating. If he was some ugly troll, she could easily resist him.

Unfortunately, he wasn't.

What made it worse was he was damn good in bed.

Unfortunately, he knew it, too.

However, it was the rest of the baggage that went along with him she wasn't so fond of...

That cut he wore proudly. The attitude most bikers had about women being property. Or the mistaken belief that anyone with a vagina was weak, helpless, and *needed* their protection.

"Does that president's special include a foot massage?"

"No."

"Oh. Too bad. That's what I really need right now instead of an internal massage."

He snorted. "That internal massage gonna make you forget your feet."

"I'm not so sure about that," she murmured. She'd been on them for too many hours today. "Do I get a refund if it doesn't?"

"Got a no refund policy. But if you ain't happy with the service, can make it right."

"How?"

"By doin' it again. No charge."

"*Oooh.* So generous. And if I don't like it the second time?"

"Then gonna do it 'til it's done right, and you're satisfied."

"How about this... I'll pass on the president's special and take a food and foot massage package, instead."

"Gotta get the whole *package.*" He grabbed his crotch and shook it. "Ain't a la carte."

With a soft snort, she dropped her head to hide her amusement because his ego really didn't need to know he was funny, too.

He snagged her chin again and lifted her face. "Don't fuckin' hide from me."

"Do you always expect women to listen to your orders?"

"Yep."

"At least you're honest about it. So... Where are you taking me to eat? A five Michelin star steakhouse?"

"Close. Dick's. Got a whole damn kitchen full of shit there and cooks we pay to make that shit, too."

"I don't like the taste of shit, but I do have a hankering for a really good chicken sandwich loaded with pickles and a side of seasoned waffle fries. Can they make that?"

"Yeah."

She shot him a skeptical look. "Are you lying?"

"No fuckin' need to lie."

"If we get there and I get frozen chicken fingers and unseasoned tater tots, I'm writing a one-star review," she warned.

His lips quirked. "Dick's ain't ever gonna recover if you do."

Maddie doubted that any bad rating the biker bar received would do any damage. Bikers went there to drink, not for the ambiance or gourmet meals. If their guts started growling, she was sure peanuts, hot wings and a cold beer solved that issue.

She eyed up his sweet Harley. "Do I get to ride on your sled?"

If she hadn't been watching him carefully, she would've missed his nostrils flaring just slightly and his body tense.

Oooh. Did he never haul a woman around on the back of his bike? Did he think doing so might mean some kind of commitment? *Interesting.*

His seat was big enough for a passenger. Not all bikes had that. She was surprised Romeo's did since he was determined to remain a bachelor.

"Not a good idea to keep your cage here."

271

Her eyebrows shot up in feigned surprise. "It's not? It's not a bad area."

"Dontcha wanna be able to smash and dash?"

Huh. Reverse psychology. He was really using his head. The bald one between his shoulders. "That's your specialty."

"Coulda fooled me." When she opened her mouth again, his twisted. "Done jawin'. You comin' or not?"

"I would hope so. You haven't failed me yet."

He didn't roll his eyes, but she was sure it was damn close. "Woman..."

She grinned and whacked him in the gut with the back of her hand. "Okay, my stomach's growling."

A cell phone appeared in his hand, and he tapped away at the screen.

"Are you looking for another date already?

He shook his head and continued to type. "Makin' sure they got chicken for your sandwich and waffle fries."

"Seasoned waffle fries."

He finally glanced up. "Seasoned waffle fries."

"And if they don't?"

"Then their asses better find some before we get there."

"Are you a dick boss like Roger?"

"Nope."

"Should I ask your kitchen staff when we get there?"

"Nope. But I ain't their boss. Magnum is." A scowl twisted his lips. "Or is supposed to be."

"As president aren't you everyone's boss?"

He grunted.

"Just like I thought," she quipped.

He shook his head. "Let's go, woman."

As soon as she unlocked her driver's door, he opened it for her. As she climbed into her Highlander, she teased, "I'd say 'what a gentleman!' but we both know that would be a lie."

"Bet a gentleman can't eat your pussy as good as I could!" The exclamation point on that statement was him slamming her door shut.

Once he threw his long leg over his sled, she rolled down her window. "This better not be some kind of bait and switch." Yes, she was up for knocking boots with the sexy beast, but her stomach needed to be satisfied first.

His answer was him revving his Harley and jerking his chin toward the parking lot's exit.

Of course he was waiting for her to drive off. She shouldn't be surprised that he wanted to follow her to Dick's. Most likely to make sure she didn't change her mind and make a break for it.

Honestly, she didn't care who led the way as long as she got her free food and uncommitted sex. A surefire way for her to forget her shitty damn day.

Chapter Twenty-Eight

WHEN HE WALKED MADDIE OUT, Romeo purposely kept the spotlights off to prevent her departure from attracting any unwanted attention. With a pair of loose sweatpants hanging off his hips, he now stood barefoot on the concrete pad outside his door as she headed to her SUV.

Properly fed and fucked, of course. One side of his mouth pulled up. He gave her the president's special, all right.

The cooks managed to make her a respectable chicken sandwich and the waffle fries she'd been craving. Seasoned, of fucking course. Because of that, and a quick five-minute foot massage—during which she moaned and groaned as if she was having an intense orgasm—Romeo managed to have the woman he'd been craving.

She ended up satisfied... He ended up satisfied... He loved it when a plan came together.

With hands on his own hips and a full grin now curving his lips, he watched the swing of her hips before his gaze became glued to her swaying ass.

Maddie looked hot as fuck naked or dressed. He preferred the first, if anyone asked.

His heart stopped when he heard her call out, "Hey, Magnum," just as she reached her SUV.

Magnum?

For fuck's sake. So much for keeping Maddie's visit on the down-low. And if anyone was going to see her, he sure as hell didn't want it to be the Knights' sergeant at arms.

A large, dark figure appeared from the shadows with his focus on one thing...

Maddie.

Fuck. Fuck. Fuck.

He sucked in a deep breath to prepare, since his good night and relaxed mood was about to go to shit.

The natural high he got from fucking a gorgeous woman, was about to drop like a concrete block from a twelve-story building.

Unfortunately, he was caught red-handed unless he could come up with some sort of excuse that Magnum would buy. Romeo just wasn't sure if he was a good enough salesman.

Wait. Did she just give Magnum a wink? A fucking wink. Did he see that right? It *was* pretty damn dark out. It could've been a simple eye twitch. Like the one he had right now.

That had to be it.

"You can keep this little secret between us, right?" she asked the massive man as she climbed into her Highlander. When she didn't get a response, she continued with, "Great talk. See you later, Mag!"

Magnum didn't say shit to that, either. Instead, he only pointed his narrowed eyes in Romeo's direction. That he *could* see clearly, despite the lack of light.

"Fuck me," Romeo groaned as his club brother began to lumber in his direction the second Maddie drove away.

Christ.

"Need a word," Magnum growled.

Of fucking course he did. Romeo raised his chin. "Which one?"

The answer Romeo got for his smart-ass question wasn't the one he expected when he found himself slammed against the door of his place with a big paw gripping his throat tightly.

He didn't even need the flickering flame of a fucking Bic lighter to see the thunder on his enforcer's face.

Anyone else's asshole would be puckered so tightly it had grown shut about now, but Romeo knew enough to stay still and keep his cool. He might be a lot younger and not much smaller than Magnum, but he also wasn't a stupid fuck.

Anyway, this wasn't some random drunk at Dick's. Someone like that would be much easier to deal with. Instead of another beer, they got served with a fist to the face.

"What the fuck you doin', asshole? Really determined to piss off the Fury, ain't ya?"

Romeo kept his tone low and steady. "Gonna only say this once, brother... Get the fuck off me. You know fuckin' better than to put your goddamn hands on your prez."

As soon as Magnum's grip loosened enough for Romeo to push his hand away, he slipped to the side so his back was no longer pinned against the door. Being caged in was never a good position to be in.

By a fellow Knight or not.

"Maddie just asked you not to say shit, so who's gonna tell the Fury? You? Says a fuckin' lot about your fuckin' loyalty to your club *and* your prez."

Magnum's jaw shifted and he jabbed a finger in Romeo's direction. "Don't you ever question my loyalty to this fuckin' club. Been a member since before you were in goddamn diapers."

That might be true, but Romeo wasn't about to do the math.

"Tryin' to protect her and our fuckin' club, asshole. And if you wanna go there, also tryin' to protect you. Shade's gonna show up in the dead of goddamn night, slice your fuckin' throat, then my ass is gonna have to retaliate. That's gonna cause a fuckin' war. All 'cause you couldn't keep your fuckin' dick in your pants. Plenty of fuckin' pussy out there without havin' to wet your dick in that one." He tipped his bald head in the direction Maddie drove away.

"She came to me." At least the first time. And second. His enforcer didn't need to know about the rest.

"Don't give a fuck. There's a goddamn word that's only got two letters in it. Don't take much fuckin' effort to say it, even for a simple fuck like you. If she was lookin' for dick, you coulda told her no and sent her on her fuckin' way. But of course, you saw an easy opportunity to get laid and jumped on it."

"Ain't like that."

Magnum's eyebrows shot up his forehead. "No? You didn't take advantage of an easy target?"

"Don't think she'd appreciate you callin' her easy."

This time Magnum's finger jabbed him in the chest. Hard. "You're the easy one, dumbass, not her. You jumped on a goddamn opportunity you should've turned a fuckin' blind eye to."

"Have you seen her?" *Damn it.* He kept digging his own hole deeper every time his opened his trap.

"Used the wrong goddamn head, Rome. In the future, you got no choice but to say no. She shows up again, tell her no. Try it."

Magnum was not his goddamn babysitter. He wasn't Maddie's, either. "No."

"See? Ain't so hard. Unlike your dick."

"Was sayin' no to you, brother."

Magnum pursed his lips as he stared at him.

Romeo did not like that stare. "Got shit to do."

Magnum slapped a hand across Romeo's chest, stopping him from heading back inside. "You want her to wear your fuckin' cut?"

"No."

"See? You keep provin' you know how to use that fuckin' word. Here's the deal... You ain't willin' to scrape her off, then your ass better head north and have a meet with Trip. Then once you got his approval, you have a sit down with Shade. Or do it the other way 'round. Ask Shade first before you embarrass your Black ass in front of the Fury's exec committee when they tell you to fuck off."

"Just fuckin' said I ain't lookin' to fill that spot on the back of my damn sled. Your old ass must be hard of hearin'."

"Heard you just fuckin' fine. You know what to fuckin' do, so do it." He tipped his ear forward with his finger. "What was that word?"

"Fuck off."

"That'll work, too."

"Again, that was for you. Not her."

"Messin' with a good thing, Rome. Told you not to fuck it up. You're hell bent on doin' that."

"Makin' this a bigger deal than it is."

"You stickin' your dick in the property of another club is

a..." Magnum leaned in until they were almost nose-to-nose. He ground out, "Big. Fuckin'. Deal." He straightened. "Thought you were smarter than that. Now I know I was fuckin' wrong."

Ouch. "How much of a big fuckin' deal was it when you did it?"

When Magnum turned his head away, Romeo could see the man's jaw working. But he did have to agree with his brother. He'd been stupid.

Unfortunately, the result of that was, as soon as he was done fucking Maddie, he was ready to do it again. And again. Never in his goddamn life did he have an itch he couldn't scratch. That was what it felt like with her. He got the itch to fuck her and once he did, he felt relieved. But every damn time that itch came back with a fucking vengeance.

Even worse, and so fucking unlike him, he couldn't stop thinking about her. She was on his mind constantly, whether she was with him or not. He swore it was turning into some sort of sickness or something. Like a virus he couldn't kick.

"Got two choices. Leave her the fuck alone or go all in. And you know what goin' all in means... A ride north and a sit down."

He wasn't willing to do either. But for now, he'd keep that shit to himself.

What really chapped his ass was that his enforcer was supposed to listen to the club president, not the other way around. This whole thing was fucked up. "Thanks for the advice, brother. Gonna sleep on it."

"Better not wait too damn long to decide. Otherwise, if Shade finds out that you're doin' his girl behind his fuckin' back, you might not wake the fuck up."

"Noted."

Magnum grunted. "Guessin' you wrote that note in fuckin' crayon."

Romeo forced out a dry laugh. Maddie wasn't the only one thinking they're a comedian. "Nah. Invisible ink."

The Knights' enforcer shook his head and turned on his boot to leave. *Thank fuck.* As expected, the man totally fucked up Romeo's goddamn afterglow.

Just as he turned to go inside, he heard, "Rome," and glanced over his shoulder.

"Know it's fuckin' difficult for you but... don't fuck up an alliance that's been solid for fuckin' years over some pussy."

The problem was, to him, Maddie was far from "some pussy."

For some fucking reason, that idea disturbed him more than the conversation he just had with Magnum.

Romeo ground his teeth and headed inside.

He told Magnum he would sleep on it, but he didn't like anyone telling him what to do. Tonight was no damn different.

———

"I SHOULDN'T HAVE to remind you that it's a privilege to work here. As well as to work for me."

Maddie sat across from Roger in his office, trying her damnedest not to gag. As usual, her boss decided she'd committed some imagined deadly sin. Like greeting a patient in the wrong tone or some such crap.

"You seem to have forgotten that."

Maybe that was because she didn't see him as some golden calf. He wasn't worth worshipping like he thought he was. He was her boss, plain and simple.

The only problem was, how connected he was in the

world of professional sports. At least on the western side of Pennsylvania. Maddie was sure that none of the sports teams in the rest of the U.S. had ever heard of the jerk.

Roger was a legend in his own mind.

Sort of like Romeo.

But unfortunately, he *was* well-known around Pittsburgh in the sports circles, so she had to play nice. She swallowed the bile working its way up her throat to say, "I appreciate you giving me this job—"

"Did I indicate in some way that it's your turn to speak?"

Maddie clamped her teeth down on her tongue to keep from spewing how she really felt about the man sitting across the desk from her.

With a smug smirk on his very punchable face.

She reminded herself for the hundredth time that she only needed a little more experience under her belt so any team she applied for would take her more seriously. Despite her education, only having a little more than a year on the job, as well as her age, counted against her.

She understood it. Professional sports teams only wanted seasoned physical therapists. They didn't want to leave their highly paid athletes in the hands of someone without extensive experience.

As it was, those jobs were well sought after, and any opening would have a lot of applicants. Right now, with her level of experience, they most likely would file her resume in a round file—aka trash can—without even looking at it.

Roger's influence and recommendation would help hers get seen. Hence, her bloody tongue and forced smile.

She was ready for him to say whatever he wanted to say... meaning, he needed to hurry and write her up for whatever perceived wrong she did so she could remove herself from his presence.

Sitting in a closed office with the man was not on her top ten things to do.

In contrast, Romeo *was* on that to-do list.

What bugged her the most, she couldn't stop thinking about him. Especially after the last time they hooked up.

She had no idea what Roger was blabbing about since suddenly, she was taken back to two nights ago.

Holy shit. That foot massage, though... The one he gave her once her belly was full of surprisingly decent food. She didn't expect that from a true biker bar. Cold beer? Yes. Lots of whiskey flowing? Of course. Good food? A crapshoot.

Once she was sated with food, he began digging his thumbs into the bottoms of her feet. She wasn't ashamed to admit she almost orgasmed. Then, when he squeezed her aching toes, she just about melted into a puddle.

As a sports physical therapist, she did a lot of hands-on with patients and she doubted her massages were anywhere near that level.

The man had very strong, capable hands.

It could've also helped that he was buck naked while he manipulated her sore feet in the best way.

Unfortunately, it didn't last as long as she'd like. But then, if he'd kept going, she might have fallen asleep. It was that relaxing.

She quickly woke up when he worked his way up her body with a searing heat in his eyes and a naughty grin on his lips right before he...

A barked out, "Did you fall asleep?" had her jerking in her chair and her eyes flashing open.

Shit. "No, sorry. I have a headache." Roger was an expert at giving her one.

"You were groaning."

"Was I?" She squeezed her forehead and grimaced to make her lie look legit. "My head is pounding." More like she was getting lost in how well Romeo pounded her. Her pussy clenched from the memory.

Roger's office was the last place she should be getting horny. *Gross.* That should be enough to make her never want to have sex again.

Should be, but it didn't.

She snuck a glance at the clock on the wall behind him. The second hand was moving too damn slowly. This day needed to be over like yesterday. "Remind me again why I'm in here?"

Roger scowled across the desk at her. "It's your quarterly employee evaluation."

It was? She had lost track. Not that it mattered. He'd find some reason not to give her a raise, even if it was for only a measly five cents an hour. Though, if she *was* going to get a raise, he'd give her something like that simply out of spite.

Actually, she was surprised that Roger didn't charge his employees simply for the "privilege" of working at his business.

Narcissistic asshole.

"Has it really been a whole three months since the last one? Time flies when you love your job," she lied. She brushed a finger across her nose to make sure it hadn't grown.

As Roger went over her employee evaluation scores, she wasn't surprised at what they were. She also wasn't surprised that she didn't get a raise, but at least today he wasn't docking her pay with some bullshit excuse.

When her cell phone vibrated with an incoming text, she dipped her head and peeked at it, trying not to be obvious that she wasn't paying attention to the man on the other side of the desk.

Instead, she was paying attention to the man who sent the text.

Dinner and dick?

Well, look at that, she suddenly had a hankering for crispy waffle fries...

A five-minute foot massage...

And a Dark Knight to deliver all of that and more.

Chapter Twenty-Nine

SOMEONE NEEDED A FUCKING ATTITUDE ADJUSTMENT.

While in one way, Maddie hating her job kept driving her into his bed. In another, he saw her bottling up all that shit and that made him want to drive his fist into her boss's throat.

Romeo wanted to see that fucker on his knees gasping for air. Even better, begging for mercy. And not the Shadow named Mercy because if he got on that man's bad side, Roger Smith would both shit and piss in his panties at the same time.

Truthfully, Romeo didn't know who he'd rather meet in a dark alley: a pissed off Shade or Mercy.

Neither, if he had to choose.

While Magnum was a badass—even at his age—he most likely wouldn't slice you open from nuts to throat and then climb into your carcass to use you as a coat.

"Fuck," Romeo whispered, thinking about how savage both men could be.

Of course, they always had a valid reason to do what they did. Romeo made sure not to give either man a reason.

Wait...

His brain glitched when he wondered if doing Shade's stepdaughter without his knowledge would really trigger a response like that.

Would fucking Maddie be a death sentence? Magnum believed it would, but Romeo had no clue how Shade's twisted mind actually worked.

As for Smith, he only wanted to crush the man's windpipe until the asshole learned a lesson on how to treat his damn employees. Even though Romeo only cared about one in particular.

The one who came to his place very tense—now on a regular basis—and, after Romeo's type of therapy, left very fucking relaxed. He was tasked with undoing any damage Smith caused Maddie.

Every time she had shown up in the last few weeks, she arrived earlier and stayed later. While that meant more sex with her, it also meant more shared meals and words.

Crazy enough, while not his normal routine when it came to women, he had actually begun to look forward to it.

His grin was quickly wiped from his face when he spotted movement out of the corner of his right eye.

Just the man he'd been waiting for.

While he had considered wearing something to conceal his identity, like a mask or similar, in the end, he decided he wanted Smith to know exactly who was delivering the important message.

His only concern about this special visit was if Maddie ended up fired. If she did, she'd probably never forgive him, and he'd never get to taste or fuck her again.

That disturbing thought almost kept him seated in the

cage he'd borrowed. If he ever wanted the opportunity to dip his dick into Maddie's sweet, wet pussy again and watch her face as she orgasmed, he should drive away and leave the whole situation alone like she insisted.

He should.

But he wouldn't.

Romeo might benefit from Smith being a bastard, but that didn't mean he'd let Maddie's boss continue to go unchecked. He was ticked every damn time he entered her apartment, or she walked into his place with her spirit crushed.

He had done time in the joint. He had seen fellow inmates get beat down. Not physically, but mentally. Her working at Smith's shouldn't be similar to doing a bid in prison.

It wasn't capital punishment; it was a goddamn job.

So, *yeah*, a little attitude adjustment was on the menu tonight. If Maddie felt the need to continue working there in order to help advance her career, then she needed a better environment to work in. Meaning, if she wouldn't leave Smith's, then Smith's had to change.

Romeo was bound and determined to help make that happen.

After unfolding his body from the driver's seat, he took long strides across the unlit parking lot. Of course, driving anything with more than two wheels, he had removed his cut. He left it in the cage after deciding it was best not to advertise his MC.

This little late-night visit didn't have dick to do with the Knights, anyway. It wasn't club business, this was personal.

Romeo figured if Smith saw him approaching, he'd either run, hide, or call the pigs. Because of that, he purposely dressed in all black, including wearing a do-rag on his sometimes-reflective bald head, and kept to the shadows as he moved quickly, but quietly, to catch up.

He must not have been careful enough, because when Smith glanced over his shoulder, Romeo knew he was made. He increased his pace at the same time Smith took off in a jog.

For fuck's sake, he wasn't expecting to break out in a damn sweat tonight. This was supposed to be a "catch and release" operation, not a chase.

A fleeting realization filled his gray matter... He should've hired Mercy to deliver the message so Romeo could stay anonymous.

But he was a cheap ass and, anyway, it was too fucking late. Now he needed to follow through and deliver that message. One Smith needed to receive loud and clear.

Just as Romeo got about five feet away from the fleeing business owner, Smith stopped suddenly and spun to face him. "What do you want?"

Should he be satisfied that the whites of the man's eyes were so damn wide that they were blinding?

"You!" Smith yelled when he recognized Romeo. "Mad's friend, the thug."

Say fuckin' what? Forget the part where the asshole called her "Mad" after Romeo warned him about that. "Callin' me a fuckin' thug?"

"Why else would you be hunting me down?"

"For a simple discussion," Romeo lied, taking small, slow steps closer. He was trying not to spook Smith since he wasn't in the mood to sprint after this fucker wearing his heavy boots.

"About what?"

"About the way you treat your fuckin' employees."

Smith's eyebrows stitched together. "How the hell is that

any of your business? If they don't think they're being treated well, they are free to get a job elsewhere. I'm not forcing them to stay."

"Ain't you?"

For every step Romeo took toward Smith, the other man took one backward, not realizing he had a wall behind him.

Stupid? Hell yes, but the fuck if Romeo would warn him. Instead, he would use that mistake to his full advantage.

His hand shot out in a blur and his fingers wrapped tightly around the man's throat. He used that grip to slam Smith against the wall. The same way Magnum had done to him a few weeks ago.

The satisfying sounds of air being forcefully pushed from Smith's lungs hit Romeo's ears. Seconds later, Smith's Adam's apple shifted under his palm.

"Take your hand off my neck."

Did Smith think he was in the position to make demands? It was time to prove otherwise. Instead of loosening his grip, Romeo tightened it. "No one's stoppin' you from removin' it."

Was Maddie's boss trying to swallow? Was he struggling to breath?

Too fucking bad.

Smith yanked at Romeo's wrist and tried to peel his fingers free, but Romeo was stronger.

More determined.

And, if anyone gave a fuck enough to ask, pissed.

One thing was for sure, he was tired of seeing Maddie beat down. And the man causing that was now in Romeo's hands.

When Smith tried to pull free again, he only cracked his own head against the brick wall.

That had to hurt.

Damn shame.

The grin he wore earlier slid right back into place. "So... Got a reason to treat your employees like shit? Besides the obvious one that you're a dick."

A croak was the only answer he heard.

Romeo turned his head until his ear was closer. "Didn't get that."

Smith's mouth opened and closed like a fish out of water.

If he had to admit it, his chokehold might not be helping this discussion. "If I loosen my grip, you gonna run? Before you answer, just a warnin'... gonna have a discussion whether you wanna or fuckin' not. Ain't gonna be able to escape it. If it ain't now, it's gonna be later. Promise you that."

All he heard was a gurgle.

Romeo loosened his grip slightly. "What's that?"

Again, he heard nothing but a strangled noise.

"Glad to hear you're agreeable and are up for a little convo. So, this is how it's fuckin' gonna go. Gonna release you and we're going to continue this discussion like two fuckin' men. Don't disappoint me by runnin' off like a little bitch. Got it?"

Smith managed a slight nod.

Romeo stared at him for a few more seconds, just knowing the asshole was going to run, before releasing Smith's throat and taking a step back. He was ready to knock the fucker to the ground, if needed. And Smith couldn't outrun a bullet. Not that Romeo was going to admit he was packing.

But at this point, the motherfucker hadn't done anything to warrant a death sentence. Now, if he had put his hands on Maddie... That would be a whole different story.

"I don't know who the hell you think you are, but I have a lot of friends in high places and you're going to regret this."

"Huh. 'Magine that. I got friends in low places and ain't lyin' when I say my friends are fuckuva lot scarier than yours. But ain't here for a dick sizin' contest. Only want to have a word."

"You could've called."

"Nah, Roge, doubt you woulda answered. And anyway, this needed to be face-to-face."

"I have nothing to discuss with you."

"Don't got the same opinion."

"I have to get home," Maddie's boss insisted.

As he went to move away, Romeo slapped his hand across Smith's chest—the same way Magnum did to him—to stop him. "Only need a few minutes of your time."

"I don't have a few minutes."

"Ain't askin', Roge."

"I was right to call you a thug."

Romeo let that slide. He didn't give a fuck what Roger Smith thought of him. He cared more about how the fucker treated Maddie. He wanted Maddie to be happy while Smith wanted her to be miserable.

The asshole got pleasure out of doing that. It was a whole damn power trip for him. Power that needed to be stripped from the pussy-ass bitch before him.

"Since you're in a fuckin' rush, lemme get to the point... You treat my girl like fuckin' shit." *Damn*, did he just call Maddie *his girl*? Had he lost his damn mind?

That had to be it.

"You know who else don't like you treatin' her like shit?" He paused. "Her family." He wouldn't mention that the Fury considered her family and if they found out about Smith's treatment of Maddie, they'd be having a conversation with him, too. Only he didn't need to mention that whole MC, just one particular member... "Ever meet her stepdaddy?"

His answer of "no" came out strained, like his windpipe had been bruised or something.

"Be glad you haven't. Only'll take one word to him, and he'll infiltrate your nightmares. Take my fuckin' word, you don't want that."

"You aren't doing her any favors by assaulting me."

"Didn't assault you. Not yet, anyway. Only havin' a discussion man-to-man. Don't gimme a reason to show you the difference 'tween talkin' and you endin' up not talkin' 'cause your jaw's broken."

"You'll end up in jail."

Romeo shrugged. "Nothin' new. But here's the thing... I'd still be breathin'. Unlike you."

"Are you threatening me?"

"Like I said, ain't me you gotta worry 'bout. Consider me the calm before the fuckin' shit storm. You don't want that shit storm, Roge. Promise you that. You might got connections but so does she."

"What the hell does that mean?"

"Exactly what I said, so I'm gonna make a suggestion you should heed... Gotta treat her and the rest of your employees better. Treat 'em with respect. Give them good references."

"I don't have to do anything you say."

Romeo went on like Smith hadn't said a word. He leaned in closer and dropped his voice an octave to make his point. "Maddie hasn't left your abusive ass 'cause she thinks you're gonna tank her career. That true? You hold that shit over her?"

"She doesn't have a career to tank."

"Bullshit. She's doin' time with you so she can move on to bigger and better things. You know what those are to her?"

Smith nodded. "She has this mistaken notion that she'll get hired by a professional sports team. They're never going to give her a first glance, forget a second. She's too much of a screw up."

"Then why didn't you fire her if she sucks so bad?"

Smith pinned his lips together.

"Thought so," Romeo continued. "Just talkin' out your ass and tryin' to control her. So, here's what you're gonna do to make up for that... You're gonna put in a good word for her with your friends. Her dream job is workin' for the Steelers. See she gets that."

Smith grimaced. "I can't get her a job with—"

"Steelers don't got a spot for her yet, then check with the Penguins. Or the Pirates. Get her in where she'll get her name known with those overpaid athletes. Or hell, give her a fuckin' choice."

Smith's eyebrows jerked up his forehead. "You think I have that kind of power?"

Maddie thought so. That was the whole reason she kept working for this motherfucker, so it had to be true. She wouldn't continue to torture herself if it wasn't. Unless he'd been running his mouth, and it was all a damn lie.

Narcissists did tend to lie often.

"Don't you? Didn't you just brag about having friends in high places?"

Smith's mouth dropped open. "I meant in law enforcement."

"Here you are lyin' to me again, Roge," Romeo said in a very low tone.

Did the asshole turn even more lily white? Good.

"Why do you think she's good enough for them to hire?"

"You sayin' she sucks at her job? You keep her on, so that sounds like another fuckin' lie. Don't like liars, Roge."

"My name is Roger."

"Don't like your name bein' shortened? Well, neither

does Maddie." Romeo drilled a finger into his chest. "Don't call her Mad again. Last warning."

"I'm done with this conversation. You didn't do Madison any favors by having it."

"Once you lay your head down on your pillow tonight, Roge, I'm sure you'll go over this conversation in your head and realize what you need to do. So, do it."

Smith shook his head and when he went to escape, Romeo didn't stop him this time. Instead, he remained where he stood and watched Smith power walk to his prissy sports car.

One side of Romeo's mouth pulled up after witnessing Smith looking back over his shoulder several times.

As soon as Smith got into his cage and sped away, Romeo's lips pursed.

That didn't go quite as planned. Did he get his message across? Or did he just fuck shit up for Maddie?

And if he did, who would regret it more?

Chapter Thirty

The second Maddie stepped through the door at Smith's Sports Therapy & Rehab Center to get her daily dose of verbal abuse, Maribeth called her over to the receptionist desk.

"Do I have a new patient?" If so, Romeo better not have sent another Knight with a fake injury.

The receptionist shook her head. "Unfortunately, no. Roger wants to see you immediately in his office."

What?

Her stomach lurched and she hoped the oatmeal she ate for breakfast didn't make a reappearance. "Did he say why?"

Maribeth quickly masked her expression. That wasn't promising. "No. He only told me that you need to go see him before your first patient arrives."

"He's in early," Maddie murmured, glancing toward the back of the building. Where Roger's office was. Where the miserable man waited.

The receptionist's eyebrows rose. "Tell me about it. He was here before I even opened this morning."

Holy shit. That was not a good sign. Roger never came in early. He usually strode in whenever he damn well pleased.

But him demanding that she come to his office first thing...

She quickly ran over all the patients she worked with yesterday in her mind. As well as everything she said to them and her co-workers. She must have done something wrong. Only, she didn't know what.

Plus, if he only wanted to insult her, he had no qualms about doing that on the floor in front of everyone. So, whatever he wanted to speak to her about in private couldn't be good.

Knowing Roger, it was most likely really, *really* bad.

Maddie jumped when Maribeth's desk phone rang. The receptionist didn't greet whoever it was, but a few seconds later only said, "She's on her way back now," into the receiver and hung up before shooting Maddie a sympathetic look.

Shit.

She was sure Roger came up with another stupid reason to dock her pay. That meant her paycheck would once again be light. That also meant she'd be financially short to pay her bills. Again.

She didn't know how he continually got away with doing so. Maybe she needed to talk to an attorney with extensive knowledge of labor laws. She wouldn't be surprised if Roger was breaking at least one of them. Most likely he was breaking a slew.

With a hand pressed to her churning stomach, she gave Maribeth a stiff nod and headed toward the rear of the building, dodging equipment, and hoping she didn't leave a trail of undigested oatmeal.

She was damn sure Roger would dock her pay if she got sick while out on the floor.

When she reached his office, the door was shut so she tentatively rapped on it with a single knuckle.

"It's open," she heard barked through the door.

Great. He already sounded cranky.

She pulled in a deep breath, opened the door and quickly stepping through.

"Shut it behind you."

She did, then turned to face the man sitting behind the desk in his big office like he was sitting on a throne. All he needed was a crown and scepter to complete the pompous look.

Good lord, she detested this man with her whole heart and soul.

As she went to settle in one of the chairs across the desk from him, Roger stopped her with, "Don't bother sitting. You won't be in here long."

Her heart was thumping so hard, she was damn sure Roger could both see and hear it. Unfortunately, he'd probably be pleased with how nervous she was since the man thrived off fear and misery. He enjoyed making his employees jump and squirm. As well as apologize and grovel for things they supposedly did.

She clasped her hands together to prevent rubbing her sweaty palms on her khakis, and waited.

Roger only had a single folder sitting next to his oversized monitor. In his hand was a pen—one of those expensive fountain pens—that he was tapping the end on the desk.

Tap. Tap. Tap.

"You wanted to see me?" she asked.

Tap. Tap. Tap.

Every tap set her teeth on edge, but she supposed that was why he was doing it.

"I didn't want to, but you left me no choice."

What the hell did *that* mean?

"Your friend visited me last night."

Her friend?

"More like cornered and confronted me."

She frowned. "Who?" It couldn't be Shade since her stepfather had no idea what was happening to her at work. She planned to keep it that way.

Wait. Romeo had better not have tipped Shade off—

"Marvin Carter. The one who faked an injury and wasted my therapist's time."

Oh shit. What did Romeo do now?

Of course she knew what he did. Stuck his nose where she didn't want it. Now *she* was in the hot seat because of something *he* did.

Son of a bitch!

Maybe she could save herself. "He's not my friend."

Roger cocked a single eyebrow. "Really. He called you *his girl.*"

Her mouth fell open. He did *what?* "I'm not his girl. Are you sure he was talking about me?"

"You're the only one who works for me with the lofty dreams of working for a professional sports team."

Her heart seized. He mentioned that? To Roger? Why?

"He demanded I put in a good word for you."

Oh no. She bit back a groan.

"I *will* put in a word but not a good one. I can promise you, after that violent attack last night, you'll never work around here again."

For a violent attack, Roger sure looked fine.

"I'll make sure every door is slammed in your face before you even have a chance to open them. And your dream of working for a Pittsburgh team?" Roger huffed out a breath. "Not a chance. You blew it."

Her oatmeal was slowly and dangerously bubbling up her throat. She swallowed, trying to keep it contained. Though, Roger deserved a whole bowl of regurgitated oatmeal spewed over his perfectly neat desk.

Her boss jabbed a finger in her direction. "You're fired. You will not be getting any kind of severance package, nor will you be getting your last paycheck. You have five minutes to collect your personal belongings and leave. If you dally, I'll have the police escort you out."

"But—"

Roger gave her "the palm," shook his head, pulled a piece of paper from the folder, and slid it across his desk. "I listed all the reasons why you've been terminated. Don't even bother to file for unemployment. I made sure it'll be denied."

The blood drained from her face. She wouldn't be able to get unemployment compensation?

This man was beyond cruel.

She couldn't survive without any kind of income coming in. In a week or two, she'd be homeless, starving and living under a damn bridge in a cardboard box.

Holy shit, what was she going to do?

Roger tapped his Rolex. "Five minutes. That starts now."

She swiped her termination memo off his desk and the second she ripped open the door to leave, she heard behind her, "And, Mad... Don't take anything that doesn't belong to you."

Like she wanted anything of his.

Fuck him. Fuck this place.

And, dammit, fuck Romeo for causing this.

She stepped out but she had one more thing to say... Turning, she crumpled up her pink slip, tossed it toward the desk, flipped him the double bird and added a, "Fuck you," before slamming the door shut.

She had nothing in this place she wanted to take with her.

Not a damn thing.

Not even memories.

Twenty minutes later, she sat in her vehicle in Dirty Dick's parking lot, staring at the bar, and gripping the steering wheel so tightly, she was wishing it was Romeo's neck instead.

Because of him, she just wasted a year and a half at Smith's. A whole damn year and a half of dealing with Roger's bullshit. For what? For it all to be gone in an instant?

This was all Romeo's fault. He went against her request not to get involved.

Men! They always thought they knew better. All he ended up doing was screwing up everything.

Now she had no job and no possibility of landing her dream job. All because of his bullshit.

She never should've gotten involved with him in the first place. She *knew* it was a mistake. She went against her gut and because of that, ended up the loser in this scenario.

The sex had been great but not enough to make it worth him blowing up her future. And that's exactly what he did by threatening Roger. Or whatever Romeo did.

Since it was still early, she had no idea if he would be in Dick's, still in bed or out and about. She didn't even know if the biker had a damn regular job. She couldn't imagine that being the president of the Dark Knights paid well, if at all.

Trip didn't get any kind of compensation in exchange for all the heartburn he got from being the Blood Fury's president. Neither did Zak with the Dirty Angels.

It didn't matter. None of that mattered. What mattered right now was confronting Romeo about his screw up.

As soon as she climbed out of her Highlander, she was

taking long strides to Dick's front door. The second she was inside; she surveyed the mostly empty interior looking for the man. She went directly to the bar, where a Knight with a name patch declaring him Sigh stood tracking her approach.

"Where's Romeo?"

"Who's askin'?"

"A woman very pissed at him right now."

Sigh chuckled. "Nothin' new. Guess you expected more than a one-night stand with him?"

"No. I expected nothing from him but to stay out of my damn business." Her voice got louder, and Sigh's eyebrows inched higher, with each word she uttered. By the end she was practically screaming and Sigh was grinning like a fool.

"You call him?" the amused Knight asked.

No, because she wanted to face him in person. She didn't want to hear his bullshit excuses over the phone. She wanted to be able to read his expressions. Maybe even kick him in the balls. "I take it he's not here, then."

Sigh shrugged. "Maybe. Maybe not. He ain't wearin' an ankle monitor, so he's not being tracked."

What? She shook her head. "Is he in his place?"

"Again, maybe—"

Maddie cut him off with a "stop talking" palm. The same as Roger gave her. With another impatient shake of her head, she pulled out her phone, found his number in her favorites— that would be changing soon—and called him.

After two rings, he picked up and before he could say a word, she demanded, "Where are you?"

Silence greeted her.

"Rome," she growled into the phone. "Where the hell are you?"

"Shouldn't you be at work?"

He had the balls to ask her that? "Maybe I am at work."

"When did they start playin' Dr. Dre? Figured that fuck only like classical."

Dr. Dre?

She paused and realized he was talking about the song *I Need a Doctor* playing in the background in the bar. She always thought it was an Eminem song. *Huh.*

She groaned. That was neither here nor there at this moment. "Where are you?"

"A few yards behind you."

Chapter Thirty-One

HE HAD JUST PULLED into Dick's lot on his sled when he spotted her Highlander. It was hard to miss at this hour in the morning when their customers were few and far between. His ringing phone displayed Maddie's number.

Apparently, she wanted a word with him.

Once he answered and entered Dick's, he spotted her standing near Sigh. When he was within a few feet, she spun with the phone still glued to her ear.

His gut twisted when her eyes narrowed on him.

Something was wrong if she was here this early. She should be at work—

Fuckin' fuck.

"Want a beer, brother?" Amusement colored Sigh's tone. "Or maybe a helmet and one of those plastic cups to protect your nuts?"

Ignoring his brother, Romeo snagged Maddie's elbow in a firm grip, causing her to lurch forward and her phone to be dislodged from her ear.

"Let me go," she hissed like a pissed off cat.

"Once we're in private," he ground out through clenched teeth. "Let's go."

"Why? You don't want to have this discussion in the middle of your bar?"

"No idea why you're here." Even though he had a damn good guess. "But whatever it is ain't anyone's business," he finished on a mutter.

Clearly, the woman was pissed. Not only pissed, he could see her eyes were red and puffy, like she'd been crying.

Of fuckin' course. He was hoping he was wrong, and she was here about something else, but his gut was telling him differently. Trying to help her out last night was about to bite him in the fucking ass. Not a sexy bite, either. This one was going to leave a scar.

He didn't need to wonder how much damage he did because he was damn sure he was about to find out. Only, not in Dick's. Not in front of his brothers, any sweet butts or the couple of early customers sitting at the bar. Of course, the few sets of eyes in the establishment were already turned their way.

"In your cage? Or my place?" he suggested.

"You sure you don't want to have this discussion right here?" She stabbed her finger toward the floor.

He lowered his voice. "Better we don't. C'mon. Let's go out back."

When he steered her toward Dick's kitchen, Sigh yelled out, "Should I send a rescue team if you don't return in a half hour?"

"Gimme ten," Romeo told him.

"He won't need ten," Maddie assured Sigh. "This will be quick."

That could be good. Could be bad. He steeled himself for the latter.

Since it was too early for the kitchen to be open, it was quiet as they worked their way through and headed back outside. It was better out there than inside since less eyes and ears would be on them.

As soon as they stood behind the building, he asked, "What's goin' on?"

"What's going on?" Her shrill voice made him grimace. "What did you do, Romeo?"

He pressed his lips together.

For fuck's sake. This discussion was about to give him heartburn.

He quickly ran through some scenarios to see how he could get out of the hot seat. Though, he was pretty sure that would be impossible.

Her expression said it all.

"What the hell did you do? And why? I told you to stay out of it. I also told you this would happen if you didn't!" she cried out, slamming him in the chest with both palms. The impact forced him back a step before he had the chance to brace himself.

He didn't give a shit that she shoved him. He was more concerned that her voice was now thick with sadness and disappointment. Add in the betrayal on her face and she might as well have stabbed him in the heart.

He kept his voice low and steady to try to keep the powder keg standing before him from exploding and leaving behind scorched earth. "Tell me what happened," he urged, even though he knew.

"I got fired."

His head twitched.

"All because of you. He'll have me blackballed."

That motherfucker. "Bullshit."

Her jaw dropped and her dark eyes went wide. "Bullshit? Do you think I'm lying?"

"No—"

"Do you think *he's* lying?"

That question was so sharp Romeo was surprised he wasn't bleeding out.

Before he could respond, she continued. "You fucked up, Rome. Big time. Now I don't have a job and most likely my career will have a permanent black mark on it. Not only that, but my dream of working with the Steelers will never happen, all because of you! You made sure I didn't even get a fair shot!"

Tears welled up in her eyes. As one spilled over, she swiped angrily at it.

"You do realize that I only put up with his abuse to help my career? A whole damn year and a half and it only took you a few minutes to screw that up. Whatever you did to him made my life and career crash and burn."

"Was tryin' to help, Maddie, not fuck shit up." He reached out to brush away the now steady stream of tears rolling down her cheeks, but before he could, she slapped his hand away.

"No. Don't act like you care, Rome. You don't care about anyone but yourself. You're no better than him!"

His head jerked back, and the knife jammed in his heart twisted painfully. "Was tryin' to help you."

He wasn't sure how to undo his fuck up. Make Smith disappear before he had the opportunity to fuck up Maddie's future?

Jesus.

"Well, you failed. I'm not sure why you'd think assaulting my boss would help! Who does that?" She lifted a hand. "Oh wait. Someone who can't control their impulses, that's who.

Someone who doesn't respect me enough to take what I say into account. I'm just a woman. What do I know, right? I need a big, bad biker to solve my problems because I'm not strong enough to solve them myself."

He unclenched his jaws. "He fuckin' didn't respect you, Maddie. Even kept callin' you by a name you don't like. He treated you like shit. Who fuckin' puts up with that?"

Fuck, was he digging himself a bigger hole?

"Me, the fool, apparently." She shook her head and pressed both fists into her tear-filled eyes. "Just like I'm a fool for ever dealing with you. I thought you of all people wouldn't get involved with my life. Boy, was I wrong, as well as stupid. You guys can't help yourself, can you?"

Damn. "Made your point," he murmured.

When she dropped her fists, her expression had turned hard. "I don't think I have, but here it is, loud and clear... Leave me the hell alone. Don't call me. Don't stop by. Don't even think about me. You've done enough and I don't need any more of your so-called help. This was only supposed to be casual sex, Rome. That's it. I didn't want anyone trying to rule my life. Or even stick their nose into it. You did it anyway without my consent and now look where I'm at."

"Maddie..." When he reached for her, she quickly moved away.

"I told you to let it go, Rome." She pounded a fist against her thigh. Not once, not twice, but too many times to count. Maybe it was so she wouldn't punch him instead. "This is exactly why I never wanted to get involved with a biker. Thanks for the reminder. I'll make sure not to make that mistake again."

"It wasn't supposed to go like that—"

Her head tipped to the side. "You know what I haven't heard yet? A damn apology. You know why? Because you guys don't want to admit when you're wrong. Not that saying sorry will undo the damage. It won't." With another shake of her head, she stormed past him.

"Maddie!" When she didn't stop and disappeared around the corner of the building, he muttered, "Goddamn it."

He rubbed at his forehead because he was getting a damn headache.

Even if gave her an apology, he doubted she'd want to hear it anyway. Right now, she was too damn pissed. He needed to give her some space and wait until she cooled off so he could explain that he hadn't gotten her fired on purpose.

That hadn't been his intent.

Did he want her working at Smith's? Fuck no.

Did he want to screw up her career? Also no.

Did he really have to pay Smith another visit? Probably. Maybe the asshole would take her back if Romeo ate a little humble fucking pie. He hated that flavor but would force a piece down if only for Maddie and to make up for his fuck up.

Once again, he realized his biggest mistake.

He shouldn't have been a cheap ass and should've stayed anonymous by hiring Mercy to pay Smith a visit.

Yeah, he should've handled it a whole different way and kept his hands clean.

His fucking mistake.

One he wouldn't make again.

———

HE WAITED A FEW HOURS—LONG enough for her to cool off a bit—before shooting her a text.

He did something he rarely ever did... Apologized.

Fucked up. Sorry.

All he got in return was radio silence. Maybe a few hours wasn't long enough. He might have to wait a few days.

For fuck's sake, he didn't want that.

Her tears had killed him. She had her heart set on working for a well-known sports team and he broke that heart.

He thought he'd done right by her when he resisted putting his hands on her boss—now former boss—at least to the point of causing any injury. What he did was only supposed to be a warning.

He didn't want to get her fired. He only wanted Smith to start treating Maddie better. Treat her like she deserved. She did not deserve to be abused by her damn boss and stressed out to the point she had to find relief by having sex with a man.

Of course, he benefitted from that stress, and he was the lucky one to help her relieve it. But she could've gone to any fucking man.

His lip curled at the possibility of her picking someone other than him. The thought of Maddie getting dick from someone else burned deep in his gut. Of having orgasms from some other asshole.

Goddamn it.

The truth was, she could've gone anywhere. But she had come to *him*.

Because she trusted him enough to do so.

The same way she had trusted him enough to take her virginity.

He broke that trust. Now he had to fix it.

Even if she didn't want that.

Even if she stuck to her guns about him staying out of her life.

He got it.

She was pissed. She was hurt. She was worried about her future. And, as expected, how she'd pay her bills until she found another job.

"Stupid fuck," he muttered under his breath as he got off his sled.

He stared at his house. He didn't need to go inside to know it was empty. Just like his goddamn soul.

He should've told her no. Just like Magnum insisted. He should've sent her on her way. Told her to run fast and far from him.

He had never been good at doing the right thing.

The evidence of that was obvious.

Maddie was right. He was a selfish fuck. He only thought about himself.

Her situation was the first time he hadn't. And, of course, he fucked that up.

Maddie said what he did was a good reminder why she didn't want to deal with bikers. Her reaction was a good reminder why he didn't like strings.

He choked on them.

Maybe he only needed to snip those fucking strings and simply let her go.

That would be the best thing. For her. For him.

Even for the alliance.

He hated that Magnum was right.

As he pulled his keys from the front pocket of his jeans, he paused when he heard a rustle nearby.

It could be an animal. A bird or a squirrel.

Fuck. Did they come out at night? He was no wildlife expert. What if it was a skunk?

Squinting, he searched the shadows while listening carefully.

Why the fuck was he still standing there? It was safer

inside where he had plenty of beer, a bong, and a baseball bat.

Only six steps away from the door, he heard something again. This time it sounded like the crunch of gravel underneath feet.

That was either one big fucking skunk or another type of animal.

One with two feet instead of four.

He reached for his cell phone to turn on the flashlight app but before he had a good grip on it, something came at him hard and fast.

Romeo didn't even get a chance to react before he found himself not only on his knees, but unable to breathe.

Chapter Thirty-Two

THAT WAS no goddamn skunk unless the striped bastard knew how to use a fucking tire iron.

He could safely say it wasn't a fucking squirrel, either.

But it *was* a pack of animals. He had no idea how many because he was now on the ground unable to get up, unable to see shit since warm liquid was blinding him.

Not tears. Thicker, like blood.

Something hard had knocked his brain loose and his head now pounded in time with his racing heart.

He needed to get up and either fight back... or escape.

Was he going to fucking die behind Dick's and only a few yards from his own damn door?

As soon as he tried to clear the blood from his eyes and right the tilting, spinning world, something slammed into his gut, dropping him flat to the ground again.

Jesus fuckin' Christ.

He couldn't even catch a damn breath when the hits kept coming. One after the other, after the other. Were they all taking a shot at him? Like a fucking piñata? The only problem was, if they broke him open, they would not find any damn candy.

He tried to roll into a ball to at least protect his most vulnerable places, but the pain only became even more unbearable when he moved. He probably had broken bones and shit.

Whoever was surrounding him was shouting at him, too, but he couldn't clear his head enough to figure out what they yelled. Not that he gave a fuck right now since he was too busy trying to stay alive.

If he survived, he'd get answers. One way or another.

A random thought made it through to his fuzzy brain. Did Maddie have the Fury come down to kick his ass?

Was one of them Shade?

Was she that fucking pissed at him? If so, while he deserved her anger, she was taking it to a whole other level.

Women could be damn good at revenge. Sometimes they were more dangerous than men.

A few seconds later he was being dragged across the ground. His arms and legs were useless to fight it. *Hell*, he couldn't lift his arms enough to cover his head to avoid the blows.

They were breaking him piece by piece.

He'd never been so goddamn helpless in his life.

The last time he'd been jumped like this was in prison. At the time, he'd been warned by his cellie that it was coming. That gave him enough time to prepare and plan a counterattack.

Unlike then, he had no warning this time.

Being behind Dick's, his only hope was that a Knight or an employee would step out back, see the fuck what was going on and get help.

Whether he continued breathing or not, he wanted these

fuckers identified. If someone killed the Knights' prez, his brothers would be out for revenge. Even if it ended up being the Fury teaching Romeo a fucked up "lesson."

He wasn't sure how long the attack lasted. It could've been a minute. It could've been ten.

Romeo's last lucid thought was that it sure as fuck seemed like an eternity.

———

ROMEO BLINKED. A bright light made him wince and close his eyes again.

With a groan, he lifted a single eyelid to double check.

When you died, you were supposed to walk toward the bright light, right?

Wait. Did he actually qualify to get through the pearly gates?

No fucking way.

Or was it a trick? An attempt to lure him to follow the light and then once the gates were slammed shut behind him, he'd find himself in a very hot spot? Burning for all eternity?

That would suck.

Fuck the light. He was going to resist for as long as he could. He wasn't going willingly. He would have to be dragged kicking and screaming—

"Romeo!"

God or Satan, he couldn't tell which, had a very familiar voice.

Damn, they were trying to trick him by using Wick's voice. He wasn't falling for it.

"Rome!"

"Not goin'," he moaned. "Fuck off." Why did it even hurt to talk? Or, *hell,* breathe?

What the fuck? Why was he feeling pain at all? He was dead. He wanted a goddamn refund if you still suffered after death.

"Rome! Wake up before I hafta call a fuckin' ambulance."

What? Shouldn't it be the coroner?

"You ain't Wick." Even saying those three words was a damn struggle.

"Who am I?"

"The fuckin' devil."

"Been called that before."

When he lifted his eyelids again, a sharp, shooting pain caused his brain to throb. "You're tryin' to trick me with that light."

"It's my fuckin' phone, you dumbass."

"Why do you need a—" He tried to block the blinding light with this hand, but his arms weighed too much for him to lift. "Am I dead?"

"Sure don't sound like it. Checked your pulse and you still got one. And since you're bein' a dick, my uneducated guess is no, you ain't dead."

That would explain the unbearable agony in every inch of his body. Or at least in the parts he still could feel.

He'd been in plenty of fights, including bar fights and prison brawls. Never had it hurt this fucking bad.

"Should get you to the hospital, anyway."

"Should but won't."

"Not sure you got a choice, prez."

"Always got a choice."

"Sure, a choice of life or fuckin' death. Could have internal injuries. Brain could be bleedin'. Lungs punctured. Who the fuck knows?"

"When the fuck did you turn into an EMT?" Every damn word uttered was a chore.

Wick huffed and threw up his hands. "Whatever, brother. Just so you know, you look like week-old roadkill right now. Musta done somethin' stupid to spark this. Got every fuckin' right to continue to be a dumbass."

Romeo could agree with that. He was a dumbass, but not because he didn't want to get medical attention. "Call Sparky."

Sparky, a fellow Knight, was also a volunteer firefighter. He sometimes could pull off some medical shit in a pinch. Stitches, cleaning up wounds from fights, pulling debris out of road rash... That kind of shit.

Romeo wouldn't trust him to do brain surgery. Or a vasectomy.

Wick huffed, "Sparky ain't a miracle worker."

With that remark, Romeo was damn sure it had to be ugly. "Don't give a fuck. Tell him to meet me at my place. He can patch me up."

"How the fuck are you gettin' to your place?"

The only thing he could move right now was his eyeballs, so he glanced in the direction of his crib and judged the distance. It was close as fuck but he doubted he could even crawl those few feet. "You're gonna help me. After you call Sparky."

Wick shook his head. "Ain't callin' Sparky. Takin' you to the hospital, Rome. And we're wastin' time by you bein' so goddamn stubborn. Your fuckin' arm's at angles I ain't never seen before and never want to see again. Got a bone stickin' out of your thigh and your boot's backward. Got blood everywhere. A goddamn butterfly bandage and a kiss on your boo-boo ain't gonna fix what you got broken."

"Gonna be pissed if you take me anywhere other than my place."

"What the fuck you gonna do, hit me?" Wick snorted. He took a step back and challenged, "Get up and try it."

The second Romeo tried to push past the pain to do just that...

He lost the fucking fight.

Again.

————

THE ANNOYING SOUNDS. The unnatural smells. The eye-searing lights.

It might not be hell, but it was damn close.

He forced open his eyes again and shifted them enough to take a better look at his surroundings.

Of fuckin' course. He kind of remembered now, even though his memory was a bit spotty. More like it had gaping holes.

He glanced down to see needles with attached tubes stuck in his cast-free arm. One of his legs was also in a plaster cast and hanging in the air using some contraption. What he currently wore was as far from his cut as it can get, except for being naked.

They better not have cut off his goddamn cut. It was one of his prize possessions.

For fuck's sake. Did he pull out in front of a tractor trailer that was traveling seventy-five miles an hour or something? Did he misjudge the distance and speed of the truck?

A noise to his left had him turning his head. And regretting it.

Bishop slouched in a chair by the bed, scrolling through his cell phone.

Now Romeo wondered where his was. Was it destroyed?

If it was, he was screwed. His whole life was stored in that damn phone.

His VP looked up, then put his phone down. "'Bout time you woke up. You've been out so fuckin' long, thought I might need to take over the gavel."

He thought *what?*

"H—" His throat felt like it was full of dust and gravel. Despite trying to clear it, his voice remained rough, and speaking was a chore. "How long have I been here?" Here obviously being a hospital.

"This is day four."

What the fuck? Four days? "Why don't I remember that?"

Bishop shrugged. "Could be the fact you've been in and out of it. When you were in, you babbled some shit that didn't make much fuckin' sense. They really scrambled your brain."

They. So, he hadn't been splattered like a bug on the front grill of an eighteen-wheeler.

"How'd I get here?" he croaked.

"Wick."

"Where's he at?"

"Not sure. We've all been takin' turns sittin' with you."

"To keep me company?"

"To make sure the motherfuckers who fucked you up don't come back to finish the job."

Romeo let that sink into his shaken and bruised gray matter.

They. Motherfuckers. Wick. Bits and pieces of the attack were slowly coming back to him.

Bishop picked up his phone again. "Gonna let Magnum know you're awake."

"Fuck that. Wanna talk to Wick first. He tell Magnum what happened?"

"What d'you think?"

His mouth and throat were so damn dry, he needed water. Though, whiskey might be a better choice.

Lifting his unbroken, but severely bruised, arm—the one with the needles stuck in both the back of his hand and forearm—he reached for the cup sitting on a rolling table next to the bed. Unfortunately, it was empty. "Water."

Bishop popped up and grabbed the pitcher, filled the plastic cup, and held it out. "Want me to help?"

Romeo swiped at the cup and missed. He tried and missed again.

Bishop held the straw to his lips. "Might take a while to get back your coordination. Remember that old commercial where they cracked an egg into a fryin' pan and said, 'this is your brain on drugs?' Your brain's sorta like that right now but instead of one egg, they broke a whole dozen."

What the fuck was he talking about?

Whatever it was wasn't important. But what was... "My cut?"

"At your place."

"It okay?"

"That's fucked up, brother. You're more worried about your damn cut than yourself?" Bishop shook his head. "It's safe and sound. Wick thought ahead and left that and the piece you were packin' at your place before the ambulance hauled your ass away."

He'd sigh with relief but figured doing so would hurt like fuck since his ribs were tightly bound for a good reason.

But... his piece? Why didn't he pull it if his life was in danger?

"I give any of 'em an extra hole or two?"

"Don't think so. Seems like the only blood that needed to be washed off the pavement was yours."

Great.

"Think it was the Fury?"

Bishop's forehead wrinkled. "Why the fuck would it be the Fury?"

Shit. "It wouldn't. You're right about my mind bein' scrambled." He quickly changed the subject. "Wick found me?"

"I just said that."

"Need to talk to him."

Bishop shook his head. "You just said that."

For fuck's sake. Did he have permanent brain damage? "What's wrong with me?"

"Listin' what's right would be shorter."

"That supposed to be a fuckin' joke?"

The Knights' VP sighed. "No, Rome, it's the fuckin' truth. Don't remember what the doctor told you?"

"Don't remember shit. Just bits and pieces of me bein' jumped."

"Then I'm sure she'll give you a laundry list the next time she stops in."

"No brain damage?"

"We asked her how we'd be able to tell when you're normally an idiot."

"No way to talk to your prez," he grumbled.

"Rather me lie?"

"Yeah."

Bishop snorted.

"Gimme my phone so I can text Wick."

"About that..."

Oh, for fuck's sake.

"Sully already got you a new one. Had the phone company transfer all your shit, so not much should be lost."

"My phone lost or did those fuckers take it?"

"Got as beat up as you did."

"Didn't get fuckin' beat up. Got ambushed."

"Your ass got beat. Badly." Bishop jerked his chin toward the hospital bed. "The proof is you bein' stuck in that bed."

Like he needed that damn reminder.

He was done with this conversation. The only one he wanted to talk to right now was Wick.

"Text Wick, then go get me my new phone, my sled and my cut."

Bishop hooted loudly. "How the fuck you ridin' your sled when you're in goddamn traction?"

"Will figure out a way."

"The only vehicle with wheels you'll be ridin' for a while will be a wheelchair."

The good news kept coming.

Chapter Thirty-Three

"SEE WHO IT WAS?" Romeo asked Wick not even two hours later and after a short, much-needed nap.

Wick leaned back in the chair and propped his boots on the hospital bed. "Kinda."

Romeo narrowed his eyes at those dirty boots until Wick dropped them back to the floor. "Was it the Fury?"

Wick's forehead creased the same way Bishop's had. "The Fury? Why would they wanna kick your fuckin' ass?... Oh... fuck... 'Cause you banged their property without permission? That hot thing belongin' to that scary fucker Shade? What's her name?"

"Wick," Romeo growled, then quickly regretted it. Coughing was not good for broken ribs. Not one, not two, but a whole rack of them. "You recognize any of 'em?"

"No and didn't see a fuckin' cut in sight. If it was the Fury, they'd be representin' to let you know it was them and make sure you know why they're visitin'."

The man was right. If it was that MC, they'd make sure

Romeo knew they were delivering that message. "Wanna hear the details."

"Not much to tell. Stepped outside to throw shit in the dumpster and have a fuckin' smoke. Saw you on the ground rollin' around. One fucker was beatin' you with some metal thing, the other two were kickin' the shit outta you."

How could there only be three of them? At the time, it felt like a dozen. "They stopped when they saw you?"

"Fuck no. They didn't fuckin' scatter 'til I took a coupla shots at 'em."

Romeo must've been knocked out by then to miss that. "You hit any of 'em?"

"Not sure since it was fuckin' too dark to see. Don't think this was random, right?"

"Could be." But Romeo doubted it.

"If it ain't, they know where you live."

No shit. "Or they think I was hangin' at Dick's." That was a long shot.

"Either way, Magnum's on it."

Just fuckin' great.

If the attack had anything to do with Maddie, he'd never hear the end of it from his sergeant at arms. The man told him to leave Maddie alone. Romeo ignored that warning and now look where he landed.

In a fucking hospital bed.

Along with Maddie being unemployed. As well as pissed at him.

He closed his eyes and breathed. Carefully.

He needed to make shit right with her.

While he hated to admit that Magnum had been right, Romeo should've told her no like he said. He also should've told himself no, instead of being so goddamn selfish.

But he didn't and here he was.

Bottom line... he fucked up.

"Just so you know, Sully was on stand-by."

Wick's words had his eyes flashing open. "For what?"

"Last rites, I guess."

"Fuckin' Sully. Don't he know I'm too fuckin' stubborn to die?"

Wick snorted. "Pretty sure I heard one of the nurses sayin' it was touch and go for a while, too."

"Well, everyone was wrong, weren't they?"

"It was close, Rome. Good thing I stepped out back when I did. If I hadn't..."

True, but it would've been even better if he'd went out back sooner. "Yeah."

"You're fuckin' welcome."

It also would've been better if Wick had better aim. Romeo kept that opinion to himself. "Thanks, brother."

"You would've done the same."

"I hope to fuck any of our brothers would've stepped in. None of us are pussies."

"Truth." Wick stared at him for far too long. "Who d'you think's got it out for you?"

"No fuckin' clue."

"Magnum's on it."

Jesus Christ. "Already told me that."

"He'll find out who those fuckers are and why they ambushed you like that." Wick tipped his head. "Might not be the Blood Fury but do you still think it got to do with that Fury chick?"

"No fuckin' clue," he repeated, but he was starting to think it was related. The only person he had a run-in with lately was...

Roger fucking Smith.

Did the fucker put out a hit on him? Maddie's former

boss probably had enough scratch to hire some crackheads to fuck him up. Since he survived, hiring some scumbags off the street would make more sense. If it had been a professional hit, Romeo doubted he'd still be breathing.

"Well," Wick started with an amused grin, "the doctor said you'll need physical therapy to help with healin'. Guess it's good you got her in your pocket."

Romeo frowned. How did Wick know Maddie was a physical therapist? "She ain't in my pocket."

Wick chuckled. "Just in your bed, then? Never knew you to chase a chick. She's gotta be somethin' special." He wiggled his fingers and his eyebrows. "She good with her hands, brother?"

Romeo wasn't liking this turn of conversation. "She ain't nothin'. She's property of an ally. That's it. Was only lookin' out for her, the same as they'd do for us if one of ours moved north."

"For fuck's sake, Rome. You really think we don't got eyes and fuckin' ears? Or brains to figure shit out?"

"What're you talkin' about?"

"Seen her comin' in and outta your place for the last few weeks. How she looked arrivin' ain't the same as how she looked leavin'. You also disappeared a few nights. Since when are you crashin' at some woman's house?" He lifted a finger. "Never. You dip the second you pull out." Before Romeo could deny it, he continued. "And the most obvious evidence? The sweet butts complainin' that you've been ignorin' them. When the fuck ain't you gettin' head from at least one of 'em at the drop of a fuckin' hat? Or zipper, more like it."

Shit. Was it that obvious? Did he have a routine?

Of fucking course he did.

"Need some shuteye. More pain killers, too." He was

starting to hurt like a motherfucker. Whatever they had him on was wearing off. Fast.

Wick burst out laughing. "Truth can be fuckin' painful, can't it?"

A noise made them both look toward the door.

Could this fucking day get any better?

Apparently not.

"Get gone," Magnum ordered Wick as he lumbered into the room.

With a grin, Wick unfolded his ass from the chair, gave Romeo a sloppy salute, a "Prez," and wandered out.

Now it was just Romeo and the big man. He braced for what was to come next.

Standing at the end of the hospital bed, Magnum jerked his chin at it. "What'd you do to cause this shit, asshole?"

"Why do you always assume that I'm the asshole and it wasn't some random attack?"

"Ain't an assumption. Facts are fuckin' facts."

"Have you figured out who ambushed me, yet?"

"Not yet but bettin' this has somethin' to do with the woman I told you to stay the fuck away from."

"Pretty fuckin' bold assumption," Romeo countered.

Magnum shook his head. "Know it ain't Shade. He don't get other fuckers to do his dirty work. He would've come silently in the middle of the night and left just as quietly after jammin' his hand into your chest and yankin' out your heart. Could still happen if you continue to diddle with Maddie."

"About her..."

Magnum groaned and brushed an agitated hand back and forth over his bald head. "I gotta fuckin' sit down for whatever the fuck's gonna come outta your mouth next?"

If he did, Romeo figured the big man wouldn't be sitting long. "So..."

"Christ," Magnum muttered.

Maybe if Romeo gave his enforcer some background, he'd be able to find the assholes who put him in the hospital a lot faster.

"She has... *had* a dick boss that was constantly abusin' her." Magnum's chest seemed to expand at that, so he quickly added, "Verbally. The fucker treats all his employees like shit. He seems to get a hard-on over making their work lives miserable. He made her work late for free, kept dockin' her pay for made-up shit..."

"Quittin' would easily solve that problem."

"For most people, yeah." He explained to Magnum about Maddie's dream of working for the Steelers, or at least one of the Pittsburgh sports teams.

When he was done, Magnum said, "Mighta been told that was why she moved down here. Didn't give much thought at the time 'cause I really didn't give a shit about the why, only the fact that she was in our area."

"Yeah, so... Maybe you should know. Just in case..."

"In case of what?"

"Any further attacks," Romeo finished reluctantly.

"Fuckin' fuck. Knew you did somethin' stupid. You make fuckin' enemies with him?"

"Was only tryin' to help the property of an ally." Would Magnum buy it? The man wasn't stupid.

"Jesus fuckin' Christ. By doin' what?"

"To help her out, had a word with her boss," he answered.

"About?"

"Don't matter what it was about."

Magnum asked, "He do that to you?"

"Not him, but... Thinkin' maybe he hired someone to fuck me up." It was the only thing that sort of made sense. If this didn't have to do with Roger Smith, then it had to be random.

Especially since he never fucked with married women or ones in relationships. It wasn't worth it. Plenty of single women out there who wouldn't turn him down when he turned up his charm.

"What gave you that clue?"

"Can't think of anyone else who'd have it out for me."

"So, what'd you do to him?"

"Like I said, had a word."

Magnum cocked an eyebrow. "Did that 'word' also include hands?"

"For a second." Or two.

Magnum dropped his head to stare at his boots for a moment while grinding his palm back and forth along the back of his neck. "So, you threatened her boss," he concluded once he looked at Romeo again.

Was his jaw popping? Because it sure as fuck looked like his jaw was popping.

That usually wasn't a good sign.

"Not quite. Just gave him a coupla suggestions."

"Wanna tell me what those suggestions were?"

"One was stop bein' a dick to his employees..."

"And?"

"And to put in a good word for Maddie with one of the teams so she could get her dream job."

"Why the fuck would he do that?"

"'Cause he got connections with the teams in the area. That's the only fuckin' reason she continued to put up with his bullshit and wouldn't quit."

"You fucked that up for her."

Since that wasn't formed as a question, Romeo should be

offended. But, unfortunately, it was true. "Could say that since he fired her."

"Then sent some goons to visit you."

"Think so."

"For fuck's sake!" Magnum barked. "Shoulda left her alone. Shoulda stayed outta it. Shoulda listened to someone older and wiser than you."

"Your opinion."

"A damn good one. One fuckin' day you're gonna realize that you should take my opinions seriously."

One day soon the big man would no longer be the club's sergeant at arms and his opinion wouldn't mean dick.

"So, what did chasin' that pussy get you?" Magnum raised a finger as he counted off. "Risked our alliance." He lifted a second finger. "Got the woman fired." A third one rose. "Mighta fucked up her dream." He dropped two of them but left his middle finger up. "Got your ass beat to fuck."

"That about sums it up," Romeo muttered. He reached for his water again but struggled to grab it. The fuck if he was asking for Magnum's help. He'd die of thirst first.

"In case you forgot, my fuckin' job's to protect our club and our brothers. Make that shit difficult when you do the fuckin' opposite of what I tell you. Told you she was a bad idea. Also told you, if you wanted a piece of her, to do it the right way. Always think you can be slick, Rome. That you can fly under the radar. This proves you ain't good at it."

"Gonna admit my life choices ain't always the best—"

A phone ringing in Magnum's cut had the big man pulling it out and glancing at the screen. With one last pointed look at Romeo, the Knights' enforcer stabbed at the screen and put it to his ear. "Yeah."

The longer he listened to the caller, the more his face

turned to concrete. When he turned away, Romeo began to worry.

Something was up and he was damn sure it had to do with him.

"For fuck's sake... Ain't that some fuckin' shit... Not sure... Gonna have to think about it and get back to you... You're right. Ain't good news but gonna have to deal with it one way or another... Thanks, brother, owe you one."

Magnum tucked his phone away, turned, set his hands on his hips, and stared at Romeo.

"That call have to do with me?"

Magnum pulled in a deep breath and shook his head. "You stirred a fuckin' hornet's nest, know that?"

"Would rather get stung by hornets than tenderized by a tire iron."

"Fuckin' hornets gonna be the least of your worries. That was Mercy. His team did a bunch of diggin'. Thing is, they didn't have to dig too deep to find out that her boss has ties, just not only the ones she knew about."

Romeo's stomach dropped. "What the fuck does that mean?"

"Ever think Smith might not be his real last name?"

"You sayin' Roger Smith ain't Roger Smith? What's his real last name?" Did Romeo even want to know?

"Russo."

What the fuck? "Asshole didn't look Sicilian to me."

"Yeah, 'cause his mother ain't. Some genes are stronger than others."

"Jesus fuck. Know Maddie had no clue that fucker had ties to La Cosa Nostra. She might be shocked just findin' out the Mafia existed in Pittsburgh. Wonder why he kept that shit secret?"

"Could be usin' that business for money launderin' and

didn't want eyes lookin' extra hard into his business dealings. Who the fuck knows? Don't give a shit about the reason why. I give a shit that he's got them at his back."

"If he's in with the Russos, why ain't I dead?"

"Good question. If you wanna be, willin' to help with that." Magnum glanced at the machines in the room. "Sure I could find a red button somewhere or unplug somethin'."

"Fuckin' funny."

"What ain't funny is the truth that my life would be a lot fuckin' simpler, Rome."

"Yeah, okay. But it's a serious fuckin' question. If it was the Mafia, why ain't I dead?"

"'Cause he wanted to keep his ties with La Cosa Nostra secret? Probably hired some idiots desperate for scratch and without any real skills. Doin' so wouldn't leave a path back to their organization. Also, him ambushin' you coulda been personal and nothin' to do with the family business."

Damn. That actually sounded like a reasonable explanation.

"How come that federal task force Ali-Cat's baby daddy belonged to didn't take out all those motherfuckers? Were they pussies?"

Magnum shrugged. "Think I got inside info on a fuckin' federal task force? Think I sit around drinkin' a fuckin' beer with one of the former members of that pig circle jerk?"

Romeo snorted. "He's married to your oldest girl. And he's pop to your grandbaby."

"So? Don't mean we have deep, meaningful conver-fuckin-sations. Only tolerate his ass 'cause I want Liyah and my grandbabies to stay in my life. That's the only fuckin' reason. You wanna know why they didn't take down those Mafia motherfuckers, call him."

"He ain't gonna talk to me."

"Yeah, you know why? 'Cause you were sniffin' after Liyah when he already claimed her."

"If that pig thinks Ali-Cat is his property, he's wrong."

"No shit. That's why she didn't want your ass. She ain't no one's property."

"'Cept yours," Romeo murmured.

"It's my blood's runnin' through her veins."

Romeo sighed. Carefully. "So, now what? We gonna go after that motherfucker?"

"And start a war with the Sicilians, are you fuckin' crazy?" Magnum growled.

"Then what?"

"Don't know yet. Gonna have to think about it."

"Can't just let this go unanswered," Romeo reminded him.

"Don't need you tellin' me how to do what I fuckin' do."

"Just sayin'... We could handle him separately. Some random shit could happen to him. An accident or somethin'," Romeo suggested.

"Said I'm gonna think about it. Whatever we do, we gotta make sure it ain't tied to us."

"But we're gonna do something, right?"

"They attacked our prez. Of fuckin' course we are. Like you said, that can't go unanswered. You attack one, you attack us all."

"Good to see you back to bein' loyal."

"Never wasn't. The Knights might not be blood but they sure as fuck are family." The last thing Magnum said as he walked out the door was, "Even you, asshole."

Chapter Thirty-Four

It took two more days before he was freed from the hospital hell where he'd been imprisoned.

Two more damn days before he could try to make amends with Maddie. Even using his replacement phone, she wouldn't respond to his calls or texts. Since she wouldn't, he planned on facing her in person.

Now that he knew her former boss used a commonly used last name to conceal his ties to the Russos, he was worried about her.

Since he was still stuck in casts, and would be for a few weeks yet, he couldn't ride his sled over to her apartment. Instead, he was having a prospect drive him around in a cage and basically be his bitch.

Booger waited down in the lot while Romeo slowly hauled his injured ass up the steps to her apartment using only a single crutch due to his broken arm. Luckily, his broken arm and leg were on the opposite sides of his body, otherwise Booger might be pushing him around in a wheelchair. And carrying him up the stairs like a new bride since there wasn't an elevator.

Propping the crutch under his arm, he leaned back against Maddie's door since he was so damn out of breath after maneuvering the flight of steps to the second floor.

At least he didn't tumble the fuck back down. That would've sucked and most likely landed him back in the hospital again.

Once he didn't feel like he was about to die, he knocked on the door behind him and put his weight on his good leg so when she opened the door, he wouldn't fall backwards and end up on his ass at her feet.

He was a goddamn mess.

With a groan, he turned around and knocked again. This time a little louder and yelled out a, "Maddie! Open the fucking door!" Fuck bothering her neighbors.

Again, he heard nothing. Not her voice. No footsteps. Not even a "fuck off."

Did she find another job already and was currently at work?

He was such a dumbass. He should've made sure her cage was down in the lot before taking on the fucking chore of climbing a flight of steps.

Yeah, he was a goddamn mess.

The turn of a lock raised his hopes until he realized it wasn't the door in front of him, but the one behind.

A blond man, maybe in his thirties, stepped out into the hallway. "If you're looking for the girl who lived here, she moved out."

She did what? Maybe she got a better job with a better salary and decided to upgrade her apartment.

Maybe he was also lying to himself. "When?"

The man shrugged. "About a week ago, maybe? Sorry, I forgot to mark it on my calendar."

Smart ass. "Did she take all her shit?"

The man shrugged again. "A bunch of guys, all wearing vests with the name of some gang on the back, were going in and out. I did notice they brought a boxed truck and a couple of vans."

For fuck's sake. Now the "apartment for rent" sign posted out in front of the building made sense.

"I had no idea she was affiliated with criminals, otherwise I would've complained to the landlord. While they were here, I figured it was safer for me to stay inside and keep my door locked."

Jesus Christ. "Sounds like you stayed inside instead of doin' the neighborly thing and helpin' like the pussy you are."

The man's gaped mouth snapped shut. "And you're trespassing since your friend no longer lives here. It's best you leave before I call the cops."

"Get out of my fuckin' face," Romeo growled. He about had enough of this asshole.

Maddie's former neighbor snorted out a laugh and eyed Romeo up and down. "Who's going to make me? You? It looks like someone already kicked your ass. Two times over."

"Know those *criminals* who made you piss your pants? I got a vest like that, too. So do more than thirty of my brothers. Now... You were sayin'?"

"I was saying, 'Hello, 911?'"

"Ain't illegal to visit a friend, motherfucker. So, go ahead, call the fuckin' pigs and see where that gets you." He adjusted the crutch under his arm more securely and hobbled across the narrow hallway. "Just remember, I know where you fuckin' live."

The closer he got, the wider the neighbor's eyes got. "Is that a threat?"

"Damn right it is." Really, there was no point in him wasting any more time here, so Romeo carefully pivoted on his good leg and hobbled toward the steps.

"I figured you're all talk," was heard right before the slam of the apartment door. Along with the turn of a lock.

"Not worth it," Romeo muttered under his breath and did his best not to break the rest of his bones while heading back down the stairs.

———

"WHERE THE FUCK IS SHE?"

"Who?" filled Romeo's ear.

"You know who," he responded impatiently.

"Ain't learned your lesson yet?" Magnum asked.

Romeo pulled the phone from his ear, frowned at it for a few furious seconds before putting it back to his ear. "Since the Russos are involved, went to check on her and she's gone."

"Yeah."

"Yeah?" Romeo echoed.

"That's what I said."

"Where'd she go?"

"Brother, you think she shares her goddamn plans with me? Why don't you fuckin' call her."

He had. Numerous times. "She don't answer her phone."

"Maybe that should tell you somethin'."

Romeo dropped his head back and ground his teeth. "She's just pissed right now. She'll get over it."

"You wanna know so fuckin' bad, call Shade and ask him. 'Cause you're callin' the wrong fuckin' person. Got no fuckin' clue where she is. My guess? She went as far away from you as she can get."

This was going nowhere, so he pivoted. "What's the plan?"

"For what?"

"To get those motherfuckers back."

Magnum huffed. "You want us to go to war with the goddamn *Mafia?*"

"Not war. Just take a coupla shots at 'em."

"A coupla shots lead to more. Look what they did to the Deadly Demons. They pretty much wiped out that MC after being crossed."

"We ain't those Deadly Dumbasses."

"Look, brother, thought long and fuckin' hard about it and decided we gotta make the best decisions to keep this club in one piece. They got a shit-ton more scratch behind their organization with access to a lot more. They also got a fuckuva lot better firepower than us. They could easily pick us off one by one 'til there ain't nothin' left of our brother-hood. That what you want?"

Magnum's response surprised him. When did that man ever back down from anything? Romeo swore he softened with age. "Assumin' you had a sit-down with the Shadows about this." That had to be where this was coming from.

"Not a sit-down but yeah, discussed our options about dealin' with that kinda organization. This ain't another MC. This ain't those fucknut Warriors takin' pot shots at us and the Angels. We'd need the whole fuckin' alliance behind us to go head-to-head with a Sicilian army and that ain't gonna happen. No one wants to start a goddamn war if we can avoid it. We got too much to fuckin' lose."

"Sounds like a bunch of pussies to me."

A loud sigh hit Romeo's ear. "Suggest lookin' in the

fuckin' mirror, Rome, and ask yourself if you're ready to go head-to-head with La Cosa Nostra in your fuckin' condition."

"Not sayin' we need to do it this fuckin' week, but we need to strike back. What he did to me can't go unanswered."

After a long pause, Magnum said, "This is personal shit, brother. This ain't got fuck to do with the rest of us."

"You sayin' you won't back your prez?"

"For fuck's sake. Ain't what I said. You stepped in shit I told you to avoid and now you want us to turn that into a shit storm? Be smart. Take your knocks for bein' stupid and let it go."

Romeo couldn't do that. He understood what Magnum was saying but he didn't have to like it. He also could handle Smith—or Russo or whatever the fuck his real name was—on his own. But he would not just "let it go." *Fuck that shit.*

And, *yeah*, it was personal.

What Smith did to Maddie. What Smith did to him.

But he was still disappointed that his sergeant at arms wouldn't have his back in this. "Old age really mellowed your ass out."

"Unlike you, the older I get, the wiser I get. Also, my head's a lot fuckin' cooler now than it used to be. Remember that I gotta look out for the whole damn club, not just you." A noise in the background had Magnum pausing again. "Gotta go. Got a baby who needs me and that baby ain't you."

The line went dead.

Maybe he should take this to Bishop and if his VP agreed, take it to the board for a vote. Magnum wasn't the be-all, end-all. He might be on the board, he might be toward the top of the Knights' chain of command, but he was only one of thirty-two patched members.

He'd worry about that shit later. Right now, he was on a

mission. He needed to find Maddie and make sure she was okay.

He scrolled through his phone for LZ's contact and when he found it, pressed Send.

"Didn't know you had my fuckin' number," were the first words out of Zeke's mouth.

Romeo wasn't calling the cocky shit to have a friendly conversation. He only needed info. "Where she at?"

"She?" Zak Jamison's firstborn asked. The kid Sophie Jamison should've swallowed.

"Know who I'm fuckin' talkin' about."

"Not sure I do."

Romeo gritted his teeth. The kid was a dick simply because he could be. "Where'd Maddie go?"

"After you got her ass fired? Where d'you think?"

"If I fuckin' knew, wouldn't be callin' your ass. She get a better apartment?"

"Without a damn job, she couldn't fuckin' afford that apartment she already had. She had no fuckin' choice but to move out, Rome. You should be the one payin' her landlord for the broken lease, not her."

"Know she moved, but where'd she go? Someone from the Angels take her in? Or did she move back north?"

"Gonna take a wild guess here... If she wanted you to know where the fuck she went, she woulda fuckin' told you."

Romeo wanted to shove one of his casts up LZ's ass. The brat had no respect for his elders. "You'll never be as good a prez as your pop."

"Could be half as good as him and still be a thousand fuckin' times better at it than you."

Romeo stabbed the phone with his finger to end the call and closed his eyes, waiting until the rage simmered down.

When it did, he tried Maddie again. As expected, it went directly to voicemail.

"Saw you moved. Lemme know you're okay. Just a text or somethin'." He hung up.

He was batting a goddamn thousand here. He tapped his cell phone against his forehead as he considered his next step.

Getting hold of Trip was out. Talking to Shade was definitely out. He went through a mental list of members in the Fury he could contact without ratting his ass out.

It hit him, then. Someone who might help.

Castle.

Black bikers had to stick together, right? And Castle would know if Maddie moved home. He also wouldn't be a damn snitch.

Did Romeo even have Castle's digits?

He scrolled through his contact list. He had a lot of numbers for a lot of bikers in the alliance, but Castle's wasn't one of them. He needed to fix that.

He wracked his brain on who might have Castle's number. Maybe Cisco. Those two seemed to be tight every time the clubs got together.

He quickly texted the Knights' road captain. *U got Castle's number?*

Twenty minutes later, the only text he got was the ten digits he needed. Twenty minutes and thirty seconds later, he called the only Black Blood Fury member.

At twenty-one minutes, he had his answer.

In one way, he was relieved, in another he wasn't because now he had to figure out a way to get his broken ass up to Manning Grove and keep it on the down-low.

Chapter Thirty-Five

MADDIE RECEIVED a text from a number she didn't recognize: *Got a job 4 u 2day if u need scratch.*

While she could certainly use the money, she had no idea who was texting her. Most likely it was some scammer.

Who's this? she asked, thinking she'd never get a response back if it was.

Sig. New phone. Lost old one.

Since when did people get a different phone number when they bought a new phone? That was so 90s.

But she had to remember that these were bikers and some, if not most, didn't give a shit about the latest technology. They also didn't care about transferring phone numbers. They could just as easily send out a mass text with their new number. Maddie was confident she wasn't on that Fury list.

Sig probably needed her to watch the kids. They had rescued Autumn's three young half-siblings from a cult and taken them in to raise as their own.

Since coming home, Maddie sent out countless resumes without a lot of positive response back. It probably didn't help that she didn't have a good reference when it came to Roger Smith. While she waited to score an interview from at least one, the Fury members and their ol' ladies had been tossing odd jobs her way to keep her busy and put a little cash in her pocket.

So far, she'd helped out at the club-owned motel, Dutch's garage, ran some errands for Justice Bail Bonds, babysat and even helped out one very busy night at Crazy Pete's Bar.

What time do you need me? she sent back to the club's VP.

ASAP was his answer.

She glanced at the time and sighed. She had plans with her younger sister Josie, but if Sig and Red needed help, then Maddie wanted to help. That was the good part of belonging to an MC. Everyone was considered family and assisted each other whenever possible.

Okay, I'll head to your place in a few.

Before she could text Josie to cancel their plans, she got another text from Sig. *Not at the house.*

She frowned at that unexpected news. Why wouldn't he want her to watch the kids at their house?

Then where?

The seconds ticked away while she waited for his answer. *The Co-Z Inn.*

The what? *A motel?* she asked. Her frown deepened.

Since she never heard of it, she did a quick Google search to find out where it was located.

It made no sense. Why the hell would Sig take the kids to a motel in Parsington?

House got bugs. Being fumigated.

Then why wouldn't they stay at The Grove Inn here in Manning Grove? Could it be booked solid?

346

It was going to take her a good twenty-five minutes, if not more, to get there.

With another sigh, she asked, *Room number?*

15.

Be there soon.

———

SHE COULDN'T IMAGINE that run-down town of Parsington was considered any sort of "destination" for tourists to visit. At least the quaint town of Manning Grove attracted people visiting the Pennsylvania Grand Canyon and in fall they came for the brilliant colors of the autumn leaves.

Only three vehicles were parked in front of rooms at The Co-Z Inn. Not one of them was Sig's sled, or his family's SUV.

Huh.

In fact, she didn't recognize the car in front of room fifteen, either. That made the fine hairs on the back of her neck stand up.

Was this some sort of set up? Was she about to be kidnapped? Or worse?

Standing outside of her Highlander, she left the driver's door open—in case she had to bolt—and glanced around. She then decided to text Sig to make sure she wasn't walking into trouble.

I'm here. Come outside.

She wouldn't even knock on the door until she knew it was definitely Sig and the kids. She knew better after the Fury had to deal for years with the dangerous whack jobs that lived up on Hillbilly Hill.

Door's unlocked.

She wasn't falling for that. No way.

She quickly texted back, *You don't come out, I'm leaving, and you'll have to find someone else to babysit.*

With her heart pounding in her throat, she was beginning to believe this really was some sort of trap.

She should go. But before she did, she found Sig's original phone number and called him. It went straight to voicemail. She texted him next just to be sure that losing his cell phone was true.

After climbing back into her Toyota, she locked the doors while waiting to see if she got a response and stared at the motel door to see if he would appear.

When the door opened, her breath seized.

When a man stepped out, her heart skipped a beat.

That was not Sig.

Not unless he changed his race, grew a longer beard, and gained fifty pounds.

What the hell?

It *was* a trap! One set up by Romeo.

Son of a bitch! Now her pulse was racing for a different reason. If she was smart, it was one she needed to ignore.

Her brain told her the man was trouble. Her heart told her it didn't matter.

The heart wanted what the heart wanted, right?

Wrong!

She needed her common sense to be stronger than her desire.

When Romeo hobbled a few steps out of the motel room using a crutch, she noticed he had casts on both his left arm and right leg. Pressing fingers to her lips, she whispered, "Holy shit."

What the hell happened? Did he crash his sled?

He stopped where the concrete sidewalk met the macadam parking lot and waited.

She remained frozen in her seat as a flurry of emotions barreled through her.

Anger.

Excitement.

Confusion.

Empathy.

And...

No.

Shut up, heart!

She should leave. The injured man waiting for her blew up her career and not in a good way. A career that required years of education so she could work hard at it for a year and a half while putting up with a bully boss. It only took Romeo having "a word" with Roger for him to destroy that career in minutes.

Romeo thought he knew better than her.

He didn't listen and leave it alone like she asked.

Despite her annoyance, she gritted her teeth and climbed back out of her vehicle to approach him as his dark eyes tracked her every step.

She stopped directly in front of him and raised her chin. "You tricked me."

"You wouldn't have come if I didn't."

No, she wouldn't have. "Were you in an accident?"

"No."

"What happened?"

He tipped his head toward the open motel room door.

Yes, it was a trap. He wanted to get her alone and convince her to forgive him. She steeled her heart because she wasn't ready to do that.

Hell, she might never be ready.

She was unemployed, desperate for a new job and had been forced to move back home because of it. Because of him.

Her eyes sliced from Romeo to the motel room and back.

She shook her head. "No. You don't get a pass on this, Rome. I don't care if you were hit by a bus." That was a lie, but he didn't need to know that.

"Damn," he whispered.

"You blew up my life, now you want me to forgive you? Just like that?" She snapped her fingers.

"Ain't askin' for forgiveness. Askin' for you to step inside so we got privacy."

Bullshit. He wanted to get her alone so he could tug on her heartstrings. "I don't think I need to hear anything you have to say. You've said enough already. To Roger."

When her phone dinged, she glanced at it. Sig texted her back: *WTF U talkn about?*

At least that proved Sig wasn't in on it. If he was, she'd never forgive him, either. "I wonder how Sig would feel knowing you pretended to be him?"

Romeo jerked his chin toward the cell phone in her hand. "That him?"

"Yes. Should I tell him you tricked me?"

"Only if you wanna make my life more of a fuckin' shit show than it is right now."

"Why should I care? You did it to me."

He sighed, dropped his head, and squeezed his forehead. "Don't gotta forgive me, Maddie. Just askin' for you to hear me out."

"You didn't hear *me*. If you did, you would've left well enough alone."

"Yeah," he admitted softly.

"Is that an apology?" Not that an apology would fix what he broke, but it would at least show remorse.

His chest slowly rose and fell. "Fucked up and regret it."

Her eyebrows rose. "Is that a sorry?"

"No. Ain't sorry. Once you hear me out, you'll know why."

She flung out a hand. "So talk."

He shook his head. "Not out here."

"I don't think anyone is going to overhear you, Rome. This place is a deserted dump." When she glanced around to make her point, she noticed something she missed upon arriving.

And that could've been dangerous if it had been someone wanting to hurt her.

"Who's in the car?" Whoever it was, was slumped down in the seat, making him hard to spot.

"Prospect."

Of course. In the condition he was in, he couldn't drive himself. Or ride his sled. But at least he didn't have some sweet butt as his travel companion.

"You're going to make him wait in the car?"

"He ain't a dog or crotch fruit. He'll fuckin' live."

She rolled her lips inward to fight her reaction for a second before quickly slapping the steel back around her heart. He'd need a torch to break through. "Why did you come up here if you're not here to apologize?"

"Wanna explain."

"You could've done that with a phone call."

"You don't fuckin' answer your fuckin' goddamn phone!" he yelled before visibly reining in his impatience.

"Then you could've written a letter."

"Jesus fuckin' Christ," he muttered.

"And included a check for all the financial hardship I'm now going through. Apparently, you're aware of that since you used it to lure me here."

"For fuck's sake, Maddie. You wanna go somewhere else, we can do that. It ain't like I'm gonna hit on you. I'm pretty fuckin' useless right now." He swept his unbroken arm up and down his body.

She considered his injuries. At least the ones she could see. He was right. He would be harmless and unable to talk her into bed with him.

She glanced at the open motel room again. Maybe she wouldn't be kidnapped but she reminded herself it was still a trap.

One she was about to fall into.

"Fine. I can't wait to hear what you have to say." She met his eyes and warned, "It better be worth it."

When she headed into the room, she heard the thump of the crutch and some muffled grunts as he followed behind her.

As soon as he made his way over the threshold, he shut the door and leaned back against it. His expression was tense, and his lips pressed together.

Was he in pain?

Damn shame, that.

Chapter Thirty-Six

MADDIE PERCHED on the edge of the bed and closely watched him try to hide his pain.

Damn it.

She shouldn't feel bad for him, but she did. Her career involved helping people, not wishing for them to suffer.

She closed her eyes and breathed until she let go some of her anger and frustration at him. Not all of it, of course, because she needed to use it as fuel to keep her heart whole, but enough to hear him out and take into consideration whatever he had to say.

With clenched jaws, he adjusted his crutch, pushed off the door and hobbled closer until he stood only a couple of feet in front of where she sat.

But the closer he got, the easier it was to pick up his familiar scent and the harder her heart thumped. That unwelcome reaction made her spew, "I'm giving you fifteen minutes. Not a minute more." She glanced at the time on her cell phone. "That starts now, so you better start talking."

Did what she just said annoy him? Good. Since she

compromised by entering his motel room, he needed to follow her rule to keep her there and listen to whatever he had to say.

She reminded him, "Time's ticking..."

He sure was leaning heavily on that crutch. Did he purposely remain standing so she'd drum up some sympathy for him?

"You were right when you said that asshole had connections. Just ain't the connections you thought."

Maddie shook her head in confusion. "What do you mean?" This was not the conversation she was expecting.

"Ol' Roger's connected to La Cosa Nostra."

Her head twitched. "La what?"

"The goddamn Pittsburgh Mafia."

That unexpected answer had her eyes bugging out. "There's Mafia in Pittsburgh?" How did she not know this? Was this common knowledge and she missed it somehow?

"Yeah, Maddie, there's fuckin' Mafia in Pittsburgh. Here's the proof." Searching where he pointed to his face, she realized it was darker than normal in some spots, like around his eyes. How had she missed that they were bruises and not a play of light and shadows. Was his nose also swollen and slightly more crooked?

She shook herself mentally to fight back the flood of sympathy. She needed to get back to the subject at hand... "How's he connected?"

"Beats the fuck outta me..." He blew out a breath, then winced. "Actually, they did beat the fuck outta me and he seems to be a Russo in disguise."

"A Russo?"

"Yeah, the Sicilians runnin' the Burgh."

"Roger is Sicilian?" None of this was adding up.

He sighed with impatience. "Woman, that part ain't

important. The important shit is his ties to that organization. They got a lotta power and a lotta soldiers doin' their dirty work. Way more than our MC alliance."

"So, why is his last name..." She bounced the heel of her palm off her forehead. "Holy shit. Of course! Smith is a fake name, isn't it?"

"Gotta be."

"But why would he need to use a fake name?"

Romeo jerked up one shoulder. "Most likely so the place where you worked wouldn't be tied to that crime family. Could be they use that place for money launderin'. Who fuckin' knows. Fact is, he's got connections. Ones you don't wanna fuck with."

"Were his connections for the professional sports team a lie?" If she suffered working for that dickhead for a whole year and a half when it was never going to get her anywhere...

"Can't say. But if so, it could also be why he's usin' Smith as a last name. Sure those teams don't wanna be tied to anyone in the goddamn Mafia."

She couldn't imagine they would. *Hell*, she wouldn't have worked for him if she knew that.

If all of this was true, Roger hid it well.

Or... was Romeo lying to her?

Did he really crash his sled and made up this story simply to get back in her good graces?

Would he stoop to that?

She studied the man before her. Most motorcycle crashes resulted in road rash. Romeo wouldn't escape getting some if the crash was bad enough to cause broken bones and other bruises.

"Take your shirt off."

His head jerked back. Most likely from not expecting that demand. "Normally, I'd be good with that. Not today."

Interesting. "I've seen you naked before." Many times.

"Nothin' to do with bein' naked. Everythin' to do with havin' broken ribs."

"What did they use on you?"

"Tire iron. Boots. Fists."

She rose to her feet and stepped toe-to-toe with him. "When it's bones versus a tire iron, bones usually break before steel does. I want to see."

"Why? So you can' poke me in the fuckin ribs? Make me suffer for fuckin' up your life?"

"Tempting," she murmured, sliding her hands under his cut, and slipping it off.

He didn't stop her, but warned her with a, "Careful," instead.

She raised his colors in her hand. "With this? Or with you?"

Something flashed behind his dark eyes. "Both."

She knew how important a cut was to club members and that she needed to treat it with respect. It represented their way of life. It represented their brotherhood, their found family, their loyalty to each other. It represented their *everything.*

Turning his head, he watched her place it over the single chair in the small room and return to stand before him. He stood quietly, with only a few winces, as she slowly and carefully tugged his shirt from his jeans and up his torso, cautiously working it around the cast on his arm and his crutch. Once his broad torso was bare, she tossed the T-shirt onto the bed and circled him, using both her eyes and a light touch to check every inch she could see.

His magnificent body was definitely damaged. It didn't look anything like the last time she saw him naked.

Just the memory of the last time they had sex, made her breathing shallow and her pussy clench.

God, why did this man make her weak? Why did she keep having to remind herself what he did and what that action did to her.

She couldn't let him off the hook easily. If at all.

She skipped over his ribs and any visible bruises, though some were harder to spot than others due to his dark skin and numerous tattoos. No road rash was found, and the visible injuries were consistent with being beaten and not crashing his sled.

He'd been truthful with her. He wasn't only making a play to get her to forgive him. But that also meant what he was saying about Roger could be true.

Was her former boss really tied to the *Mafia*? Was that from where his arrogance stemmed? Was he more of an awful person than Maddie ever realized?

Romeo said that the people who jumped him had beaten him with a freaking tire iron. She couldn't wrap her mind around how he wasn't worse off. Or dead. "Jesus, Rome. How didn't they not break any more bones than they did?"

"Pretty damn confident when I say Jesus didn't help me. Guessin' he thought I deserved that ass kickin' as a warnin'. If it wasn't for Wick steppin' out back for a smoke, it woulda been worse."

Thank goodness for Wick! "Do you plan on retaliating?"

Romeo would never simply let what happened to him go. He'd want revenge despite his statement that La Cosa Nostra had a bigger army than the MC alliance. And between the three clubs, that combined biker brotherhood was pretty damn large and powerful.

They also had Diesel's Shadows at their backs. Even though those six former special ops guys were getting up in age, they still were more dangerous than more than a dozen bikers.

"Can't do shit right now."

He didn't say he wouldn't eventually do it, either. But... would he try to handle it on his own? She couldn't imagine that Trip or Zak would want to go head-to-head with the Mafia and start a huge war. Right now, things were quiet and content in their worlds. Their expanding clubs and families were safe.

"Are you worried that they'll come after you again? I don't know much about the Mafia except for what I learned from movies and TV. I can't imagine that's an accurate portrayal."

"Pretty damn close."

If that was true, Romeo being a target of the Mafia was more than concerning. "They could've killed you, Rome." What was that mysterious sting in her eyes?

She refused to cry over the man who blew up her future. No matter how injured he was. No matter if what happened to him was some kind of karma. Karma she did not order.

She would never want him badly injured or dead. Despite what he did and how she'd suffered since.

With his good arm, he reached out, snagged her chin, and tipped her face up to his. "Would you have missed me if they did?"

"That's not even funny, Rome." If he wasn't injured, she would've pushed him away because of his attempt to play on her emotions. Instead, she tried not to let his touch chip any more away from the steel coating her heart.

"Yeah, no shit. Wasn't fuckin' laughin' when I was ambushed, but laughin' right now would really fuckin' suck." He paused before saying, "They weren't out to kill me. They were givin' me a warnin', makin' a statement. They wanted me dead, wouldn't be here right now. Easily could've been picked off from a distance, shanked in a crowd or run over by one of their fuckin' garbage trucks while ridin' my sled."

"Romeo," she breathed, trying not to imagine any of that.

He dropped his head even lower, locking their gazes. "Yeah, you'd miss me."

Being beaten badly certainly didn't curtail any of his cockiness.

She stepped back and freed herself from his grip. "You misunderstood. I don't want anyone hurt or killed like that. Not just you." *But especially you.*

"Bullshit. You know what sucks the most about all this shit?"

"The pain?"

"No. The worst part is I can't fuck you."

Of course. Fucking was a higher priority than even breathing for this man.

"Your injuries aren't what's preventing that, Rome. It takes two to tango and this woman isn't in the mood to dance with you. You said you were going to explain why you're in Parsington and why you tricked me to get me here. I still haven't heard an explanation, and your fifteen minutes are about up." She needed to hear what he had to say, this way she could leave before her resolve completely crumbled and she fell for his charm.

Or lack of charm.

"Gonna tell you 'bout my momma."

Well damn, that was a complete change of subject. But with the way he said it, she had a feeling she wasn't going to like this "explanation." She once again settled on the edge of the bed.

"She's the reason I got involved even when you told me not to."

"You said she was gone."

"She is. Still miss her every fuckin' day, too."

Her throat tightened from the painful loss in his tone and expression on his face.

More evidence that she wasn't going to like this story. Not at all.

"Saw what happened to you happen to her."

What? "With her boss?"

He shook his head. "Her last man."

Her last man. She frowned. "Like a boyfriend?"

"Yeah." He sighed. "She knew how to fuckin' pick 'em. Even the bastard whose nuts I spawned from. Swear she was a magnet to every fuckin' loser and user. But that last one..." He shook his head and pulled in a breath. "With him, I watched her lose herself little by little 'til nothin' was left but a goddamn empty shell. That motherfucker had her fuckin' brainwashed with all that gaslightin'. Made her think things were true when they were a complete fuckin' lie. Nothin' I said would change her mind and all of it was hard to watch. Begged her to leave him. Tried like fuck to convince her. But his influence was helluva lot stronger. He made her think she was useless. She was a nothin' without him. Eventually she became a shadow of the mother that I remembered. It got to a point where she couldn't take anymore..."

When he stopped talking, she waited a bit before prodding him with, "You said she was gone."

"Yeah."

She debated whether to ask this—or even how to ask—but she needed to know the whole story. "Did he kill her?"

"Not by his hands."

She blinked and let her mind sort out what he said before concluding softly, "But by her own."

"Yeah."

Holy shit. "How old were you?"

"Ten."

Holy shit! "You didn't... find her, right?" *Please say no. Please say no. Please say no.*

"Asshole did. And the fuckin' kicker was, she wrote him a goddamn note. Left nothin' for me."

She slapped a hand over her heart because an arrow had pierced through the steel.

The picture hanging on the wall in his place flashed through her mind... "That's when your aunt took you in."

"Yeah."

"Where's he at now?"

His chin rose and his expression turned into concrete. "Where you think?"

Of course. "I couldn't imagine you'd let that slide." Just like she wouldn't expect Romeo to let what Roger and his "family" did to him slide.

"Shoulda done it sooner. She might still be here."

Oh sure. It was perfectly normal for someone younger than ten to make his mother's lover disappear. It wasn't even normal for adults! "You were a child, Rome. On the other hand, your mother was an adult. She made her own decisions, whether good or bad. She stayed with him despite how he treated her."

"Like you did?"

Her situation wasn't quite the same as his mother's. Roger had been her boss, not her significant other. If she had to deal with Roger twenty-four/seven... "You mean until you took my choice away from me."

"Didn't mean for shit to go down like it did. You came to me 'cause of the stress that motherfucker was puttin' you through. I saw it, woman, with my own two eyes. Can't say I hated you slidin' into my bed 'cause of it but hated the reason why."

"Are you touting yourself as a hero for getting me fired? I want to make sure I'm clear about that."

He huffed, "Ain't a hero. The fuck if I was gonna sit back and watch that asshole continue to do to you the same as what that motherfucker did to my momma. People are scared about gettin' beat the fuck up physically. Bein' beat up mentally's just as bad, if it ain't worse. My broken bones will heal within weeks. A broken mind can't heal that fast. Sometimes it never recovers."

"I'm sorry that happened to your mother. I'm sorry there are people like that in the world. I'm sorry you didn't tell me about what happened to your mother sooner."

His eyebrows rose. "That've made a difference?"

"I don't know," she answered honestly. "I was determined to work toward my dream job, and I thought working for Roger would make that happen. But even if I was wrong and he couldn't or wouldn't help, without a good reference..."

"And I fucked up your good reference."

"It wasn't only a reference, Rome. That was only one piece of the puzzle." She ticked off the rest one-by-one. "I needed consistent employment, the right experience, and the necessary hours to even be considered for that type of position. They were never going to look at anyone with the limited amount of time I had working with patients."

"Not sure how to fix it."

Holy shit, did he sound sincere? Did he really feel badly about what he did and wanted to make amends?

Could she forgive him? That remained to be seen. "I don't think you can. I can only hope someone will give me a chance so I can rebuild my resume. But, honestly, if Roger really did have connections to those sports teams, then I'm shit out of luck in that respect. If I want to continue working toward my dream—and I do—then I might have to move to a different state with different teams. Teams Roger won't have any influence with."

She really didn't want to do that, though. While she didn't want to live with her family, or even in Manning Grove, she also didn't want to move far enough away so it was more of a chore to visit. She was close with her family and wanted it to remain that way. Plus, she'd have no one at her back if she needed someone.

Add in the fact that Shade would not like her being so far out of reach. He never hid the fact that she, Josie, their mother, and Jude belonged to him now. They were under his protection, and he took that seriously.

If anything happened to any of them, he would leave behind nothing but scorched earth.

Chapter Thirty-Seven

"I'VE BEEN SENDING out resumes all over. Without a good reference, I'll have to take any interview I can get, no matter where it's located."

The fuck if Maddie was moving to some other fucking state. That was some goddamn bullshit.

"Shade ain't gonna let you leave this side of the state," Romeo said with more confidence than he felt. He hoped to fuck what he said was true.

"He might not like it, but he doesn't rule my life." She shot him a pointed look. "No one does. And what you did left me between a rock and a hard place, Rome. It's not a decision I want to make, but I might not have a choice."

"Always got a choice," he grumbled.

She hated that pat answer because it wasn't always true. "Oh sure. You mean the choice of working at one of the Fury businesses for practically free or wiping down tables at Coffee and Cream for minimum wage? That's not what I went *years* to school for. Sorry, but I'm not giving up my dream or career goals because of Shade." She then added, "Or you."

He needed to come up with a plan to keep her in western Pennsylvania. "Got a gig for you."

She rolled her eyes. "Sure you do. Doing what? Being a line cook or tending bar at Dick's? If I wanted to do that for a living, I could work at Crazy Pete's."

"Need your expertise."

"My expertise?" Her voice raised a pitch. "For what?"

"Doc said I'm gonna need a physical therapist once these fuckin' casts are off."

"I can recommend you a good one."

"Already got a good one."

"I'm sure I can find you a competent one closer. No need to drive hours north to see me."

"Not true. Got plenty of other fuckin' reasons to come see you." Not only did he have to convince her to take charge of his PT but to move back south to do so.

"Name one." Maddie lifted a finger and added, "Other than sex."

"Got a whole list."

"Okay, let's hear it."

Shit. He wasn't expecting to be called out on that claim. He should've known better. Maddie was smart and no pushover. But...

If she thought he would cut himself open by giving her that list... *Fuck that.* He already was doing shit not normal for him just by driving north to see her. By telling her about his mother. He never shared personal shit with women, and he certainly didn't chase them.

Fuck. If that wasn't a reality check...

He still didn't understand his obsession with her. Why he couldn't stop thinking about her day and night. What made

Maddie different from the rest of his conquests? The answer *should* be "nothing."

Only, it wasn't.

His chest tightened when unexpected panic began to set in. "Ain't my fifteen minutes up?"

Her eyebrows raised. "I'm willing to extend your time limit for this."

Jesus Christ. "Missin' the point."

"I doubt that I am."

"Maddie, I couldn't just sit the fuck back and watch him abuse you like that." Anyone who cared for her wouldn't. If any Fury member knew about Smith being a total dick to her, they certainly would've stepped in and handled it.

"Well, you definitely solved the problem. Only not in the manner I would prefer. It would've been much more karmasmic for me to leave his employ once I got my dream job. I would've relished seeing that asshole's face when handing in my two-week notice."

"Karmasmic?" That was a goddamn mouthful.

Her lips curled slightly at the corners as she explained, "The satisfaction of seeing karma in action."

"It give you a karmagasm?"

A smile flitted across her lips before she pinned them together to smother it.

Fuck, did that make him want to see her orgasm again. Unfortunately, that wouldn't be any time soon.

Unless he got creative.

Of course, she wouldn't be open to that right now. He had more work to do...

His brain had to be scrambled. He still couldn't understand why he fucking cared that she had ignored all his texts and calls.

Why did that bother him so fucking much?

And why did his heart do some crazy shit when he saw her parked out front?

Or getting out of her Toyota.

Or stepping into his motel room.

Those were signs he was fucking broken, right?

In the past, he'd been relieved when women simply disappeared out of his life. No "goodbye" was necessary. Truthfully, if they left quietly on their own, it made his life a fuck of a lot simpler.

No whining. No screeching. No stalking.

No fucking drama at all.

So, why the fuck was he here?

He said he had a list of reasons. Really, there was only one.

Her.

"You're right. Your fifteen minutes is up." She rose from the bed. "I need to go. Thanks for the explanation and I'm sorry for what happened to your mother. I'm sorry you lost her in that manner. But what happened to you, Rome, is your fault. What you did was reckless. I didn't tell you to rough up Roger. You did that on your own. I told you to a thousand times to stay out of it, but you couldn't. Now, not only am I unemployed and possibly blacklisted, you were broken into pieces." She headed toward the door. "Have a great life, Rome. I'll try to do the same."

He raised his crutch and used it to block her path. He wasn't done with her yet. "Could give you a great life, Maddie. Could give you whatever you want."

Her eyes bugged out. "Whatever I want? I think you tried that already and look where it landed. Are you really willing to give up your title of Supreme Stud? Are you feeling okay? Do you have a fever?"

"Got a few aches and pains," he answered. "I get that you

don't think I'm bein' serious, but I am. You could come back with me."

Her brown eyes got even wider. "And do what?"

"Wear my cut."

For fuck's sake. Did that really come out of his mouth? He never wanted an ol' lady and figured he'd die a bachelor. Remain free to the very fucking end.

No one to answer to. No woman going on and on about bullshit in his ear. No long honey-do lists. No...

He pulled in a breath.

No Maddie.

The tightness in his chest returned.

All of this was proof Smith's goons knocked his brain loose and scrambled his wiring.

A dry laugh burst from her. "Why? You don't need me. You have sweet butts to do your bidding."

She was right.

But also very wrong.

He did need her.

Not to baby him or be his nursemaid.

Not only for sex.

"It'll tell everyone you're mine."

"But I'm not."

"Only need a little convincin'."

"You think that's all it will take? If so, you're simple."

"Like a simple life."

"Then you should live one, but I know being an MC president is far from simple. For years I've watched Trip lead the Blood Fury. It's hard work and a lot of responsibility. Now that I think about it, how the hell did you become president?"

Damn. That was a low blow, but not the first time he'd been asked that. "Got skills."

"*Mmm hmm.* What skills are those? The ability to remove bras with one hand? Or talk a woman out of her skirt? Eating pussy?"

The last one was definitely one of his greater skills and he wasn't shy to admit it. "You forget how good I eat pussy? Need me to remind you?"

With pursed lips, her eyes sliced him up and down. "I don't think you're in any shape for that, but thanks for the offer."

"Ain't gonna be like this forever." His brain might be broken but his mouth wasn't. It would only take some careful planning.

"I guess you didn't get the hint when I moved home and blocked your number."

"'Bout that—"

She raised a palm. "Look... Even if I was interested in being your ol' lady, it's common knowledge you could never commit to one woman, *Romeo.* It's not in your nature and I'm also not stupid. *If* and when I settle down, I want it to be with a man I love and respect and who does the same in return. Someone who supports my decisions, whether he likes them or not. Someone loyal and only has eyes for me. Someone who won't get bored and cheat. I don't think you fit that bill."

He opened his mouth to tell her that she was wrong, and she would be the exception, but he quickly snapped it shut. Never in his goddamn life did he think he'd have to work so damn hard to get a woman to wear his cut.

And why would he? Again, what the fuck was wrong with him?

His plan hadn't been to come to Manning Grove to get her to wear his cut, to become his ol' lady, it was only to...

"Right," he finally muttered.

"I thought so. Now... since you clearly don't need babysitting, I should go."

Once again, he blocked her exit by using his crutch. "Since I'm injured, a babysitter couldn't hurt." Especially if it was her.

"You have one already. He's waiting in the car," she tipped her head toward the door, "and he's free. I charge by the hour."

"What's your hourly rate include?"

"Microwaving chicken nuggets and turning on your favorite cartoons."

One side of his mouth pulled up. "Don't fuckin' threaten me with a good time."

She finally cracked a smile, too. "Thanks for proving that you *are* simple."

"Said simple life."

He needed to come up with a better plan. Winging it wasn't working.

He wracked his brain. What the hell did women like?

He had no idea. He never "dated." He never had to "romance" any of them to get them naked.

He only ever wanted one thing from them, and he preferred women who only wanted the same from him.

Dinner? Drinks? Movies? He had no fucking clue. But everyone had to eat at one point or another, so... "Have dinner with me."

Her head snapped back. "What? Why?"

That request shouldn't have been so damn shocking. *Jesus.* "Why the fuck not? We both gotta eat, right?"

"But you want us to eat *together*. Like at a sit-down restaurant?"

"What the fuck, woman?" he muttered with a shake of his head.

"When's the last time you took a woman out to dinner?"

Never. "We ate at Dick's together."

"We shoveled food into our mouths while standing at one of the prep tables. That isn't the same."

"Depends on who you ask."

She stared at him with that elusive smile long gone. "What are you doing, Rome?"

"What d'you mean?"

"What. Are. You. Doing? What is all this?" She fluttered a hand around in the air. "Why are you suddenly wanting me to wear your cut? You, a known womanizer and perpetual bachelor."

"Maybe that ambush woke me up and got me realizin' life's too fuckin' short."

"I'm sure you knew that before you were introduced to a tire iron."

"Maybe it hit it home."

"Is that supposed to be a joke?"

"Maddie..."

"Rome... I just... don't understand this coming from you. Just because we had sex—"

"A shitload of times," he interjected.

"Doesn't mean I want to be your ol' lady," she finished. "Are you stoned?"

"Ain't high. Ain't drunk..." He lowered the crutch and jerked his chin toward the door. "Never fuckin' mind. Said you gotta go, then go."

She stared at him for far too long with her forehead creased in confusion.

He was done trying to enlighten her. She either got it or she didn't. And it was clear...

She didn't.

However, she paused instead of immediately sprinting

the short distance to the door. "Let me think about dinner. How long are you staying up here? Do you have a meeting with Trip?"

If he did, he certainly wouldn't be staying in some shit-bag motel. He'd be at The Grove Inn, instead. But he was keeping his presence in the area on the down-low and preferred no one in the Fury knew he was up here chasing Maddie. Especially the Fury's president, as well as Shade.

"Not sure how long I'm stayin'." He had planned to stay long enough to convince her to head back south with him.

Unfortunately, it was looking like that wasn't going to be easy and he couldn't stay up here forever. His absence from both Dick's and his MC would raise red flags in his own brotherhood.

"You let me know. When you do, either gonna be here or ain't."

"If you aren't, I know where to find you," she said as she headed out the door.

"Doubt you'll even bother to look," he muttered to the door after she shut it behind her.

If he was goddamn smart, he'd to head home and forget this woman ever fucking existed.

But he was simple and forgetting her would be impossible.

Chapter Thirty-Eight

A MUFFLED SOUND, sounding way too fucking close, had his eyes flashing open.

What the fuck was that?

Roaches? A rat?

"Booger?"

The prospect didn't have a key to his room, so it had to be fucking roaches. This motel grew them as big as fucking ponies.

Before he could turn on the bedside lamp to make those bastards scatter, he found himself pinned down to the bed.

"What the fuck?" he shouted.

Jesus Christ! Did La Cosa Nostra track him down up here in Parsington? Were they here to finish the job?

Where the fuck did he put his gun? Could he even shoot with his left hand since his right arm was fucked up?

Whatever he was going to do, he needed to do it now. He wouldn't willingly go back into the hospital.

Or six feet underground.

It fucking sucked because, with broken ribs and without full use of one leg and arm, he was basically helpless. He couldn't fight like he normally could and was at their fucking mercy.

From what he could tell in the dark and by the number of hands holding him down, it was only two men. Maybe Wick had shot and killed the third motherfucker who ambushed him. Assuming these were the same losers.

Neither intruder said a word, and both wore dark clothing along with hats pulled low. Unfortunately, the little he could see disappeared the second they yanked him up into seated position and tugged what felt like a pillowcase over his head.

Why the fuck weren't they saying a goddamn thing?

This was not good. "Who the fuck are you? Did that asshole hire you?"

No surprise, he didn't get a response. Instead, they yanked him off the bed and to his feet. Or, more like it, foot.

He saw stars when he bucked hard against them, trying to pull free. "Lemme fuckin' go. You're makin' a fuckin' mistake you don't wanna make. Promise you that. You're gonna be hunted down like fuckin' rabid dogs."

He couldn't hide his grunts of pain as they wrapped a rope around his bare waist and manhandled him so they could bind his good arm to it. Clearly, they didn't give a shit that he was already fucked up and, for the most part, unable to fight them off.

Jesus Christ. Was he going to die only wearing his skivvies? In a goddamn roach motel?

He released a searing curse when they tightened the rope even more, causing sharp pains to radiate from his broken ribs.

"Booger!" he shouted, hoping the prospect could hear

him in the next room since the walls were thin. So thin that last night he could hear that stupid shit whacking off to porn. Not just once, but five fucking times. "Booger! Goddamn it!"

There was no way these assholes would let him keep shouting for help. But it was so damn whacked that they didn't order him to shut up. So, until they stopped him, he would use his fucking voice since that was all he had.

"Booger! Wake the fuck—"

———

ROMEO GROANED. His tongue was as dry as a goddamn desert from whatever was tied around his mouth, effectively gagging him. He couldn't see shit since the pillowcase was still in place.

However, it was pretty damn clear *he* was no longer in place and unwillingly on the move.

No voices could be heard, only the sound of an engine and road noise. And, of course, his own pounding heartbeat.

His head throbbed at the point where they knocked him out to shut him up. His good leg was now bound to his casted one, trussing him up like a turkey ready for the oven on Thanksgiving Day.

He had no idea who kidnapped him.

He had no idea where he was headed.

He had no idea how to fucking save himself since he couldn't rely on his goddamn prospect. Apparently jacking off five times in a row made you sleep like the dead.

If Romeo somehow survived this, he would make sure Booger never got his fucking colors. Not after this. And if he did die, then his MC would make sure Booger wouldn't need colors where they sent him for failing to protect his prez.

A mortal sin for a prospect.

Romeo grunted when the van, or whatever he was in, stopped suddenly and he rolled forward.

For fuck's sake, just the trip alone was torture due to the pain.

He listened carefully to keep track of what was happening so he would be prepared in the slim chance he had an opportunity to escape. He logged all the sounds in his throbbing noggin.

The silencing of the engine.

The opening and slamming shut of both the driver and passenger doors.

The slide of a side door, confirming he was right about being transported in a full-sized van.

Wheels rolling towards the van. Not another vehicle. Something smaller. A cart? A gurney?

Suddenly, hands were on him again, sliding him across the van floor, lifting him up and dropping him onto a flat surface. His plaster casts slamming into the thin metal echoed through the night.

He gritted his teeth to endure the bumpy ride over what could be pavement, then up some kind of ramp. They took him into the cool and quiet interior of a building. Only the wheels rolling along concrete could be detected.

Why would La Cosa Nostra take him to some building in Manning Grove? That didn't make any damn sense.

Had he been passed out longer than he thought? Had he been taken to Pittsburgh instead?

When the cart came to an abrupt halt, he was surprised he didn't shoot off the end to be rudely introduced to the floor.

Without warning, he was jerked off the cart and onto some other metal, flat object. But this surface wasn't solid. It felt more like a grate with holes against the bare skin of his back and cast-free leg.

The possibility of escape was flushed down the fucking toilet the second they lashed his ass down to whatever the metal grate was.

A moment later he heard a loud whoosh. Something—he had no fucking idea what—had been fired up.

What the hell was going on?

Was this the end for him?

Unexpectedly, the pillowcase was yanked over his head and the gag sliced free of his mouth with a big-ass knife.

He blinked and checked out his surroundings as best as he could. *What the fuck was this?*

Wait...

He twisted his neck to see where the heat was coming from that was searing his skin.

Holy fuckin' shit.

He didn't think the situation could get any worse until he realized he was on some sort of rolling pan that slid into a large oven.

He was right. He *was* a Thanksgiving Day turkey about to be cooked.

Christ. He did not want to die by being incinerated.

When he recognized his two abductors, it hit him where he was.

It wasn't La Cosa Nostra. He hadn't even left Manning Grove.

He was at Tioga Pet Crematorium, a business owned by the Fury. They had bought it for a good reason. And what they were about to do to him was one of them.

Son of a fuckin' bitch.

Did Maddie go running to her goddamn stepdaddy? Did

Shade know Romeo fucked her? Or even worse, popped her fucking cherry all those years ago?

With his eyes wider and his asshole pinched tighter than he wanted to admit, he asked, "Tell me what the fuck I did to deserve the death penalty?"

"Your past actions prove you're a dog," Shade answered in his slightly slower pace. The Fury member spoke much better now than when Romeo first met him. It was more obvious years ago when he had to carefully choose his words. "Know how many dogs we've turned to ashes in this very oven?"

"What's one more?" Easy wore a fucking grin that Romeo wished he could wipe off the other Fury member's face.

Holy fuckin' shit. "You're gonna fuckin' burn me to death?"

Both the heat and the thought of being turned into a pile of ash was causing him to sweat. If he had to die, this was not the way he wanted to go. *Hell*, they could incinerate him, flush his ashes down the toilet and his own club members would have no fucking idea what happened to him.

Here one day, flushed the next.

He threw out a hail Mary. "Don't you think that's gonna fuck up the alliance?"

"Who's gonna know?" Easy asked. "You simply disappeared one day. *Poof*, you went up in fuckin' smoke."

"Ain't gonna be nothin' left of you. No fuckin' proof what happened here tonight," Shade added.

Romeo knew Shade was "off," but to kill a president of an MC that was part of the Fury's alliance? That was totally fucking whacked.

"Know your reputation, Romeo," Shade growled. "Know you like to use women for your own pleasure, then kick them to the fuckin' curb. Maddie ain't a sweet butt. She ain't for you to take advantage of. Hell, she ain't for you. Period."

"She tell you I took—" He slammed his mouth shut. He needed to carefully negotiate with them, not give them shit so they were tempted to say "fuck it" and push the rolling tray with his Black ass on it into those fucking flames.

He stifled his shudder at the prospect of burning to death. That had to be one of the worst fucking ways to die.

Stay calm. Keep your fuckin' patience. Don't let 'em see you sweat.

Too late for the sweating part since beads were already covering his forehead and rolling down his temples just from the heat alone.

"Love my family. Will fuckin' do anythin' for 'em. Last thing I want is for my girl to get burned by the likes of you. You got plenty of women to fuck with. Leave Maddie the fuck alone."

That sounded like a warning for the future and not the threat of imminent death. Was this whole thing some sort of sick fake-out? He wouldn't celebrate yet. "You had to go through this bullshit to tell me that?"

"Needed to make a statement. One you wouldn't forget."

Romeo could guarantee he'd never forget this shit. Not sure he'd ever forgive it, either.

"You fuckin' tell her to leave me alone, too? Or do you just think it was one-sided?" he asked Shade.

"Don't give a fuck if she wants to marry you and have your goddamn babies. Ain't gonna happen. Find a reason to cut her loose."

Didn't he know that Maddie had already cut ties with him? "How's she gonna like you interferin' in her life?"

Shade didn't answer, but Easy did. "Ain't for her to know and you ain't gonna tell her, either."

One side of Shade's mouth pulled up and it wasn't in a smile. For the first time in his fucking life, a sliver of fear slipped down Romeo's spine.

He could hold his own if the threat came at him from the front. But it was well known among those in the alliance that Shade was quiet and deadly. Unlike Diesel. Unlike Judge. Unlike Magnum.

Shade was more dangerous than all of them. He was on the same ass-puckering level as Diesel's Shadows.

You'd be dead before you know what hit you.

He needed to convince Shade to reconsider his plans. "She tell you about her dick boss? And why I stepped in?"

"She tell you not to get involved?"

Ah, fuck.

"But you did anyway, didn't you?" Easy asked next.

The two Fury members were tag-teaming him.

Shade tipped his head at Easy. "Slide him in."

"Wait!" Romeo shouted. "Does Maddie know you're doin' this?"

"Not up to her."

"She might have a fuckin' opinion."

"Opinions are like assholes," Easy said on a dry laugh, "everyone's got one."

Fuck Easy. Romeo needed to concentrate on Shade. Easy was just that psycho's sidekick. "She didn't wanna tell you about that dick she worked for. She was afraid somethin' like this would happen to him if she did. So, I took care of it, instead."

"By gettin' her fired."

How much did Maddie tell him?

"You should be fuckin' thankin' me for handlin' that asshole. Only wanted to teach that fucker a lesson for abusin' her. Was tryin' to help her goddamn career not fuck it up."

"Well, you fucked it up," Easy said. "All those goddamn years of college and now what? She's back to livin' at home and takin' odd jobs. All 'cause you couldn't respect her decisions."

"What the fuck this gotta do with you?" Romeo bit off.

"She's family," was Easy's answer. "We're all fuckin' family." He leaned closer. "You ain't."

"Shoulda came to me," Shade said.

"About that dickhead? Just said—"

"To ask permission," Easy interrupted.

"To fuck up that motherfu—"

"To fuck her."

Son of a fuckin' bitch. "This shit ain't got nothin' to do with you, Easy. Stay the fuck outta it."

Easy smiled. "Those are some strong fuckin' words for a broken man."

"Untie me and we'll see how fuckin' broken I am."

"Enough," Shade quietly interjected.

Romeo pulled in a breath to cool off his temper. Easy was right. He was in no fucking condition to threaten anyone. Not only was he injured and wearing casts, but he was tied down.

He needed to keep his head.

"Need you to know you ain't my choice for her," Shade said next.

"Gettin' that."

What sucked was, Romeo still had no idea how much Shade knew. He didn't want to dig because that could raise red flags. And his Black ass was still parked in front of a human-sized oven.

Now was not the best time to talk about Maddie's sex life and how he was involved.

"Seems as if what I want for her is different than what she wants," Shade continued.

Hold up. What the fuck did she want?

"But that don't mean I can't tell you what I want anyway..."

Oh fuck.

Romeo needed off this goddamn rollercoaster. They either needed to kill him or—

"You to be true to Maddie. Meaning... No side pieces, no sweet butts, no nothin'. I hear you stepped out on her..."

"Ain't gonna do that."

"Havin' a hard time believin' that with your history."

"She changed me." *Holy fuck.* Was that true? "For the better," he quickly added. "Want her to wear my cut."

"She said," came Easy's unwelcomed response.

Christ, now he couldn't back out. Was he going to be stuck with one woman for the rest of his fucking life?

And if he fucked up, he'd get incinerated?

That sounded worse than life in prison.

Was the sweat gathering on his forehead from him having a fucking panic attack because his life as he knew it would be over and not because of facing death?

If it was anyone other than Maddie...

He closed his eyes and tried to slow his racing heart.

But it *was* Maddie.

He wasn't being forced into taking an ol' lady.

He didn't have to offer her his cut.

But he did. Before this threat.

Why?

Because his real panic began when he found her gone. After she moved back to Manning Grove.

He had been and still was afraid of losing her.

Christ. Who the fuck was he? How could a lone female make his life do a complete one-eighty?

"Now... My ol' lady invited you to dinner."

He opened his eyes. *What the actual fuck?*

One minute the man was threatening to reduce him to a pile of ashes, the next, inviting him to share a fucking meal?

This whole damn thing was messed up.

Chapter Thirty-Nine

NEVER IN HIS goddamn life did he think he'd be sitting around a table and having dinner with the parents of a woman he fucked.

Like this was normal. Like they were normal.

None of them were normal.

Not a fucking one.

Despite his broken ribs, leg and arm, he had a hard time sitting still.

He might have escaped being cremated long before it was his time, but he was still paranoid about this dinner invite. This whole thing had to be a damn trap, and he wouldn't be surprised if Fury members stormed in at any goddamn second, dragged his ass out and buried him out in one of their fields, never to be seen again.

He glanced at his still full plate, then up at Maddie sitting across from him. She chewed away unbothered like Romeo shared dinner with them every night.

But no one was saying a damn word.

Shade sat at one end of the dining table, Chelle at the

other. Romeo sat along one side next to Jude, while Maddie sat next to her sister Josie.

"Why aren't you eating?" Maddie's adopted brother asked him.

Maybe because a few hours ago he was only a cunt hair away from being turned to ashes.

Or because both he and Maddie were being closely watched by Shade.

Or because Maddie's younger sister kept giggling under her breath. Most likely from the awkwardness from this whole fucking situation.

He told Maddie he wanted to take her to dinner. Only, he didn't expect it to be at her family's house.

"You don't like the chicken?" Shade's ol' lady asked him.

Romeo glanced at Maddie's mother, then again at his plate. He picked up his fork and knife, cut off a small piece of the roasted bird and shoved it into his mouth. "It's great," he answered Chelle as he chewed, not even tasting it.

He had to gulp down some water just to swallow that small piece since his throat was tight.

Across the table, Josie giggle-snorted and elbowed her older sister.

"Stop," Maddie whispered, not finding this situation as entertaining as her sister.

"How'd you get injured?" Jude asked.

The kid had to be in his late teens or early twenties by now. He'd grown like a fucking weed since he first arrived in Manning Grove.

"From not mindin' my own business."

Jude chuckled and stabbed the last potato wedge on his plate with his fork. "I'm assuming you killed them for what they did."

Maddie's fork clattered to her plate, and she dropped her head in her hands with a groan.

Shade's expression remained unreadable.

Josie's eyes grew as wide as her plate before she burst out in a peel of laughter.

And Chelle scolded, "Jude! Not at the dinner table!"

But on the couch would be perfectly okay?

Jude shrugged and grinned. "That's how we'd handle it in the Fury."

Romeo frowned. "You a member now?"

The kid's chest puffed out. "Prospect."

Romeo grunted and glanced at Maddie again. She rolled her eyes at her younger brother's boasting.

Apparently, Shade hadn't schooled his "son" on how club business should remain within the club. That meant patched members only. "Guessin' you haven't learned yet, you don't mention that kinda shit in mixed company."

"Like they don't know what—"

"Jude!" Shade barked.

Jude pressed his lips together.

"He's right," Shade murmured. "Runnin' your mouth's a good way to get your cut pulled."

Romeo got whiplash when Jude quickly switched topics. "You eatin' your potatoes?"

He slid his plate over to Jude. "All yours." He watched Jude shovel the crispy potato wedges into his gullet as fast as he could.

"Sorry that you didn't enjoy your meal," Chelle apologized softly.

Shit. "Ain't that. The pain's fuckin' up my stomach." And, of course, his pain right now was a level ten out of ten because of being manhandled by Shade and Easy. But he took his own advice and wouldn't mention that shit in mixed company.

It wasn't only the pain that made him lose his appetite. It was the fact he had no idea about the point of this dinner. He really needed to get Maddie by herself later and have another convo. Let her know he wasn't blowing smoke up her ass about wanting her to wear his cut.

Maybe she believed it as much as he did.

He definitely lost his goddamn mind.

When he looked over at her, she was smiling at him behind her glass of water.

Had she forgiven him or was that some evil smile because she knew this was to be his last meal?

Was this her idea of revenge for him fucking up her future?

A buzz had his heart jumping out of his chest.

Everyone at the table checked their phones except for Chelle.

And Romeo. Because he wasn't taking his eyes off anyone.

With his phone in hand, Shade slid his chair back. He turned his dark eyes to Romeo. "They're waitin' for us."

Say what? "Who?"

"Let's go," was Shade's response, along with a jerk of his head toward the front of the house.

For fuck's sake. This day was turning out to be all kinds of fucked. "I got a choice?"

"No."

"Can I go?" Jude asked.

"No," Shade repeated.

Maddie's expression told him nothing.

Shade's face told him shit.

The taste of dread in his mouth was bitter. "You know what this is?" he asked Maddie.

She shook her head. "No. But you're in good hands."

She wouldn't be saying that shit if she knew what game her stepdaddy played with him in the middle of the night.

He grabbed the crutch leaning against the table and used it to help himself stand.

"Bye, Romeo!" Josie yelled as he followed the long-haired Fury member to the front door.

He paused when he heard Chelle call out, "Good luck!"

Romeo had no idea what the fuck was going on, but he was damn sure he could use all the luck he could get.

———

Limping his way up the stairs to the second floor at The Barn, the Fury's church, had sucked. When he stepped inside the Blood Fury's meeting room, he found the officers already sitting around the solid wood table with the club logo carved in it dead center.

Shade hadn't been shitting him when he said "they" were waiting.

Trip was leaning back in the chair at the head of the table at the opposite end of where Romeo stood leaning on his crutch.

He damn sure didn't like being in the hot seat. Though, he wasn't invited to actually sit, despite having two obvious broken limbs.

"Came to claim Maddie, huh?" Sig, Trip's brother and the club's VP, asked.

"Doin' this backward, ain't ya?" Cage, their road captain, asked next.

"Didn't have to do it at all," Romeo told them.

Trip cocked an eyebrow. "That right?"

It wasn't, but the fuck if he was changing his answer. He had the utmost respect for Trip and the rest of the Fury members, but he wasn't some damn chump. He was the goddamn president of the Dark Knights MC. He didn't answer to them. He was only here out of respect.

And possibly because Shade insisted.

Forget the fact it was also strongly suggested by Magnum for the good of the alliance.

Fuck.

"Touched Fury property without askin' first," Ozzy, the club secretary, announced like it was breaking news.

"Think she'd disagree with her bein' your club's property. She was an adult when Shade hooked up with his ol' lady."

Ozzy, one of the Blood Fury Originals, came back with, "Don't matter. She don't gotta be born into the club for her to be our property and under our protection. Bottom line is, she is and that's all you gotta know."

Funny how Shade, standing next to him, wasn't saying shit.

Still, why did this feel like a goddamn shotgun wedding?

"Maddie didn't agree to wear my cut," he told them.

"She don't gotta agree," Trip said. "We either approve of you claimin' her or we don't. You know how this shit works."

Romeo really fucking doubted that Stella, Trip's ol' lady, would've been forced to wear his cut if she wasn't willing.

They might all pretend their women didn't have a choice, but the reality was, they sure as fuck did. The ol' ladies had more power than any of them wanted to admit.

At least out loud.

"Yeah, but you also know how it works when a woman's pissed the fuck off 'cause she's forced to do somethin' she don't wanna do," Romeo reminded them.

Some of them murmured their agreement, while Deacon muttered, "No truer words."

His ol' lady was another one who wouldn't be railroaded into shit. Reese was the kind of woman who'd neuter her ol' man if he fucked up.

He glanced around the table. In fact, none of their ol' ladies were spineless.

Having a strong woman at their side made them more powerful. Having a weak woman hiding behind them, while waiting to be told what to do, did the opposite.

But he wasn't bringing that shit up right now.

He only knew, if he was to share a life with someone, she needed to be able to think for herself and know the life.

Maddie fit that bill.

Add in the fact that she was hot as fuck and smart. She wasn't into drama or hysterics. Any fucking man would be lucky to have her. Even when she was upset with him, she didn't shriek or scream or scratch his fucking eyes out.

Or knee him in the nuts.

Even if he deserved it.

Truth was, he didn't want anyone else having her.

He didn't want her name crossing any other man's lips.

He didn't want her saying any other man's name.

Of course, not during normal day to day shit, but at night. When it counted.

His name and only his name should be heard when she was coming.

His name and only his name should be called when she needed some dick.

Jesus Christ, he was fucked.

Standing in front of this crew, it hit him that his life as he knew it was now over. He would be joining the "ol' man's club." A club he never wanted to be a card-carrying member of.

He never understood why anyone would want only one woman for the rest of their life when there were so fucking many out there to choose from. Until now.

Every man sitting around that table, even the man standing next to him, knew that when you found the one, you did whatever was needed to be done to keep her.

He could've had Booger drive him back to Knights territory after Easy and Shade dropped him back off at the roach motel early this morning. He had an opportunity to escape all of this.

He didn't.

Instead, he put on his damn clothes and had that asshole prospect take him over to Maddie's home earlier.

To sit down to dinner with her fucking family.

"Second thoughts?" Cage asked on a laugh. "Betcha his asshole's puckered so damn tight he'd explode if he had to fart."

"Same as yours when your surprise baby was dropped off at your fuckin' doorstep. Right?"

"Speaking of... How many kids you got out there?" Trip asked.

Romeo could honestly answer, "Zero. Know how to prevent crib lizards." He glanced at the Fury's road captain and added, "Unlike some others."

"Damn," Deacon whispered and dropped his head to hide his chuckle.

"All right, let's get back to business here," Trip ordered. "Got better things to do than listen to you assholes trade insults. Let's wrap this shit up."

Romeo agreed. He had better things to do than be there.

Like talk to Maddie and figure shit out. She was easier on the eyes than any of these motherfuckers.

"Just to be clear," Trip continued. "You're claimin' her, right?"

Was he finally pulling the trigger? "Yeah."

The Fury prez glanced at Shade. "You good with that?"

It took forever and a fucking day for Shade to answer. In fact, they waited so long that Ozzy finally yelled, "Jesus Christ, brother! You good with this one claimin' your girl or not? A simple fuckin' question only needs a simple fuckin' answer."

"If that's what she wants but need some guarantees first."

But was that what *she* wanted? Or was she being forced into this? Or did she make up her mind in the time between their discussion in his motel room and sitting down to dinner?

"She tell you that?"

Shade turned to look at him. "You fucked up her life. You gotta fix that shit."

"Becomin' my ol' lady's gonna fix that?"

"It better," Shade answered.

He had no fucking clue how that would work. He guessed he'd figure it out.

Or be stuck with a woman bitter about being stuck with him.

Like a goddamn arranged marriage.

Ice slithered down his spine.

He tried to swallow but it was close to impossible.

It was happening. His bachelor days were coming to an end. He'd no longer be able to smash and dash.

"Already can guess what those guarantees are," Trip said impatiently, "so let me get to them so we can get the fuck outta here..." He met Romeo's eyes. "Gonna keep your dick in your pants? No sweet butts, no hang-arounds, no randoms?"

"Hope to."

Someone made a loud buzzing noise. "Wrong fuckin' answer."

Judge.

"What's it to you?" he asked the club's sergeant at arms.

"Musta missed the part where Maddie belongs to us. Not you. Unless we hear the answers we wanna hear and," Judge circled his finger around the group, "we say she can."

"Get that you wanna protect her..."

"From womanizers like you," Shade said quietly.

Both Deacon and Ozzy snorted.

"Gonna tell you guys somethin' I ain't told anyone. Know I got a reputation. Know that reputation was true. But..." He pulled in a breath. "Ain't been with any other woman since runnin' into her."

The silence was deafening until Shade asked, "Not even a sweet butt?"

"No."

"She know that?"

"No."

"You plannin' on tellin' her?"

That would probably be a good fucking idea.

Chapter Forty

MADDIE FIDGETED on a stool at the Fury's private bar in The Barn.

Where she waited impatiently.

As soon as Shade and Romeo left the house, she hopped into her SUV and kept enough space between the two vehicles so they wouldn't spot her tailing them.

Shade didn't run any of this past her, but she knew exactly what he was doing.

Putting Romeo on the spot.

Making him put up or shut up.

Making him declare in front of the club officers whether he wanted to claim Maddie as his ol' lady or not.

The only problem was, Shade never asked her if that was what she wanted and, truthfully, she was still torn.

If she was using her head and not her heart, she'd reject his ass. Especially after he butted into her business and screwed everything up.

Plus, he had never been a man to stick with one woman.

She did not want to tie herself down with a cheater. Not now, not ever.

She wasn't sure Romeo was even the type of man who *could* be loyal. Maybe he'd start out that way, but eventually?

Was it worth the risk of heartburn and heartbreak?

Another issue was the most obvious one... He was a damn biker. Not only a biker but a president of an entire club! Did she even want to deal with that shit? In the past, she purposely avoided hooking up with bikers. And here she was, about to get claimed by one?

She sighed and dropped her head in her hands, trying to sort through her ping-ponging thoughts.

She would eventually want children. She had no idea where he stood on that subject. She had no idea if he'd even be a good father.

The "what ifs" were endless when it came to the man.

Did she even love him?

Did he love her?

She wanted to spend the rest of her life with someone who loved and cherished her. Supported her decisions.

She didn't want a man forced to be with her. She was damn sure if Romeo had to pick one woman to spend the rest of his life with, he'd want it to be one of his own choosing. Anyone else would be a recipe for disaster and not a good one for a solid relationship.

She worried she'd never be able to trust him one hundred percent. If he had to head out at an odd hour or if he came home late, would she always be wondering where he went, who he was with?

There was so much she needed to think about. So much for them to talk through.

When she moved out of her apartment and back home,

she didn't ever want to see or talk to him again. She had tried to push him out of her mind and her heart.

Was she successful? Hell no, but she knew with enough time and distance her feelings toward him would eventually fade away.

As long as she didn't see him, hear him, touch him, kiss him...

Have sex with him.

She groaned when her gut began to burn, and her heart started to ache at the thought of never doing any of that with him again.

She tried to resist. She truly did. She told herself time and time again, what she had with him was only sex. Only physical.

Emotions weren't involved.

At first, she also thought their encounters would only happen a couple of times. But two turned into four, then into eight and sixteen before she lost count.

During all those times, she refused to admit it wasn't just sex. That Romeo wasn't simply some horny dog. That she wasn't only using him as an escape from her stressful job and bully boss.

Before she knew it, she began to look forward to seeing him, hearing him, touching him, kissing him...

Fucking him.

But all of that was the polar opposite of being someone's ol' lady. Being permanent fixtures in each other's lives.

Living a life together.

Forever.

Could she wake up next to him every day?

Could she watch sweet butts, and random women hang all over him, trying to tempt him? Because she knew that was a reality.

She'd seen it.

On the other hand, she'd also seen Trip nip that shit in the bud quickly. Zak, the DAMC president, also did the same. No one questioned how loyal those two presidents were to their wives.

But how many would look her way and feel sorry for her for being stuck with a man not known for keeping his dick in his pants?

Would there be whispers?

Would distrust and rumors eventually force a wedge between them?

She blew out a breath, trying to settle her stomach, trying to rein in her thoughts.

She was only twenty-seven. She had plenty of time to find someone to fall in love with. To have children with. Someone responsible. Someone who was good husband and father material...

The sound of thumps had her lifting her head and glancing toward the stairway leading to the second floor. Romeo was slowly and carefully making his way back down.

Seeing him struggle twisted something inside of her. But it was when he paused on the steps and his eyes locked with hers was when she realized...

All her concerns were only that. Worries and not facts.

The real fact was, she didn't want to spend her life with anyone else.

No matter how flawed that man was. No matter his history.

He only approached Roger because he was trying to help *her*. If he didn't care about her, he never would have done that. Instead, he could've just gone about his life and not taken any action on her behalf at all.

If he didn't care about her, he wouldn't have had a

prospect drive him north so he could smooth things over with her.

If he didn't care about her, he could've refused to face the Blood Fury's executive committee.

He did all of that without her asking.

The cliché "actions speak louder than words" was so damn true in this case.

To be fair, she had to at least give him credit for that.

She sprung off the stool and rushed over to him as he used his crutch to continue working his way down the steps. "You need help?"

He paused and shook his head. "Stay there."

She held her breath as he made it down the final four steps without tumbling down and breaking more bones.

When he stopped in front of her, she finally breathed. "Are you okay?"

"Didn't fall on my fuckin' face."

Obviously. "I meant after being upstairs."

He ignored that by asking, "You bring your cage?"

She nodded.

"C'mon, let's get the fuck outta here before they all come down."

"Where are we going?"

"Somewhere we can have a conversation without any of those... *them*," he jerked his chin toward the ceiling, "bein' nosy fuckers or givin' us a fuckin' opinion we didn't ask for."

That sounded like a plan she could work with. "That's a good idea. I already have enough people in my life who like to make decisions for me." She lifted an eyebrow in his direction.

His mouth twisted. "Point taken. Let's go before you got a fuckuva lot more."

She matched his slow pace as they crossed The Barn and

headed out the front door. "Stay here, I'll grab my car and pick you up."

His jaw shifted but he gave her a single nod.

Huh. Did he not like relying on a woman? Too bad.

She jogged to her SUV, which was parked around the side of the building, and was pulling up to where he waited within less than a minute.

After placing her vehicle into Park, she jumped back out and flung open the passenger door.

When he eyeballed the interior and growled softly in frustration, she urged him to, "Hang on," before stepping behind him to help him slip out of his cut. Once he was free of it, she folded it neatly and placed it on the back seat while he hauled himself into the passenger side with an accompanying grunt and a few groans.

He had to be going nuts not being able to ride his sled. She swore their motorcycles were an extension of their body and if they couldn't ride, it was like lopping off a limb.

While he was getting settled, she slammed the passenger side door shut and rushed around the front of the Toyota to jump in. They needed to get out of there before they were seen and stopped.

Once her Highlander was in Reverse, she asked, "Where to?"

"You know this area a fuck-ton better than me. Somewhere it's only me and you."

Only me and you.

Where could they go besides the awful motel in Parsington? There had to be somewhere closer. When a lightbulb went off in her head, she quickly put the SUV into Drive and drove off the farm.

Not even five minutes later, she parked in a secluded

tobacco field owned by the Fury but farmed by the local Amish.

Once she shut down the engine, they sat in uncomfortable silence. Her pounding heartbeat the only sound in her ears.

Someone had to get this conversation rolling.

"Rome—" she started at the same time he said, "Maddie—"

If he wanted to speak, she'd let him since she was dying to hear what he had to say.

"Never saw my life takin' this direction."

"I didn't, either," she responded.

"Never wanted an ol' lady," he continued.

"I never wanted to be one."

"Didn't think it was in my blood to settle down."

When she countered with, "I never wanted to settle," his brow scrunched low.

"Bein' with me would be settlin'?"

She must have struck a nerve. "Well, first off, I'm not *with* you. Second, I don't want to be forced into anything. I also don't want to be with someone forced to be with me."

"Ain't..." He shook his head. "No one's forcin' shit."

"Then, what happened up there?"

"Truth is, want no one else to have you. Wanna make you mine. Claimed you at the table upstairs. Now wanna claim you in front of the rest of the world. Want everyone to know you're 'property of Romeo.' Now and forever."

"Property of Romeo?" Her question came out in a squeak.

He muttered a "fuck."

She cleared her throat to bring her voice back to normal. "Do you think a college-educated, independent woman wants to be property of anyone?" Especially a *man*.

"What's the difference between wearin' a man's cut and a weddin' ring? Don't both tell others that you've been claimed?"

"Are you proposing?" she half-joked, but her stomach churned at the thought of the man sitting next to her proposing to anyone.

Romeo, a husband?

She leaned forward and looked up at the sky through the windshield.

"Whatcha lookin' for?"

"Pigs flying."

"You didn't answer."

She unclipped her seatbelt and turned in her seat to face him. "Neither did you."

"Told you that I want you to wear my cut."

At the time she only thought it was a knee-jerk reaction and when the reality hit, he'd change his mind. "Did you get their approval?"

If he did, she'd believe he was actually serious.

"Once I agreed to their terms."

Her eyebrows pinched together. "Terms? What terms?"

"That I ain't gonna dip my dick into any other female."

She lifted a palm. "Hold on... You only agreed to that because they demanded it?"

"That's the thing..."

Three heartbeats later she prodded, "What? Spit it out."

Why did it look like what he was about to say would be painful?

"Haven't been with anyone else since I spotted you at Bangin' Burgers."

Chapter Forty-One

*H*AVEN'T BEEN *with anyone else since I spotted you at Bangin' Burgers.*

"What?" she whispered. How could that be? "Why? Was your dick broken?"

He scowled. "That a fuckin' joke?"

"I only want the truth, Rome, so I can make a good decision about where we go from here." If anywhere.

"Just so you know, they made that decision for you."

"That's what they think, but they don't rule my life. I won't have some man forced upon me. They don't get to vote on who I spend the rest of my life with. Or even who I sleep with."

"So, you don't wanna be with me," he posed that as a fact and not a question. Unfortunately, his expression gave nothing away.

"I didn't say that. What I said isn't only about you."

"I'm the only fuckin' one in this goddamn cage, woman." He jabbed his finger toward the floorboards. "I'm the one sittin' in this seat. I'm the one who had to face your Fury family. I'm the one givin' up my free—" He swallowed the last part of the word, and his face pinched like he swallowed something sour.

"Were you about to say freedom?"

He sneered, "That was some goddamn bullshit."

She blinked in confusion. "What was?"

"Goin' in front of that fuckin' firin' squad."

"Like the Knights don't do the same shit."

"Not even fuckin' close. If one of my brother's wants some woman to wear his cut, more fuckin' power to him. He wants to give up his freedom for some pussy, then..." He grimaced.

There was that freedom word again. Did he consider being loyal to one woman as restrictive as prison, where he truly lost his freedom? "Go on. You weren't done. Finish."

"Done."

"Didn't sound like it to me. Look, I get it. You're afraid of losing your freedom. Guess what, Rome? You missed the point about you not being the only one this would affect. I'm involved in this, too." Now she was about to dish some hard truth. "Here's the bottom line... I won't be with a man who doesn't love me. One who doesn't respect my decisions. I want a partner in love and life, not a damn dictator."

His volume cranked up a notch. "You sayin' I put up with all that goddamn bullshit for nothin'?"

"Did they make you sweat?" she asked calmly.

"Not up there."

Not up there. That was a strange answer. One that made the fine hairs on the back of her neck rise.

"Then where?" When he didn't answer, she prodded, "Where, Rome? Did Shade do something? Tell me the truth. Are you being forced in some way?"

"God-fuckin'-damnit," he muttered under his breath

before saying more loudly, "No, woman. Ain't bein' forced to do shit." He closed his eyes, visibly pulled in a breath, and when he reopened them, they met hers. His intense gaze never wavered when he went on with, "Came to Manning Grove willingly. Asked you to wear my cut willingly. Went upstairs willingly. If I didn't want you bein' my ol' lady, never woulda came up here at all. Woulda been happy you skipped town without a fuckin' word. We coulda went our separate ways and none of them woulda known anythin' happened between us. Both of us coulda moved on and lived our damn lives. But here I am..."

"Wow. I'm finding you very hard to resist when that was one of the most romantic speeches I ever heard."

Romeo sucked his teeth.

"Tell me. *Why* do you want me to be your ol' lady, Rome? I haven't heard a good argument for that yet."

"Ain't obvious?"

"Honestly, no."

He scraped fingers down his bearded jaw. "Maybe 'cause this is all fuckin' new to me, Maddie. Not sure how to act. Not sure what to do. Not sure even what to fuckin' say. Already pissed you the fuck off when I had words with your asshole boss. Tryin' not to step in shit again."

"The answer doesn't have to be complicated."

"Not complicated? Sure fuckin' feels like it to me."

"You mean, figuring out what to say to me?"

"No, this... relationship shit. It's worse when you're makin' it pretty damn clear you don't feel the same 'bout me."

Her head jerked back. "What? How do you know how I feel?"

"Guessin', 'cause you ain't said shit."

Her eyebrows rose. "Have you asked?"

He pressed his lips together so tightly they became a slash.

She sighed. "Yes, I was pissed at you, Rome. But deep down if I didn't feel anything for you, we both wouldn't be sitting here right now having this discussion. No one—and I mean *no one*—could railroad either of us into doing something we don't want to do. Do you agree?"

"You kept mentionin' me bein' forced."

"Because this is my future we're talking about. Yours, too. I want to be sure this is what you want."

"But you're sure now." Funny how he didn't form that as a question.

She laughed softly. "Look, this whole... situation has been confusing. For me as well as you. All I know is, despite me being hurt and angry at you, I still missed you." Surprisingly enough, it was a load off her shoulders to reveal that.

"You ran off."

"My heart ached for you," she admitted next.

"You blocked my goddamn number."

She shrugged. "Then, I guess I did us a favor by making us both realize what our lives would be like without each other."

"Truth? Didn't fuckin' like it. Also don't like needin' anyone as much as I need you."

Holy shit. He really did want this.

Romeo. The infamous womanizer.

The man known for bouncing from bed to bed his whole adult life had stopped doing that after the chance meeting they had at a hamburger stand.

She had witnessed other bikers clean up their hound dog ways after meeting "the one." Was she "the one" for Romeo?

An awkward laugh slipped from between her lips. "We're a mess."

"Ain't gonna argue that."

"Will this even work?" She still had some doubts. Actually, more than some. He'd been set in his ways for a long damn time.

"Not sure."

At least he was honest about that. "Is it worth trying?"

He hesitated before admitting, "Ain't gonna be easy."

It sure wasn't. "Our lives will be completely changed," she warned.

"Not completely. But it's for fuck sure gonna be different."

Again, he wasn't lying.

"If we build a strong foundation, we can grow from there." *Holy crap*, were they really doing this? Would Romeo become her ol' man? Would she be his ol' lady?

Something neither of them wanted.

Until now.

"Maddie..." He lifted her chin and forced her to look him directly in the eyes. "Wanna make this fuckin' clear, then we need to move the fuck on. Doin' this for one reason and that one reason is you. Ain't doin' it 'cause I'm forced to, doin' it 'cause I want to. Can't see myself with anyone other than you anymore. Thought those motherfuckers scrambled my brain when they knocked me in the head, but the truth is, it made me see shit more clearly."

She stared at the man with only inches separating them. The man she gave her virginity to so long ago. The man she gave her heart to more recently.

Her heart and her head might not be totally at peace with all this yet, but they were finally in one place.

"This snuck up on me," she whispered.

"Yeah. Same."

"This is not how I envisioned the direction my life would take."

"Yeah. Same."

"I never thought I'd end up with someone like you."

"Yeah. Same."

She grabbed his beard and tugged on it. Dropping her voice an octave, she echoed, "Wanna make this fuckin' clear, then we need to move the fuck on. I'm doin' this for one reason and that one reason is you. Ain't doin' it 'cause I'm forced to, doin' it 'cause I want to. Can't see myself with anyone other than you anymore." When his mouth opened, she pressed a finger against his lips and shook her head. "You said this was complicated, so let me simplify this for you... I love you, Rome."

It was finally out there. She could never take it back.

"Yeah..."

She held her breath, waiting.

"Same."

She released it in relief.

He might not have said the actual words, but he didn't need to. Because she felt it instead, enveloping her like a warm hug. She didn't want to let that feeling go.

How did her life take such a crazy turn?

Oh... She knew.

It was all due to the man in her passenger seat.

The one she kissed long and hard.

The one who whispered promises against her lips of all the things he'd do to her, all the things she had missed, once his casts were removed.

She couldn't wait.

———

AFTER THEIR TALK in the tobacco field, she drove him back to the motel in Parsington. Once he grabbed his stuff with her help, he sent Booger on his way, and they headed back to Manning Grove to a much better motel.

The Fury-owned Grove Inn.

She told him there was no way she was sharing a room with roaches since they still had a lot to discuss and settle between them before any major decisions could be made.

She helped him undress and get into bed. Once he was comfortable, she joined him only wearing her bra and panties.

Even though they had a lot to figure out and a future to plan, she ended up distracted since the casts, his tattoos and a snug pair of boxer briefs were all the man wore.

She'd be much happier if he wasn't stuck in casts. Or had broken ribs.

So would he.

But then, they wouldn't be doing much talking at all.

She curled around him, being cognizant of his ribs as he slowly combed his fingers through her loose hair.

Using a fingertip, she slowly traced his many tattoos as well as the lines of his muscles. When she was done exploring, she stroked the back of her fingers down his beard. Brushing her thumb over his slightly parted lips next, his warm breath drifted over the pad of her thumb.

He snagged her hand to stop her. "Makin' me hard."

With a lift of her head, she saw he wasn't lying. "Well, it's proof that's not broken."

"That breaks, just shoot me."

"I don't think a broken penis warrants euthanasia."

"The fuck it don't. Would be a humane way to put me out of my misery."

411

"Sex isn't everything."

"Speak for yourself. 'Cause, for me, bein' inside you is."

She hid her grin against his warm, dark skin. When she could finally control it, she said, "Never expected you to be such a romantic."

"Surprises the fuck outta me, too."

She rolled her eyes. "I know how to get rid of that hard-on."

His eyes heated. "No shit. So do I." He dragged the pad of his thumb over her lips the same way as she had done to him.

"I had another idea."

He patted his bare thigh. "Don't mind bein' on the bottom and lettin' you ride me like a mechanical bull."

"That wasn't it."

He pursed his lips, most likely trying to come up with another idea that wouldn't aggravate his ribs too badly. Unfortunately, those options were limited.

"Jerkin' me off?"

"I was thinking more along the lines of making sure we're both on the same page."

"That don't sound as good as you jerkin' me off."

"Deal with it."

He chuckled softly. "Don't get sassy with me, woman. Or your ol' man's gonna have to teach you a lesson."

"You're not my ol' man yet." She playfully nipped at his nipple, making him jump.

He groaned, "Fuck. That didn't help my ribs."

"What do you think will happen if I blow you or jerk you off? Or ride you like a mechanical bull?"

"This fuckin' sucks. Just for this reason alone, Smith needs to..."

Her pulse sped up. "Needs to what?"

"Nothin'."

"That's one of the topics I want to discuss. We need complete honesty between us. No secrets."

"Maddie, there's shit that's gonna happen in my life you do *not* need to fuckin' know. Better for you. Better for everyone involved."

"Club business isn't my business, isn't that right?"

"You know how it fuckin' works and don't act like you don't."

"Look what happened last time you confronted him," she reminded him needlessly.

"And that needs to be addressed."

"We're talking the *Mafia* here, Rome. This isn't some group of juvenile delinquents spray painting the side of Dirty Dick's."

"Know who the fuck they are, woman. Know what they're capable of. Let's get this straight, you can't question my actions. I'm the goddamn president of the Knights and you gotta remember that. Gonna be actions that need to be taken you ain't gonna like. Bottom line, you got no say on club business. If that's gonna be a problem, then we're gonna have a problem."

"Roger had nothing to do with club business," she reminded him. "That had to do with me. That means I should have a say if you're planning some sort of payback."

"Maddie..."

"I don't want you getting hurt again or even killed. I don't want you to make me a widow before you even make me your wife."

His brow dropped low. "Think I don't know how to handle my business?"

"Well... If we want to go there..."

"Jesus fuck," he muttered.

He was getting pissed and this was getting nowhere. "I thought we're here to hash things out?"

"Only agreed to that to get you naked and in bed."

Chapter Forty-Two

Maddie sat up. "If that's what—"

Romeo grabbed her wrist and jerked her back down next to him. "How 'bout we talk first, then we do a whole lotta not talkin' later."

"Because our mouths will be busy? I bet straddling your face won't mess up your ribs."

His anger quickly dissipated, and his lips curved into a grin. "Fuck yeah. Wanna practice first? Miss the taste of your pussy."

That same pussy clenched at the memory of all the times he made her orgasm only using his very skillful mouth. "You know how to make me lose my mind and I won't be able to think straight afterward, so can we get through this conversation first?"

"If we gotta," he muttered.

"Yes, we have to because I need to know where we go from here. I need a place. I need a job. And, frankly, I need... you."

"Got me—"

"In one piece," she added.

"Got a place, too, so that's covered. That's the foundation you talked about. Gonna work on the rest."

"Sounds like you expect me to come live with you behind Dick's."

"For now, 'til I find some place better."

"Do I have a say in where we live?" she asked.

"Long as it's in Knights' territory."

She could work with that. It would also be nice to live close to Zeke, as well as Gabi again since they were her two closest friends after her younger sister Josie.

"The next problem is my job situation. And don't you dare tell me that by being your ol' lady I won't have to work. Or that I can work in one of the Knights' businesses. I worked long and hard to earn my license as a sports physical therapist. That's what I want to do, Rome. That's non-negotiable."

"Everything's negotiable."

"Not this." She sighed long and loudly. "I get your heart was in the right place when you confronted Roger, but you didn't think it through."

"Ain't gonna deny that."

"If I'm returning to the Pittsburgh area, that's going to limit my chances of doing what I love and fulfilling my dream, especially if I'm blackballed with the Pittsburgh teams. Possibly even the whole industry. No one is jumping to hire me, Rome. Hell, I can't even get an interview."

"Gonna fix that for you."

He was going to do what? She groaned. "You're going to fix it for me? I'm not sure I like that answer." She waved a hand down his body. "Look what happened last time. I'm unemployed and you got your ass kicked."

"What the fuck," he muttered. "How many fuckin' times

I gotta say this? Only 'cause I was fuckin' ambushed and outnumbered. In the goddamn dark."

Boy, someone was touchy about that subject. "Okay, so explain... how are you going to fix it for me?"

"Remember when I said there's gonna be some shit you don't need to know? This is one of them."

Her stomach twisted. "Rome..."

"Maddie, lemme handle it. Need you to trust me. This shit ain't gonna work between us if you don't. Gonna fix what I fucked up. Owe that to you and gonna make sure you get what you're owed."

Right then and there, she realized he was going to do what he was going to do, no matter what she said. "At least promise me you won't get killed?"

"Won't get killed. We done talkin' yet?"

"You only want to move on to the next part."

"Said you wanted me to be honest, so here's me bein' honest. Want you to wrap your lips 'round my dick and stop flappin' them 'bout shit I'm gonna handle."

"I'm really feeling the love," she said dryly.

"What you're 'bout to do ain't got shit to do with love. Me fixin' what I broke will."

Well, then... She guessed they were done talking. For now, anyway.

She shifted on the bed until her mouth hovered over his semi-hard cock. She watched it grow right before her eyes.

Both of his hands drove into her hair, and he whispered, "Fuck yeah."

"I haven't even done anything yet."

"But my dick knows what's comin'."

"You?"

"Damn right. Then it's gonna be your turn."

Where there was a will, there was a way, apparently. She

only hoped giving him head wouldn't cause him more pain than it was worth. However, he had no trouble using his mouth, so he could tell her to stop if it became unbearable.

After slipping his boxer briefs down, she fisted the root of his cock. Then she lowered her head and took him into her mouth as deep as she could without choking.

As her head and hand moved in sync, it caused the tiniest twitches of his hips. If his ribs were healed, she had no doubt he'd be driving into her hard right now, most likely making her gag.

If it was true that he hadn't had sex with anyone else—unless he jerked off in that time—he hadn't had a release recently. He'd be more than primed and ready to go. Or blow.

That also meant it wouldn't take long for him to get to that point.

The grip on her hair tightened. "That's it. Deeper. Squeeze my fuckin' balls."

She gently tugged and kneaded his soft, delicate sack.

After licking down the thick ridge, she dragged her tongue back up to suck the tip. The salty tang of his precum hit her taste buds before she moved on to circle the base of the crown.

"Fuck, woman," he groaned. "Take me deep."

She swallowed him as far as she could. The man might not be huge, but he sure was girthy.

With the way his fingers flexed, she knew he was fighting the urge to shove her head down and impale her throat on his cock.

She was grateful he had enough control not to do that.

But like she predicted, it didn't take long for Romeo to reach his limit.

Not a few minutes later, with a deep grunt, he shot his load down the back of her throat as well as coated her tongue with his release. She kept him in her mouth until his cock stopped twitching and his muscles relaxed, then she slowly let him slip free.

His head dropped back on the pillow and between ragged breaths, he growled at the ceiling, "Fuck, woman... Wanna fuck you so fuckin' bad."

If anyone understood his frustration, it was her right now. She was soaking wet and would love to be able to straddle his hips and ride him until she came. But instead, she'd have to be happy with him using his mouth and fingers instead of his cock.

She never hated Roger more than that very moment. Her only consolation was, Romeo would make him pay for the damage he caused. Both to her and to him.

She thought of herself as a good person, always wanting to help others. To stay true to herself, she really should discourage him from exacting revenge on her former boss. But, *damn it*, deep down, the thought of Roger getting taught a valuable lesson gave her some satisfaction.

Maybe living amongst badass bikers had rubbed off on her and made her more cutthroat than what she should be. Or maybe it was simply the fact that Roger Smith deserved everything he had coming his way.

A big ol' slice of karma served by her future ol' man.

Hearing him demand, "Sit on my face," pulled her from her thoughts about that asshole.

Fuck Roger Smith.

The only man she should be thinking about right now was the one whose face she was about to sit on.

They might not have figured everything out yet between them and she knew their relationship wouldn't be easy, but in the end, she was confident it would be worth it.

Chapter Forty-Three

"She know where you're at?" Shade asked him.

"Fuck no."

"Gonna tell her?"

"Fuck no," Romeo repeated.

Shade nodded. "This is one time I ain't gonna care that you're keepin' her in the dark."

"Glad to get your approval," he said dryly. "Bet you ain't tellin' your ol' lady, either." When Shade didn't respond, Romeo followed up with, "Thought so. Just like Chelle don't know you had me strapped down in front of a dead dog oven."

"Always gonna be secrets you take to your grave," Shade said matter-of-factly.

Romeo would bet his fucking balls that Shade had plenty of those.

It had taken over two months to get to the point where his bruises had faded, his broken bones healed, and his casts removed.

His life was pretty much back to normal. His new normal, anyway.

The one where Maddie now lived with him in his place. At least until he could find something bigger and better. A place where she wouldn't bitch every time she climbed up and down the steep stairs—what she called a glorified ladder —to their bed.

She also had a permanent seat on the back of his sled. She was the first and would be the last woman to ever sit there.

Despite them settling into their relationship, she was stressed because she still hadn't been offered one fucking interview.

He hated seeing her like that.

Except for the part where he volunteered to help relieve some of her stress.

One side of his mouth pulled up.

"There he is." Shade's head was turned as he stared out of the passenger-side window.

Romeo squinted, trying to make out the man on the move. "You sure that's him?"

"You fuckin' tell me. You've seen the motherfucker in person. Not me."

But Romeo had texted Shade enough pictures of Roger Smith that the long-haired Fury member should recognize Maddie's former asshole boss.

Shade now also knew everything that Smith had done to her, making him even more motivated to pair with Romeo to deal with the motherfucker. They both agreed to keep it on the down-low from their clubs since this retribution was purely personal.

Magnum didn't need to know what they were doing. Neither did Judge or Trip.

To keep her hands clean, Maddie didn't need to know the details, either.

"Ready?" Shade asked.

"Yeah. Can't wait," he murmured, watching Smith—or Russo or whatever his real fucking last name was—climb in his overpriced douche-mobile. As soon as he headed out of the parking lot of Smith's business, Shade put the plain white van with the fake license plate into gear and followed.

Their plan was simple. Make Smith disappear.

Romeo could confirm that Shade had the perfect way to do that. They only had to get Smith up to Manning Grove without getting caught along the way.

This needed to be handled as quietly and cleanly as possible. No evidence left behind besides an abandoned sports car. The last thing they wanted was the Sicilians finding out what happened to Smith or by whom. It could spark a war between the MC and the Mafia, and no one wanted that. It was one reason they left their cuts at home since they would easily identify them.

The goal was also to keep his ass out of prison. He doubted he'd be permitted conjugal visits, even if Maddie agreed to them.

"He's takin' a left," he told Shade, like Maddie's step-daddy didn't have two perfectly good eyes in his messed-up head.

No surprise when Romeo got zero reaction from him. Shade was a man of little words and had perfected the poker face.

They followed that motherfucker for two hours as he ran errands in very public places. Romeo worried that if one of Smith's stops wasn't in a good spot for them or the asshole headed home before they could intercept him, they'd have to abort their mission and do this shit all over again another night.

Neither of them wanted to do a repeat. They wanted to get this fucking shit over with. Tonight. This way they could move the fuck on with their lives and forget Smith ever existed.

The tricky part to this plan was leaving behind no DNA, witnesses, or video proof. This had to be handled with skill. Following him home and taking the guy from his driveway or house would be fucking stupid since the motherfucker probably had a security system with cameras.

As they watched Smith throw dry-cleaning into his cage, Shade said, "Might hafta make our own opportunity."

"Thinkin' the same thing. Got any idea on how the fuck to do that?"

"Yeah."

Romeo waited for him to explain and when he didn't, he asked impatiently, "Wanna fuckin' share?"

"Could run him off the road but damage and paint transfer would be evidence. Need to leave his cage whole and make it seem like he abandoned it."

That wasn't a fucking solution. Maybe Romeo needed to call one of the Shadows and get some advice. If anyone could make someone disappear without a trace, it was Diesel's guys. They'd also know a good technique to isolate their target.

But, if it could be avoided, he'd rather not share what was going down tonight with anyone.

"Still haven't heard your idea."

Romeo ground his teeth when Shade only grunted a reply.

The Fury member removed his foot from the van's brake pedal and stepped on the accelerator to follow Smith's

Porsche out of the strip mall, where the dry cleaner was located, and out onto the road.

They knew his home address, so as soon as Smith turned onto a road that would eventually lead to his gated—and guarded—neighborhood, he warned, "Better get your idea in fuckin' motion since he's headed home."

Of course, nothing but engine noise answered him.

He had to trust that Shade knew what the fuck he was doing.

Shade hooked a right so hard that Romeo had to hold onto shit so he wouldn't be thrown into the passenger door. He was not spending another six weeks in casts.

"Smith's goin' straight," Romeo announced.

"Yeah."

The Fury member sped down some unknown, dark road while keeping one eye on the GPS app on the phone attached to the dashboard in a holder.

He blew through a stop sign and slammed on the brakes in the middle of an intersection, almost launching Romeo through the windshield.

"Warn a brother, will you?" Romeo yelled. "Jesus, don't wanna fuck up this pretty face."

Shade turned to look at him. "Get out."

"What?"

"Get out, go hide on the side of the road and when the asshole stops, jump in and we'll drive somewhere more isolated."

"Then what?"

"No time for fuckin' questions. Headlights are headin' this way."

Romeo glanced down the road and saw a glow in the distance. *Fuck.*

In a flash, he pulled on his leather gloves, kicked open the van door, jumped out and hid behind a tree that never would've hidden his ass in the daytime. Thank fuck he blended in with the dark night.

With his pulse racing, he peered around the slim tree trunk and tracked the oncoming vehicle. He sure as fuck hoped that Shade picked the right cross-street, and this wasn't some random driver approaching.

Once the vehicle came over a small rise, the Porsche came to an abrupt halt, despite not having a stop sign. The vehicle remained there for a few seconds before Smith laid on the horn, rolled down his window and began to curse at Shade. "Get that hunk of junk off the roadway!"

Time to move. Romeo needed to get in that vehicle before Smith put his douche-mobile in reverse and found an alternative route.

As soon as Smith ducked his head back into his cage, Romeo jerked open the passenger door and jumped in. "Drive."

"What the hell? You! You can't be serious! Get the fuck out of my car!" As Smith reached for his cell phone in the center console, Romeo grabbed it first and slipped it into his back pocket.

While he was back there, he pulled his gun out of the holster tucked in his waistband at the small of his back. He wasted no time pressing the end of the barrel into Smith's temple to show the asshole just how fucking serious he was.

Smith raised both hands in surrender, pleading, "Don't shoot me."

Proof the narcissist was nothing but a pussy under the surface. Being related to the Russos didn't change that fact.

"Fuckin' drive!" Romeo shouted and jammed the business end of the barrel harder into the side of his head, making

Smith flinch. "Now, or I'll splatter your fuckin' brains all over this piece of shit."

He was tempted. So fucking tempted.

Shooting the motherfucker would be the simplest way to deal with Smith but too fucking messy. Not only would Romeo be covered in Smith's DNA, he'd have to worry about gunshot residue.

It would be too risky to take him out like that. But that didn't mean his finger didn't caress the trigger as that fantasy played out.

"Drive!" he shouted again.

"Didn't you learn your lesson the first damn time?"

What a cocky bastard. "You admit you sent your goons after me."

"And I'll do it again."

"Doubt that," Romeo grumbled.

"You don't know who you're messing with."

Fuck this asshole. "Pretty sure I do. Know your real last name ain't Smith. Know who you're connected to."

"Then you have some balls to do this."

"My balls are pretty fucking nice, if I gotta say so. Now quit flappin' your veneers and drive."

"And if I don't?"

"Don't and find out. Your choice." He then warned, "Choose wisely."

Smith slammed his hand on his steering wheel. "Never should've hired that bitch. Knew she was trouble from the start."

"Don't remember askin' for any of your fuckin' opinions. Now... Drive!" he barked.

With a tight jaw and him mumbling curses, Smith shoved the shifter from neutral into first gear. When he lifted his foot from the clutch, the car lurched forward.

"Follow that white van," Romeo ordered, watching Smith's hands carefully. The fucker could be packing on his person or in the cage. He kept his own gun glued to the man's temple. "Better watch for potholes."

Did Smith's Adam's apple just jump? Good.

It was an uncomfortable twenty-minute ride. For a while he wondered if Shade was fucking lost. His arm was getting tired from holding the gun steady and his hand was beginning to cramp.

When Shade finally pulled the van over, it was onto a dirt road in some corn field. No streetlights. No traffic. And the corn stalks were high enough to hide the Porsche easily.

Perfect.

Maybe he needed to give Shade more credit than being just a sociopath. It was possible he was smart, too. Romeo wouldn't form a final opinion on his future stepdaddy-in-law until he knew him a lot better.

"Set the e-brake and shut this piece of shit down."

"This car isn't a piece—"

"Don't give a fuck. Need to remind you that your shitty opinion don't matter. On anything."

"Now what?" Smith huffed after the engine went quiet.

The driver's door was ripped open, and a gloved Shade reached in, grabbed Smith, and yanked him out of the vehicle.

The ground wasn't far, but he still hit it hard with a grunt.

"That's what, motherfucker!" Romeo yelled. He quickly tucked his gun away, hopped out of the Porsche and joined them, where Smith was still on his ass in the dirt with Shade standing over him, a roll of duct tape in his hand.

He probably kept a whole box of duct tape in that van.

With a boot to Maddie's former boss's back, Romeo

shoved him face first into the dirt, drove a knee into the fucker's back, leaned all his weight into it and yanked one of his arms in a direction it normally didn't go.

"What the hell!" Smith yelled.

"Shut up," Romeo ordered Smith before telling Shade, "Gonna hold him down, you tape him up."

With Romeo's help, Shade made quick work of securing Smith's wrists behind his back and taping his ankles together.

"You will regret this!"

They should really gag the asshole. Romeo was tired of hearing his pussy-ass whining.

"Nah. Don't think I will." He glanced at Shade. "Will you?"

If he would've blinked, he would've missed Shade shaking his head.

Romeo jerked the man to his feet and shoved him. Smith, unable to use his legs, toppled forward and once again landed in the dirt, unable to break his fall.

Damn shame.

"Lemme help you up." Romeo grabbed Smith's arm and pulled him to his feet again.

"You need to let me go!" Smith's panic was evident in his voice.

As Shade grabbed Smith to assist taking him to the van, Romeo stopped him with, "Hang on, brother." Then he stepped in front to face him and hauled off and slammed his fist into Smith's nose. So much for not getting Smith's DNA on him. He'd have to burn the blood-splattered clothes he was wearing. "That's a message from the *bitch* you hired."

Smith really deserved more than only his nose broken but that would have to do for now. What was coming next would be worse than any fucking broken bones.

"All right. Now that's been settled..."

"Before we load this motherfucker up…" Shade held out a bandana and Romeo snagged it from him. "Don't wanna listen to his fuckin' whinin' for the next three hours."

"Three hours?" Smith screeched. "Where are you taking me?"

When Romeo was finished tying the bandana around Smith's mouth, he put his mouth near the fucker's ear and whispered, "To the fiery depths of hell."

Epilogue

"HAPPY NOW?" Romeo asked Magnum. "You were worried about fuckin' up our alliance. Like you bein' with Cait strengthened it with the Angels, me bein' with Maddie strengthens it with the Fury. We're closer to being bullet-proof. You're fuckin' welcome."

"Goddamn lucky you didn't find yourself skinned, filleted and hangin' upside-down by your ashy feet," the big man grumbled.

"My feet ain't ashy!"

"That's the part you're worried about? Not bein' skinned or filleted?"

"Hell no. My future stepdaddy-in-law loves me." Romeo grinned.

Magnum snorted and shook his head. "Later, asshole." With that, the Knights' sergeant at arms lumbered toward the exit.

Romeo watched him go for a few seconds before snagging an unopened bottle of Jack Daniels from behind the bar at

Dicks and heading through the kitchen to go home to his woman.

It wouldn't be home for long. He was passing it on to Bishop, his VP, and soon they'd be moving into a larger crib not far from Dick's. They found a three-bedroom, two-bath house with a garage big enough for both his sled and her SUV. Even better, it had no damn stairs.

It even had a backyard large enough to hang out and barbecue. Just like a real domesticated motherfucker.

He turned the knob to make sure the door was locked—since that was a requirement for her safety and his sanity—and was relieved to find he needed to use his key to go inside.

When he did, he found Maddie—now officially his ol' lady—curled up on the couch with her laptop, most likely scouring job postings and sending out a fuck-ton of resumes.

He told her multiple times to not freak out about earning scratch—he had them covered—but she was determined to get a job as soon as possible.

She glanced up from the computer and shot a smile at him as he slipped out of his cut and hung it near the door. "Hey, baby."

Her smile grew bigger as he went directly over to her, grabbed her face, leaned down and planted a kiss on her mouth.

Actually, it was now *his* mouth since it belonged to him.

"Is that supposed to be foreplay?" she teased.

"What, that didn't get you wet?"

"Wrong lips," she advised.

"Will take care of that fuck up later." His gaze dropped to her laptop. "Any luck?"

Her smile faded. "No."

He glanced at his phone, saw the time, and muttered a curse under his breath. He almost missed it.

Snagging the remote from the cushion next to her, he quickly changed the channel from some brain-rotting reality show with a bunch of catty bitches to a local station that covered the Pittsburgh news.

Roger Smith's mug was plastered on the screen with the caption: New twist in the case of a local man missing for a month.

"Oh my God!" Maddie yelled, closing her laptop and sitting up. "Turn it up!"

The news anchor behind the desk wore a serious expression. "Local business owner, Roger Smith, has now been missing for almost four weeks. The only sign of Smith's disappearance was his Porsche 911 found in a corn field about five miles from his home. With this new development, law enforcement is now labeling his sudden disappearance as foul play."

"What new development?" Maddie yelled at the TV.

Romeo dropped his ass on the couch next to her, cracked open the whiskey and swallowed a generous mouthful.

As if the anchor heard Maddie's question, he answered, "Several sources are telling us that Roger Smith is an alias, and he has ties with the Russo crime family."

Maddie turned toward him with wide eyes as the newscaster droned on in the background.

"Police are looking for any tips from the public. If you've seen Roger Smith, or know his whereabouts, please contact the 800 number on your screen."

Guaranteed, Romeo would not be calling that toll-free number.

With a dropped jaw, she asked, "I wonder how the media uncovered that connection?"

Romeo shrugged. "No clue. Might be good for you, though. His word is now shit."

She bugged out her eyes at him. "What did you do?"

"Didn't do dick."

"Rome..."

"Look, woman, don't fuckin' ask questions you don't want the answers to. Told you I was gonna make it up to you—"

Her lips flattened out. "So, you did have a hand in this."

Not only with his "disappearance" but the leak to the media. "Karma can be one independent bitch."

"Does karma happen to be a six-foot-one Black biker?"

"Can't confirm."

She whacked his bicep. "Rome!"

He shrugged again and swallowed another mouthful of Jack before offering the bottle to her. She shook her head, rejecting it.

"All I know is, now that his ass has been exposed for being tied to the fuckin' Mafia, those professional teams will be cuttin' their connections with him as fast as possible."

She grabbed his forearm and squeezed. He had to assume with excitement. "How do you know that?"

"Educated guess."

"Bullshit," she said.

"You're a helluva lot smarter than me, so bettin' you can figure out what this shit all means for you. Ain't sayin' there's a guarantee one of them's gonna hire you, but at least his opinion will be considered fuckin' worthless."

"And they might give me a fair shot."

They might, but he was afraid she'd get her hopes up and then be devastated when it didn't pan out. "Got us covered financially so you might be able to get your foot in the door with one of their internships. Then once they realize how fuckin' valuable you are—"

She grinned. "Like you did."

"They're gonna want to hire you permanently. They don't, their loss." Like it would've been his loss if he didn't chase her down in Manning Grove.

He had zero fucking regrets on making her his ol' lady.

She wasn't a jealous bitch. She wasn't a dumb cunt. She didn't screech non-stop. She was super responsive in bed. Looked great naked. But, best of all, she had eyes only for him.

She was damn near perfect.

Him? Not so much. He got the better end of the deal than she did. He wouldn't deny that.

"I think we need to celebrate."

He lifted the Jack Daniels. "Why I brought this."

She narrowed her eyes on him. "So, you knew we'd have a reason to celebrate? Or was that another educated guess?"

"Got a degree in guessin'."

With a soft snort, she put her laptop aside, grabbed the bottle, took a long swig, then plunked it on the coffee table before climbing onto his lap, straddling it.

He immediately planted his hands on her luscious ass since that was the best place to put them, besides her tits.

She wiggled in his lap. "How are you hard already?"

"Don't take much with you."

The corners of her lips twitched. "That's the nicest compliment I've ever received."

"Got plenty of 'em."

She wrapped her arms around his neck and locked gazes with him. "Let me hear some more."

"Your tits are the fuckin' bomb. Your tight pussy's addictin'. Your mouth can suck me off better than a Shop-Vac."

"That's *sooooo* much more romantic than flowers or a

435

candle-lit dinner," she teased. "Wait a minute! How do you know that my mouth is better than a Shop-Vac?"

"Just told you I got a degree in guessin'."

"You sounded pretty damn confident about it."

"Confident about a lotta things."

She poked at his gut. "Like what?"

He reluctantly released one of her ass cheeks to cup her face. "Like how much you made my life a whole lot fuckin' better."

"And?"

"How I'll do anythin' to protect and take care of you."

She bent her ear forward. "And?"

"How much I love you?"

Her eyebrows pinned together. "Why did you make that a question?"

"Ain't a question. It's true. Just didn't know if that's what you wanted to hear."

She grabbed a handful of his beard and tugged gently. "I always want to hear that."

She wasn't the only one. But he knew he never told her enough and needed to do better. Telling her didn't cost him a damn thing and it made her happy.

And he only wanted her happy and to never regret being with him.

"Who knew that my craving for a burger and fries from Bangin' Burgers would alter the direction of my life."

"Gotta agree, a Bangin' Burger is life-changin'."

"So is 'karma' in the shape of a big ol' biker."

"*Your* big ol' biker," he reminded her.

She leaned in until her lips hovered near his. "And I think I'll keep him."

Thank fuck for that.

Sign up for Jeanne's newsletter to learn about her upcoming releases, sales and more! http://www.jeannestjames.com/newslettersignup

---

Magnum: A DKMC/DAMC Crossover

Out of the dark comes a knight she least expects.

He's the sergeant at arms for the Dark Knights MC. He enforces the rules and gets his hands dirty.
She's the daughter of a biker. Property of another MC.
She's young. He's not.
He's lived a life. She's just finding her way.
She's a bad idea.
A very bad idea.
One which can quickly turn allies into rivals.
One war is over, he's not ready to begin another.
But the temptation might make it unavoidable.

Turn the page to read the first chapter of Magnum: A Dark Knights MC/Dirty Angels MC Crossover

Magnum: A Dark Knights MC/Dirty Angels MC Crossover

Chapter One

With a twist of his wrist, Magnum downed the rest of his whiskey, slapped the shot glass on the worn, scarred table in front of him, planted his boots onto the floor and sat back in *his* chair, crossing his arms over his chest.

He did this all while staring at the young blonde across his bar. That was right, *his* fucking bar.

He knew she wasn't scouting.

He knew she wasn't gathering intel.

Why she would show up at Dirty Dick's, his club's bar, he had no fucking clue.

Why she would sit down and make herself at home in the Dark Knights MC hangout, he didn't know.

While he needed to find out, he was in no rush to see what her angle was. Fuck no, he'd wait a bit and see how it all played out.

His club brothers were eyeballing her, but none had been stupid enough to approach. So far.

Why? Because they all knew who she was. And like Magnum, had no idea why she was there.

But it spooked the ones who knew who her father was. A member of an ally MC, the Dirty Angels.

She was young when Magnum first met her and now, even ten years later, she was still too young.

One good reason to avoid her should be her father being a member of another MC.

Add the fact that she didn't grow up in that MC. Fuck no, she grew up in a rich neighborhood, attending private schools. Attending a good college.

The problem was, she was his type. Long legs, long blonde hair, green eyes and fair skinned. Not to mention— and hard to ignore—curves in all the right places. So, he couldn't help but watch her for the past few years. Once she became legal, of course.

Because he did not fuck, or even eye-fuck, jailbait. Never had, never would.

It wasn't her youth which drew him, anyway. Once she'd matured and filled out, it was those very curves, the confidence she carried and her *capture-your-soul* green eyes she pointed at him.

But even then, he had only watched her. At poker runs, at the DAMC parties, at the Toys for Tots drives, at Ellie Walker's fundraisers for the Walker Foundation, which helped needy amputees.

He'd seen her at them all.

But he'd kept his distance. For the most part.

And for good reason.

But why had he caught her attention?

He had no fucking clue. Because they couldn't be more opposite.

Was she still too young? Fuck yeah.

Did he want her anyway? Fuck yeah.

Was it smart? Fuck no.

But his undeniable interest in Caitlin was a no-fucking-go.

Not unless he wanted to cause a war.

For almost the last decade, shit had settled, and the Knights had made strong allies. Not only with the Angels, but also with the Blood Fury MC up north.

Between the three clubs, they ruled the western half of Pennsylvania. So currently, life was easy.

It wouldn't remain that way by Cait showing up solo at Dirty Dick's.

Dawg was protective of his daughters, whether they were five or twenty-five. Whether he claimed them at birth or at almost fifteen.

You did not fuck with a brother's daughter, whether from your own MC or another's. At least not without getting permission first.

And if you approached that brother, you'd better be damn sure you planned on taking that relationship seriously. You did not approach a brother just to ask to bang Daddy's little girl. Fuck no. Not if you wanted to keep, not only your throat intact, but your nuts securely in your sac.

So, it made him wonder why the fuck she walked into his bar and sat at one of his tables.

He waited to see if any of his brothers dared to approach, in case she was there to meet one of them.

What was fucking crazy, she didn't even scan the room. Not once. She'd walked in, sat at an empty table and, after one of his girls took her order and returned with a drink, she took a long swallow and then stared at it with her eyebrows pinned together.

This did not give him the warm fuzzies. Especially with someone as outgoing and outspoken as Cait.

He raised his hand and motioned Nina over.

Nina hurried over to him, ran her long pointy nails across the skin at the back of his neck and asked, "What do you need, Big Daddy?"

For fuck's sake, Nina had been trying to get his dick for months now. She wasn't going to do it by calling him Big Daddy. She wasn't going to do it at all. Nina wasn't his type.

His tastes ran elsewhere.

His eyes slid back to Caitlin, who'd now almost finished her drink.

He jerked his chin up toward the blonde. "Why she here?"

Nina lifted a slender shoulder. "Didn't ask. Should I have?" Her claw-like nails dug deeper into his neck.

Normally that shit would get him hard. Just not from Nina.

"Yeah, get 'er another drink and dig."

"Want me to tell her to leave?"

"I fuckin' tell you that?"

Nina made a face. "No. But whatever you need, Big Daddy..."

"Told you what I fuckin' need. When you get 'er another drink, tell Wick to get me another shot."

"I'll get that for you now."

As she spun away, Magnum reached out and snagged her wrist, jerking her to a halt. "Problem with you, Nina, is you don't fuckin' listen. Told you what to do. Now do it."

Nina's nostrils flared and her jaw got tight, but not as tight as his. Then a second later, she nodded and, *thank fuck*, kept her mouth shut.

Magnum released her and she scurried away. He watched her long enough to make sure she was doing what she was told, then his eyes sliced back to Cait.

With her gaze still directed at her glass, she was clueless

two of his brothers were moving in. Like two fucking panthers stalking a doe at a watering hole.

He caught Cue's eye and cocked a pointed eyebrow at him. Cue slapped Cisco's arm and both quickly fell back.

Smart move on both their parts.

Nobody from his club was touching her. No-fucking-body.

Not even him.

Nina approached her table again and set down a fresh drink. She hovered for a few, trying to make convo with Cait.

A few seconds later, Nina's mouth became pinched and her lips flattened out before she swiped the empty glass off the table and headed back to the bar.

She was beside Magnum not a minute later, putting two more shots in front of him.

Magnum downed one, then waited. Of course Nina just fucking stood there. She was a beautiful woman but he swore she was missing shit upstairs. Another reason he wasn't into her. He might not be very educated, but he liked a woman who had more than two brain cells to rub together.

"Jesus fuck," he muttered finally and shook his head.

Nina's hands flew up and she huffed. "No fucking clue, Big Daddy, she wouldn't say much besides thank you."

Christ.

"Maybe she's waiting for someone."

Maybe.

"A date or something."

Magnum raised his eyes to hers. "When the fuck you ever seen someone in here on a fuckin' date?"

Nina shrugged. "Don't know. I don't really pay that much attention to it."

"Especially a white girl in a Black biker bar?"

Nina pursed her full lips and rubbed the back of her

neck. "Plenty of white girls in here. With one of the brothers."

"She with a fuckin' brother?" he just about shouted.

"Not yet."

His fingers curled into fists and he stared at them, trying not to lose his shit. "Go. Go back the fuck over there an' bring 'er here."

"But—"

"Now, Nina."

Nina huffed again and headed back over to Cait's table.

Nina said something to her and Cait's head raised, she answered, then her neck twisted toward him. Nina jerked her chin towards Magnum and the blonde stood and, without an escort, headed in his direction.

She took her time, all eyes in the bar on her, which annoyed Magnum more than it should.

Since she was taking her sweet time, so did he, running his gaze from top to toe.

Yeah, that fourteen-going-on-fifteen-year-old who Dawg discovered was his and claimed, was no longer that thin, petite blonde young girl. She'd graduated fucking high school, she'd graduated college and she was beginning to carve her way in the world. And along that way, she'd developed into a woman, attitude and all.

Made no sense why she was in Dirty Dick's. None at all. But he was about to find out.

"Hey, Mag," she said softly with a *barely-there* smile that got him smack in the middle of his gut.

Trouble, nothing but fucking trouble, he reminded himself. "Sit the fuck down."

That start of a smile slipped upside down as she plunked her drink down on the scarred and scratched table—*his* fucking table—and yanked out the chair opposite him.

Magnum waited until she settled her bones. Once she did and opened her mouth, he threw up his hand to stop her.

He shook his head, then locked his gaze with hers to make sure she was listening. "Story time. Long time ago a really fuckin' hot redhead did a stupid thing. She walked into this fuckin' bar. Didn't know she was DAMC property at the time. What she did wasn't smart, and it really pissed off her man. That man, you know as Jag, dragged her ass outta here. Ivy came in scoutin' for info. See if we were doin' a territory grab. We weren't, but it still coulda caused a shitload of problems between your father's club and mine. Luckily it didn't because we were busy dealin' with a bunch of fucksticks called the Shadow Warriors. We had a common enemy and goal. Now we don't. Wanna keep it that way, Cait. You showin' up here, especially when you stand out the way you do... Blonde, green-eyed, with great fuckin' tits and ass..." He sucked in a breath and shook his head again. "History's proven wars have been started over less."

She opened her mouth again and he cut her off, making her eyes narrow and her lips thin, but he didn't give a fuck.

"Likin' the peace right now. All I gotta do is protect my brothers from themselves, not protect them from an enemy. You fuckin' showin' up here can make us an enemy. You hookin' up with any of my brothers will start that war. Your daddy ain't gonna like you're here. Pretty sure he'd expect me to squash any shit you start with one of my brothers."

Her voice wasn't so soft this time when she announced, "I'm not here for any of your brothers."

He leaned forward, still keeping their gazes locked. "Then what the fuck you here for?"

"You."

His brow dropped low. *Bullshit.* "Why didn't you

approach first thing? Why'd you sit over there if you're here for me?"

One of her long slender fingers with a light pink painted nail distracted him as she traced the word "KNIGHT-HOOD" raggedly carved into his table by someone's knife. "I was gathering my thoughts... and..." The breath hissed softly from her.

He raised his eyes back to her green ones, the color reminding him of a gemstone. "An' what?"

"And my courage."

His head snapped back. "Nobody more confident than you, Caitie."

Fuck. He didn't mean to call her that. It was just a slip of the fucking tongue. Just like what happened at Diesel's wedding. A slip of the goddamn tongue.

If she was here for that... If she was here for more...

Whatever this was, whatever she was here for, he needed to shut this down. And do it right fucking now. "Already lived half my life. You're just startin' out. You don't need the hassle that comes along with a man like me. Got your whole life ahead of you. What we did at D's weddin' was a mistake. Told you that. Thought you understood."

"I'm not here about that."

Yeah, it was over a year ago, but he still hadn't forgotten it. Still hadn't rid himself of the memory of how sweet she tasted on his tongue. It was the one and only time he did something more than watch her.

He did something he shouldn't have. And he was lucky he hadn't been caught. Once he realized what a stupid fuck he was being, he got away from her and stayed away.

He didn't need that temptation.

But here she was.

Her lips twisted. "I mean, you're hot and all that. But you're not irresistible."

He cocked a brow, pursed his lips and sat back in his chair. "I'm pretty fuckin' irresistible."

"Mmm." She tilted her head and made a show of studying him. "Jury's out on that. Irritable, more like it."

He surged forward, slammed his palms on the table and growled, "Didn't..." He flared his nostrils and sucked air deep. She played him. *Jesus fuck.* "Woman, spill it or get the fuck out of my bar."

She glanced around. "This is *your* bar, Magnum, or the Knights' bar?"

"The Knights', which means it's mine. Talk, Cait."

The flame in her eyes suddenly extinguished.

As much as he didn't want to see her in Dirty Dick's, he also didn't like seeing that light dim.

His chest tightened as she leaned back in her chair and closed her eyes, her fingernail now nervously picking at the carved letters and making little shavings. If she didn't stop, she'd shred her nails and they weren't very long as it was.

Something was up and he didn't like it. He didn't like it one fucking bit. "Cait!" he barked, because he couldn't take much more of her hesitating.

Her eyes slowly opened, and they looked troubled. That did not help his damn soaring blood pressure at all.

"I need your help."

Those four words made his heart seize, then begin to pound as loud as a bass drum in his ears. Why the fuck was she coming to him? What the fuck was going on?

Keep your shit together, brother. Keep it the fuck together. "Don't need my fuckin' help, Cait. Got a whole club at your back. And it's not mine. Like I said, don't need a fuckin' war."

Goddamn it. He didn't need anything to cause tension between the Knights and the Angels. No fucking way.

"I can't go to anyone in the club with this. It'll create more of a... a mess than it already is."

Goddamn it. "The Shadows."

"They work for Diesel who won't keep shit from Dad."

Goddamn it. "The pigs."

She sighed. "Axel. He'll tell Bella and Bella will tell D or Dawg."

Jesus fuck. She was probably right, Axhole would run to his wife like the pussy-whipped pig he was. "Yep, screwed no matter who you go to."

"Except you."

He could debate that, too. Because there was nothing more he wanted to do than pound her like a nail into the wall.

He downed his remaining shot, slammed his hand on the table, making his empty shot glasses jump, as well as her Jack and Coke—or whatever the fuck she was drinking, or actually not drinking—spill over the rim. "Nina!" he bellowed and lifted two fingers. "Now!"

Not even a minute later, Nina rushed over with two more shots and slid them both in front of him. She gave Cait a frown, who gave her an answering shrug and then scurried away.

The woman was at least smart enough to know to stay away from him when he was not in a good mood. And right now, he was on the wrong side of a good anything.

He downed one double shot, then the next, and waited for the warmth to hit his gut and his pulse to stop raging. But it ended up being more of a searing burn which turned his stomach. "So far, you haven't told me shit. And not sure I wanna hear it if you can't tell anyone in your club. You belong to them, Caitie. You're Angels' property. I can't step in and interfere."

"I'm not property of the club."

Her cheeks were now flushed, and her eyes held a hard glitter. She was getting pissed. Good. Because so was he.

"Babe, you became property of the DAMC the second your daddy's swimmer hit your momma's egg."

Fuck yeah, she was getting pissed.

"I didn't know my father until I was almost fifteen!" she shouted.

"Don't fuckin' matter."

She shot to her feet. "Fine! If you don't want to help me, I'll go elsewhere."

Oh, *now* she was getting an attitude. *Fuck that.*

He reached out, grabbed her wrist and jerked her back into her seat. "Sit the fuck down and fuckin' spill it, Cait. Least tell me what the fuck's goin' on that's got you all fucked up."

"You have to promise not to tell anyone."

He almost rolled his fucking eyes. And it took a lot for him to do that. "Not promisin' shit."

"Then, fuck you." She tried to surge to her feet again, but he still held her wrist. That outburst had him tightening his grip to keep her in her seat.

"Woman, you walk into this fuckin' bar, try to get me involved in shit and now you're gettin' an attitude with me? That shit ain't gonna fly."

When she squeezed her eyes shut and her wrist trembled within his fingers, he knew that very fucking second he was not letting her leave without knowing what the fuck was going on. Even if he couldn't help her, he wanted to know.

He *needed* to know. Because now his thoughts were spinning, and his gut was a raging fire.

"Cait, you're killin' me here." He had done his best to soften his tone, even though he was ready to flip the fuck out. "Cait!" he barked so loudly, she jumped and opened her eyes.

What could be so bad, she was afraid to say it?

What happened to her unwavering confidence? What the fuck happened to *her*?

He rose from his seat, not releasing her wrist. He was not risking her running out of that bar and him being left in the dark. Because he could not chase her down if she did that. Especially if she ran back to Angels' territory and back to Dawg's house in the DAMC compound.

That would raise way too many red flags. And he hated the color red.

No, he was getting to the bottom of whatever the fuck was going on and he was doing that right now.

Get the rest of Magnum's story here: Magnum: A Dark Knights MC/Dirty Angels MC Crossover

If You Enjoyed This Book

Thank you for reading Romeo: A Dark Knights MC/Blood Fury MC Crossover. If you enjoyed Romeo and Maddie's story, please consider leaving a review at your favorite retailer and/or Goodreads to let other readers know. Reviews are always appreciated and just a few words can help an independent author like me tremendously!

Want to read a sample of my work? Download a sampler book here: BookHip.com/MTQQKK

Also by Jeanne St. James

Find my complete reading order here:
https://www.jeannestjames.com/reading-order

Standalone Books:

Made Maleen: A Modern Twist on a Fairy Tale

Damaged

Rip Cord: The Complete Trilogy

Everything About You (A Second Chance Gay Romance)

Reigniting Chase (An M/M Standalone)

Brothers in Blue Series

A four-book series based around three brothers who are small-town cops and former Marines

The Dare Ménage Series

A six-book MMF, interracial ménage series

The Obsessed Novellas

A collection of five standalone BDSM novellas

Down & Dirty: Dirty Angels MC®

A ten-book motorcycle club series

Guts & Glory: In the Shadows Security

A six-book former special forces series

(A spin-off of the Dirty Angels MC)

Blood & Bones: Blood Fury MC®

A twelve-book motorcycle club series

Motorcycle Club Crossovers:

Crossing the Line: A DAMC/Blue Avengers MC Crossover

Magnum: A Dark Knights MC/Dirty Angels MC Crossover

Crash: A Dirty Angels MC/Blood Fury MC Crossover

Romeo: A Dark Knights MC/Blood Fury MC Crossover

Beyond the Badge: Blue Avengers MC™

A six-book law enforcement/motorcycle club series

COMING SOON!

Double D Ranch (An MMF Ménage Series)

Dirty Angels MC®: The Next Generation

WRITING AS J.J. MASTERS:

The Royal Alpha Series

A five-book gay mpreg shifter series

About the Author

JEANNE ST. JAMES is a USA Today, Amazon and international bestselling romance author who loves writing about strong women and alpha males. She was only thirteen when she first started writing. Her first published piece was an erotic short story in Playgirl magazine. She then went on to publish her first romance novel in 2009. She is now an author of over sixty contemporary romances. She writes M/F, M/M, and M/M/F ménages, including interracial romance. She also writes M/M paranormal romance under the name: J.J. Masters.

Want to read a sample of her work? Download a sampler book here: BookHip.com/MTQQKK

To keep up with her busy release schedule check her website at www.jeannestjames.com or sign up for her newsletter: http://www.jeannestjames.com/newslettersignup

www.jeannestjames.com
jeanne@jeannestjames.com

Newsletter: http://www.jeannestjames.com/newsletter signup
Jeanne's Down & Dirty Book Crew: https://www.facebook.com/groups/JeannesReviewCrew/

TikTok: https://www.tiktok.com/@jeannestjames

facebook.com/JeanneStJamesAuthor

instagram.com/JeanneStJames

bookbub.com/authors/jeanne-st-james

goodreads.com/JeanneStJames

Get a FREE Sampler Book

This book contains the first chapter of a variety of my books. This will give you a taste of the type of books I write and if you enjoy the first chapter, I hope you'll be interested in reading the rest of the book.

Each book I list in the sampler will include the description of the book, the genre, and the first chapter, along with links to find out more. I hope you find a book you will enjoy curling up with!

Get it here: BookHip.com/MTQQKK

Printed in Great Britain
by Amazon